I0715122

ARCANUS
PRESS

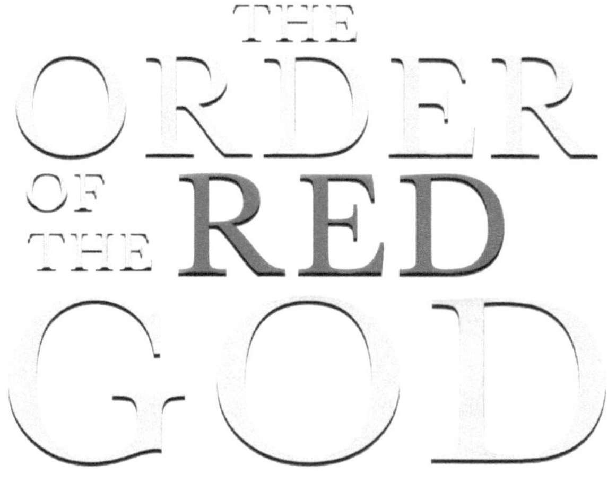

Book II of the
Seagrass Maggie Trilogy

Charles Allen

Arcanus Press ®

dba of *Emmergen, LLC*

Post Falls, Idaho

Any questions, comments or reviews: arcanuspress@gmail.com

Author's website: www.charlesdallen.com

Interior Layout by EK Morris

Internal Illustrations by EK Morris and Elmo Rocko

Cover design by Matt Seff Barnes

Library of Congress Cataloging-in-production Data has been applied for.

1st Edition

ISBN (hardcover) 978-1-7354705-5-9

ISBN (paperback) 978-1-7354705-6-6

ISBN (ebook) 979-8-3305-1154-9

To Jen,
for saving me in more ways than one.

Tír na nÓg
Tór Mór
(Fomorian Territory)
Falias
Ildathach
Gorias
Tech Duinn
Temple of Lia Fáil
Crann Lár
Finias
Hy Brasil
Magh Mor
Lake Dulcinea
Murias
Mag Mell
Tír Tairngire
Tír fo Thuinn
The Land of Eternal Youth

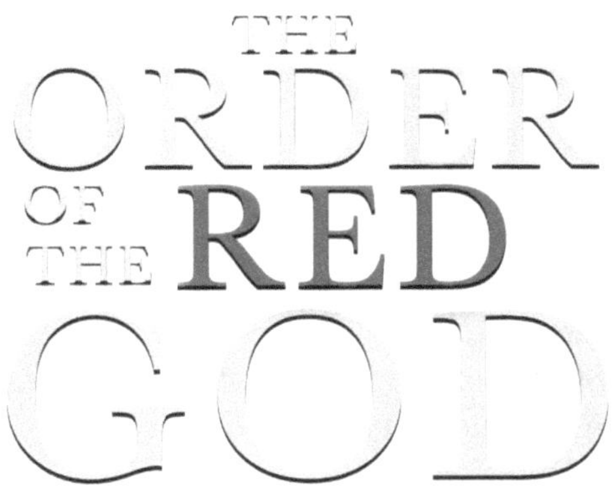

CONTENTS

Part I
Dreams
&
Nightmares

Dark Visitations

July 1855

1

The air was brisk, filled with moisture from the western sea, and the cliffs stood proud against the crashing waves below. There were several herring gulls looking for shelter against the rocks, seals making their way among them along the coastline, and the sprites in the air stirred, sensing the pungent likes of the Deep Dens.

They were coming.

Malformed, ghastly arms reached out from beneath the waters and grasped the rocks with their clawed hands. The horribly twisted and ominous-sized creatures lifted their hulking bodies from their natural element and breathed in the air as if grasping for something that they never knew they needed.

Inside their heads, the Fomorian King—Elieris—spoke to them.

Find her. Bring her back, or kill her if you have to.

They started the climb up the cliffs, their tongues flicking over their sharp teeth. Oh gods, *this* was their *divine purpose*, and it thrilled them more than the savagery of copulation. Serving Elieris served themselves in almost every way.

No one fools me, Elieris said to them. *She is mine.*

2

Thunder was sudden around her, and she could feel the electricity in the sea air. Thrilled, Maggie looked behind her, having left Oona in bed for the night, hoping no one had seen her leave home. Luckily, Cuán, the absolute love of her life, was off in Dublin, where he was setting up a home for them. He knew her very well, and if he knew she was out here, he would probably fret and criticize her for being so careless.

She wore a simple white gown and nothing else, though she hung the straps of an old, beaten leather bag (that belonged to Oona's husband—now gone, *gods rest his soul*) over her shoulder. At the cave, she pulled her gown over her head and stuffed it in the bag, leaving it in a dry spot as close to the exit as she could. Bare-skinned, she delighted in the wind and went running for the swelling waves. Her naked feet *splipped* and *splashed* through the cold water, hitting her calves and then her thighs. Soon the swells were around and between her legs, pushing her back and then pulling her toward its dark, leviathan form.

Diving forward, she allowed her body to change. Her skin darkened to a deep sea-green, and the symbolic scars she received from the Fomorians when she was but a babe deepened. Her hands and feet both grew webbing between the digits and long, black claws. Her mouth grew jagged, incredibly sharp teeth. The Fomorian scratches etched upon her body started to glow a cyan, revealing their occult significance. Along the top of her skull through her curly red hair, and down her back she grew purplish spiked fins that continued down her long tail that swung between her legs, helping propel her quickly through the oceanic waters.

She was a human-serpent hybrid—*Seagrass Maggie.*

The sea life around her spread out, sensing her predatory instincts, though she was not inclined at the moment to hunt them. She dove deep, following the island's bottom as it deepened into the Atlantic Ocean. She felt the pressures increase around her, and she could feel her body easily adjusting to them at the same time.

Maggie had come to realize that she was a powerful creature, and though she knew there were worse things alive around her, she learned that she was not easy to kill. Living all those long years with the fomori in the Deep Dens had changed her natural mortal body, touching her with the fae essence, transforming her into something different. Having escaped the Fomorians with the help of the Cailleach, she found herself hunted by a sorcerer working for the Fomorian King, Elieris, who wanted her back for breaking the Great Contract. The sorcerer was Doran Dunn—a maniac that also happened to enlighten her, that she was now a Maris, a Demidian of the oceans. Someone with divine blood.

Over the next couple of years, once Dunn was dealt with, Maggie and her lover, Cuán, explored more of her powers and sought others of her kind. However, these were no longer like the ancient times—the fae all but retreated to the Otherworld, leaving only a few behind after the Great Contracts made with the Milesians.

Swimming still deeper, moving swiftly between a few basking sharks and the hairy-looking orange blob of a lion's mane jelly-fish, she thought about Killian. He was the only fae she had met who actually spent a lot of time socializing with mortals in their world. While he refused to say too much about himself, he was the only one she really learned to trust. Other fae creatures lived in the shadows, refusing to speak. They were spread out, usually living hermit lives, mostly running away as she approached them. Even though she could sense their natures, it was still difficult to find them, and even more difficult to communicate.

Over the last few months, however, she swam farther from the island. Farther and deeper. Beyond the Celtic shelf, she encountered other beings. Humanoid and yet alien. Some were as frightful look-ing as the fomori; only, unlike those terrible creatures, they were often beautiful in some alien way that not even Maggie understood. They also had these gorgeous red bio-luminant veils about their heads—gelatinous and transparent, they opened like balloons about their heads before folding and collapsing when they moved about. Their *cohuleen druith*. In folklore, it was described as a red cap and Maggie could see why some may think that.

The creatures kept themselves mostly hidden, staying in the murky veil in the distant waters, but they looked at each other for as long as each dared and then they would be gone before Maggie could find the courage to approach them.

She suspected they were the merrow.

As Maggie approached the last location she'd seen them—only a few nights before—she stopped and hid amongst the rocks on the seafloor. They stood up around her like standing stones. There were so many that it was easy to hide within them, making her feel certain that she couldn't be seen.

She waited, hoping to see one again. Maggie wondered what Cuán would say about all this. She truly wanted to show him these marvels, and she often wished she could bring him down here with her. Except, after the dangers Doran Dunn put them through, he was reluctant to let her do anything treacherous.

A coldness ran through her. Maggie's body always adapted to both the pressures and temperatures of the ocean, so when she got a chill, it wasn't the waters. It was something in them. Her senses told her she might be in danger.

Maggie looked around, frightened that she had let her guard down, not realizing her life could be in immediate danger until it was too late.

She froze when she saw it: the smooth head, the shiny silver eyes, and the masculine torso. It was alien to her. Almost metallic, like a school of shimmering bluefin tuna. Only it was a beautiful man with fins and a wide mouth, ribs fanning the waters as he breathed. There was a tendril of red behind his head; his *cohuleen druith*. He watched her for a moment and then dashed away. Behind him, several merrow that she didn't even know were there, followed him just as quickly. There were females with long flowing hair, naked breasts, and long, elegant and colorful-fined tails. (*Mermaids*, Maggie thought). But they were gone almost as quickly as she noticed them.

Maggie swam out of her hiding spot, wanting to communicate that she wasn't a danger to them, but she waited there and didn't see them again. She swam around the rocks with her powerful tail swishing back and forth through the waters, feeling the ocean rush through her hair and her fins, and looked for them.

They disappeared, leaving no trace of their existence.

Disappointed, Maggie decided she would try again another day. Beneath the waves, Maggie often lost track of time. For all she knew, Cuán could be over to have breakfast and wonder where she was.

Maggie started back, swimming as quickly as she could. The muscles in her body jetted her to the coastline in very little time, her supernatural vigor outlasting any ache that she would normally imagine. On the shores, she let her body shift back to its human form: the short, freckled redhead with ghostly pale skin. She could not see the sun on the horizon, but she was sure it was soon upon her.

She climbed up the rocks to her cave and went to her bag.

Only the bag was not there.

In the deeper, dark part of the cave she heard a sloughing breath. Its unnatural sound scared her. Maggie didn't know what to do, so she stepped back toward the mouth of the cave. She was naked and alone with no weapons to protect her.

"Seagrasss Maggie!" came a deep, sloughing voice.

"Who the feck is there?" she said. Maggie told her body to change, and in a moment, she had her claws, her fins, her tail...

"Oooooh, Maggie. You don't remember us?" The mouth that formed the words sounded like it popped and sloughed again.

"*I'll rend you in two, you shite,*" she said, letting her voice turn into a growl. "*Ba chóir duit teith, nó bainfidh mé do cheann díot!*"

Out of the darkness—where the Cailleach first approached her many years before—a slouched, slimy-skinned creature appeared. Its face was as horrid as the angular fish—jutted and toothsome. Eyes red and bugging. It had crustacean arms and claws, black hairs, and algae all over him.

Behind it came the echo of another, its voice gargling and sloughing as well. She could not yet see it, but she knew it was there.

Two of them?

*Jaysus Christ...*What was she going to do?

Don't show them fear, she told herself. If you show them that, they will feed on it and use it against you.

"Elieris invokes the Great Contract, girl. He owns you by right," the first creature said. "He will have you again, and you will serve him as he commands."

Maggie realized the second creature—now coming out of the darkness—held onto her bag. Her pocket watch was in that bag. The one Cuán gave her when they first met. Her gown was in there, too. She meant to have it all back. But instead of waiting to let them make their move, Maggie decided she needed to go first.

Maggie ran at them, crying out in anger, letting the monstrous throat of hers shriek its horrible noise. The caves echoed it back, the high pitch almost hurting her own ears.

It worked. The fomori grabbed their ears, giving Maggie time to rake her claws across a fomor's eyes. The eyes were sliced in two, blood pouring out of them at once. The fomor cried out, and she ran past the other, snatching her bag, going deeper into the cave. Hoping for a place to hide rather than draw them toward the village. At the back was a small chamber with a crack in the ceiling and a tunnel traveling upward. It didn't go high enough to reach the surface, but it was a place to climb and hide. Her claws easily found grip and she scampered up into its darkness.

The fomori were quickly behind her. She could hear their iterant and sloughed breathing.

They were not talking this time. They kept quiet, feeling out the air around them. Maggie knew that she was not in the perfect hiding spot, but what else could she do? She hoped they'd give up and go away without looking up.

Do you really think they're that bloody dumb, Maggie? Cuán said inside her head.

Well no, actually.

And do you think it was a good idea not taking precautions when you came down 'ere? You know the fucking things are looking for you.

Fuck off, Cuán. I don't need your shite right now.

The bag was tucked under her arm, but she had to open them a touch to keep hold of the rock around her. It slipped, and after biting her tongue, she tightened her armpit, sighing. Her left foot then slipped a little.

Shit.

Damn it, Cuán. Why did you have to be in Dublin? Ye could have caught me last night, so I wouldn't do something so stupid.

A fomor came up beneath her. It started looking up...

Just do it and stop IT now, she thought.

Maggie jumped down on it, wrapping her legs around its neck and grabbed hold of its head with both her arms. Her bag fell somewhere, but she gathered her strength and twisted with all she had. Eventually, the muscles in the neck gave, and she turned the head sharply. She heard its spine crack, and then it fell over. She rode the body down until her bare feet hit the ground, and she quickly scampered away, grabbing her bag when she saw it.

The other fomor screamed at her, but she started running toward the mouth of the cave, leaving it behind.

It's going to follow you home, Maggie.

Fuck all, Cuán. I don't need you crawlin' 'round in my head right now.

Maggie stopped and turned around. The blind one with the crablike claws shuffled behind her, eyes still bleeding. She could run, but Cuán's 'voice' wasn't wrong. It would follow her. Oona and Cuán would be in danger. The village. She couldn't have that.

Maggie bared her teeth, dropped her bag, and then chopped at one of its arms with her claws. The claws sounded like teeth clacking when they collided with the shell-like armor, surprising her. Its other claw came around, snapping around her waist, clamping down, crushing her. She hardened her muscles in return, but the grip was draconian. She thought its next move would be to simply cut her in two with another crushing squeeze, but the creature held her firm.

Maggie grabbed its other clawed arm and shoved it up into its own face. The claw drove into its flesh, and it screamed as Maggie pulled it back and then shoved the arm up again. When the claw smashed into its face, it tore its cheeks wide open, and its tongue lolled out.

The claw around her waist loosened briefly, which was long enough. She pulled the claw open, and as it tried squeezing back down, she slipped out and climbed onto his arm. She grabbed its jutting chin as it opened its toothsome mouth, pushed it up, exposing the neck, and then she sunk her teeth into its throat. She felt her teeth sink in and its esophagus and larynx, snapping and tearing between them. Its bitter juices filled her mouth and ran down her chin.

With a hard yank, she tore her mouth away from its neck, taking a bloody chunk of its throat away between her sharp teeth. The thing dropped dead as she climbed away from it. She spat out the bloody matter in her mouth and wiped the blood away on her arm.

Maggie's ribs ached from the claw, bruising and tearing some of her skin. Her mouth drooled out strings of blood.

How the fuck was she going to wear her white gown over this?

Maggie went to the ocean and cleaned herself off. Not being able to see herself, she hoped she got most of it. In her pale human form again, she pulled the gown over her wet body and grabbed her bag.

Climbing up the path toward Oona's, she checked her pocket watch, winding it the while.

A quarter till six.

Maggie sighed. While she didn't have to worry about Cuán right now, Oona could be awake, but Maggie thought maybe she could get in without being seen.

After a moment, she stopped and turned back toward the water.

3

Maggie went back down to the coastline, pulled the skirt of her gown up her legs to keep them from getting wet, and squatted to touch the water. She pushed out her senses through the Hollow and the sea and found the place where they intertwined. Over time she had taught herself to hone the sensitivity of her mind to feel the vibrations in the waters for anything that had different energies other than life's vital forces.

She sensed no other Fomorians nearby, so she relaxed and breathed. If there were more, they probably would have swept over her by now.

Throwing her bag over her shoulder, she headed for the path through the rocks, letting her gown fall back around her ankles as she went.

Hopefully, Oona hadn't noticed her absence.

Maggie & Cuán

1

Cuán was already on the wagon before the sun rose, so when it came up and he found the day pleasant, it made him breathe easier. Today was an exciting day. He'd been gone almost a month, and he couldn't wait to get back to his girl. Of course, he wanted to see his ma and da, Oona, and the others, but he desperately wanted to throw his arms around Maggie. He wanted to feel her body, smell her hair, and listen to her sweet voice again. He missed everything about her.

When Kilkee village came into view—the familiar rooftops and the expanse of the sea behind it—Cuán stood up, holding onto the seat behind the driver. Colum, who'd made the special trip to Galway to pick Cuán up at the train station, clicked his tongue at his horses. As they got closer, Cuán could see a few doggers as little black dots out at sea. His da probably one of them.

"I 'ear you're taking our Maggie to Dublin?" Colum said.

Our Maggie. Yes, the village adopted her as if she were an orphan, as if it knew that she was special and knew she needed protection. Cuán thought that if he were to die tomorrow, this town would take care of her, and he was glad for it.

But it also didn't stop him from wanting more from his life. For several years now, he wanted to attend the university, and because of one thing or another, he found himself pushing it off.

Now was the time, he thought. He and Maggie had to go, even if Kilkee would always call them back. It comforted him, knowing that even if all went to shit in Dublin, this village would always wait for them. A home behind their home.

"Aye. But don't worry. I'm sure we'll make a visit every year or so. We'll miss all of you," Cuán said. He was sincere too. Especially since Colum—unbeknownst to Colum himself—was Maggie's biological father.

It was one of those strange stories. Everyone, Cuán believed, had one or two of these. A family story that is passed from one generation to another, something one often tells others when offering little interesting facts about one's life. Only in this situation, Colum and his wife were left in the dark to keep them from realizing a truth that would shake the foundations of everything they knew.

The truth?

Maggie was taken from them when she was a babe, and they raised her changeling without even knowing...a *siofra* that had replaced her while she was away. Once the Cailleach had rescued Maggie from the Fomorians, Maggie wanted to return to her family, but how does one go about that without proving who they were in the first place? Oona, Cuán's mother's best friend, took her in. When they discovered the *siofra* was a fae trapped in a curse and was also ignorant of her situation, Maggie found that she couldn't take revenge on her. Instead, they helped free her from her curse, which, unfortunately, ended in the fae's death.

Once it was all over, neither of them knew how to explain the story in a way that anyone in the village could believe. No, not telling Colum and his wife was easier. And even though the changeling—Deirdre—passed away, it was easier for them to know that their daughter had always been theirs.

This, of course, didn't mean that Maggie couldn't get to know them and treat them like her parents. Colum and his wife, Mona, appreciated her, especially after they lost their daughter. And while Oona had taken her in and loved her, Maggie had plenty of love to share. It was infectious, and the whole village eventually fell in love with her too.

Cuán would be jealous if he wasn't so damn happy for her.

Colum stopped the wagon downtown, and Cuán hopped out once he tossed his bags onto the road, carefully aiming to miss piles of horse dung.

Colum grabbed one of his bags to help him out.

They went across to the road to Cuán's house, where his ma would wait for him. Colum followed behind him.

"Ever since ye left, yer father has been employing young Jacob. Says Jacob is doing an excellent job," Colum said. "Though I can see that yer father misses you out there."

Colum talked about being out with his father on the dogger, fishing. Something Cuán could say he didn't miss at all.

"Me and my da were out there for a good many years. I'm not surprised," Cuán said. "We'll always have those memories, eh?"

"Aye."

Inside the home, his ma came running, grinning ear-to-ear when she heard the door: "Cuán! My boy! How was Dublin?"

He hugged his ma and kissed her cheek.

"Swell, Ma. The university accepted me, and I got Maggie and me a pretty good house on the west side of town. It'll be easy to visit if you can ever escape the village to come see us."

His ma held his arms tightly as he stood there with the big dumb grin. He could see the pride in her eyes, and it felt good though he was abashed by it all.

"I knew you could do it," she said. "I knew it...my boy was smart as they come."

And a tear rolled down her right cheek.

That hit him. "Ma. Don't cry."

His ma laughed then, wiping away the tears. "Don't be daft! Me? Cry? Not in your life."

She saw Colum then. "Thanks for picking up my son. Quite a trip to Galway, aye?"

"Aye, Misses Foley. I'll put your bag here, Cuán. You two catch up. I'm off to get fed and maybe catch a draft before bedtime."

Cuán thanked him again as Colum shuffled out the door.

His ma grabbed his arm, turning him around.

"So, do you really got it? You didn't say in the letters..."

Cuán smiled at her, knowing exactly what she was talking about. He opened the corner pocket of his bag, where she could see its case.

"Can I see it?"

Cuán nodded, letting his ma take the case out, popping it open between them.

"Oh my God, Cuán. She's going to melt. Oh my God, it's so beautiful." She opened her arms again and hugged him tighter. "Oh, son, I can't believe you're so grown up now."

"A'right, 'nough ma," he chuckled, filling a little too smothered. "Do you really think she'll say yes?"

His ma looked at his eyes. "Oh, Cuán...if you could only see how she looks at you. I've no doubt at all."

2

Oona and Maggie were beside each other in the wagon, where they helped Mona Ó Fionnáin load the buckets of sugar beets. Since she'd been sick for a while and uninterested in seeing doctors, Mona was often too unwell to do the work all by herself. Normally Mona's husband, Colum, would be there helping them, but he had gone to Galway for Cuán. They were expecting him anytime now, and Maggie wasn't sure if she could bear it any longer. It was one of those flutters one gets, a flutter that comes from the excitement of seeing someone you desire coupled with the uncertainty of having not seen them for longer than you're used to. Maggie loved it and hated it at the same time.

"There he is," Oona said, elbowing Maggie lightly in the shoulder.

Colum's wagon came up the road to the farm. Of course, Cuán wasn't with him. Colum would have dropped him off at his home first. No, Maggie had to wait until they took this last trip to the store in town.

But Maggie did have a big smile on her face. She knew it and was sort of embarrassed by it as well. She was obviously a goof.

Maggie wiped the smile from her face before Mona picked on her.

"A'right then. I suppose we should get the last few buckets quickly so that Mona and Colum can rest," Maggie said.

"Tsk! Maggie. Don't forget your pay from the last load you made. Ten pounds. You get this load to the store and come back tomorrow, and you'll get the rest."

"Thanks, Mona," Maggie said. It really was hard not to call her mother. She still ached to say it from time to time.

Colum passed them with the wagon, stopping the horses nearer the stables. He came down and walked on over, giving Maggie and Mona a hug.

"Cuán is very happy to be back. Not happy enough to stay, though. I bet you have something to do with it, aye lass?"

Maggie tried not to blush. "You're terrible, Mister Ó Fionnáin."

Everyone laughed but her, though she did smile despite herself. Maggie grabbed the last two buckets of beets and put them on the back of the wagon.

Mona coughed into her handkerchief, and Maggie saw blood. Colum frowned at this but stepped between them to take the conversation elsewhere.

"Horses well-fed, Oona?"

Oona nodded, smiling at Colum. Since they didn't have much money, Colum liked to help them whenever he could.

Oona gestured at the horses leading the wagon. It was the only two horses that Oona and Maggie owned. "Do you want me to drive the horses, or would you like to do it?"

Maggie was never a good teamster, but wanting to get better, she said, "I'll do it, Oona. Ye rest up, eh?"

"Aye. Well, don't go too fast. I know you're excited to see Cuán, but me arse can't take these bumps in the road like it used to."

While Oona climbed into the wagon, Maggie gave Mona and Colum another hug.

"Don't forget I love ye all. And I appreciate the job. The spare cash comes in handy," Maggie said.

Colum patted Maggie on the shoulder. "Go now before it gets dark, Luv."

"Take care of yourself, Mona," Maggie said. They waved at each other before Maggie turned to go.

Her mother looked so pale.

3

Once the sugar beets were unloaded at the store, Maggie turned to see Cuán standing there, watching her from across the road. She was filthy, but she grabbed her curly red hair and tried pulling it back, hoping to at least contain some of the wildness of it. He looked handsome there with his dark seal eyes, dark brown hair swept over, and his hands in his pockets, gazing at her like she was everything.

Oona saw them but sat in the wagon as Maggie made her way over to him.

"Cuán."

"Maggie."

"I look a mess."

"I see that. But you're still beautiful."

Maggie didn't know why, but she always blushed when he said that. Did she believe that she could be so beautiful to him? She didn't know what to think, but she loved how he always came back, and always wanted her.

"Well, ye look handsome yerself, of course. Always do."

Cuán laughed, and he took her up in his arms. She buried her face in his chest and wrapped hers around him. Hearing his heartbeat, feeling the strength in him—it was very satisfying.

God, it *was* satisfying.

"You done 'ere?" he said.

"I suppose." She looked back, and Oona waved at her, smiling. It was her way of saying to go ahead. "Yes." Maggie looked back into Cuán's big brown eyes, and she let herself push her lips against his.

The kiss was strong, but it lasted only a few seconds. Cuán pulled away from her, breathing heavily.

"I want to take you to the cave. I have something to show you."

"Me? Somethin' from Dublin?"

"Aye."

On the way toward the cave, Cuán told her about the university. It was the second time he'd attempted to get in. The first time went well all the way until Doran Dunn ruined their lives. This time he was sure things would be different.

Maggie didn't mind Dublin, but the longer she stayed in Kilkee, it became more of her home. Though she'd never wanted Cuán to throw away his dreams of going to school, she sometimes wished that he'd change his mind and stay.

He was right, though. There wasn't much of a life for Cuán here. Day in and day out, Cuán was with his father on the fishing doggers. What else would he do?

No, Cuán belonged in Dublin. At least for now.

But did she belong there?

They climbed down the path carefully to the cave. Cuán stopped at a spot closer down by the rocks and stared at it. Maggie remembered seeing Cuán's Irish Wolfhound, Ponc, in that spot a couple of times after the poor dog had passed away. Ponc's ghost. She followed him into the sea and into the cave.

"What are ye looking at?"

Cuán took a deep breath and smiled at her. "This is where I found you. Naked and wrapped in algae. It was like fine hair, wound all around yeh. I pulled most of it off you and then took yeh into the cave when you begged me to tell no one."

Maggie nodded. "I remember."

It had been a day or so after the Cailleach had raised her out of the Deep Dens. She was disorientated—her mind plagued with delirium from the Otherworld like the seaweed that had tangled her up. At first, she thought she was lost, and then as her memories began to return, she started noticing the place the Cailleach had left her. And there was Cuán, rescuing her.

Maggie took his hand and squeezed it. He squeezed back.

"That day changed my life forever, and I look back on it as the best day of my life. Not because it was happy or anything, I was frightened for you. But I knew when I found yeh that I needed you to change my life, and I was ready for it."

Maggie smiled at him, but he didn't smile back. He tugged on her hand. It felt awfully disconcerting, and she worried at it. She didn't know what to think.

"Come on."

Holding her hand, he guided her up the path to the cave. They only just stepped in, staying mostly in the light. He then took her other hand and turned to face her.

"You want to make love here, Cuán?" Was that what he wanted? She felt so dirty!

Cuán chuckled. "I always want to make love to you, Maggie. But right now, I have something different in mind."

Maggie was a bit confused, and then she remembered he wanted to show her something. Why such secrecy?

"Is this a sex toy?" she grinned.

Cuán laughed. "No. Maggie. Stop. I'm trying to be serious here."

Maggie stuck her tongue in her cheek and then wiped away her smile. "Okay. Sorry."

Cuán, still smiling, dropped to one knee, still holding both her hands. Even before he reached for his pocket, a cold wash flowed through her entire body. The humor inside her flushed away, and her heart stopped.

When Cuán pulled out the little box, Maggie's hands started shaking and she wanted to cry.

"Maggie. Will you marry me, lass?"

He popped the box open, and she saw the ring, the diamonds—It was gorgeous, and she realized tears were already flooding down her cheek. Her heart started again, beating so hard in her chest that she thought she'd faint.

"Oh my God, Cuán!" She wanted to be angry with him for surprising her like this, but she also wanted to cry and scream in joy. "Are ye daft? Jaysus, yes. Yes, I will."

Cuán, upon hearing what he wanted to hear, smiled and took the ring out of the box. He took her shaking hand and carefully put the ring on her finger. It was agonizingly slow because she wanted to pull him into her with her arms. He was about to stand up, but she fell to her knees and threw her arms around him as quickly as she could. She sobbed and laughed as she held him tight.

"Ye fucking do such terrible things with me emotions, Cuán! How can ye make me so happy and yet ache this badly? Holy Jaysus!"

"I take it you like the ring?"

"I love it."

"No bullshit?"

"No bullshit. You're what I want forever."

"Same here, Wonderful. Same here."

Once Maggie could feel her legs again, she and Cuán left the cave. He helped wipe her tears away. They kissed. Her body pressed into his, but then Maggie realized the shadows had grown long.

"We should really get home. Will ye walk with me?"

"Please. I'd love to walk you home."

There was some silence between them for a bit. Maggie had to assuage the strong feelings—the urges, the joy, the terror—and breathe in the fresh air, let her body relax.

"We should get married fairly quickly," Cuán said. "The university starts soon. I, uh, I found us a place that I figured would be nice—"

Why did that make her want to cry again? She wiped away the tears.

"You found *us* a place? You've been planning this for a while?"

Cuán nodded. "I have. I hoped you'd come with me to Dublin."

"My place is always beside ye, Cuán," Maggie said. "Forever."

Cuán held out his arm, and she took it, and they made their way back across the Strand toward the village. Once they were at Oona's house, Maggie went up to the door.

"You want to come in?"

"I do. I'd love to see Oona again." He smiled up at her.

Maggie turned and opened the door, seeing Oona, Brian, and Orna all there.

"Was it a yes, Cuán?" Orna said.

Maggie looked back at Cuán, who nodded.

Maggie found that her mouth was open, so she closed it, and grinned at everyone.

"Did you all know?"

Everyone laughed.

Cuán's father, Brian, popped open a bottle of whiskey. "I think it's time to celebrate, aye?"

"I can't believe ye all kept this a secret from me fer so long," Maggie said. "Especially you, Oona! Yer like the town gossip!"

"Oh, shut it, Maggie," Oona laughed. "I keep my secrets, too."

They congratulated them, and everyone hugged each other. Maggie loved times like these—when everyone seemed like one big family. And they were *all* her family. It was beautiful.

She couldn't see a life without any of them.

The Dead Dog

1

Maggie lay in her bed in her white gown, back to her pillow, gazing at the ring on her finger. The ring was Cuán himself, wasn't it? It's what is symbolized. Having a connection to the one you love, saying to the world you are bound to the love of another.

Beautiful humanity. Out of the darkest things mankind had brought upon the earth, this show of bonding and love seemed like a powerful thing. At least it was inside one's own heart. It could also be fragile, too.

How could something be so strong yet so fragile at the same time?

She let her left arm fall to the bed, feeling happy about everything. Maggie yearned for nothing more but to end this distance between her and Cuán once and for all. She wanted to roll over in her bed, wrap an arm around him every night, and feel him there beside her for the rest of her life.

Maggie rolled over, putting a pillow between her legs and she gazed out her window into the night. In the distance she could see the sea and its waves. When Oona first offered her this bed, Maggie didn't entirely know who she was or where she was headed.

Now everything seemed so clear.

Something moved in the yard. It was big and dark. She could see it out her window.

Maggie sat up, her happiness sobering. She bit her bottom lip.

Was it the fomori?

Not seeing everything well, she opened her window. The cool night air pummeled in, blowing the curtains and her hair all about.

The dark thing was a spirit hound—a partially transparent, vaporous dog with glowing white eyes.

Breathing her relief, she saw now that it was Ponc.

Ponc turned around three times and barked at her, seeming to say, *Come on. No time for lying about. We must go.*

Maggie climbed out the window, noticing right away that the ground was cold and that she had forgotten her shoes.

Ponc panted, tongue lolling aside his jowls, and then barked again. *Hurry.*

"I'm comin'," Maggie said. "I'm a little tired, ye know."

Ponc took off down the road, so Maggie followed. She walked through the green fields, moving through a spectral fog that surrounded her. As soon as she thought she had lost Ponc, she saw him again, just on the edge of her vision.

"Slow down, Ponc," she said. "I'm not sure where yer takin' me, and I don't know if I like it."

Ponc didn't reply. The blue-gray wolfhound continued to hurry through the fog.

He had never taken her this way before. Ponc usually led her to the cave or into the ocean. This was different, and she wasn't sure why.

They came to the Ó Fionnáin's farmhouse. There was an orange glow in the bedroom window. It occurred to Maggie that this was impossible. The Ó Fionnáin farmhouse was about an hour's ride by wagon from town. How could she already be there?

It was true, though. She felt the rough, cold stone of the house walls and followed it to the window. Colum was on the other side of the window, looking right at her, and Maggie's heart leaped in her chest.

No. He couldn't see her. He was looking through her at the sugar beet fields. Behind him, Mona sat in bed, coughing into her handkerchief. There was more blood in her sputum.

Hearing this, Colum went to her and picked up her tea, helping her drink it.

"Will you be a'right?" he said.

Instead of answering him, Mona started coughing and convulsing. He hurried and put the tea on the table and then wrapped his arm around her, helping her to sit up and cough. Blood splattered her white gown, all over her chest.

Mona, very weak, spoke with a soft, rough voice: "I don'na think I'll make it, Colum. I'm so tired, and all I want to do is sleep."

Tears were running down Colum's face, and he shook his head.

"I cannot 'ear this now, Mona. You're all I have left."

Maggie's heart ached, and she felt sudden warm tears burdening her eyelids, and she sniffed, knowing they couldn't hear her. She wanted to wake from this, go to them—"I'm ready to see Deirdre. I'm ready to die," Mona said. "Don't cry for me. We'll be watching over you, you damn fool."

"No, *NO*, Mona! Don't do this to me. Please!"

Mona coughed again, settling.

"I love you. Tell everyone I love them. Tell Orna, Maggie and Cuán. Tell them I love them all, and one day we'll see each other soon, aye? Do that for me, Colum."

Colum let out an ugly whimper.

Mona closed her eyes.

Maggie pulled herself from the window, unable to take it anymore. She wiped her wet eyes, feeling hot rage well up inside her. It wasn't fair...Not at all. She didn't feel as though she even knew Mona enough to have her gone so quickly.

"Ponc! Ye fuckin' dog! Why would ye show me this?"

Maggie kicked a nearby bucket, stomped, and screamed at the night around her.

"Fuck all!"

2

Maggie climbed through her window onto her bed, then turned and shut the window tight. Her tears were now dry, and she was out of emotions. All she wanted to do was sleep.

No more ghosts.

No more fomori.

No marriage.

Only sleep.

Then she woke.

Ponc lay on her bedroom floor. He didn't move.

"Ponc? Ye 'ere to sleep with me? I may be in fer that—"

Ponc wasn't moving. She smelled something foul in the air.

"Ponc?"

Maggie climbed to the edge of her bed for a better look. Ponc lay dead. His ruddy bowls were cut from his body and laying between his legs, blood pooling about him. He was rotting there on her floor.

Her gut wrenched. "What the fuck is this?" —Not him too!

She climbed out of bed and stepped over the body. Should she touch it to see if it were real? Maybe this wasn't Ponc? Maybe it was another wolfhound? What if someone was trying to frighten her? Or threaten her?

Maggie couldn't do it—She couldn't look at the dog's corpse, so she backed out of the room and made her way down to Oona's. When she opened the bedroom door, there was only blackness... and like a vacuum, it lifted her off the floor and sucked her right into it.

In the strange invisible mirrors around her, she could see her body warp and transform into an infant. She shrank and was caught in hideous, scaly arms with slime and blood coating them. Some creature was there in the shadows, mostly hidden in the darkness, and it grabbed her by the back of the neck and dangled her little body, naked over the oblivion around her.

Maggie cried out and she sounded like a babe. She had no words, just terror thumping madly in her chest.

The creature buried its sharp teeth, and it pushed a claw into her pale stomach. It pushed until the tip of it broke the skin and pushed deep inside her guts. The pain was immeasurable, and Maggie could do nothing but scream and convulse. The claw tore downwards, tearing open a wide wound, where her intestines fell out in a pile to dangle half a foot below her feet.

She awoke, sitting up in bed, her head wet from all the sweating.

"What the hell?" she said to herself.

Maggie looked at her floor. The dead dog wasn't lying there anymore. As if it had never been.

Was any of it real?

If it wasn't real, then what about the Ó Fionnáin's?

No, it couldn't be real. Right? It's too far to walk. *Had to have been a dream.*

Maggie looked out her window, looking for any sign that Ponc might have been there.

Not seeing anything, she opened her window and crawled out. She went to the road and crouched where she found a footprint.

She put her foot in the print to gauge its size.

It was her footprint.

"What the feck is happenin' to me?"

Maggie crawled slowly into bed with Oona, who woke only to say, "Nightmares?"

Maggie whispered back: "Nightmares. Ghosts. I don't know."

"It's a'right, Maggie. Try to get some sleep."

Maggie shifted down to get comfortable and pressed her body against Oona's, letting her sleep.

3

In the deepest fathoms of the Otherworld, in the shadows of the Deep Dens, Elieris grinned. Before him was a Fomorian advisor, holding the Derdriu Shard aloft so he could manipulate the girl's dreams. It was the very device that he used to watch Maggie, to invade her mind.

"She will never understand it," his advisor said. "She does not know how the *píos anam* was taken from her essence and made into the Shard."

"Yes, but I do love to play," Elieris said. "If you don't throw the mortals a bone once in a while, they sit there stagnating like the horrible creatures they are."

The Fomorian hissed, looking simple now, and Elieris was disgusted.

"Be gone now."

The advisor left him, and Elieris recalled taking a piece of Maggie's spirit essence from her when she was but a babe. The event was very similar to the nightmare she had. They cut open her spirit, and some of it spilled from her in strands. His minions then clipped a piece—the *píos anam*—which was already changing from the weave of the Otherworld and the serpentine blood they'd given her. After all, the Otherworld was the closest thing to the Primordial, and transformation there was near effortless.

Elieris also recalled part of the *píos anam* escaping their grip and floating off elsewhere. The Fomorians tried to retrieve it, but it proved impossibly swift and was lost. With the piece he had, his Soulforger, Fangtooth, used the *Eagla* to transform into the Derdriu Shard. An artifact that would always be linked to the girl it came from.

The Shard bonded them, and Maggie didn't even know it.

The Bridge

1

Bridget was sure she dreamed. She was in a park where families often went for some summer sun, basking away when they had any, but what made it different was the path and the woods.

There weren't any woods in Dublin normally. But here she stood on a dirt path that led into a deep, verdant forest with numerous animal sounds that unnerved her. It was a path she was certain didn't exist in the real world.

She watched a red fox, who sat there on the path, watching her from afar as if he wanted her to follow him. Bridget left her mother and father as they chatted about their tedious adult lives and trailed after him. The red fox stood up and started down the path, never letting her get too close as they went.

Da had told her that wild animals did not like to be come upon, but she really wanted to embrace its soft red down and gaze closer into the wild blue—and possibly very cunning—eyes.

"Come on, fox. Let me hold you," she said to it. "My ma don't like it when I stray too far from them when we're on an outing."

The fox ignored her and continued on.

The forest seemed to wrap itself around her, and that's when she was very, very certain that the wood was a dream. She thought about turning back, but when she did, the road forked off in many directions. Of course, this puzzled her because she didn't recall once seeing other paths dividing out on her way into the forest.

"I'm frightened," she told the fox, who sat down on the path, waiting for her to make up her mind. "Why would you bring me here?"

The fox got up again and trotted on. Not wanting to be alone, she followed the fox until she came to a bridge. A boy with blond, shaggy hair and blue eyes, who was perhaps her age—eight or nine—looked over the edge of the bridge, down at the rumbling waters.

When she looked for the fox, it was gone.

"Boy! Boy!" she said. "Have you seen a red fox?"

The boy looked up at her, startled.

"You frightened me!"

"I'm sorry, but I'm lost. I was following a fox. Have you seen it?"

The boy came closer to her, shaking his head.

"You lost too?"

"Aye. My name is Bridget."

"Aedán."

They shook hands. The boy did seem proper.

"Do you know the way to the park?"

"I'm not sure there's a park anywhere near here. I was following a path past the ruins. I don't remember there being a path before…I mean, normally."

"Would you like to help me find my parents? I'm frightened, and I don't want to do it alone. Please? I have an apple in my lunch. You can have it if you'd help," she said.

The boy scratched his head, thinking about it.

"I suppose there's no harm in it," he said.

Bridget took him back the way she thought she came. The two tried each path, backtracking again and again until Bridget started to feel scared. What if she lost her parents? What if she'd never see them again?

"Try not to think about it," Aedán said. "We just keep trying. That's what we do."

They tried more paths through the woods. They saw deer, rabbits, squirrels, and several kinds of birds, but they never found the path to the park. The sun went down, leaving a full moon above them. For the first time they came across a sign next to the path.

This is the Land of the Red God

"Who is the Red God?" Bridget said.

Aedán shook his head. "I don't know, but it sounds creepy."

"Bloody hell."

Aedán looked shocked at her. "Does your da allow you to swear?"

Bridget tried not to cry. "I just don't care right now, Aedán."

Aedán sighed. "Ah, me neither."

When Bridget awoke in her bed, she sighed relief and grabbed her teddy. She never wanted to be lost in real life again. She didn't want to sleep either. Not for a while, anyway.

Bridget crawled out of bed, a part of her needing to prove to herself that she wasn't dreaming or lost any longer. She went to the window and peered out, seeing the city. Dublin was quiet because it was late, but it was there.

"Dear God," she breathed again and climbed into bed. She looked at her teddy—his old, worn ears and the plastic eyes—and said: "I will never travel down a road I don't know. Never again, Grá. Never. Again."

2

The girl with the long, straight hair like golden cotton and the bright blue eyes sobbed at the bridge. She was sitting all curled up, face buried in her crossed arms, knees tight up. Funny, wasn't it? He had never seen her before in his whole life, and he came across a girl on a bridge named Bridget.

Aedán went to her, sitting beside her.

"Ever since we both entered these woods, we've been trapped here. You think it's strange?"

Bridget looked at him—her face pale white, and her eyes were red and puffy.

"I don't like it at all," Bridget said. "Strange doesn't even begin to bloody describe the situation."

Aedán nodded. "True."

They sat there a while, and then he got up to look down at the river below the bridge. It dropped down several feet. Probably over fifty feet. He wondered how deep the river was, or where it went.

What he needed to do was get her mind off being lost.

"I suggest this. Actually...it comes from my foster-da. What if we follow the river?"

He got Bridget's attention. "The river? Why?"

"Well, my foster-da says that if you follow a river, you're sure to find a town or village. People often make their places along rivers, so they have easy access to water."

Bridget nods. "That's pretty smart, actually."

Aedán held a hand out to her. "We'll be together, and we'll help each other out, okay?"

"Aye. Sounds splendid."

Aedán smiled at her and then he led her around the bridge. They left the winding paths and followed the decline around the rocks, making their way down along the river.

Bridget stopped, suddenly reluctant.

"But what if something happens?"

Aedán sighed, thinking about it. "Well, then we have an adventure. I heard they're good for stories. Our friends would love to hear them."

Bridget nodded and pulled back her hair. "Then we have the adventure."

"Aye."

"Okay. Let's do it then."

They went on, finally reaching the river, and they followed its flow.

"What if the town is closer the other way?" Bridget said.

Aedán laughed and pointed at a loose stone he almost stumbled on. "Be careful of that one."

"I see it."

After a long moment of quiet, Bridget said, "Aedán, right?"

"Aye."

"I'll never forget this, Aedán."

He didn't know what to say. He liked the girl, and he thought they might make great friends. But he wasn't sure why he dreamed of the woods or the girl. She couldn't be real. He'd never seen a girl like her.

It'd be bloody weird to make friends with a dream.

"**W**hat's that?"

Aedán turned around to see that Bridget had stopped, looking around in the trees.

"What's what?"

"I heard something. Over there." Bridget pointed toward some trees where the sun would set. "Do you think this forest is haunted?"

Aedán thought about it. "Well, I'm sure there's animals out there, and they can make noises."

Bridget groaned. "I got lost following a red fox. I feel so bloody stupid."

"A red fox?"

"Yes. God."

He had followed a red fox from the St. Albeus ruins to where he found the path that took him to the bridge. Could it be a coincidence?

No, he told himself. Of *course*, she followed a red fox. She's a figment of your dream, remember? She's recalling what you're recalling. Things are getting mixed up.

It's a dream, Aedán.

Then he saw something move in the wood, and he realized why Bridget mentioned the red fox. Whatever was out there was red, and it moved amongst the trees. He saw it for a split second, and it was gone behind all the vegetation.

"Bridget. Did you see that?"

"I told you. And you looked at me as though I was daft!"

He saw it again. It was red and black. Like he would have envisioned a hell-sent demon. Aedán didn't want to move. His eyes shot around the trees, the bushes, the tall grass...

There was an animal whooping some awful noise that echoed around them. He didn't know what it was. It could be the creature he'd just seen.

"Bridget. Maybe we should run?"

Bridget nodded at him, and he grabbed her hand.

They ran, trying to stick to the river.

Then the red thing moved out from behind the trees just a few feet away. It was on them—its skeletal face yawned wide, and its eyes were black pits. It had a black cloak that unfurled, rippled, and fell, exposing its rotten features and old armor.

Aedán screamed and tried to grab Bridget, but there was suddenly another of those things behind him. It was fetid but powerful. It swept him up in its arms and Aedán's heart almost burst in his chest.

3

Several years passed, and Bridget couldn't escape the same dream.

Well, not the same dream exactly. She was always lost in the forest with the boy, Aedán, and always chased through the woods by the red specters, but what happened changed from day to day. Over time she started to appreciate the dreams with Aedán, and her teddy, Grá, became an afterthought. When she lost him one day, she never even thought to look for him again.

Aedán, however, was always there for her.

When they realized they could not leave the forest, they started playing games. They laughed and cried together. They sang, climbed trees...and when the red skeletal creatures appeared, they always ran together.

Sometimes she couldn't find Aedán right away. These were stranger dreams. She always walked between standing stones, which were huge and reached into the skies like the trees in the surrounding area. There was a woman in white, holding a dagger, standing in the center with a naked man on his knees before her. All he wore was a golden torc around his neck. She cut the man's throat as two other men watched. One with almost glowing yellow hair, looking regal, even in his solemnity. The other—who stood outside the stone circle—looked triumphant, as if he'd just won a battle. The wind lightly played with his dark hair.

Sometimes she would try to run to stop it, but they would only disappear. The whole scene would vanish. Most of the time, she just ran away.

At the bridge, she and Aedán kissed, trying to forget the nightmares that seemed to randomly appear from time to time. She dreamed herself into a beautiful emerald dress with intricate braids throughout her hair. It was like a fairytale. He could be charming and funny, and he liked holding her. In the end, that's what she appreciated most. Her da was so distant most of the time. When Aedán wrapped his arms around her, she felt safe and comforted. Something she had always wanted from a male in her family.

It was too bad he was just a dream, she often thought. Yet despite him being a dream, they embraced, and she loved it.

Hugging led to kissing.

Kissing led to exploring each other's bodies, and eventually, they pressed themselves together in a discord of urgent heat. Bridget would often wake with her fingers between her legs, her thighs squeezing down as her body trembled.

The orgasms woke her.

Bridget hated it. She would wake, leaving the dream lover, losing his body as hers raptured exquisitely. But he wasn't there, and she could not bury herself in him after she finished.

On the other hand, there were many times they didn't make love. Sometimes he brought a quiet sorrow, and sometimes she would bring her own life's burdens with her. This is when the Red Knights—as they came to call them over time—would find them, terrorizing them.

***

"This may be funny. But how old are you?"

They were laying naked in the grass in one of the forest clearings. A spring burbled nearby. Aedán laid on his back beside her, hands interweaved behind his head, and she was on her stomach, turned so that she overlooked his well-muscled body. His eyes seemed to be interested in the shape of her buttocks.

"Twenty," Aedán said. "You?"

"Nineteen. You probably already know this since you're a dream figment and all, but I'm from Dublin."

"Dublin? I'm from Wexford. Not too far south."

"Wexford? I've never heard of it. I don't...travel...much."

"What's wrong?"

Bridget stopped. She really hadn't ever heard of Wexford.

"How does a figment know of a place I've never heard? I made this all up," Bridget said, confused. Had she heard of Wexford in passing and somehow remembered it in her dreams?

"I assure you, I'm very real," Aedán chuckled. "You're the figment. A dream lover."

She looked at him, grinning, knowing that he wanted to crawl atop of her now. Bridget reached over and grabbed his manhood, which laid erect over his stomach, and then she climbed on top of him, putting it into her. Enjoying every movement inside her, she grounded herself onto him.

She awoke.

Bridget rubbed herself to a finish and then stretched out her legs and arms. The sun peaked on the horizon, so she crawled out of bed and opened the curtains. She was naked, but she didn't care. She wanted the warm light to bathe her nakedness.

Then, suddenly, she remembered her dream lover saying he was from Wexford. Where did he say it was?

Dublin? I'm from Wexford. Not too far south.

Bridget washed up and dressed. At breakfast, her ma sat quietly, and da grumbled while the billows of smoke from his pipe came wafting up from behind his paper.

"Where is Wexford, da?"

Her da briefly looked up at her from his paper. "South dear. Farther than we'll ever go."

She looked at her ma.

"Why is this? Are we cursed to stay in Dublin forever, or—"

Her ma looked sternly at her. "Don't be such a fool, Bridget. Dublin has everything we need, and the country isn't worth seeing. It's full of foul people who make their living in the dirt."

Bridget sighed. "That seems to be a disgusting way to look at it to me."

Her da slammed down his paper, biting his pipe. "You will respect your ma, Bridget! You're not a child anymore."

Bridget looked down at her plate, which didn't seem so appetizing anymore. Fuck 'em, she thought. She'd figure it out for herself.

4

Bridget couldn't wait to share what she found with Aedán as she crawled into bed. Her excitement plagued her that night, though—she couldn't sleep. Her mind rolled over what she had learned repeatedly.

Wexford in County Wexford. It was right there in the library books. In the maps.

And the books almost mentioned an old Wexford family there— the Ó Cuinns. Aedán had mentioned that his father was Lord Cuinn on a few occasions. She was sure now that Aedán might actually be real. Somehow, they shared the same dream.

But...*How?*

She didn't know. Whatever was happening—the reoccurrence of the dreams, being lost, the forest, and meeting each other on a bridge—it was happening to two real people. Bridget was sure of it. All her life she had been filled with a depression...something inside her that she never figured out that somehow always seemed to drag her down. Maybe she could escape her sadness by making her dreams real. Maybe her dreams were real!

When she fell into her dreams, however, she entered one of the bad ones...

She could not find the bridge along the paths. The paths changed in every dream, but one always led her where she wanted to go: to *him*—her dream lover. It was like an instinct.

This time would be different. No matter which path she tried, she found herself nowhere. The forest canopy made everything darker, and there was a heavy wind wafting through their branches.

The forest creaked and crackled.

Creatures howled.

Bridget slowly made her way, calling for Aedán.

Horrified, she found him. There was a tall pike driven into the dirt path right in the center. It held Aedán's head on it. His eyes were lifeless. Flies buzzed and crawled around the bloody stump of his neck.

"Aedán?" She threw a hand to her mouth, unable to hold her terror and sorrow back. "Aedán! God, no!"

Aedán's eyes opened and turned on her, scaring her.

How was this possible?

It's a dream, dummy, she told herself.

"Run, Bridget. Run."

Bridget turned around, seeing one of the Red Knights behind her. This time its mouth was filled with bone-white teeth, and spiders crawled out of its black eyes.

"What have you done?!" she cried.

"We call the *Red God!*" the creature moaned.

Something gripped her hair, and—

Beyond the nightmarish creature, she saw a naked man with a golden torc around his neck, holding a spear. He was just watching her, and he was so familiar. She didn't know why, but she thought *Cridhinbheal!*

***

Bridget woke up screaming.

Her head rattled the skeletal voice: *We call the Red God!*

Bridget sobbed, kicking off her blankets, and ran down the hall, throwing open the door to the bath. She had to find someone who knew who the Red God was and why she had these nightmares.

Was Aedán dead?

She didn't know. But there was more to these dreams than she first thought. It wasn't just some fairytale. Something else was happening to her.

Maybe she was going mad. She didn't know. She couldn't even remember the strange name that came to her lips just as the nightmare ended...

Deep inside her, she hoped Aedán was real, and she hoped he was alive. Aedán was the only thing about her life that felt real, even if he was only real in her dreams.

If not, she thought, *I'll kill myself. Yes, that's what I'll do. I'll cut my veins open.* Because who could live like this? Mad and always so desperate?

The Way is Short...

1

The sun shone brightly through his window, and he opened his eyes, feeling its warmth on his face. As reality set in, he thought he heard women weeping. Cuán rubbed his eyes, threw a robe on, and went down the stairs, beginning to feel anxious.

He found his mother crying at the table, sniffing into a handkerchief. Maggie stood in the kitchen corner, clutching a wide brim hat in her gloved hands. Her eyes were red. Her chin trembled.

"Maggie? What is it?"

Maggie looked at him only for a moment, tossing her hat aside, and then ran to him, grabbing him in her arms. More tears poured freely down her pale cheeks.

"It's Mona. She died of consumption last night. Colum is visitin' the undertaker now."

"Oh God, Maggie. I'm sorry." He held her tight, feeling her tremble.

"Let us know what we can do," his ma, Orna, said. "You're in our hearts, Luv. You're in our prayers."

"You should go with him. Be there. Help anyway you can," Cuán said.

Maggie nodded. "You'll come?"

"Of course. By 'you,' I mean 'we.'"

Maggie let him go, and he grabbed her hat for her, and then he reached for his jacket.

They walked with Colum, helping him make some decisions: which casket, which marker, which plot. By midday, Colum broke down, shaking. He lit himself a cigar and said, "I just can't do it anymore. What should she be buried in?"

"Oh, Colum. I'll choose the dress," Maggie said. "Ye don't have to do anythin' ye can't. You understand? We're 'ere to help."

Colum took her hand in his.

"I wish Deirdre was here, Maggie. And since she's not, you bein' here is actually just a great comfort. I want you to know that."

Maggie broke into tears.

"Da," she said and wrapped her arms around him.

Cuán didn't know if she realized what she'd said, but Colum welcomed her arms, and they sobbed together for a moment. Cuán had to look away, fighting back the tears himself, hating seeing either of them in so much pain.

"Cuán. Don't think this robs you of your celebration," his da said later that night. "You and Maggie will be married, and it will celebrate life, showing the village that though we walk so closely by the waters of death, we live, and we can be happy."

"Where's yer clerical collar?" Cuán said, grinning from ear to ear so that his da knew he was trying to make light. "You've a preacher in you, now?"

His da squeezed his shoulder, and it made his heart break.

All Cuán could think about was poor Maggie. Poor fae girl with the wild hair and the heart that's so full of life. Cuán was never one to cry as much as others, but this time, he couldn't stop himself.

"It's okay, Son. We try to be strong for the women, but we need our time too. I'll tell no one."

"I'm not really worried about this ruining our wedding day," Cuán said. "I'm afraid Maggie will feel like she's lost a part of herself. Here I am, da, trying to complete us by bringing us together, and—Ah, I don't know."

His da nodded. "Why don't we go on down to the pub and have a pint? It's on me."

Cuán nodded. "I won't argue a pint."

2

Cuán packed some of the things he did not want to be without. He plucked a lemon drop from a bag on his dresser and plopped it into his mouth as he went. He had crates he borrowed from one of his da's dockside buyers, and he filled them with old clothes, baubles, and other childhood things.

His childhood was gone now. If they were going to make a life in Dublin, it was time to take it seriously. Maybe when Mona's funeral passes, and their wedding is also behind them, Dublin will help them get a new breath of air.

Maybe.

Hopefully.

Someone knocked at his door, and he opened it, finding Maggie there. She was in a simple turquoise dress with gloves on. Her hair was braided up nicely, and she held her wide brim hat in her small hands...just as he'd seen her when she told him the bad news. Only this time she wasn't crying. Somber, giving him a weak smile, she seemed together now.

"Maggie. You a'right?"

Maggie nodded, giving him a bigger smile. His eyes traced over the freckles from one cheek, over her small nose, to the other cheek, and then he shot to her eyes. They never wavered from his.

"Colum is all set. The funeral is tomorrow."

"Aye."

"I thought our weddin' day is in a few days, and there's a lot of work to do. Would ye go with me to the bakery? Oona said that she had the money for any fancy cake we want."

Cuán smiled at her, tossing some of his old clothes on his bed.

"Sounds wonderful."

Maggie held out her hand, and he took it, and she led him from the house joyfully.

It took them a bit over an hour to talk about cakes with the baker. Maggie paid up front, and then they walked the beach of the Strand.

"I think we should have our wedding here," Cuán said, "overlooking the bay."

Maggie looked around. "With this wind?"

"Maybe the gods would be kind and give a right sunny day."

Maggie laughed. "We know *that's* not happenin'."

Cuán grabbed her hand and spun her around, suddenly pulling her in close. Maggie giggled and Cuán tried not to let her fall, laughing the whole time.

"I'm not as agile as you are," Cuán said. "But I'm flexible. We can have it anywhere you'd like."

He wondered what she was thinking. Was she thinking about Mona? Colum? Was her mind really on their wedding, or was she just trying to get through everything? Cuán wanted to ask her, but maybe that would be insulting?

God, Cuán didn't know what to do except be there for her. But he wanted to do more. He wanted to ease her mind.

Cuán held her close, and she laid her head on his chest. Their fingers intertwined.

"Maybe we could have it simple. We could do it in Oona's cassie. She has a lovely field. The sea isn't too far. The place is filled with love," Maggie said. "That's the kind of place I want me wedding."

"I do love you, Maggie."

Maggie grinned up at him. "I do love you, Boyo."

When they returned to Cuán's home, his ma was out shopping, so he tossed her onto his bed, lifted her dress, and pulled down her knickers away from her long legs. They opened for him, and it made his blood burn.

"An Aussie kiss, is it then?" Maggie said with the cutest smile.

"Aye." Cuán grinned back.

He moved between her legs and started to kiss and lick the moist flesh between her legs. He craved her, and his mouth watered. She moaned and grabbed his head, pulling him in. When she couldn't take it anymore, she begged him to take her. He withdrew his excruciating erection from his slacks and buried himself inside her greedily. They made love in a mad dash to the end, holding each other in their gratifying throes. Fingers burying into muscled flesh. Bodies crushed together.

Finished, they lay on the bed beside each other, catching their heavy breaths.

"I needed that," Maggie giggled.

She turned onto her hip, looking down at him, putting an arm on his chest. Maggie ran her hand over his firm pecs.

"You and me forever?"

Maggie laughed in a short spasm. "Aye. You and me forever."

She ran her fingers over his jawline, and she looked at him. Then she drew her finger along different places on his face, around his eyes. Her smile slowly turned into a frown.

"What is it?"

Maggie stopped touching his face.

"Nothin'. There's just so much happenin' right now. All at the same time. It's overwhelmin'."

Cuán grabbed her hand, laying on his chest, and kissed her fingers.

"We'll manage splendidly. I know we will."

Maggie smiled at him. Again, it was fragile. She was remembering her anguish, and Cuán could understand it.

3

Early the next day, they had the wake in the Foley's parlor. This was so that the village didn't have to travel so far to the Ó Fionnáin's farmhouse. Orna and Brian were both happy to help Colum out, offering their whole home to the event. Orna, Oona, and Cuán offered refreshments, cakes, or crumpets to those who came by to see Mona one last time.

Mona lay in a simple wooden casket, but Maggie had chosen the woman's most beautiful dress, and she looked splendid. Maggie and Oona dressed her before the undertaker put her in the coffin. Brian, Cuán, and the undertaker managed to get the coffin into a wagon, and then they unloaded Mona to the Foley parlor from there.

Mona was covered in white linen with black and white ribbons. People had brought flowers and they filled the coffin around Mona. Lit candles were set all around her. Boxes of tobacco and snuff sat nearby so that the men could take a puff upon visiting her.

Between thanking the villagers for coming and helping his ma, Cuán took a moment to take a puff of the tobacco, looking at Mona for one last time.

"You meant a lot to Maggie, Mona. You were her mother, and it hurt her so much to keep it a secret so that you could live with the happy memories of Deirdre. When Maggie tried so hard to be in your life, you could have pushed her away as some stranger, but you didn't. You welcomed her with open arms and treated her like a daughter, even though you didn't know the better. For that, I learned to love you as well, and you will always have my respect," Cuán said softly to her.

He saw Maggie visit her as well later that day. She spoke to her for a long while and then sat with Colum. She never left her da's side unless to visit the bathroom or to help another in some way. Cuán gave her space. This was her moment to grieve, and he didn't want anything to sully that.

He waited until that afternoon when Mrs. Donoghue—a somewhat tall and slightly plump woman—came in with a harp. Many of the villagers gathered inside the house around Mona or gathered outside for their turn, all waiting for Mrs. Donoghue's Ullaloo. After a moment of clearing her throat, she started to keen softly:

> *Mona Ó Fionnáin. Mona dear.*
> *We gather here for your day has come.*
> *Mona Ó Fionnáin. Mona dear.*

Why did you die, leaving us sorry, dear, Mona Ó
Fionnáin? Dear?
Even though your spirit is now set free?

Was your husband faithful, dear, Mona Ó Fionnáin?
Dear?
Even though he had many long days on his feet?

Was your daughter chaste, dear, Mona Ó Fionnáin?
Dear?
Even though she, too, went before her time?

How did your gardens tend, dear, Mona Ó Fion-
náin? Dear?
Even though hard times were had by all?

Did your husband warm your bed, dear, Mona Ó
Fionnáin? Dear?
Even when he worked so late into the night?

Mona Ó Fionnáin. Mona dear.
We gather here for your day has come.
Mona Ó Fionnáin. Mona dear.

Everyone clapped and cheered.

Colum stood up then and sorrowfully said, "I want to thank all yeh for comin' out 'ere fer Mona. She would have felt well-loved. She loved all of 'yeh. She was a good mother. A good wife. Thank you all."

At Mona's graveside, her coffin closed and lying next to the hole dug for her, the villagers gathered around Colum, Maggie, Oona, and the Foleys. The young, bald Church vicar, in his black robes, poised beside the coffin. A pall of heartbreak hovered over the crowd.

"May those who love us, love us; and those who don't love us, may God turn their hearts; Death leaves a heartache no one can heal; Love leaves a memory no one can steal," he said. "Amen."

"Amen," many said.

Cuán stood next to Maggie with his arm over her shoulder. She looked so heavy and delicate at the same time.

Once the vicar had said his prayer, the town began to go their own way. The day was on the cusp of giving into the night, and all that remained was for the undertaker to lower and bury Maggie's mother.

They stood there until everyone was gone, except Colum.

Colum turned to them and kissed both of Maggie's cheeks.

"Thank you, darlin', for helping me get through this. You're an angel," he said. "You promise not to keep an old man lonely?"

Maggie grinned, but her eyes weren't in it. Tears still sat on her cheeks. "I'll visit ye as often as I can," she said. "Besides, who's goin' to help with the sugar beets?"

Cuán shook his hand. "Anything you need, Colum, and we're there fer you."

"Thank you, Cuán.

"Don't think that because of all this, I've forgotten the happy occasion. I'll see you at the wedding, aye?"

"Aye," Maggie said with a warmer smile. Cuán watched her eyes water up again, glistening.

After Colum left them, Maggie went over and touched the coffin.

"I said me peace with her," Maggie said, "and yet I still don't want to leave."

Cuán kneeled beside her and put a hand on her back. He could feel her shallow breathing.

"I'm right here with you, Maggie, so long as you need."

"Bein' with her seemed so short of time. No matter how long it is, the way is short, isn't it? And then it's gone," Maggie said. "Forever."

...And the Road is Dark

1

Etna had always had bad dreams as a child. Only they weren't about monsters coming to get her or awful things happening to her. In these bad dreams, she did awful things to others. She realized that she liked to strangle things in her hands, feel them struggling as their soft necks give to her strength, and then relax as they perished.

She dreamed of dark forests, rotting remains, and ghouls coming up to pleasure her while she laid before them in the peat.

When she woke up, it was a different matter. Etna McCarna always woke up horrified by the mind that would think such things.

This is why she sometimes stayed up late. It was near midnight, and she was still going over the needed papers and organizing files to get them ready for the dig at the St. Albeus ruins, named after Saint Ailbhe—one of the disciples of St. Patrick, who went on to become a preacher and a bishop. He was not directly acquainted with monastic ruins except through the legend of wolves. Many claimed he became lost in the woods and then suckled by a wolf, which is why later, an old she-wolf came to him for protection as a hunting party tracked her.

The brotherhood that once walked the halls of St. Albeus used the wolf as their emblem. Not many knew why.

One of the noble lords in the area, Lord Grady Ó Cuinn, said that he had the privilege of knowing why this was and hired Etna to do further research on this ancient site. He was also funding the whole excavation. She learned from her own research that St. Albeus was built in the 7th century and rebuilt over and over again until it fell out of use in the 13th century.

All this took her mind off the nightmares. It's why she dove so thoroughly into her work. She changed the lantern oil more than once. If Lord Cuinn knew more, she wanted him to tell her. A part of her wanted to leave at once, wake him, and demand to know all he knew.

But that was ridiculous, wasn't it? She was just obsessed.

Maybe she should try to sleep.

Etna heard something behind her. She was in the cottage alone. She knew her assistant, Mary, had left for the night. Well before ten.

She turned around, listening quietly.

Something shuffled outside her door. There was a brief light, but it snuffed out.

Was she being robbed? Was someone there, or was it her imagination? She just wasn't sure.

Etna tip-toed to the door, putting her ear against it, her mind racing with all the things she thought she must do. Go out the window. Shout for the police. Demand the interloper leave at once. Find a weapon to defend herself with.

Something slowly creaked down the hall.

Why did she feel so cold?

It could be Mary. Maybe she forgot something, and could not leave it here, and returned for it?

But *no*...something inside her could *feel* what was on the other side of the door. Cold. Dark. Malice. The hair on her neck crawled like spiders.

She was sure that this person had no right to be there and did not have good intentions.

Etna could feel that in her blood.

The sound of wings fluttered. She thought she heard a chicken's high-pitched clucking.

Fluttering?

Whatever it was, it had a chicken.

Don't be a fool, she told herself. *You're just scaring yourself. Go out there and confront him.*

Him?

Her—Whatever, whoever. Confront them.

Etna grabbed the doorknob and turned it. And stopped.

What if they had a gun? What if they meant to harm her in some way?

Before she could catch herself, a part of her went for it anyway: "Hello! Anyone there?"

No one answered.

Etna could hear the birds fluttering, clucking away.

Whoever was there—was *still* there.

Etna touched her throat, telling herself, *Stop being such a coward!*

Etna opened the door and grabbed her parasol from the coat closet.

"Mary? Is that you? It upsets me that you would be in so early and make such a ruckus!"

Out the backdoor window, she saw a skeletal face. Its horrid beaten look and rotting features made her gasp. Her long black hair billowed in the air about her skull, and she stuck out her gray, chewed tongue.

He's here for you, she said. *And he wants a taste of you.*

Etna backed away from the door and turned around. When she looked back, the specter was gone.

She followed the noise and walked into the kitchen, where a lamp sat on the counter—its light pulsing on the walls. Next to the large sink basins, a tall man stood in a long dark coat and a peaked cap with captain bars. In one large hand, he held onto the legs of a panicked hen, which beat its wing furiously to escape.

"Good God, who are you?" she said.

The man grabbed the hen's neck and twisted the head off. Blood gushed from the head onto the floor, and he moved it over to the sink. The blood splattered his nice coat, but he didn't seem to care.

"Get out, or I'll beat you with this! I'll call the police!"

The man laughed. She could feel the depth of his malignancy. It made the room smell of grave dirt and rosemary. It made her skin bristle. Her muscles tightened as if she were being watched from every direction by unseen things. Things that would mean her harm.

"Your threats are weak," the man said, tossing the chicken into the sink. "I came for you, Etna. I came to help you."

The man turned around. She could not believe how handsome he was. How sexy his eyes were. Out of all the terror she felt for him, she realized she was also drawn to him. That's why she found she couldn't say anything to him.

From his pocket, he placed on the table what looked like a sausage, but on further inspection, she realized that it was a large, bloated severed finger. It had that brownish mottling of the skin that made her think that it had been preserved and kept for centuries.

"What is that?" she said.

That's when she realized there was a boy huddled under the sink basin, holding his knees and quivering, tears of blood threading down his cheeks.

Etna backed up, rubbed her eyes, and looked again.

The boy was gone.

The man moved closer to her. "Sreng's Finger Bone. It will help you achieve yourself."

"I have already achieved yourself—uh, *my*self."

Etna then saw that her hands were shaking, and holding her parasol between them seemed such a weak gesture.

"Oh. But you are wrong," he said, slowly pushing the parasol away.

In the blink of an eye, his body lay against her, and she looked up at him, and into his black eyes. His teeth were unnaturally white, and his canines seemed like they were two or three inches long. The tips were pointed more like bird talons than teeth. It frightened her in a way far more extreme than she'd ever felt before.

"You are a dark dominion. Like Satan himself," she said.

"I. Am...the Commination," he said, and licked her lips.

His tongue was cold, but the touch of his saliva made her lips tingle. She didn't even realize that she had opened her mouth for him. She wanted the Dominion inside her. She wanted HIM inside her, filling her up. And somehow—though part of her was against it—she wanted him to tear her apart. Etna wanted his large, powerful hands to rend her to pieces.

Her body quivered at that idea.

"I don't understand this," she said.

The man grinned.

"You are more than one. You are not entirely yourself, but you are also all there is."

"Not very clarifying," she said, breathing heavily now.

"Well, the road *is* dark..."

The man grabbed the front of her gown and tore it aside. It didn't all come off her, but the fabric fell away in tatters, exposing her breasts. He traced a vein along her left breast, which ran close to her nipple, and then trailed off.

He was teasing her.

She remembered the ghoul outside her door: *He's here for you. And he wants a taste of you.*

"You must be cut asunder," he said and grinned again.

Etna lifted her face to him, opened her mouth, and let her tongue dart out. It was an offering to him, and he pressed his mouth to her. His teeth bit down on her tongue, and she cried out, but instead of releasing her, he sucked on her tongue. Swallowing her blood.

Her mouth tingled and then became numb, and as her heart raced, her mind spun back into blackness.

This was all a dream, she thought.

The world was black and smelled of sulfur, which burned into her nose, making her head ache. Goat-legged demons with bloody red flesh were crawling on her, using their black claws and black teeth to tear and bite at her skin. It was hot, stifling, and she couldn't breathe.

This was Hell. The idea terrified her so much that she screamed and begged for the Dominion to save her from it all, but she did not see him. She only felt the heat, the claws, the teeth, the burning of her flesh as it opened and bled.

The Dominion pulled away from her, his lips dripping with her blood. Etna fell back against the kitchen wall. Her tongue started to throb painfully as it wet her mouth with its iron taste.

The man wiped his mouth and then grabbed his chicken.

"Thank you for the chicken. I'll see you soon. Aye?"

He started to leave but turned back for a moment. "Don't go into the Hidden Place unarmed."

The man left her, and Etna started to sob.

It was so exquisite and terrifying. She didn't know what to do with any of it.

Then she saw the preserved finger on her kitchen table. The fat, bloated thing felt like the Dominion, and she wanted more of it. She went to her room, closed the door, and pulled her gown over her head. Falling back on her bed, she pulled her knickers aside and shoved Sreng's Finger Bone inside her. It felt like a cock, and she imagined it being the Dominion himself. She started to drive it into her body until she squeezed her thighs shut tight. Her body shook out the nicest feeling she'd ever had.

Exhausted, she fell asleep.

2

The next day, Etna and her partner, an archaeologist from Dublin named Doctor Alastar Macguire, went to the ruins to mark the sites for random sampling. He was a short, stocky man with very little hair on his head and a mustache. They worked together to choose the spots where they'd dig, measured them out, and staked them off.

With a few diggers who arrived early, they helped put up a couple of tents in the field on the west side of the monastery to store supplies, records, and to report and store artifacts as they found them.

Once that was done, it was later afternoon. Alastar went with a couple of diggers to collect the supplies—the trowels, hammers, shovels, etcetera—leaving Etna to start the logbook. She used a ruler to divide columns on sheets of paper, trying to get well ahead so that she wouldn't have to do it often.

When she woke up earlier that day, she put a leather strap around the severed end of Sreng's Finger Bone. This way, she could put the strap around her neck, letting the finger bone lay between her breasts. Her dirty mind liked the idea that it felt like a hard cock between them, and it excited her. It made her feel as though the Dominion was with her.

She didn't know why she liked this. It should terrify her...and maybe it did a little...but it also made her feel more alive than she had in years. However, after Alastar left for the equipment, the Finger felt like it moved between her breasts. She grabbed it there, gasping, unsure of what was happening. When she let it go, the Finger moved again.

Etna looked around, wondering if HE was back, but saw no one around. She stepped out of her tent, looking.

Nothing.

The Finger moved again.

Etna pulled the collar of her dress forward and reached in with her other hand, grabbing the Finger and pulling it out. It rose in the air in front of her, pointing...

What the bloody hell was this?

Etna couldn't believe it.

She started walking, seeing that the Finger pointed toward the St. Albeus ruins. It was leading her inside.

Etna swallowed hard. The Dominion hadn't come to just *please* her...No, HE came to lead her to something.

She followed the Finger into the chapel and then around to a half-fallen cloister. Once she approached a tall stone, it dropped back onto her chest. Etna touched the stone. Looking at it carefully, she realized that the stone wasn't part of the monastery structure. It was a separate thing: a standing stone, and it was probably older than the ruin itself.

"Holy shit," she said. "What are you trying to tell me?"

Etna clutched Sreng's Finger Bone, taking it off from around her neck. She couldn't leave it there anymore. It was too distracting.

She went back to the tent, wondering what the Dominion expected her to do or wanted her to understand. Etna was sure it was more than his desire for her blood or her death. It was much more than that. She just couldn't think of what it could be yet.

In the cottage Lord Cuinn offered her during her stay in Wexford, Etna sent Mary home right after supper. She couldn't wait. Unable to stop her cravings, she undressed and crawled into bed with the Finger. She rubbed her wetness around between her legs and then rubbed it against each of her nipples, and when she couldn't wait any longer, she drove the Finger inside her again.

Letting her muscles relax as her chest heaved for breath, Etna rolled over and saw that she was sweating.

No, not sweating. Her flesh seemed like it was melting.

The terror of it made her heave. She tried to gather her melting flesh, but it poured through her fingers like molasses.

Etna cried out, her breath seizing.

Had she gone too far? Wasn't this what the *damned* Dominion wanted of her?

Etna thought, *I don't want to die. What have I done?*

Oddly, she had skin that did not melt away, but the skin that did started shaping itself into another feminine form. It had the same form as she had: it was as tall as her and had the same shaped arms, legs...face.

Face?

Etna crawled out of bed.

What witchcraft was this?

Dark hair grew out her scalp, her pits, and between her legs. Her flesh also kept reshaping itself. Etna could see green eyes forming, nipples, and a cleft between her legs. Fingers. Toes.

The other body convulsed, and then it gasped for breath.

The form was made into another woman—a woman who looked exactly like her. She was a copy in every way.

The woman looked at her, saw her expression, and laughed.

"Who the bloody fuck are you?" Etna said.

The woman laughed again. "Carman, silly bird."

Carman looked herself over, rubbing her body with her hands. Her flesh remained the same as if this woman hadn't just sprung from her own flesh.

"I do look good, aye?"

She felt herself between her legs.

Etna couldn't even look away.

"I am hungry, though," the woman said. "You have anything?"

Etna barely understood what she said.

The woman laughed, crawled over to her, grabbed her hands, and pulled her close. The other woman felt like any other human. Alive.

Carman kissed her on the cheek.

"See? I'm no danger to you."

The room started spinning, and before she knew it, Etna fainted.

The Tomb

1

Carman watched as Etna passed out onto the floor. She picked the woman up and laid her on the bed, covering her up with the blankets. Carman gave her another kiss on the cheek and whispered, "*Codladh sámh.*" She then saw Sreng's Finger Bone, which had fallen on the floor in Etna's hurry to leave the bed. It still glistened with her wetness. Smelled of her sex, too. Carman picked it up by the strap, letting it dangle, and then slowly, the Finger rose, pointing toward the bedroom window.

It was saying, *Go there. Go now.*

Carman couldn't remember much. She knew she was a witch, and she remembered losing her sons, but she couldn't remember where she was or why she was there. She knew that the woman beside her was an avatar—a spiritual aspect of her that she had somehow made flesh. It was in her blood that she was able to hide.

But something inside her wasn't complete, and she didn't know what it was.

Carman did know of Sreng's Finger Bone, and she thought that it might have been left for her so that she could complete herself.

In essence, Carman had been Etna, and had all her memories and dreams, and could now put context to the Dominion—the vampyre that brought her the Finger, and said, *It will help you achieve yourself.* It helped divide them as they needed to be, and she was sure it would lead her on her path to glory.

And what was glory? she thought.

It was freeing her sons from exile and punishing the children of Bres.

Yes, that's what glory was.

Carman, holding the Finger by the strap, found the door and left the cottage.

She passed by a farm as she walked the road, following where Sreg pointed, and she remembered what the Dominion had told Etna. *Don't go into the Hidden Place unarmed.* Carman thought she might find something helpful there and walked a few minutes to the barn and dug through its contents quietly. Then she found a broad-bladed sword that looked a little unwieldy, but it would work just fine. Using Etna's memory, Carman realized it was a machete—blades made for hacking away wild growth. Farmers used them to hack away unwanted shrubs and things from their fields.

With the machete tight in her hand, she followed the Finger as it pointed away from the barn and to an old ruin she had never seen before. It took her around the partially collapsed walls of the cloister to a standing stone.

A standing stone?

Carman touched it. The stone was made by Bres and encrypted with a *Song of Eagla* by the white sorceress, Bé Chuille. One of the daughters of Bres and one of Lugh's sorcerers. Her anger surged. Why would this power be here other than to mock her?

Carman yelled like a wild cat, tears fleeing her eyes.

Damn them all to Dá Derga's Pits in the very bowels of Duinn!

She heaved, catching her breath. Carman wiped away her tears, wishing then that she had access to her gods. Here in the land that once belonged to the Tuatha Dé, no other gods could purchase.

Carman hated them all, and she missed her sons terribly.

She touched the stone again and she saw that inside, a blurry, monstrous apparition laid in wait. They entombed it, trapping it there beyond the Hollow of the ruin catacombs. No mortal would be able to find it, but she was no simple mortal. She was a witch, and she stripped half the world of its occult knowledge, and she now wielded it against her enemies.

Carman just couldn't remember how to use them now.

Shame ran through her.

How could she not remember her power?

Carman looked up at the standing stone, thinking. She started turning in circles, opening her arms. She was naked still, not even realizing her nakedness, knowing only that as she danced, she was with the world, and the world was now flowing through her. She twirled, dancing widdershins around the stone. When she completed three revolutions around the stone, it hummed in her mind, and she let her arms drop to her sides.

Before, the old walls of the monastery were solid and thick, but there was a black doorway that now beckoned her. She could feel the monster's breaths. Each breath was shallow, but it was inside, awaiting her.

Carman didn't have her powers. She was merely a naked woman standing there like a fool. Going in there would be a terrible idea...But she *did* have her machete. Maybe it was enough. Without thinking too much about it, she descended the stairs to the catacombs beneath. As she walked to the back chamber, she heard nearly inaudible whispers.

Carman stopped, not knowing what to do. One of the voices sounded familiar. A male voice. It spoke to her somehow, though she couldn't place it at the moment.

Don't let this place haunt you, she told herself. *You must conquer your doubts in order to conquer your enemies.*

2

At the back of the chamber, something moved. It was a *she*—a woman with mottled purple and blue skin. She had dark, avian wings. Her black hair covered her face, but what light there was, showed her mutant features, which horrified Carman.

The monster looked up at her, and its eyes shot fear. Its mouth widened, and it hissed, *"Nooooo! Stop! You don't know what you're do—"*

But Carman knew she couldn't think too much about it. If she did—if she paused for *one moment*—the opportunity would be lost.

Carman raised the machete over her head, shouted a battle cry, and attacked the creature. She hacked at its face, driving the machete half through her skull and then again, cutting her down to her neck.

The creature continued to scream like it could not die.

Carman knew it had to be destroyed. The Dominion was giving her this, and if she desired her sons and her revenge, then HIS will *must* be done.

Carman repeatedly hacked at the creature until it fell to bloody pieces, blood spraying everywhere until it just poured. When Carman finished, the creature lingered as a pile of chopped meat and feathers as she gasped for her breath.

The image of the creature's face—*those eyes*, especially—gave her a cold shudder, but it was now dead at her feet. Some of its blood ran in rivulets down Carman's pale, naked flesh.

She caught her breath, throwing the machete aside.

Someone was behind her, she thought. Carman could feel it.

"Good," he said.

It was HIM. The Dominion. He came up behind her and his large hand grabbed her between her legs from behind, his palm squeezing down on her buttocks. The sensation was delicious.

Carman saw some blood on her finger and licked it off.

The man behind her smiled at her over her shoulder. He squeezed again, and she moaned.

"You have set yourself on your path," he said. "This will benefit both of us."

Carman turned to him, planning to ride him, but HE was no longer there. Just...gone.

Too bad for him.

She grinned.

Though she did not feel the creature's power enter her, she was sure that she took its place somehow. It was now up to her to figure out how she would use this to get what she wanted. And Carman knew it was only a matter of time, so she wasn't going to worry about anything now.

She left the catacombs and the Hollow. The night air was crisp.

Etna's memories reflected on her nakedness again, and Carman decided that she needed to make herself more modest for the day and age. She also recalled the St. Albeus research information, the dig, Lord Cuinn, and the Order of Bres.

As she walked back to Etna's cottage, Carman considered all of this.

Ponc's Omen

1

At the pub, Brian raised his pint, and everyone there followed suit, quieting down. "In a couple days, my son, Cuán, and his beloved, Maggie, are getting married. Here's to them and the life they'll make in Dublin!"

"Here's to a long life and a merry one. A quick death and an easy one. A pretty girl and an honest one. A cold pint and another one!" another man exclaimed.

Maggie was a wee bit pissed, but she knew enough to say, "Now come on, save some of those blessings for the actual day! Don't want to go about and muck up a perfectly good fortune!"

Men and women laughed.

Cuán brought another pint to the table.

"*Ack*, I don't know if I can manage another. I'll be passed, and ye'll have to throw me over yer shoulder."

Cuán stumbled a bit. "Yeah, well. As I bloody see it, we deserve a little too much tonight."

Maggie smiled at him and then said, "It's a game then. Whoever passes first carries the other."

Cuán held up his pint. "It's a contract."

"I'm betting on the lass," someone said. "She's a might pint short, but not short on the might, aye?"

More people laughed, and Cuán stood up. "Oh yeah? Well, I know yeh don't know...what I know, and that's that...I am *perfectly* stubborn enough to meet this match."

More laughter. Maggie grabbed the back of Cuán's slacks, pulling him back down his chair. "Don't mind Cuán. He's speaking out his tin-faced arse."

***

She helped Cuán stumble home, regretting that second pint. Cuán had never been a real drinker, so when he was pissed, he was utterly useless. She loved the lug, but she had to remember he wasn't a particularly heavy sponge.

Cuán twisted from her arms and fell back on his ass onto the steps of his home. Orna would be inside. Maggie hoped she was asleep so she didn't have to witness this.

"I'm sorry, Maggie. I just needed a moment of not feeling, you know?"

"Ye feeling anythin'?"

"Well... yes, honestly. I feel like shite. I might hurl, Luv."

"Please, no."

Cuán leaned over, and he sprayed the ground with black stout. Maggie had to look away as he continued to empty his stomach. When she heard him spitting, she turned to see him wiping his mouth.

"*Hup*. It came up." He grinned at her.

Maggie grabbed his jaw and looked at him. The last time she looked at his face she saw the faint lines of aging on him, and she was beginning to be disturbed by it. He was twenty-six now. Soon he'd be thirty, and then forty, and eventually, he would die of old age. Like Mona, and eventually Colum and Oona, she would lose him too.

And her?

Maggie had done the math. If she'd stayed in Ireland and not spent ten years in the Otherworld, trapped with the Fomorians, she would have been the same age as Deirdre—the *siofra* who took her life. When Deirdre died fighting an *Arrachtaigh*, she was twenty-eight. She'd be thirty now.

Maggie was thirty years old, too, really. But she didn't appear that old at all. When she came back from the Otherworld, she was eight years old when she should have been eighteen. She thought this gave her longer life because of her absence from the material world, but over the last two years, she realized that once she turned eighteen, she stopped aging altogether. She didn't just have a longer life. Maggie might even be immortal because of the loathsome serpentine blood running in her veins.

Even if Maggie aged to twenty-two, which would have been her age if you don't count the eight years she grew up in the Deep Dens, she would have something to show for it. But she didn't see it. The reality was: if she was going to live much longer than Cuán, perhaps even live an immortal life, what would that life be without him? He was there in the beginning when she woke up, tangled in that algae. He should be there in the end. Nothing else was fair to her, and it hurt her to think it.

"Why are you looking so sad at me, Maggie? You look at me like that sometimes. It breaks my heart," Cuán said.

Maggie didn't want to tell him—*couldn't* tell him. She let go of his jaw.

She smiled, though she really didn't feel like it.

"It's not sorrow," she lied. "It's just a lot of love and hope stirred together, making things confusin' but right somehow. Let's get you inside."

Maggie helped him up, and he leaned on her as they went into the house. Orna watched her as she dumped Cuán in bed, covering him up.

"You're so good to him," Orna said. "I hope he's what you deserve."

Maggie tucked Cuán in and then sat on the bed, looking back at Orna, smiling. "He's proved himself to me already. I think we're right fer one another, as mushy as that sounds."

Orna grinned. "Good night, Luv."

"'Night, Orna."

2

When Maggie left the Foley house, stepping outside, she looked up and saw the gray wolfhound across the street, staring at her.

Ponc.

"What are you doing here, boyo?"

Ponc just looked at her for a moment. Then he sniffed the ground and started prancing off. Maggie started following him. The large dog took her once again to the cliffs and down the path to the rocky shoreline where Cuán once found her washed ashore.

It was no surprise, of course.

But she wondered what it was this time.

Ponc barked and then started walking on water like the Jesus of dogs. Maggie took off her shoes and walked until her feet were in the icy water, waves washing over them as they lapped back and forth.

She pulled up the skirt of her dress and squatted down. Flattening her right hand, she touched the water and sent her senses out.

Instead of feeling the normal vibrations and sensations of what was in the water, something redirected her mind through some other path in the Hollow. It wound her somewhere, but she wasn't sure where.

And then, all at once, it opened on a moment in some room somewhere. She recognized herself, though perhaps her face changed a little over time. She looked impossibly sad as she buried her head in the chest of the old man lying in bed in front of her, a black cat on her lap with golden eyes.

Maggie looked closer at the man and saw Cuán's beautiful seal eyes, but his face was cracked with age and mottled skin. His hair was a dark gray.

He coughed, and Maggie watched the very youthful version of herself help lean him up, and then she tried to give him some water off the bedside stand. Tears were running down her cheeks. She knew—could *feel*—Cuán was dying.

Maggie stood and stepped back from where the sea gave her the omen.

There she was: youthful, full of energy, and looking no older than she did now. Cuán was old now, fading away—she would lose him soon.

She couldn't stop herself from crying again.

Mona's death, still so fresh and sharp in her mind, was still an open wound, so seeing Cuán perishing now was a blow that she didn't want to take right then.

Ponc looked at her as the waves washed through him.

He was a ghost, after all.

Ponc was showing her the vision, letting her know that her worst fears were true. The damn faithful dog was looking out for them. Looking out for her.

"How do I fix this?" she asked the wolfhound.

Ponc barked. *I don't know.* And then the wolfhound ran toward the sea and disappeared from her sight.

Maggie looked back at the rocks and then at the cave.

After Maggie and Cuán's experience in the village with the Devil's Breath, Maggie attempted several times to return to these caves and call the Cailleach—the Winter Queen who saved her from the fomori after having kidnapped her for several years. Each time she attempted to call the ancient goddess, Maggie failed.

Maggie went back to the caves, angry and sobbing.

"Where *are* you?!" she said. "Cailleach! CAILLEACH! Tá tú ag teastáil uaim! Le do thoil, tá tú teastáil uaim! PLEASE!"

The cave just echoed the words back at her...

... lease... ease... ease...

For fuck-sakes. Help me, she thought. She prayed.

"If I cannot save Cuán, then I will find a way to die!" she screamed. "I will find a way to *die!*"

Maggie left, kicking dirt and rocks as she went. She screamed at the sea, and then she turned around and went home. Oona slept soundly and didn't stir when Maggie walked by. In her own bed, Maggie found it hard to fall asleep. Her mind reeled.

How does one find mortality? How did one *clean* their blood?

Maggie needed help from someone, and the only fae creature she could think of was Killian.

The Athenian Witch

1

Etna startled awake. She was lying in bed naked, wrapped in blankets. Her doppelgänger lay beside her, unmoving at first. The woman sensed that she was awake and turned over, holding Sreng's Finger Bone up.

"This makes you happy?" Carman said, grinning.

Etna crawled out of bed, feeling humiliated. "You're still here. It wasn't a nightmare?"

Carman looked her over, not answering her. "I always wondered what it would be like to make love with myself."

Etna could hear Mary working down the hall. "Shh. She cannot hear you."

"Oh? The servant woman? You frightened of her?"

"No!" Etna groaned. "I don't want her hearing our business."

Carman got out of bed, tossing the Finger onto Etna's bedside stand. "You can keep that and enjoy it as much as you like. I'll need some of your clothes."

Etna reddened. "You can have whatever," Etna said. "Just go."

Carman looked back at her and slowly shook her head. "Oh no, Etna McCarna...You and I are One. You are a reflection of me and nothing more, do you understand?"

"Don't think I won't escape you," Etna said. "I am much more than that! I will have a life. I will—"

"'Will' what?" Carman laughed. "You are nothing but a shadow, and without me, all your efforts will be for not. Even your children will be shadows and expire early and with no importance. You... Etna...are what I choose you to be, and nothing more."

Etna knew this woman could kill her, *would* kill her if she had to. She was sure that the woman could conjure dark forces, let alone the Dominion, and she didn't want to be her next victim, so she nodded enthusiastically. "If we must."

"Good. Once I'm dressed, I'm going to be looking for my sons. Keep your eyes and ears open because I think St. Albeus has more to offer me than mere monsters."

Etna looked at her, shocked, but she vaguely remembered seeing it in her dreams. Carman going to the monastery, finding a door by a standing stone, going into the catacombs, and slaying some creature there. The Dominion was there with her, too.

That's when she realized that she somehow psychically connected to Carman as well. If they were connected, then she wouldn't be able to run far without Carman hunting her down.

"Whatever you'd like, Carman."

Carman opened her closet and started picking through her dresses. She pulled a white one and showed it to Etna.

"Will you help me with this?"

2

As the sun rose higher, the grassy fields warmed around the ruins. Diggers started in their zoned areas, and Etna supervised by making her way around. Doctor Macguire sampled in one zone, carefully guiding the other diggers in the more fragile work.

About mid-morning, Lord Grady Ó Cuinn arrived in a carriage. Etna knew that he funded the dig, but he was also her High Priest in the druidic Order of Bres. She was certain that he knew more than he told her, so she approached him before Dr. Macguire had a chance to notice his arrival.

"Lord Cuinn. May I have a short word with you?"

The man was tall and old enough to have the whitest hair. He wore a suit with a top hat and carried himself much like most nobles that she knew.

"Of course, Etna. Anything for you," he said.

Etna walked beside him as they walked down the path toward St. Albeus.

"I know we spoke of this site's significance with the god Bres, but in my research, I came across the name of a woman. I'm not sure if she was a god or what, but it made me curious. Could it be possible that this site also has some historical connection with a woman named Carman?"

Lord Cuinn smiled at her. "Possibly. There's a local legend of a witch from Athens. I think she was buried somewhere in Wicklow, but Leinster has local festivals in her honor—*Óenach Carmán.*

"Something about a curse. Oh yes! As she lay dying at the feet of Lugh, she demanded that they have a festival in her honor, or Leinster would be cursed with famine, so ever since then, the Tuatha Dé would honor her on Lughnasad. When the Tuatha Dé made the Great Contracts with the Milesians, the people of Ireland took over the festival."

"A witch of Athens? Has anyone tracked her past to Athens? Is she represented by any of the Greek gods?"

Lord Cuinn shook his head. "Not that I'm aware of."

The man pulled a cigar out of his jacket pocket and popped it between his lips, and then pulled out a match and lit it.

Could it be possible that Carman escaped her tomb in Leinster through her? Only to meet with Bres after these long centuries?

It sounded crazy.

"What's the significance with Bres?"

"Well, young lady, Bres designed her tomb once she fell at the hands of Lugh and his companions—the poet, Aoi Mac Ollamain, a white sorceress, Bé Chuille, and a satirist, Cridhinbheal. He designed it to imprison her until the end of her days. They say she died of longing for her three sons that Lugh exiled from the island after battling them."

This only explained a little of why Carman was here. She said she wanted to find her sons, but what monster hid in the catacombs below the ruins? She wanted to ask Lord Cuinn, but she decided that it may not be a good idea just now.

"We're to meet at the manor in a few days, correct?"

Etna nodded. "Aye. We are."

"Let's not be too late, Lass."

Etna let Lord Cuinn continue on to St. Albeus to meet up with Dr. Macguire. She decided to look around the cloister. The standing stone was obvious enough. It was standing in the courtyard near the cloister walls. She went around through one of the main doors, attempting to keep track of where she was, and went down the long hall, counting her paces. She took her time.

When she stopped, she turned toward the wall.

It was obvious to her now that the wall was broader here. Why would they build it like that? The expense of quarrying extra stones of this size wouldn't be cost-effective for a church, unless it was desperate. Why would they do this? She couldn't think of any archaeological reason.

Etna thought about the Dominion coming to her. She remembered the dream of demons as he drank her blood. Could the Church have trapped a demon under the monastery, using the holy ground to contain its evil? Had Carman found the entrance?

Etna walked back around to the standing stone and touched the solid wall where she remembered Carman finding the door. She wished her memories—or her psychic vision, if that's what it was—were clearer, less vague. But it wasn't her that entered the catacomb and slaughtered the creature within, was it? No...It was Carman. And Carman was going to be a problem.

3

Later that afternoon, Etna left the dig and rode into Wexford. In her research over the last year to prepare for this dig, Etna learned that many of the Catholic artifacts, including their texts, from St. Albeus, were never turned over to the Catholic Church and were handed over to St. Iberius, which belonged to the Church of Ireland. The Catholic Church wanted them back and attempted a few times to reacquire them, but with the Penal Code so restrictive since the late 17th century, the Church of Ireland kept everything Irish in Ireland.

If she wanted more answers, she thought she should look there.

Late that night, eyes dry and burning from all the reading by the lantern, the vicar came in wearing his pajamas, telling her that she must leave and come back in the morning to continue her research.

Dreading seeing Carman again, she reluctantly left and rode home—not wanting to be thrown out for good when she knew that if there were answers, they were hidden in those vaults.

Two days after visiting St. Iberius at night, Etna came across a journal from an unnamed monk. He spoke of dreams of the ghostly demon that often wandered the halls with raven wings and milky eyes.

> *A thyng of unnatyral evyl. A dymon of womnh'd. It shakes its mylky brests and scratchys thee walls wyth its clahs late into thee nyte.*

The monk went on to say that it tried laying on him to steal his seed so that it could do unholy things with it, including giving birth to a hell-born child for its unholy motivations upon the earth.

While it shows that a few monks knew of the demon, it didn't say who it really was or even mention Carman.

This was a dead end.

There had to be some other way.

The next day, after leaving the dig for the afternoon, she rode to the home of a historian named Rían Ó Suaird. He was a man in his fifties. He had the kindest face she's ever met, and he welcomed her into his home for a later supper.

"I was hoping you could tell me some details about a mythical woman named Carman," she said.

"Well, now. That's a little outside my expertise, but knowing the local history and participating in the local festivals, you're in luck. I happen to know a lot about Carman."

"Really? Tell me, Mister Ó Suaird."

Rían went on to tell her a lot of what she already knew, but he said something else that she didn't know about.

"Carman was never part of Ireland. The Tuatha Dé fought both the fir bolg and fomori for the rights to rule it, and when they had won it, they bound Ireland to its own magic. Outsiders would not be able to come along and learn the *Eagla*. They would have to be born to it."

"Eagla? Isn't that Gaelic for 'fear'?"

"Oh yes, the Milesians were very much afraid of the magic of the Tuatha Dé, so when they came across their magic, they often called it the Scary. It's said that the Tuatha Dé adopted the word, embracing its description because it kept the Milesians from poking around the Hidden World. Some now call them the Eeries.

"Anyway, when Carman came to the island with her sons, she knew that to conquer the Milesians—who were now very much protected by the Tuatha Dé—she would need to learn the mystery of the *Eagla*."

Etna was confused. "But she couldn't learn their magic because she wasn't born here."

"No, not at first. For you see, the real secret of the *Eagla* is that it's bound to the Irish geas—the spiritual prohibition that was created by their very essences...of their fate. In order for Carman to learn the Eagla, she would need to—"

"Change her fate," Etna said, starting to understand it.

Rían nodded and raised a wine glass to her. "She would have to take on a geas, so she had one forged into her spirit through fae blood."

"But who would do such a thing?"

Rían drank his wine and then shook his head. "Nobody knows. But somebody did because Carman learned the *Eagla*, and it made her even more powerful. She used it to make her sons powerful, and she proved difficult for Lugh to kill. Of course, the Tuatha Dé succeeded, didn't they? We know how the story ends."

Etna thought, *Do we? Really?*

Maybe the story never ends.

"So, what is her *geas*? I mean, it's her weakness, right?"

"Oh! She was a clever one! She knew that the geas could be used for her weakness, so she tricked whoever forged her *geas* into making it something that was impossible to do."

"Which was?"

Rían looked at her, biting his lip for a moment. Why wouldn't he just come out with it?

And then he did: "It's said that she cannot deny the commands of her father. Except, her father died when she was sixteen. No one in this world could command her anymore without him. She was free to do whatever she liked, knowing there was no weakness man could take advantage of."

Etna was shocked.

This wasn't good.

"She's invincible."

Rían laughed. "No, I mean, Lugh handled it, didn't he? Bres forged a prison for her, and she died in it many years later."

They ate in silence for a short while, and then she told Rían about her dig at the St. Albeus ruins. She didn't tell him about Carman or how she hunted a demon beneath the monastery, but she did tell him about the unnamed monk's letters.

"Have you heard of a demon such as this? In the folktales, or—"

"As I said, Etna, I'm not a folklorist. I'm a historian. I know some about the monastery—you probably know everything I know, but I have never heard of any demons there. It is interesting, though. Even ghost stories seem to have their own little lives, aye? People believe in them, and then the stories fade in time, and then not even the ghosts survive.”

Etna nodded and finished her food.

“Thank you for supper. It was good of you.”

“Come back any time, Etna. Be safe out there.”

Etna stood up to leave.

“Oh, and is Lord Cuinn doing well?”

Etna shrugged. “I suppose so.”

“Tell him I said hello, will you?”

“Of course, Mister Ó Suaird.”

The Whisper in the Shell

When he last dreamed, he couldn't move, unable to look around him, save down the path, and then he saw Bridget's reaction when she found him. The Red Knight was coming up behind her, grabbing her head to lob it off with a sword. He shouted at her: *Run, Bridget. Run.* Aedán woke up with a panic attack, thinking the red Knight was going to kill her, too. He couldn't calm his heart. His whole body felt frozen, making it all even worse. The flies that buzzed around him in his dream were almost like the black dots that floated just on the edges of his visual periphery.

He had to close his eyes and lay there, slowing his breaths, calming himself. Just being.

Aedán wasn't sure what had happened, but a few days later, he found his way back into the dream.

He went to the bridge and waited for Bridget, sitting with his legs dangling over the edge. When he saw her coming down the path, he stood up and opened his arms to her.

She ran to him and threw her arms around him.

"I thought you were dead! I saw your head on that stake and..."

Aedán sighed. "I—I wasn't sure what was going on. I couldn't move. I didn't know what was happening to me. But I'm fine now. It's over."

Bridget pulled away from him. "Why is this happening to us? I mean, you're real. I'm real. We're both dreaming in the same dream world. This isn't natural. How did this happen to us?"

"I don't know, but if you're real, then we should meet in the waking world, away from this Lost Place."

"I agree. Wexford is a day's journey by carriage. I looked it up."

"If we do this, I'll find a spot for us to meet. I can also find you a place to stay."

Bridget looked at him gratefully.

"Then I'll try to leave the day after tomorrow. We'll get together, and we'll figure this out."

Aedán sighed. "Do you think we're cursed? Maybe that's why we're lost here? What if there's no sane way out?"

Bridget shrugged. "We'll worry about that if it's a problem. For now, we'll take it a day at a time. Sound good?"

"Aye, Bridget. It sounds wonderful. I can't wait to meet you in life. Who knows how much this place changes us?"

Bridget got close to him, and kissed his bottom lip slowly.

"We'll see, won't we?"

It was a good night to dream. Aedán woke up just after making love to her and smiled.

She was real.

Or was she? Dreams were never logical places, and they could make you believe things, only to wake up and realize *it was nothing but a dream*. How many times in other dreams had he thought he'd gone to school without pants or that he made a grievous mistake and shamed himself in front of other people? Then upon waking, breathed a sigh of relief that none of it was real?

Plenty of times, that's the answer.

Laying there for a moment, he started missing his real da. He reached above him to the shelving and grabbed the small conch that was lying there. It was said that you could hear the ocean in the shell if you put it to your ear, but this was a special shell. Not even Lord Cuinn knew about it. Aedán called it his Macalla Shell. When he put it to his ear, he heard his da's voice. The man was long dead, but he could hear him as if the conch itself captured his voice, and it somehow got caught in the twisting, pinkish posterior canal.

I won't see my son grow, will I? I'll be dead any minute now. Dead, and my son will never really know.

No! NO! Put that away!

And then someone else spoke, almost inaudibly. Aedán figured he'd never know who it was.

Goodbye, Desmond.

When he was younger, this made him sad. After a while, he became angry, wondering who could have murdered his father in cold blood, and then it just became a reminder that his father loved him and that he was here because of him. Thanks to Lord Cuinn and his father being the closest of friends.

Sometimes he carried the shell on him, believing it to be lucky.

Aedán put the Macalla Shell back on the shelf and then crawled out of bed to take a bath and dress for breakfast. Generally, he wore simple slacks, a blue shirt, and a jacket.

At the table, an attendant served Lord Cuinn his newspaper. His two daughters—twins, and both seven years of age—sat next to each other across the table already eating, and the maid told Lord Cuinn that their breakfast would be along soon.

"Thank you," Aedán said, nodding at her.

"Aedán, my boy! How is your morning?" Lord Cuinn said, looking briefly at him before straightening out his paper in front of him.

"I slept well."

"Good. We have a long day ahead of us. I'm going to show you how to run the books on the various businesses. My hopes that in a year or so, you will take over this tedious task when you take on with the company," Lord Cuinn said, now scanning the newspaper in front of him for things to read.

Just then, Nevan entered. His hair was still a mess, and he hadn't bothered to put on shoes. He was like a younger brother, only a year younger than Aedán. But unlike Aedán, who was adopted by the Lord Cuinn, Nevan was his true son and therefore seemed to come down harder on him.

They both noticed him, and Lord Cuinn huffed.

"You can't even come to the table decent?"

"Sorry, sir."

Nevan took a seat next to Aedán and gave him a smile. "Guess what?"

"She said yes, didn't she?"

Nevan chuckled and nudged him with his elbow. "Emera is a right beauty. She said she's excited to spend more time with me. Can you believe it? A messy sod like myself catching her?"

Aedán laughed. "Congratulations, Nevan. Now all you have to do is not piss in her drink. The toughest part, if you ask me."

Nevan laughed.

Lord Cuinn cleared his throat. "That's enough, talking about girls that way. Especially with your sisters present."

Aedán and Nevan chuckled again, and the twins stuck their tongues out at them.

"And what are your plans with this girl?"

Nevan scratched his head and said, "Well, Emera is very interested in the dig going on at St. Albeus, so we thought we would take a stroll around this weekend or after class on Friday...Whatever works best for her."

"Just stay out of their way. They're busy people working out there, and they don't need a couple of kids stirring up problems or prodding around being distracting."

"I hear you, sir," Nevan said. "I promise, we'll be on our best behavior."

Lord Cuinn nodded, apparently okay with the answer, and went back to his paper.

The maid brought them their breakfast: eggs and sausages. Aedán didn't know how hungry he was until he could smell the warm food, and he thanked the maid and dug in.

The Bronze Coin

1

At midnight, Maggie ran naked into the sea and transformed.

Using her powerful finned tail, she made her way to the rocks where she'd seen the merrow more than a few times now. She hoped that if they became accustomed to her being there at the same time, they would eventually want to communicate. Hoping for the best, she swam evenly between the rocks, watching out for them.

It was difficult, no doubt. They were swift and aware of everything around them, and their reflexive instincts were far superior to any creature she had ever met.

Maggie waited for them, trying to remain as friendly looking as possible—though she knew that her Maris form was a monstrous visage, she hoped they'd see past how dangerous she appeared and saw her calmer nature.

I'm not a threat to you, she said telepathically. Something she relearned when she was in conflict with brine vampyres a few years before.

Nothing. Only the silence of the depths.

Sighing, Maggie gave up and went back to the island. She resumed her human form, her pale skin slick and wet, making her almost shine in the moonlight. Her red hair was glued to her scalp and neck, but she rang it out so that it would dry easier in the light breeze.

For a moment, she enjoyed her naked connection to the wind and sea. She could feel the sprites in them, moving and dancing around her.

And she tried not to think about her troubles.

She found her bag in the cave and pulled out her pocket watch. There was plenty of time to get home, load the horse, and be off before Cuán realized she was gone.

I'm sorry, Cuán, but this is really for you. You just won't understand it yet.

She left that on the wind and then pulled her gown on so that she could make her way home.

By the dawn of the sun, she was on a horse and galloping down the road to Galway. It took her just over twelve hours to arrive after having made stops to let the horse graze and rest for a few minutes over the course of the day. When the buildings and homes of Galway came into view, she was tired and wanted nothing more than to sleep. With some earnings she had saved up from working for the Ó Fionnáin's, she could pay for a stable to keep the horse to let it rest overnight in the Latin Quarter. With a couple of shillings left, she had enough for the pub and one room at the flophouse nearby.

She cleaned herself up a bit at the flophouse and then went to *The Quays* pub in the center of the Quarter. It was full of people drinking, dancing and listening to fine folk music. It was smoky and boisterous as most pubs and bars were—the air thick with meats and drink. Luckily, they served food, too, because Maggie hadn't eaten all day.

"What a fine doll you are," a young man said, and he tried to pop her on the ass as she walked by.

But she caught his hand, grinning at him. "You've a fine hand 'ere. If ye don't want me drink on yeh, I'd watch where yeh put it."

She let him go.

Men and women laughed around them, and the young man joined them to save face. He didn't stop smiling despite himself.

"You're wild. I like that."

"I am wild, and I bite, don't yeh know?"

"Yeah, I see that."

"Good."

When she turned around, a tall man stood there with lighter red hair than her. It was curly and he wore a dark red suit. His face was pale, and he had large blue eyes, the kind that could steal your soul, Maggie was sure.

"Killian."

"Maggie. Would you like to have supper with me? And a drink?"

Maggie held up her pint. "I already have a drink, and my order should be up soon, I'd suspect."

"Well then, join me, aye?"

Maggie smiled at him. "Of course."

Maggie was not one of the *sióg*. She wasn't particularly bound to anything or a part of something other than her own fate. Killian, on the other hand, was pure *sióg*—his *fata* essence was woven into the very wood, the coin, and the drink of *The Quays*. And he was powerful. He oozed the *fata* essence and vibrated in the material world on levels Maggie couldn't understand.

To the local patrons, Killian was just a typical employee that always seemed to be there, and to the employees, he was a typical patron. And neither of them would think to even question it otherwise.

They took a seat at a corner table, a quieter spot on the fringe of the raucous. Killian sat opposite her, a plate and pint already in front of him.

"The good thing about being *sióg*, Maggie, is that you don't have to pay for anything," he said, grinning. "My money accumulates, and I don't spend a dime of it."

"Out of curiosity—if you don't mind me asking, that is—do you have a pot of gold like in the stories?" Maggie grinned at him.

Killian smiled back.

"Rainbows don't last very long 'ere, Maggie, and I am immortal, but...there is some truth to it. I am 'ere, but I am also in the Hollow at the end of the colors. I'm a color no human will ever discover or could even begin to understand. Just out of reach of comprehension, aye? Some even could say I *am* the *gold* at the end of that rainbow."

"And if I catch you, do I get a wish?"

Killian gave her a gorgeous grin. "My *Eagla* have the tempers of earth, hearth, and the stars. I know them well, but it does not make me a god."

"Just kind'a a god," Maggie said.

Killian frowned.

"Look, I have a deeper question for ye. You and others have told me that I have no *fata* essence, and I'm as human as others, but yet, I'm fae-touched—a Maris Demidian."

"Aye. You have a strong *Vitalitas*—vital essence. You are very much a living being that belongs to the material world."

Killian drank, and Maggie's plate of smoked salmon came to the table. They waited for the server to leave before Maggie added: "So how do ye explain me inability to grow older? I had an omen that I would look exactly like *this*—have this *youth*—and will watch me lover die of old age. How do ye explain that if I have a human body?"

Killian shrugged, chewing his food.

Maggie decided to let him chew, and she took a bite out of her salmon. The pain in her stomach eased a bit, and it made her take another bite.

"The thing is, girl, is that you still have fae blood. *Fata* is woven into the vital fluid, and it changes you. And it's powerful and goes a long way. Truth is, you *are* mortal, but the serpent's blood could keep you alive for centuries. I wish I could tell you more about being a Maris, but only those that live in the waters know the details about it," Killian said. "I can only tell you of the general things."

"Could I learn the Eeries? What is the old word? The *Eagla*?"

"Some form of it, perhaps. Why do you ask?" Killian said before stuffing his mouth with more boiled bacon and cabbage.

"I want to separate myself from the fae blood, if I'm being honest," Maggie said. "I don't want to live forever. I want to grow old with me fella—not watch him decay and die. And then live centuries after him? Jaysus, no. I want to go naturally."

Killian looked at her, swallowing his food.

"Oh well, now that is another thing," Killian said. He took a drink from his Guinness, and then belched the stout.

Maggie smelled it and wrinkled her nose. She fanned in front of her face.

"Lord, Killian. Your gut smells like rot."

"My apologies, girl. Anyway, what was I sayin'?"

"Not much, actually. What's the *thing* you were talking about?"

"Ah. Yes. I was going to say, there is your *anam chara.* When I first learned of you, I did some digging around in the Hollow to learn more about you, and I found an interesting piece of information. When you were taken as a babe, the Fomorians wanted a piece of your spirit. When they rent it from you, the *píos anam* was not fully contained. Some of it escaped, which is something that often occurs, aye? One's *píos anam* is not so easily gathered once freed from the soul.

"Anyhow, when this happens, it tends to slip away to the Otherworld and bonds with a sprite—they become your *anam chara,* your spirit-sister. Think of her like a soulmate, a spiritual guide."

Maggie was stunned. "I have a spirit sister?"

"Yes. A water sprite—an *undine.*"

"Does she know of me?"

"She would be able to feel you in some ways but know about you? Maybe no. Maybe yes."

"By Lugh..." Maggie said.

"Now, if you were to seek her out in the Otherworld, perhaps she would know how to free you of the fae blood," Killian said, sitting back and pulling out a cigar. He lit it with a match and started puffing.

Maggie waved the smoke away.

"The only problem with that is that I don't know how to go beyond the Hollow into the Otherworld."

Killian grinned again. "That is trickier, isn't it? The reality is, you can't. When you're in the Hollow, it's your *psychic self* that moves through it. Sure, there are doorways through the Hollow into the Otherworld, but you'd have no physical presence there. Naw, if you want to go to the Otherworld, you have to find the right sort of threshold."

Maggie cocked her head. "And do ye know of any thresholds?"

"Depends on where ye want to go."

Maggie sighed in frustration.

"Well, how the bloody feck am I supposed to know where my *anam chara* is?"

Killian laughed. "Calm down, calm down, girl. I understand. Listen, a'right? To get there, you'll need a token that can guide you through the threshold. Being a Maris, I would say the best threshold would be *thar an naoú tonn*."

Maggie's eyes widened. "Beyond the Ninth Wave?"

"Aye. Where the merrow are."

"I have been trying to communicate with them, but they don't seem to have any interest in me as of yet," Maggie said. "Drenched snobs, I suspect."

"That's fine. You don't need the merrow. If you have the token and go past the Ninth Wave, you should slip right through without a problem. Just be careful. If the merrow think you are a threat, they could make your trip very short, if you catch my meaning."

Maggie nodded, sighing again. She waved more smoke away. "Do ye know where I can get this token?"

Killian nodded, puffing away. "I sure do."

2

The next morning Maggie met Killian outside *The Quays* with her horse. They climbed onto the horse and rode out of town while the sun was just peaking. With Galway behind them, Killian led her to a hilly green field about a half-hour ride.

"Stop 'ere," he said.

Maggie slowed the horse to a stop, and Killian tapped her hips. She climbed off, and Killian joined her on the ground. Killian took the reins from her and led the horse to an old wood post sticking out of the ground.

"The horse will be fine here. Come with me, Maggie."

Maggie followed the large *sióg* down a hill to the other side of the field, and then she started seeing that the lower hilltops were not really hills. They were man-made.

"What's this place?"

"This is an ancient *sidhe* mound—a tumuli. Strange enough, humans have forgotten it and don't know it's here. One day, it'll be found again."

"Were you around when it was built?"

"Aye. This place used to be more of a forest, but I remember it well. This mound was the resting place of an old Irish king. A once-friend of mine, actually. This was when the land had many kings, just after the *sióg* left the island to the Milesians. He was a great man and loved by the Tuatha Dé, and so they claimed it as one of *their* places."

Killian led her to an opening, an entrance into the mound. He moved some of the stones in the way, using a strength that she could only imagine giants having. She had to remind herself that Killian was a *sióg*.

He also uncovered a piece of oak wood from the dirt in front of the entrance. Killian's eyes flitted over it for a moment.

"Humans forget that knocking on someone's door before entering is an old tradition," Killian said, "of knocking on wood to cleanse any evil spirits that might be attached to you before entering their house."

Maggie was surprised, and yet it made perfect sense.

"This token will be in there?"

"In the Hollow of the mound," Killian said, nodding. "Knock, Maggie, before you enter."

Maggie nodded at him and then went to the entrance, grabbing the rocky side of it. Unsure, she looked back at Killian. "Is it safe?"

Killian shrugged. "Hell if I know, girl. I haven't been inside."

"Then how do you bloody know this token is in there?"

"It's always in there. Now go."

Maggie sighed and decided that she had done probably more dangerous things than this. She walked down the long tunnel, which opened into a room holding back the earth with huge, ancient stones. In the center was an altar stone.

There was nothing else here.

Maggie called back down the tunnel. "I don't see anythin'."

"Oh yes. Yes. That is because you need to recite the Contract Between Worlds."

"What?"

"The Contract—Between—"

"Yeah, yeah...I know *that* part. But I don't know the words of the Contract."

Killian sighed, but he didn't come in.

"A'right, girl, say it after me."

"Aye."

"Ón saol seo go dtí an saol eile."

Maggie nodded, repeating it exactly as she heard it: "Ón saol seo go dtí an saol eile."

"Scartha ach nasctha."

"Scartha ach nasctha."

"Oscail an doras atá eatarthu."

How long was this fecking Contract?

"Oscail an doras atá eatarthu."

Killian didn't say anything else.

Maggie looked about, not seeing anything. She repeated the Contract between Worlds: "From this world to the next, separated from but connected, open the door between."

Then Maggie saw it laying on the altar stone—a bronze coin. She picked it up and looked it over. It was smooth, nothing etched or hammered there.

"I think I found somethin'," Maggie said.

"Yes?"

Maggie went back down the tunnel and stepped out of the *sidhe* mound. As she did, a whoosh of air blew around her, almost as if she was being sucked into the material world all at once.

The gust lasted but a moment.

Maggie held the coin between her fingers and held it up to Killian, who nodded and smiled when he saw it.

"This it?"

"Aye. The token you'll need."

"And all I have to do is go Beyond the Ninth Wave with this coin, and I'll find the Otherworld?"

Killian chuckled.

"I don't need to repeat myself, do I?"

Maggie smiled. "No. No, of course not. Thank you, Killian."

"I'll see you soon. Be careful of the journey, Maggie. Dangerous things live in the Otherworld. Some even seem friendly at first. But many mortals find the wrong path or eat the wrong thing, and they perish. I'd hate to learn of yer demise."

"Thank you Killi—" Maggie looked from the coin to Killian, but he was not there. Killian was the *The Quays* pub, and he was no longer needed here.

<h1 style="text-align:center">3</h1>

Maggie put the coin inside her hem pocket on the inside of her skirt and then went to climb on her horse. As she made her way back to Kilkee, she was sure she'd be home before sunup. She had told Oona to tell Cuán she'd be back in a couple of days, and that it was something she had to do, but she also knew that Cuán still wouldn't be happy about her running off.

"Wait until I tell yeh about all of this," she said aloud. "That's goin' to make you blow yer top."

He won't like her wanting to leave again.

And she couldn't let Cuán go with her. It'd be too dangerous, wouldn't it? How was he going to react to that?

Maybe she shouldn't tell him. Yes, he'd be mad. But when she succeeded in dividing herself from the fae blood, he'd understand, wouldn't he?

Yes, he would. Cuán would know why she had to do it. She was sure of it.

After riding for about four hours, Maggie stopped to rest the horse and let it graze. She lay in the grass and took out the bronze coin to look at it again, feeling its weight.

Maggie then started looking around.

She felt like she was being watched, and it was a familiar feeling—a terrible feeling, and she only remembered it because it was how she felt when Elieris was around.

She felt his demonic soul.

Maggie didn't want to tear her dress, so she quickly started removing it over her head. Luckily, she couldn't see a settlement around her that would see her getting sky-clad. Once she stuffed the dress in a saddle bag with the coin, she moved away from the horse so as not to startle it, and then she transformed into her Maris form—the dark green skin, the tail, the teeth, and claws.

As usual—whatever came—she would fight savagely and fight to the death if need be. She waited, prowling around the area, looking for trouble.

After several minutes of looking around, she realized she didn't feel Elieris anymore.

"Stay away from my soul!" she yelled, her monstrous voice booming louder than she realized it would.

Calm down, she told herself. She wasn't that close to the sea. It was safer here. If Elieris was going to make a move, he'd wait until she was nearer the coast. It would be quicker that way.

Trying to catch her breath, she closed her eyes and stood there, wishing to adapt her human form again.

Relax, she told herself.

She opened her eyes and looked down at her body. It was still in her Maris form.

What was going on?

A little anxious now, she tried again. Her eyes closed. She felt the wind blow through her curly hair, tickling her shoulders. She listened for the birds and the chittering of small animals.

Calm yourself and know that everything will be okay. Everything will be fine. You are not in any danger.

Her heart rate slowed. She was breathing naturally.

And yet her body was still in Maris form.

She looked at the Fomorian scratches—the ancient symbols that were scarred into her Maris form for the rest of her life. The black claws stood sturdy at the tip of each of her long fingers. The fins on the back of her forearms with the purplish tinge of the near-transparent spots.

"What the *arse*-licking, *sheep*-fucking *hell* is going on 'ere?!"

Cuán would never sleep with her again, looking like this ugly creature! Despite what he had said in the vampyre's cave when he'd first seen this horrid form.

No, Maggie, calm down. If you let this scare you, you'll never get back to being human again. Cuán loves you, and even he'd understand...better than anyone else, in fact.

True. Sure. Maybe...

Maggie rubbed her clawed hands together, breathed, and then closed her eyes again. She hummed to herself, telling her body what she wanted, willing it to happen, but thinking about it calmly, carefully.

Sighing, hoping for the best, Maggie opened her eyes and looked down at herself. Her skin was pale. Her claws and teeth were gone.

Maggie groaned in relief and went back to her horse to fetch her dress before someone saw her.

Not sure why that happened. Going to have to learn to calm my shite, she thought.

Nerves

1

It was nearly the end of July, their wedding was just around the corner, and Maggie had to fly off somewhere. Bloody woman!

Cuán was hot, upset, and couldn't stop thinking about how she had the gall to just run off like that, going somewhere and keeping it all a secret.

Oona thought maybe it was a secret because she wanted to get him a gift from the city. Cuán thought it possible, but at the same time, something gnawed at the back of his mind. With Mona passing away and the stress of getting ready for the wedding, he still recalled how Maggie sometimes looked at him. At first full of light and love, and then its slow fade into that worried frown.

It didn't matter that with those freckles across her nose—smile or frown, she was beautiful—it only mattered that she wasn't trusting him enough to tell him what was on her mind.

Maybe it was just him. Maybe he was being a right caffler, but he wouldn't be this way if she'd been open with him.

It was time for them to have a talk.

Since Maggie was gone, Cuán spent the day on the dogger with his da, helping where he could. Da's new hire, Jacob, was a few years younger than Cuán, but he knew what he was doing. The boy learned quickly, and Cuán found that he was a good replacement. He could let go of some of that guilt he felt for disappointing his Da by leaving the business.

Still, after they docked, Cuán went home tired, and his mind swung back around to his problem with Maggie. He tried not to think about it, but he was still fuming.

He decided to go with his da and Jacob to the pub. They had a pint, chatted with the other fisherman, and then when Cuán was drunk enough, he found his bed, passing out quickly. He slept hard and woke the next morning, not remembering his dreams.

The next day was a repeat, but instead of the pub, Cuán sent their first payment to the lodgers they'd stay with while in Dublin. He wanted to secure the place so that moving would be easy for them.

After that, he went to see the town priest at the *Church of the Immaculate Conception and St Senan*, Father Carroll. They spoke for some time about the requirements of marriage. He assured the Father that there were no impediments that would disclose them from a proper Catholic marriage.

Neither Cuán nor Maggie went to mass, but he assured Father Carroll that they were both Catholics and baptized in the Church. It was only partially true. They were both baptized but were only Catholics by name/birth. Nether practiced or had strong faith in it. Maybe, Cuán thought, it was out of social expectations rather than anything else. He wasn't sure.

"And have you procured the bands of marriage?"

Cuán was confused at first but then realized what he was saying.

"Oh. Aye. The rings. I have, Father."

Father Carroll sat back. "Then we only have the ceremony to perform, though I would like to meet your fiancé before the big day."

Cuán scratched his chin. "Of course. Perhaps I will bring her in tomorrow so that you can meet her."

Father Carroll leaned forward again, tapping one finger on his desk. "If it's been some time since your last mass, it would be good to go to confession and absolution for your sins. Clean your soul before you go into this marriage under the House of God."

He imagined their souls all dirty from all the bad things that they had done or had done to them—washing that all away and being clean as they moved forward with their life. Maybe having your soul cleansed before entering their union would be a good idea.

"Maybe we will," Cuán said.

2

The day after, Cuán saw Colum dropping off more sugar beets at the store. He waved, and Cuán went over.

"Maggie told me to tell you that she is home," Colum said. "Once I finish unloading, I'll be working with your folks on other wedding supplies. You feel ready for all of this, Cuán?"

"Ready? Oh shite, I'm feeling like a fool eegit, to be honest."

"Why's that? Because you're flying low?"

Cuán checked his slacks, seeing that his zipper was down. "Ah, yeah, you see what I mean?"

He turned around and zipped up.

"It's just the nerves, lad. You need to calm down, is all."

Cuán checked this pocket and found a lemon drop in his spare handkerchief—used just for the purpose of carrying his drops—and he put it in his mouth. The sour taste gave him a little shake.

"A'right. Better. I'll help yeh out, and then I'll fancy a visit with the Connells."

Colum nodded. "I wouldn't deny any help right now."

Maggie stood there in the kitchen—all cleaned up and in her nice turquoise dress. Her feet were crossed, and she just looked at him, looking terrified. Not because he'd ever hurt her, he was sure, but because she knew he would be mad. He wanted to be furious with her, but— "Ah, fuck, Maggie."

He took her in his arms and kissed her.

She kissed him back. If it weren't for Oona being in the living room just on the other side of the wall, he would fuck her right on the table.

But Maggie pulled away, breathing heavily.

"I'm sorry, Cuán. I know yer mad."

"Aye, furious, but I'm not going to shout or carry on. I just want to know why you'd do this to me, just a few days before our wedding?

You know I'm scared of losing yeh—scared out of my mind. You're everything, and I have no idea what I would do if I lost you."

"I promise you. We'll marry. I just— I sometimes worry about who I am sometimes. I don't have everythin' figured out, ye know? What am I to the *sióg*? How will my blood affect me in me life? Will it affect our future?"

"Please don't leave me, Maggie."

She ran her fingers through his dark hair, grabbed his head, and pushed their foreheads against each other's. Looking up into his eyes through the tendrilled veil of her curly red hair, she said, "I will never leave ye, Cuán. You are all I know and have."

She bit her lip, and he found this very sexy, and he pressed his lips against hers again. They kissed long and hard before Cuán finally forced himself to let her go.

"I'll hold you to it," he said.

Maggie smiled and nodded. "Ye do that. Just, yeh know, please understand that I have things I have to do that sometimes take me away. But if I go, I'll always be back. Always, ye 'ear me?"

"Aye. I hear you. I do. It's just…difficult."

Maggie told him she was going to go with Oona to his house, where they'd meet his parents to work on the wedding supplies.

"Are ye comin'?"

"Of course," he said.

As they made their way through the town, holding hands, Cuán couldn't help but think that Maggie wasn't telling him everything. He could just feel it in his gut. But he didn't want to bring it up in front of Oona or ruin the mood for Maggie. He wanted her to look back on all of this and have only good memories. Maybe he should just wait until after the wedding to prod her further.

That sounded like the only right choice.

So, he let it go.

3

When Cuán rushed up to kiss her, Maggie relaxed, relieved that there would not be a fight.

I will have to tell him soon, she thought.

Just not right now.

"...You know I'm scared of losing you—scared out of my mind..."

Maggie felt her hand shift, and she briefly looked down when Cuán's gaze wandered from her for a moment.

The skin of her hand was a light teal. Black claws extended from the tips of her fingers.

Shite!

Maggie moved her hands behind her before Cuán's gaze returned to her.

"...You're everything, and I have no idea what I would do if I lost you."

Maggie felt the claws on her hand run over the skin of her other hand. They were still there. She wished them away.

Think, quick— "I promise you. We'll marry. I just—I sometimes worry about who I am sometimes..."

Go away, go away, she told her hands, feeling like a plonker for talking to them. Luckily, it was all in her head.

It was in her head, wasn't it? She couldn't really say.

"...I don't have everythin' figured out, ye know? What am I to the *sióg*? How will my blood affect me in my life? Will it affect our future?"

Maggie felt her fingers and couldn't find the claws.

"Please don't leave me, Maggie."

He had the saddest seal eyes. Cuán was afraid of losing her.

Of course, he was.

Maggie wanted him more and more every day, and he didn't even realize it. How could he not?

Maggie ran her fingers through his dark hair, grabbed his head, and pushed her forehead against his. She needed him to know—*to understand.* "I will never leave ye, Cuán. You are all I know and have."

As they walked hand to hand to the Foley's, Oona a short way in front of them, Maggie wondered what was happening with her. Why was she losing control of her body? Its transformations?

She looked at him, and he looked back at her. He smiled and she returned it.

Maybe there was another reason to seek her *anam chara*. What if whatever was happening to her could get worse?

How will Cuán deal with this?

All she knew right now was that she didn't want to say anything yet. She didn't want to upset him while he was so focused on the wedding, finally weaving their lives together tighter.

She really did respect how much he cared for her and wanted her. Maggie only hoped that he would understand that being together wasn't the only thing she needed.

XIII

The Festival

August 1st—1855
Lughnasadh

1

It was midnight when Etna McCarna was allowed into the servant's door on the east side of the mansion. Only one of Lord Cuinn's retinue knew of the Order of Bres—Damhán, who let her in and took her to the study.

Lord Cuinn greeted her warmly, saying, "A brandy? Scotch? A lager?"

Etna blew out a sigh. "Aye. Perhaps a scotch."

She recognized the other gentleman in the room: a disheveled man. Large, rough-looking, but somehow handsome in that wild way. He was one of the dark ones: hair, eyes, and soul.

"Mister Kelleys," she said, acknowledging his presence.

"You can call me Brogan. I'm nah one fer formal titles, Luv."

Etna said nothing but took the glass of scotch from Lord Cuinn and took a seat at his table. Lord Cuinn took its head. Brogan remained standing in the corner of the room. He was in sight, but he didn't seem to want to join them. It bothered her.

"I have a question for you," Etna said. "Did you know about Carman?"

Lord Cuinn sat back. "What do you mean?"

"Tell me this isn't some sick joke that I'm a part of," she said.

"You're confusing us, Etna," Lord Cuinn said.

"You didn't know that Carman was hiding inside of me? It wasn't the reason you made me a member of this Order?"

The men looked stunned and then at each other.

"Look. Etna. We knew you were part of her bloodline, which was fortuitous for us, but we don't know what you mean that Carman was inside you," Lord Cuinn said.

Etna needed the whiskey and took a drink. Once the rush of feeling went through her, she sat the glass down and told them about Carman—how she entered the world through her and how she found a secret Hidden Place at the monastery. Leaving out, of course, the Finger and other sordid details.

"What has she been doing since then?"

"Mostly learning. She's been going around town, talking to people, reading books, things like that. She's catching herself up on a world that has changed a lot since she was buried. She seeks her sons," Etna said.

"Can we meet her?" Lord Cuinn said. "She could be handy for us."

"Or...she could get in our way. Wasn't the Red God—"

Lord Cuinn nodded. "Yes, yes. He designed her prison once Lugh defeated her."

"So, if the Red God returns..." Brogan said.

"...then she would be a wonderful sacrifice to him," Lord Cuinn finished.

"She commands me like some minion. She feels that she owns me like I was born to bring her forth and serve her throughout her new life. It's revolting, some of the things she does," Etna said, taking another drink of the strong scotch.

Lord Cuinn leaned forward on the table toward her. "Let's watch her, but let's do it quietly. We don't want to alarm her, do we?"

Etna shook her head. "No. That would be dangerous."

"Do as she says...for now. We could learn a lot from her."

Etna sighed. "Very well."

Brogan then came over to the table, leaning on it.

"And why am I 'ere, Cuinn?"

Etna noticed the distinct lack of title in those words. She knew who Brogan was, but could he really get away with showing this sort of disrespect? Cuinn didn't seem to react to it. Either he was used to it, or he feared the man. Probably a little of both. Lord Cuinn cleared his throat and put a hand flat on the table. "That is our primary matter, isn't it? Please sit down, Brogan."

Brogan just stood straight.

Lord Cuinn turned his chair a little to face the man better. "It's Aedán. It's time to follow him."

Brogan smiled.

"It's happening?"

"Yes. While he was dreaming last night, I spied in and found him talking with the Three. And he went to that girl—"

"The MacCailín?" Etna said.

"Yes. She is coming."

Brogan grinned like a wolf. "It's about time."

Etna found his grin terrifying. It was more than mere joy. It was a hungry grin—all sharp teeth.

"Once they are together, they will return the Red God to us, and the Tuatha Dé will see their mistake," Lord Cuinn said. "I think the next full moon is the time."

Etna took down the rest of her whiskey. Wiping her mouth, she said, "Can I have another?"

2

Colorful tents were erected in the open areas of town, farmers brought in food for the markets, entertainers set up their booths, the bands gathered, and droves of people meandered about Wexford for the Óenach Carmán festival.

Aedán got ready that morning, both excited and more nervous than he'd ever been in his life. All he could think about was that Bridget was on her way there, and today they would meet outside of dreams—they were going to really look one another in the eyes, and they would see each other as real human beings.

Odd, he thought. All these years, she was nothing but some dream girl living inside his cursed mind, and then everything flipped, and she was real, and reality was suddenly just as strange as his dreams.

After grabbing the Macalla Shell for good luck and placing it in his pocket, he left the Cuinn estates by horse and rode through the festival. People seemed so merry, gathering and listening to music, looking through the markets. And he'd soon join them once Bridget's carriage arrived.

They chose to meet at the steps of *St. Iberius*. He sat on the steps, waiting, knowing that she'd be there soon. In their last dream together, she told them that she planned on leaving the evening before, so she paid a driver handsomely to drive her throughout the night so that she'd be there in the morning.

He didn't know how long he had waited, but a blue-washed post-chaise arrived with the MacCailín crest. It stopped before the steps. Aedán noticed the one luggage back and the dark blue window curtain being parted.

She was just like in his dreams: Bridget looked out, scanning the church, and her beautiful blue eyes fell on him. His heart started pounding as he smiled at her, going down the steps to meet her.

Bridget didn't wait for the teamster to step down to help her. She threw open the door, pushed her dress aside, and climbed down as quickly as she could.

By the time she was out, he was face to face with her, smelling her flowery perfumes, feeling her hot breath, and not knowing what to say.

"Aedán Ó Cuinn?" She beamed up at him.

"Bridget Rose MacCailín, I presume."

He threw his arms around her, and their mouths met. Aedán forgot about her luggage and didn't even notice the teamster retrieving it for the lady and putting it down beside her. The man cleared his throat until Aedán let Bridget go so that she could turn to the man.

"Yes, thank you, Patrick. We agreed on the need for reticence in this matter? The money is enough, yes?"

"Yes, the money is quite enough, milady. Hardly needed, really. I wish you well." The man looked Aedán over and added: "Do be careful."

Aedán nodded at Patrick. "I promise to take care of her."

Patrick sighed. "I would hope so."

Aedán picked up Bridget's suitcase, finding it lighter than he'd imagined for a lady of her class.

"I'll be off. Send me a wire directly, and I will come to collect you as soon as possible," Patrick told Bridget.

"Thanks again, Patrick."

Aedán helped Bridget onto the horse and gave her the luggage to hold in front of her, and they trotted down the road at a lazy pace. He really wanted the experience to last so they could chat.

"Have you given any thought as to my sleeping arrangements?" Bridget said.

Aedán noticed right away that she was a little different from herself when they were in the Lost Place. More ladylike. More formal. Maybe it was because when you dream, you could let yourself go and be freer than you ever really could be in life.

"I have. I would love to have you at the estate. It's much closer. But for now, I'm afraid my father wouldn't approve. But we do have a cottage just south of town, where my stepmother would go when she wanted an escape from the 'domestic politics,' as she liked to call them. He'll never know you're there."

Bridget sighed. "I don't like all the secrets. It's not like me."

Aedán chuckled. "Nor I. I figure we see how this goes, get to know each other a little."

"Get to know each other *in this world*," Bridget agreed.

Aedán's arms were around her, controlling the reigns. He could smell her. See the long curve of her neck and the wisps of her hair fluttering in the light wind. Even though they made love in dreams, feeling her warmth and breathing in her scent was far better than any fantasy. The reality of her was almost overwhelming.

Aedán smiled. "We couldn't have picked a better day. It's Lughnasadh! The festival runs all day, and we can delight ourselves if you feel up to it."

"Why would I not?"

"I figured with the long journey—"

"Oh, please. I can sleep through anything! I had a good night's rest, though I would like to freshen up a bit first."

"Then I'll take you to the cottage, and I'll have Áine—one of our maids I've sent to aid you—help you freshen up. We could then maybe meet for lunch?"

Bridget laid back into him, her head resting back on his shoulder. He could see her eyes, her nose, her lips...

"That would be wonderful."

There it was, he thought, feeling warmth flow through him. That part of her that wanted his touch. But he knew if he were to be improper, it would probably ruin it, so he held himself back and let her rest against him as they made their way through town.

Aedán took her suitcase, and Áine was already waiting for them. She took the case from him as Aedán gave her instructions. They then led Bridget through the small cottage, showing her its layout and the room Áine made up for her.

"Áine, once she's freshened up, do you mind guiding her to the festival market, down by *Clery's*. The cobbler. I'll meet you two there."

"Yes, Sir."

Aedán kissed Bridget's hand. "I'll see you soon."

Bridget gave him a long look. Was that longing on her face? Did she want him as much as he wanted her here?

Thank God for Áine being there. He wouldn't be able to stop himself.

"Thank you again, Aedán. I'm looking forward to it."

3

Lughnasadh celebrated the beginning of the harvest season. After meeting each other again at the cobbler's, they made their way about to watch or participate in the celebrations. Adapted from the old *Tailteann* Games, there was an offering of First Fruits, feasting,

handfasting rituals, the fair, and a few athletic contests—long jump, high jump, running, hurling, spear throwing, boxing, and more.

Bridget's favorite was King Puck. A blond-haired schoolgirl named Catrina was named Queen of the Puck, and Aedán explained to her that three days ago, she named one of the goats 'King Puck'. The goat was then put into the cage, but at midday, they gathered around to watch Catrina take a crown and place it on the goat's head. Everyone cheered and the music began.

A farmer then tied a rope around the goat's neck and started walking him through town, taking him back into the mountains.

"That's Catrina. She's one of my brother's friends," Aedán said.

"You have a brother?"

Aedán laughed. Of course, in the Lost Place, they didn't talk much about anything beyond their own experiences in the woods and each other. He never told her much about his family.

"Yes. Nevan. When Lord Cuinn adopted me, he already had one son. But we grew up like brothers. I think it was easier for me, being older. There was no jealousy that I couldn't remedy."

They went to watch the archery contests. They watched the archers shoot at the targets on hay bales. Bridget, enjoying Aedán so much, almost didn't notice the man who she found staring at her. He looked wild, but he was well dressed. There was something in his eyes that was seductive and yet dangerous.

For a moment she was just stunned that he would be so improper to look at her in such a way, but then it made her angry. She tried pointing him out, but the crowds shifted, and then she didn't see him again.

"Did you see him?" she said.

"No, I don't see anyone."

"He was wearing a jacket. His hair was a mess, and it was black," she said.

Aedán shrugged. "Sorry, Bridget. I didn't see him."

"He was staring at me."

Aedán grabbed her hand. "There is no one around here that is dangerous. And you're definitely safe with me."

Bridget relaxed.

"You're right. I shall calm myself."

After having some Shepard's Pie—minced meat with a crust of mashed potato—and watching some traditional Irish dancing, Aedán asked if she was getting tired.

"A little. It feels like it's been a long day."

"I have one more place to show you," he said.

Bridget looked into his deep blue eyes and knew no matter how tired she was, she wanted to look at them for much longer. "I have a little strength left in me. Show me."

Aedán helped her onto the horse, and they made their way a short way west. Not twenty minutes later, they were out of the town lights, looking at the green fields as dusk began to approach. In the fields, like a bent and rusted crown, were very ancient ruins. Half crumbled, but some of it remained standing and impressive against the emerald landscape.

"Saint Albeus," Aedán said. "It's a monastery that dates back several centuries. Archaeologists are digging there now," Aedán said.

"Archaeologists?"

"They are from Dublin. They dig up old locations to find artifacts and other clues so that they can learn about history," Aedán said. "At least, that's how I understand it. Lord Cuinn sort of explained it to me a while ago."

They stopped at a tree nearby, and Aedán tethered the horse to it.

"We're alone now?"

"Aye. Most are taking the day to enjoy the festival."

"It's dark."

Aedán dug into his saddle bag and pulled out a lamp. He took some matches and lit it. Not too much later, he then took her hand and walked her toward the ruins carrying the lamp for them.

"It's amazing—these old places—still standing there, reminding us how ancient our blood really is," Bridget said.

Aedán nodded. "And how blood can be made new."

Bridget smiled at him. She watched him breathe—his chest rising and falling—and looked over his square jaw and kind eyes. There was nothing she wanted more than to take him, but it would be different in real life, yes? In the dreams, they envisioned the task, and their bodies responded only through chemicals.

It was exciting. She was a virgin in the waking world, never experiencing anything outside her dreams besides her own touch. Bridget was sure that he brought her here to make their first time special, and when they touched each other, everything would be made real.

They didn't go inside. Probably because Aedán thought she'd be too frightened to go in—and he would be right. He did find a nice place between the walls in what used to be the courtyard, which protected them from the cool breeze. Aedán laid out his coat, and they laid upon it, kissing. His hands touched her face, and then he ran a finger over her lips, and then they went down her neck and over her breasts as his mouth returned to hers.

His tongue was wild and playful, and she loved it. His free hand massaged her left breast, and then his mouth moved to her neck.

It was a familiar move from him, but it was real...and the sensations she was feeling were far better than in her dreams. His breath. His lips. They were pleasure.

Aedán's hand traveled down her belly, down her left thigh, and pulled up her skirt. His hand then slid between her legs, and his fingers started rubbing her wetness through her drawers.

That sensation made her body stiffen, her toes curl, and she let out a soft moan that surprised even her.

Yes, this was far better than any dream.

"Do you want me?" he said softly in her ear.

"Y-Yes," she said, finding her own breath had quickened. "Fuck me."

Aedán started pulling her drawers down, and his mouth found her inner thighs. He sucked in her flesh, and her jealous sex ached for its own attention. After a moment, he was pushing down his slacks and pushing eagerly into her.

She cried out a little. Part of it was the pain, but most of it was the thrill of having his cock introduce itself inside her and the wonderful pleasure it drove throughout her body. He started thrusting, his mouth finding hers again, and she rode the revelry all the way through.

Nothing like a dream, she thought. *Nothing so holy as this.*

He rolled her over on top of him, and the top of her dress fell, exposing her small breasts. She found it much easier to grind against him in this position, hitting all the perfect spots...and the air seemed to warm around them.

She looked at the standing stone near the cloister.

Closing her eyes with her face drawn to the warm sky, she suddenly wanted to scream.

Failures

1

It is always good to be on the hunt. When the moon waxes, the tides rise, and the trees shiver at its mercy. Blood rushes icily through their veins, and their hearts quake, all at our very presence. We are the night. We are also the teeth in the night. We crave that blood. We almost worship it, Fáelad said. The varga-spirit—its wolfish form invisible to all others, save Brogan.

Brogan had to agree with his varga. There was nothing better than the hunt, but he did not entertain the Order of Bres for mere pleasure. They had gods they served and demands that needed to be met. The Red God had always chosen the wolves of Ireland as a symbol of power and distinction. Brogan could only honor him now.

"For as long as it serves the Red God, we will return them to the Order," Brogan told the varga.

Fáelad huffed. *Fine. But we will need to sate our thirst soon, or I will take my rightful charge.*

"As soon as I am able. I promise, Old Friend."

Brogan was on horseback, trotting along far behind the horse in front of them, going on the western path toward St. Albeus.

The varga-spirit ambled alongside the horse. The horse was unaware of him.

This road is very old, Fáelad said.

"It's the road to the old monastery."

Ah, Saint Albeus. He honored the wolves. This site is sacred to us.

"Indeed," Brogan said.

From the distance, Brogan watched as the couple climbed off their horse, and tied it up to a tree. Brogan knew he could be seen if they turned around, so he drove the horse in between the meager woods.

There was enough to cover them, and this is where he climbed off and tied his own horse. After patting the horse's nose, he started making his way through the trees, sniffing the air.

He could smell the boy and the girl.

He had known the boy since the boy was young. They never spoke, but Brogan knew who he was and watched him carefully for Lord Cuinn.

The blond girl was a new scent, and he enjoyed the smell of her. She was a virgin. And he could smell her in the air. She was in heat, and her skin smelled nervous. It would be her first time. Once upon the ruins, Brogan went into the darkness of the monastery and crept through the darkness. By the time he peeked out a window, they were already rutting and kissing.

The boy rolled the girl on top of him, and she happily took over.

Their sex filled the air, making Brogan's stomach growl. It made him want to tear them apart and taste their flesh. It would be spicy with their odors, and it would go down his throat well. He was sure of it.

I hear your stomach. Don't think I don't. You want to devour them, too. I can feel it.

Brogan ignored the varga, watching the couple mate. He decided: once they were through, they would start to cover themselves. They wouldn't be expecting him, so he'd make his move then. He'd knock the boy out, and then he'd take care of the girl.

Only the varga growled, and it was nothing like his stomach. It was a warning.

Something was there with them, and it watched them.

When he turned to look around, he saw the blue flame floating in the doorway of the room Brogan hid in. It just floated there as if looking at them.

The air became warm and balmier.

Stingy Jack, Fáelad said.

The flame started to slowly leave the room.

Many tales spoke of the Stingy Jack, and many of them spoke about how they were specters of portent. As it moved, Brogan couldn't let himself miss the opportunity. He started following it down the dark hallways of the ruins until it took him through a door to the woods.

But these woods weren't the same woods. They smelled different. This forest was primal and savage. He could sense it deep in his bones.

How could this be?

Brogan turned around. His varga-spirit turned with him.

There was nothing left of the dark hallway. Only a piece of ancient doorway stood up behind them. The whole monastery was gone, save this pile of rocks.

Brogan didn't know why, but he panicked. He ran through the door and found that he had only gone through the other side. Whatever forest obtained him, it was not the scant sprawl of trees of west Wexford. And this stone doorway was not St. Albeus.

Where the fuck was he?

Brogan also realized that he did not see the couple Lord Cuinn asked him to follow.

When he looked around again, he saw the blue flame hovering between the forest foliage as if waiting for him. When Stingy Jack moved again, it made its way deeper into the woods.

Follow the corpse candle, Fáelad said, *or we may be lost forever.*

"Where the fuck are we? Do you know this place?"

The varga huffed again. *Oh, yes. This is the Lost Wood of the Otherworld. It is very dangerous.*

Brogan followed the Stingy Jack to a glade, where the sunlight beamed down in all of its midday glory. Several mountain goats grazed here. Flowers bloomed in multiple colors, and some were very large, like he'd never seen before. Once the Stingy Jack found the middle of the glade, it just disappeared.

Brogan reached out his hand where the blue flame disappeared. There was no heat and no smoke. No sign that it was even there.

A goat walked up to him with its black slitted eyes as it chewed on grass.

Brogan. All the goats are black. Did you notice that?

2

Nevan Ó Cuinn was hurt, choleric even, and he didn't know how much more he could take. His father, Lord Cuinn, was behind his desk in his study, throwing a book across the room.

"I am *sick* and tired of *your* failures!" his father spat. "Your teachers say you're smart, but you *refuse* to do your work. You're sloppy and have *no pride*, and *I swear*, it's because of how much you like to dis*res*pect me!"

"I'm sick of this," Nevan shouted back. "I'm tired of all of this!"

"Then why do you sleep here? You know your responsibilities. If you don't want them, then why stay? What the *fuck* are you still doing here? Oh, let me see, it's because you know nothing of life and couldn't possibly live outside these walls without me spoon-feeding your *lazy arse*!"

"Da, would you stop?!"

"Why the bloody *feck* can't you be more like Aedán? At least he respects me."

In tears, Nevan got up from his chair and threw it aside so that it crashed loudly against the wall.

"How *dare* you!" his father shouted. "Don't think that you'd be so old enough that I wouldn't be able to give you a few lashings!"

"Fuck you, da!"

Nevan stormed out, slamming the door. His father shouted after him, telling him to get the rod, but Nevan was having none of it. He left the mansion and went down to the stables. There he readied a horse and left the estates as fast as he could. He didn't bother looking back.

His father could very well fuck off in his fucking castle and die a fucking horrible death as he choked on his fucking dinner.

By the time he made it to town, it was dark. He had spent the whole day at the festival with Emera, only to go home to a father raging about his grades and the lack of his 'follow through' in life.

Nevan sighed. Yeah, he lacked follow-through because he didn't want any of it. Though he didn't want to be exiled from the house, he didn't want to live there either. The only thing he could think about was Emera and their future together. Everything else seemed like a pale shadow to him.

As he rode, he noticed the festival winding down. Marketers were almost all packed up in their wagons, and most people had dispersed to their homes.

He rubbed his eyes and hoped he didn't look like he was brought to tears, stopping in front of Emera's home. He knocked on the door, and Emera answered it.

"Nevan?" She came out, mostly closing the door behind her so that nobody inside could hear them.

"I'm sorry. I needed to get away," Nevan told her. "My father and I had a fight."

Emera rubbed her head through her thick dark hair. He let his eyes glaze over her soft, pale skin, but he did notice her worry.

"I don't know," she said. "My parents wouldn't be happy."

"Please," Nevan said. "It won't be long."

"Emera! Is there someone at the door?" It was another woman's voice. Her mother, no doubt.

"No, I'm just going to the well to fetch some water. I'll be back," Emera said. She gave him a quick look and then went back into the house, only to return with a bucket. She closed the door behind her.

Nevan followed her to the well.

"I'm sorry, Nevan. I don't know yer da well."

"Aye, I know," Nevan said. "He's damn right malicious at times. I can say that."

At the well, Nevan scooped her up in his arms and kissed her. She let him hold her and seemed to enjoy the kiss, but then he felt her hand on his chest, and she gave him a small push to break them. It was a little uncomfortable, knowing she could do that so easily.

"Can we still go to Saint Albeus tomorrow?" she said.

Nevan smiled, raising the bucket in the well for her. "Not even my father can stop me."

Emera smiled back. "I can't wait."

Nevan couldn't look away from her gentle face.

"I'm glad you let me look at you. I think somehow when I'm with you, you erase all my pain," Nevan said. He dumped the water into Emera's bucket as she held it in place on the side of the well.

"Ssh." Emera said, putting a finger to his lips. "If you talk like that, someone might think I'm a witch."

Nevan laughed. "Well, you are enchanting."

Emera blushed, her cheeks getting very red. "Oh, now, ye need to stop."

She kissed him on the cheek.

Nevan grabbed the bucket for her. "I'll walk it up to the door for you."

"That's very considerate," Emera said.

I Can't Breathe

1

He was an old man. His head was in a pillow. His breathing was very slow, very light. She could feel the fragile lungs getting tired. His skin was cracked with age, mottled with spots, and he couldn't hold his bladder anymore. Over the years, she took care of him. Most people around them thought she was his granddaughter or great-granddaughter. But they had always been in love, had always been lovers until he was too fragile to enjoy the act any longer. Now she was an intimate caretaker, and she didn't mind at all. Her love for him still swelled in her chest, and though seeing him like this was hard, she was certain she'd be okay taking care of him forever.

Just don't die, she thought. *I can't lose you.*

At the same time, she knew she could no longer prevent him from dying and that it would be any minute now. They had gone to the Otherworld, and they could have stayed there, but Cuán could not leave the world behind. It was still too important to him. And then it was too late.

She put her ear to his chest, careful not to leave the weight on him—she didn't want to impede his breathing in any way—and she heard the faint heart. She could hear it weaken with every beat.

Cuán.

Maggie thought she had been prepared for this. She went over it many, *many* times in her head. Cuán was expiring. The last breath retiring from his lungs with the weakest rattle. Tears poured down her face.

There she was—having aged so slightly that hardly even she could tell—and Cuán was already rotting.

The black cat laying on his legs looked at her with its big gold eyes and meowed at her.

***

Maggie woke up, the tears still flowing. Her face was wet. Her pillow was wet. She let herself sob for a while and realized that Cuán was still young. Still alive. She forced herself to calm down and take a deep breath. *Fucking dreams.*

She kicked her feet from under her covers and stepped into her shoes. From the bottom of her sock drawer, she pulled out the bronze coin that Killian had helped her find. A glamour token. Maggie held it tight in her left fist and went downstairs in the dark. At the table, she gathered paper, inkwell and a fountain pen and started writing a note to Oona. Once she was done, she closed the lid on the inkwell and left it on the note so that Oona would see it, and the inkwell would hold the note in place just in case of a draft.

Still holding the coin and not bothering to change out of her nightgown, she made her way through the night to the Foley's cottage. Maggie knew how to be quiet. She could move without making noises, opening and closing doors and windows so that they never gave her away.

Maggie was good at being a ghost.

She made her way inside the house and up to Cuán's room. Maggie wanted to see him just once because she didn't know how long she would be away. Hopefully, it wouldn't take her long, but she realized now that if she were going to do this, she needed to go before Cuán got much older.

The two of them needed to grow together. And die together. Naturally. It's how it always should have been.

Maggie didn't like lying to him or leaving without him, but she knew that the Otherworld would be dangerous and—after all—Cuán was only human. She couldn't risk his life. Just couldn't do it. Witnessing his death in her visions, she in no way wanted to experience that feeling again so soon and for real.

Maggie couldn't forget how she felt when the vampyric girl came out of the Feast Pit near the cliffs of Séala Bán, grabbing Cuán and dragging him back down into it before she could grab him—save him. He disappeared down into the darkness, and she thought she might have lost him forever.

No, Maggie needed to do this alone.

She sat on the edge of his bed. He shifted, but it didn't wake him. Cuán was still young for a man, and he breathed easily and was so full of life and health. He looked adorable and sexy with his mussy hair and was still all she ever really wanted. Maggie leaned over and kissed him on the forehead.

He stirred a little, but he didn't wake.

She whispered, "I'm sorry, Cuán. Know that I did this out of love and that this will be best for both of us. I know you'll be angry now, but I'd hope that everythin' we've been through, you'll trust me."

Cuán sighed in his sleep and turned over.

Maggie buried her nose in the back of his neck, feeling his hair brush her face, and she took in his smell.

Yes, he smelled so full of life...of masculinity and strength.

That's the memory she wanted to hold tight to as she made her way to her *anam chara*. Hopefully, it'd be the same memory she returned to when she came back completely mortal and free of the fae blood.

Maggie then stopped and looked at her hand. It was a light blue-green tone, and the sharp, black claws jutted out from the tips. She looked at her face in the window, and she saw the horror of her hybrid face.

Frightened, she quickly withdrew from the Foley's house and made her way through the brisk night. After a few minutes, she stood at the shoreline with her bronze coin still tight in her hand.

Her *normal* hand. Somehow while making her way, it seemed that her hand shifted back to its human form. She touched her face and could feel the softer, delicate flesh of her human face.

She caught her breath and turned back to see the village behind her. Kilkee. Dear gods...*home.*

"It will be nice to return to you," she said, "I will. I promise."

Maggie shed her white gown and walked down naked to where the ocean sprayed her. This time she forced the change, and her body took on its horrid, hybrid form: the dark sea-green flesh with the glowing sigils clawed into it, her powerful, spike-finned tail, and the large, pointed teeth that turned her mouth into a death-maw.

She looked at the bronze coin, a slight moment of uncertainty coming over her, and then closed it tight with her final decision—*No. I must do this.* Looking at the roiling dark sea before her, she ran into it and dove into its waters. Her tail propelled her forward like a missile, shooting her through her element as it accepted her wholly.

2

His ma was out, having left with Oona slightly before he woke, but his da made him some potatoes and eggs. They ate together.

"Everything ready in Dublin?" his da asked.

"Aye," Cuán said, grinning. "I got the letter yesterday. We have a small place to stay, and it's not too far from the University."

"So, you're off in a month's time?"

"Aye. Ah, yeah, Da, I'm gonna miss you guys. You know I will."

His da nodded and sat back in his chair. "Aye, I know, boy. It's just Dublin seems so far away. But at least you'll be together. Married. Happy. Just make sure that when the grandkids are in the belly, you let us know so we can be there when they're born. It'll mean a lot to your ma."

"I hear ye, Da," he said. "I promise we will."

When Cuán stepped outside, he saw his ma and Oona standing a few feet from the door.

"Oona. How's Maggie? Hope the Lazy Bones is up, so she's not late—" Then he stopped, seeing their faces. They were long, and Oona looked as if she had been crying. "What is it?"

Oona had a letter in her hand. "I'm supposed to tell you, but I can't. I think maybe you should just read this."

Icy fear rushed through Cuán's veins. Cuán ran past them and up the road. He ran as fast as he could go, hardly feeling his legs in his state of shock. He pushed through Oona's front door—"Maggie! Maggie!" He went to her room and pushed open the door.

The bed was made, and Maggie wasn't there.

Cuán went through the house, room by room.

"You bloody fecking girl, you better not have left me. Please, you can't have left," he shouted.

Maggie was nowhere in the house.

He ran to the caves. He followed the cliffs.

On a rock near the shoreline, he found a gown. He sniffed them, knowing that it was definitely Maggie's. He bunched it up and cried into the soft cotton, trying to draw her in with every breath.

Sobbing, looking out to sea, Cuán yelled, "You *promised* me you *wouldn't* leave! MAGGIE! You feckin' bitch! How could *you* do this to *me?!* MAGGIE!"

He didn't know how long he was gone. Cuán returned to the village and to his ma's house, still carrying the gown. His da smoked a pipe at the back door. Oona and Orna sat at the table, waiting for him to return. The note was on the table between them.

"Maggie has always been a mystery to us in a way, hasn't she?" Oona said. "The girl that seemed to come out of nowhere. We raised her, loved her, and I know she loves us. Especially you Cuán. I know it."

She held the note out to him, and Cuán took it, wiping his dripping nose with his hand.

> *Dear Oona,*
>
> *I know this will be hard for everyone, even Cuán. I know today is the day I was to give my hand in marriage to the one I love, and I know that missing this day will hurt many people. And for all of this, I'm sorry. I don't think of this as the*

*end. I want to come back to all of you, but there's something
I have to do. There's somewhere I have to be. I know it's quite
cryptic, but I promise to explain when I come home.*

Make no mistake. This is my home.

*I think Cuán is a wonderful man, and he deserves the very
best out of the woman he marries. I know him to be gentle,
protective, caring—all those things that show me that he
loves me like no other can. So, while I know this will break
his heart, I have a strong hope that his love is strong enough
to endure missing me for a short while longer.*

*I will return to you. I will return to him if he will have me.
God, I hope that you both will have me back.*

*Unfortunately, I have no idea when this will be. I wish I
did so I could give you an expected day, so you won't have
to worry, but where I'm going makes all this difficult for
me to explain.*

*Please tell Cuán that I know I have broken his heart, but
I will come back and heal it with all I have. It's a promise
greater than the pull of the sea.*

All my love,
Seagrass Maggie

"You notice that she keeps mentioning a broken heart?" Cuán
said. "She's so full of herself."

He meant to be angry and spiteful, but the words twisted in his
stomach so harshly he had to move outdoors before he threw up.
She *did* break his heart. It *did* hurt. All he could think to do was
scream it out of himself, but he wouldn't put on a show for the village. Instead, he sobbed quietly on his hands and knees in the grass.

His mother squatted beside him and rubbed his back.

"I know it hurts. Don't let it twist you into something you're not,"
she said. "She says that she knows you deserve the very best. Always prove to her that she's right. Prove to her that she can hurt
you, but you're unafraid of it. Show her that that is the strength of
your love for her."

"Ma—It does *hurt*. I *can't* breathe."

She continued rubbing his back.

"I know."

3

I can't breathe. The words echoed in his heart as he made his way with Oona to her home. She held onto his arm, and Cuán could see how badly she was stricken as well. Oona began sobbing again.

"The bloody girl. She is fae, isn't she?" Oona said. "One of the Mysterious Folk."

Cuán couldn't tell if she was being figurative or if she was really catching on to Maggie's truth. While Maggie was not fae, she was almost more a part of the fae world than the mortal world.

"Do you mind if I look?"

Oona studied him, looking confused.

"Couldn't she have clues in her room, or somewhere in the house, to where she might have gone?"

Oona stood with a nod, and then squeezed his arm. "I will help you search. We'll find her."

If Maggie was going somewhere and didn't know when she would return, Cuán thought there could only be two places worth considering. Either the Deep Dens to face the Fomorian King, or maybe to the Otherworld itself. He didn't know why she would go to either place. Both would be dangerous, and he didn't see any specific motivation to go to either. Where he found the gown made him pause and think perhaps the Deep Dens would be the best bet. She had gone into the sea.

Cuán recalled her touching his face, looking at him, and frown-ing. Was she thinking about leaving him, knowing that she would soon hurt him, and being unable to tell him?

This thought made him a bit angry.

I can't breathe.

God's sake, Maggie could really piss him off sometimes.

In the house, Cuán put Maggie's gown, which he found at the shoreline, on her bed and started digging around in her dresser. Normally digging through her drawers would have been a little exciting, but he was on a mission. There had to be something here, and if there was, he was going to find it.

There was a small chest under her bed. He pulled it out and popped open the lid. There was some jewelry here, love letters that Cuán had given her, and then he found a printed yellow card. It was a wire from Galway.

THE NAME IS KILLIAN IF YOU WANT TO CONNECT STOP THE OTHERWORLD IS A STRANGE PLACE STOP THE QUAYS STOP BRING A GOOD SCOTCH STOP

Who was this Killian? The Otherworld? Cuán was right. Why was she connecting with a strange man in Galway, and what did it have to do with Maggie? Why had she kept this all a secret?

"No, Maggie, whatever you're doing, you're not doing it alone," Cuán said, putting the card in his back pocket.

Whatever it took, he would find her.

Cuán looked under Maggie's bed and found a bottle of *John Crabbie* scotch. Nothing else.

"It's like you knew I'd do this," Cuán said, grabbing the bottle.

"What is the bottle?" Oona said when he came down the stairs.

"Scotch."

"Did you find anythin'?"

Cuán didn't know if he could tell her about any of this. Not yet anyway. Oona deserved the truth, and maybe it was time to tell her. But should he?

A part of him told himself, *No, not now. You must find her first.*

"Naw, not yet. But I have a couple of other ideas that might get us some answers," he said.

"Care to share one?"

Cuán shook his head and then decided to say, "There's a guy she knows in Galway. I don't know much about him. I thought I'd ask him and see what he has to say."

"What would she be doing talking with a strange man in Galway?"

Good question, Cuán thought, but he didn't say anything.

"Find her Cuán. Please. She's all I have," Oona said, a fresh tear running down her cheek.

"I will. I promise."

Damned Children

1

Elieris had long ago become a part of the Deep Dens. He was a titan now—his whole being carved into the labyrinthine catacombs around him. His being was at its heart—a giant hybrid man with tentacles and crustaceous claws, blending into the purplish and pink logarithmic whorls, apertures, and twisting spires of the Den. His Fomorian brethren made their homes in his vastness and traveled his nightmarish tunnels.

The Fomorian advisor—man-sized and floating up to the face of his titan king—held up the Derdriu Shard for Elieris to see Maggie traveling through the waters. If she weren't going to be so useful, he would have overrun her now with fomori, dragged her back to the Dens, kicking and screaming...and hopefully bleeding, too.

Beyond the Ninth Wave, the Shard could no longer see her exactly.

"It is done," his advisor said. "She has crossed over."

"And what of Carman?"

The advisor took the Shard and held it to himself like a ball.

"She continues to seek her sons out," the advisor said.

Elieris grinned. She would never find them because she didn't know that Elieris had them here in the Deep Dens. Upon leaving the island, he had the fomori snatch them up and brought them there. He had been keeping them for a day such as this.

Elieris created himself an aspect. The naked man floated before him, curled up in a fetus position, as one does when they are first-born. This was Elieris, but it was also something other. It was his avatar for him to speak through, since his true form had carved the

Deep Dens out of his own being long ago, trapping him there. When the man opened his eyes, Elieris planted his knowledge within him.

"Do you know who you are?"

The avatar nodded. "I am Elieris. King of the Fomorians."

Elieris then sent his avatar to the island and planted in him what needed to be done.

2

Carman had been to the libraries and the churches and had gathered as many books as possible that she could find on the ancient history of Ireland. The problem was most of it had been lost to time. There were fragments of those who had told the tale from another that had gotten it from someone else, so on and so forth for centuries, and she realized there was nothing more depressing than mortal memory.

Most of this was useless trash.

Carman kept thinking of her father and mother when she was raised in Athens. She was born Katerina Metaxis, named after the goddess Hecate, and it was strongly whispered that out of all their children, Carman might have been Hecate's daughter. Katerina's father, Mihalis, an *aristoi*, was known for his many infidelities, and Hecate was thought to have cursed their family when she discovered that Mihalis had another wife. In disgust, Hecate left the unwanted baby with Mihalis, and Katerina was raised and hated by the family.

She grew up with them spitting on her, ganging up on her to beat her senseless, and ridicule her whenever the opportunity arose. When Mihalis' wife asked Katerina's father to remove her from their home, Mihalis couldn't abandon her—even though he did nothing to stop the wickedness from the rest of his family.

Mihalis Metaxis was a coward, and she learned to hate him just as much as the rest of her family.

Katerina went to Hecate, and it was Hecate that said if she kept her father's name for her, she would not help her. Katerina asked Hecate for a name from her, and Hecate called her Carman.

Carman told her true mother what happened at the house, and Hecate took pity on her and taught her the dark arts—powerful Aegean sorcery that would see that Carman would not be victim to any more blows and other family abuses.

Carman, having found herself and her confidence, fell in love with a sailor named Ioannis. Together they had children, three sons: Skotádi, Kakó and Vía. But when Ioannis did not return from Hyperborea, Carman used her sorcery to locate him. She learned of the ship meeting foul weather as the Morrígan raised a storm, which turned the sea against them and sunk his ship. Ioannis, her true love, drowned and she felt the agony as he suffocated in the frigid waters of the northern deep. In terror, she went seeking funds from her father, only to learn that Mihalis Metaxis did not want to see her. Carman used her magic and killed or transformed their armed guards, transforming his wife into a rat, and just as she was about to cast a curse upon the youngest daughter, Irida, her father called from across the chamber: "No stop! Come to me, Katerina! Please. Come to me and let us talk."

"You have betrayed me, and you have betrayed my mother. You have betrayed your wife, and you have betrayed your children!" Carman remembered shouting. "You are worthless, and I have come to kill you should you not help me now!"

"Come here, Katerina. Please. Don't hurt anyone else. Please. I will do as you say!" Mihalis said softly. "Harm no one else. Please, darling. You are loved by me, and I will do anything for you."

Carman cast the daughter, Irida, to sleep so that she would not have to remember all the things that occurred to her that night. She moved to her father, who still begged for her to hurt no one. His eyes were full of tears that had not yet fallen.

"You promise to help me?"

Mihalis nodded. "I do. What do you need, Katerina? I will help you."

Carman wiped her own tears away. "I want to go to Hyperborea, where the druids are found. There are people there who have murdered my husband, and I want to go there, find them, and kill them. But I need money. I need a couple of ships for a small army."

Mihalis nodded, holding out one hand in self-defense.

"Yes, yes...I will help you. I will give you three ships, yes? And I will give you the money to pay for mercenaries out of Sparta. If you leave my family alone, I promise you all of this now. Okay, Katerina? Is this good for you?"

That's when Carman noticed that he was holding the other hand behind his back. In the reflection of a polished bronze shield, she saw the warped length of a dagger in his hidden hand.

He was trying to get close enough to surprise her. Her own father! He was willing to kill her!

Carman grabbed the knife with magical force, tore it from his hand, and then had it fly to hers. She grabbed it out of the air, holding it in front of his face as he looked at her in horror.

"You have just *damned* all of your *children!*" she cried. Carman swung the dagger quickly across his neck. Blood spurted, and he tried to stop the flow with both his hands.

Mihalis Metaxis dropped to his knees in front of her, drowning like Ioannis. Her only regret was that he suffocated on his own warm blood and not the cold, harsh waters of the sea.

With that, she turned and went to the sleeping Irida, still holding the dagger. She made sure the child would never wake up again before Carman went to her father's coffers and took what she needed—and *only* what she needed. After all, she was not a thief. She was a woman whose fate was cruel, and who now only had one mission in her life: to destroy the Hyperboreans or bring them to their knees.

Carman remembered hiring the soldiers from Sparta and taking her father's boats and making her three sons their generals. Nobody knew what had happened to the Metaxis family. Few only speculated. Nobody but Hecate knew what Carman was capable of.

Unfortunately, she and her sons failed as Lugh, and his companions, slowly killed every soldier, sank all their ships, and finally gathered up her and her nefarious sons along with her. Bres imprisoned her, and they exiled her sons from the island. All in a span of a few years.

Was Carman the same woman now?

No, she felt different somehow, even though she could not place it. But her hatred and her anger—*it* was *all still alive within her*, and she knew that as soon as she had her sons back, they would have a second chance to rewrite their destinies.

As she poured over her books, trying to find her sons, she heard the door open. It wasn't Etna who was already sleeping in her bed. No, this person had a powerful vibration about them. It wasn't the malignity of the Dominion, but it was husky with the deep.

Carman got up, wearing only her long, flowing gown, and went out to the hallway, and she saw him. The handsome man in black. His hair was mahogany, and his eyes were large and black.

"And who might you be?"

"I am Elieris," he said, holding his hands in his jacket pockets.

"The King of the Fomorians? Seriously, now?" she scoffed at him with a short chuckle, but he did not look ashamed by this. Instead, he just looked at her. She felt his energy. "Yes, yes…You *are* Elieris, aren't you?"

"I want to be helpful, Carman. After all, it wasn't I who destroyed your ships or imprisoned you. That was the Tuatha Dé."

"How do you think I can help you?" she said, not knowing his game.

"I have a person of interest I think you might be able to capture. If you draw her out with the power of your sons, then I would be very thankful," he said, stepping closer to her.

Carman took a step back, trusting no one.

"Do you know where my sons are?"

Elieris gave her a big smile then. "Oh yes. Let's just say that once they were exiled, I picked them up, thinking they might be useful to me one day."

Carman didn't like this at all. "How dare you?! Release my sons at once!"

Elieris nodded, frowning now. "Oh, I will. If you agree to our terms."

Carman sighed, understanding now. "Why didn't you just use my son's power to fetch the girl if you already have them?"

Elieris shook his head. "They are foreign magic. I mean, sorcery is all the same, isn't it? But every language has its codes and secrets, and I simply found that they were a little harder to crack than I would have hoped."

Carman laughed and leaned back against the wall.

"Your honesty is refreshing, Your Majesty," Carman said. "Would you like to come in for some tea?"

Part II
Tech Duinn

The Other Island

1

The deep sea accepted her body as she darted through its waters. Her body was a hydrodynamic lance with a powerful tail moving her forward. Maggie had a heightened sense of the waters around her, and she could feel the surges within the waters as she passed under the waves above.

Seven...

Eight...

Nine...

And with the bronze coin tight in her grip, she felt the water change in pressure and temperature. It got lighter and warmer. She could see the light from the sun above, showering the seafloor with mercurial caustic lights, making magic all around her.

It didn't last long. It started getting dark, and as she looked up, she saw that something had begun to cover the sun.

Maggie surfaced and used one webbed hand to push back her matted red hair from her eyes. Storm clouds were sweeping in, and in the distance, she could see a small island. Not Ireland. It was much smaller and filled with forestry.

Lightning flickered about the island erratically like skeletal fingers dancing on its surface.

Could she have gotten lost?

Could this be Bishop's Island to the south of Kilkee or Mutton or Mattle to the north?

No, she thought. She swam straight west. If she were near the mainland, she would have sensed it as the sea waters reacted to the land. Maggie would even be able to sense it now.

The waters had also changed. They felt different on the skin somehow. The detail was minute, and perhaps no one else could sense it, but those who knew the sea would.

The storm clouds grew thicker, and the waters around her started reacting. She started rising and falling in its grip, so Maggie dove deep to get away from the volatile nature of the surface and made her way to the island. When she came to its rocks, she swiftly avoided them, making her way through the waters like a dance of knives or fire. If you knew how water moved—in every way—you could know how the waters reacted to the land and the rocks around it. You could use them to be in the right place at the right time, and if you move swiftly enough, you could use the waters to slide between the dangers and to the safety of the shore.

Maggie climbed on all fours onto the gritty shore, weakened a little by all the work. After a moment of catching her breath, she stood up and looked around the island. She saw several trees, and moss growing over everything. Even the black rocks were dappled with the growth.

But the trees could not hide the sudden rise of the island itself, the rocky mountain that went into the sky. From one of its high cliffs, she could see a large castle made of the same stone she saw around her. The lightning struck surfaces around it, crackling through the thick, rainy air.

When she took a step, she felt something hard beneath her feet. It made a sharp noise and when she looked down, she realized she had stepped through a skull. There were a few other human bones lying around, some half buried by the shoreline sands.

Where the hell was she?

Wanting to get out of the rain, she made her way under the canopy, but the water still dripped and poured around her. She found a hollow tree and climbed into it, huddling inside as she wondered what to do.

If she was in the Otherworld, how did she go about finding her *anam chara*—the undine that supposedly shared a part of her soul? Did she just search for someone who could point the way? Did she make her way up to the castle?

What seemed obvious also seemed dangerous. She was in a different place, and the stories she heard reminded her just how dangerous it could be. There were stories of people getting lost in the forests, never to be seen again. Stories of monsters and witches that could trick you into multiple horrible situations, including nightmarish curses and being eaten alive. She wasn't sure which would be worse, really.

None of that seemed okay with her.

She jumped when she heard the sudden screaming and moaning. There were high-pitched cries that thundered sharper than the sporadic lightning around the island. Some of it rumbled out deep.

Maggie peeked out, the rain splattering her face, so she had to shield her eyes with her hand and looked up. She saw forms moving through the clouds, riding the storm. Their skin was slate gray or pale white, and they were covered in tattered black robes. They rose the gray and black clouds around the island, crying and wailing. She could hear their pain, their sorrow, and their terror in each wretched cry.

"Fer fuck sakes," Maggie said, sinking back into the hollowed tree, hoping that they could not see her. She tried to regulate her terror as it rose in her chest.

She was sure they were the *sluagh*—those damned by Dá Derga and reigned by the Dullahan. Maggie remembered Mrs. Donoghue saying that there was an island that sometimes appeared and disappeared, taking people who visited the island with it. The island of Tech Duinn was where Dá Derga judged souls.

The human bones on the shore. The *sluagh* were riding the storm above. This was Tech Duinn, and she thought she couldn't be in a more dangerous place. She was *afraid* to leave the hollow of the tree; in fact, she found herself frozen to her spot.

The Dullahan was like Dá Derga's marshal or bounty hunter. Dullahan hunted the souls down who dared attempt to escape with a whip made of human spines. Could this specter be somewhere around her?

Maggie didn't want to think about it, but she knew it was true.

Maybe she should make her way back to the water? There, she could swim until she found another land. There had to be something around nearby…

Except that wasn't true, was it?

In the reality of being in another plane of existence, the sea around the island could be infinite and only a border planet to other worlds. She didn't know how any of this worked, and she could find herself lost in the water forever. No, swimming away might be more dangerous than the island itself.

Ah feck, she thought. *I cannot believe this.*

A moment later, she heard someone shuffling near the tree. When she looked, she saw several people walking along, making their way up the mountain path. Some of them were bloody. Others were very old. Some looked very sick and weak. She even saw one woman missing half her skull, her brains clearly visible through the blood-matted hair.

Maggie gagged.

The…*dead.*

She closed her eyes and tried to will her form back into human shape, but when Maggie opened her eyes, she found that she was still in her hybrid form. Damning her luck, she tried again, but nothing.

She wasn't sure if it was her or the being in the Otherworld.

Should I try talkin' to them? she thought. Maybe they knew where they were or knew something about how they were there. It couldn't hurt to try. Taking a deep breath to control her fear, hoping her worries about the Dullahan were spurious, she stepped out and touched one on the shoulder. The woman looked back at her. Half her jaw was missing and a part of her nose. She smelled of sulfur and phosphorus.

"You can light 'em up anywhere," the woman said. "Light 'em up. Strike 'em up."

"I'm Maggie."

The woman leaned closer. The necrosis on her gums had eaten away at much of her mouth. Maggie wanted to look away, but the woman grabbed her and moved that terrible mouth closer to her, whispering, "Our matchsticks are the very best, my darlin'. Cigars, pipes, and cigarettes. Light 'em up. Strike 'em up. Anywhere you go!"

The woman let her go and continued walking toward the castle. There was nothing there except the horror of what she brought with her.

"Our matchsticks are the very best! Cigars, pipes, and cigarettes. Light 'em up!"

Maggie looked at her claws and then at a large oak tree. After placing the bronze coin in her left cheek beside her gums, she started climbing the tree until she was halfway up, able to see more. There were more ghosts traveling up the path toward the castle. Lightning flashed again—a deep rumble came a moment later behind it.

Maybe she should get closer to the castle. Though she wasn't sure about this, she began to believe that her only hope of figuring this out was to find one of the *sióg*. One that might not bite her head off and spit it into the dungeon of Duinn.

Just don't go through the front gate. Find another way in, she told herself.

That sounded like the best idea.

Her claws were really coming in handy now.

2

Bridget breathed heavily, her toes curled, and she kissed Aedán deeply. The orgasm was intense, and it took her a moment to recover from it. She just wanted to kiss him as long as she could. It wasn't until a moment into their kiss that she realized the warm sun began to be covered in storm clouds. And it should have already been dark...

"Aedán? What's going on? Wasn't the sun setting just a moment ago?"

They both looked up and realized that Aedán was not leaning back against the stone walls of a monastery but a large, dead tree. Its branches reached out as if it were trying to catch the storm gathering above.

"What the bloody hell?" Aedán said, trying to sit up.

Bridget climbed off him so that he could move, and they stood together, looking around them. This was not the county of Wexford.

"Aedán. What happened? Did we fall asleep? Are we back in the Lost Place?"

She followed Aedán around the trees to a small clearing. They looked up the mountain, seeing lightning striking around a blackstone castle on the cliffs.

"We must be dreamin' again," Aedán said. "That's the only explanation."

Bridget scanned the trees and other vegetation around them, looking for the Red Ghosts. She thought she would see their hideous faces any moment and that maybe she should look for something to defend herself with.

Aedán, on the other hand, looked up at the castle, looking at the path. When she saw this, she joined him.

"What is it?"

Aedán pointed at the sky, and she looked up.

Did she see people in the storm clouds, riding the terrible weather?

"Have you heard of the *sluagh*?"

"Sounds familiar, maybe. Why?"

"I think that's what's in the clouds."

"Are they dangerous?"

Aedán shrugged and looked at the path. "We should follow the path."

"To the castle? Are you crazy?"

Aedán chuckled, but she didn't know if he really thought she was funny. "What else do we do?"

Bridget had to agree with him. If they were dreaming, they had never seen this castle before. The Red Ghosts would be looking for them soon.

"Okay."

Bridget grabbed a stick from the ground. It looked sturdy. She stepped on one end until it split, and then she twisted it until the piece that hung onto it fell off. That end was nice and sharp like a spear.

While she made it, she wondered. Maybe the castle would protect them? Maybe there was a warm hearth as well? Could they be so lucky?

Aedán looked at her, smiling.

"Just in case. You never know," she told him.

"Yeah, a'right."

Going up the path, they started bumping into others, but they realized right away that these people weren't normal. There was a man with his neck hanging from his shoulders, his neck clearly broken. There were sick people coughing up blood or had skin that had rotted off their bones.

Bridget was afraid of them. She gave Aedán her pointed stick and then clung to his arm.

"Who are they?" she whispered.

"I think they're ghosts, Bridget. They're all going up to the castle."

"Are you sure we should?"

Aedán shrugged again and then put an arm around her.

"We'll go carefully, and we'll watch for anythin'. Right? We're used to it, you and I, being hunted almost our whole lives."

Bridget knew he was right, but she still had a bad feeling about this…

Dáiríne

Brogan took a seat and held out a hand. The goat, munching on grass, came closer and Brogan stroked the rough fur on its head between its horns. His varga-spirit sat quietly by, waiting for him.

Be careful, Fáelad said. *Nothing is as it seems here.*

"Like this goat," Brogan said. He suddenly grabbed it by its neck and then he saw its human hands and hoven legs as it struggled to be free of him.

It was a *púca*.

"I'll let you go if you tell me why you are here," Brogan said. He looked around him, and all the goats were now hybrids between humans and goats. Men and women, all with goat eyes and the turned-back horns.

One of the female *púca*, wearing a crown of flowering wreaths, stepped forward.

"Do not harm him," the *púca* said. "He is one of my flock."

"Then what is with the Stingy Jack?"

"We sent for you. We were approached by the voice of Bres through the *fata*," the woman said.

"Bres himself?"

"Yes."

"And who are you?"

"Dáiríne. Shaman of my people." She gestured to the *púca* that Brogan had by the throat. The creature was still struggling in his grip.

Brogan let it go and the creature ran away on its hooves. It then cowed behind a larger *púca* that Brogan noticed carried a spear.

He took them all in and he realized that he was outmatched. He might be able to kill some of them, but not all of them. They would eventually win, even if Brogan called his varga-spirit.

Brogan decided to play this safe.

"I mean you no harm. I don't know this place, and I know little about the *sióg* or the *púca*. If Bres did speak through the *fata*, what did he say?"

Dáiríne looked him over and said, "All our information comes at a price, don't you know? Come with me." She gestured to him to follow her, and she led him through the wood. Several Stingy Jacks were hovering about between the verdant green foliage around him. The other *púca* followed, some showing him their spears to keep him in line.

Fáelad followed beside him.

In a few moments, they came across a small river, being filled by a small waterfall from the hills beside them. Dáiríne went up to the waters and gestured him over again.

"You must give me an oath, Brogan Kelleys."

"How did you know my na— Never mind."

"You must give me an oath. Repeat this after me," she said, grabbing his hand and putting it into the water. "I swear that in my heart, I mean no harm amongst the *púca*."

Brogan carefully looked around at the hybrid shapeshifters. They all watched him in return, not turning their strange slot-black eyes away for a second.

"I swear that in my heart, I mean no harm amongst the *púca*."

"And that I will bring no harm amongst the *púca*."

"And that I will bring no harm amongst the *púca*."

"For any harm done to them will be harm on me three-fold," Dáiríne said, raising his wet hand in between them.

"For any harm done to them will be harm on me three-fold," Brogan said.

Dáiríne placed his wet hand between her small breasts upon him, saying 'three-fold', and then she turned his hand back on him and placed it on his chest. He was still watching the water drops running down her chest and down her stomach, and he bit his bottom lip.

"It is done," she said.

"Now, you will tell me?"

Dáiríne let go of his hand and said, "The Red God says to sacrifice the lovers here before you leave Tír na nÓg. If you do not, then the *kintráth* along his return will become much more difficult."

"Kintráth? What does that mean?"

Dáiríne shrugged. "We are not your allies, nor do we owe you anythin' more."

Brogan almost kicked her, hitting a tree root. A clod of dirt exploded and fanned out in a heavy cloud at their feet. The púca started laughing around him as their bodies faded away. Like apparitions: eventually they were like smoke and were gone in the air.

Twerg scum! Fáelad growled.

"Have you heard of this kintráth?" Brogan asked his varga-spirit.

Fáelad shook its head. *Does it matter? The message was clear. And it was from the Red God himself. The lovers need to die.*

It did matter, Brogan thought. What if the *púca* lied? What if this was a trick to ruin his mission?

He looked around again and wondered what to do or where to go. Then he saw the waterfall that filled the virgin brook. He crawled up the side of the cliffs on the side of the small fall, and when he got to the top, he saw a winding creek that had carved itself through the wood.

"Always follow water when you're lost," he told Fáelad, who probably already knew this.

III

The Fresco

Emera surprised him. Instead of dressing up with a large-brim hat and with all the laces, she wore a practical and simple dress that she could move in and a simple bonnet. Her smile was beyond gorgeous, though, and Nevan gave her his arm so that he could lead her around the St. Albeus site.

Diggers were hunched in their excavations that were divided into zones, and many of them were several feet deep at this point. They didn't bother anyone as they worked hard, only walking around and exploring what had been found and was now carefully brushed off for them.

Some found nothing, but others found pottery and a few 16th Century coins. One digger even found a silver platter with a Celtic knot border around its rim while digging in a zone near one of the fallen walls of the monastery.

"Where was this wall from?" Emera said.

"I believe it was part of the refectory," Nevan said. "According to Doctor Macguire."

"Doctor Macguire? May I meet him? Is he from Dublin?"

"I believe so," Nevan said. "He should be around here somewhere."

Emera got down on her hands and knees to look down into the carefully dug pit. At the bottom was a fresco that had fallen over with the wall and buried over some time. It was remarkably intact, showing a painting of Jesus breaking bread for a crowd of hungry people, and beneath it were some ancient Irish symbols—hash marks by any quick glance of it, but Nevan knew that it was ogham.

"What are these chicken scratches under lime plaster? Scratched into the tiles?" Emera asked, pointing as she went.

"It's actually a coded language that the druids used. It was sort of the first known Gaelic writing on the islands," Nevan said. "Doctor Macguire calls it ogham."

Below the ogham, he could see there was more lime plaster, which was probably yet another fresco underneath. Nevan imagined it erect and realized that the painting of Jesus that was visible would have been the top half of the wall, and it would have been above the monk's heads in the refectory as they ate their suppers.

"Does Doctor Macguire know how to read it?"

Nevan shrugged and squatted beside her so that he could see it better himself. "I don't know. All I know is that he said that you could find the language written on many standing stones across Ireland, Scotland, and Wales. It has even been found on the mainland in Europe."

"I'd love to read what someone had to say all those centuries ago," Emera said. "Do you mind helping me find him?"

Nevan smiled at her. "Of course."

They found Dr. Macguire in one of the tents, cleaning off artifacts and making sketches and notes in a journal. He was a gray-haired man with cracked, weathered lines on his face. The doctor wore a pinstripe suit with a black jacket and bowtie. Nevan cleared his throat so that he would see them. He looked a little upset at first when he was interrupted, but when he saw Nevan, he forced a big smile.

"Ah! Nevan. How are you doing, lad?"

"Good, Doctor Macguire. Good. I just wanted to introduce you to my girlfriend here, Emera Ó Damháin. She finds yer work 'ere very exciting, I should say."

Dr. Macguire shook Nevan's hand and then took Emera's and kissed her knuckles. "Please, no need for formal titles. It's Alastar. Nice to meet you, Emera."

"I am very happy to meet you," Emera said. "I find our history very appealing. I like the mystery of it, and the work you're doing here sounds so amazing."

Dr. Macguire beamed. "Why, thank you, young lady."

"I was wondering about the ogham underneath the breaking bread fresco. Do you know how to read it?"

"Well, it's quite something, Emera, but to explain it to you is difficult. You say you're excited about all this?"

"Oh yes."

"We do need help around the site. I have plenty of diggers, but I don't have anyone to clean and log the artifacts that we find in an efficient manner. If you and Nevan were to come after school and assist with this, it would help me, and we might find time so that I can teach you how to read ogham."

Nevan didn't know Emera could get any brighter, but her smile took over her whole face. She looked at him, grabbing his shoulders.

"Oh, we should, shouldn't we? Please!"

Nevan laughed, even though he knew that this would be harder work than it first seemed. "Why would I ever deny your pretty face?"

Emera jumped up and down and said, "I'm okay, if you'd like us to start now. My parents don't expect me until supper time."

Dr. Macguire got up and had them follow him to another table. There were a couple of ceramic vats filled with water. Brushes lay beside them. On one side were a few artifacts that were tagged and a blank book with a pen and inkwell.

"Let me show you how it's done," Dr. Macguire said.

Emera looked at Nevan, still beaming, and Nevan tossed out the ideas he had for any afternoon shifting with her. It didn't matter, he thought. As long as they had something to do together...so they could *be* together. *Yes, that was a'right.*

The Dar'gone

Maggie took the difficult route up the side of the mountain, not wanting to run into the ghosts or even the creatures that might be leading them along the grim path toward the portcullis of the black castle. The bronze coin still sat in her left cheek, where she kept it safe.

The climb wasn't easy. It was raining, making everything slippery, and the *sluagh* never rested, twisting and churning through the gray, devilish vapors. As she climbed, she could even see them better, and what she saw would probably haunt her for the rest of her life.

Most wore caul-like jellies over their faces. Their fingers were long and spidery, and their eye sockets were filled with chunks of ice. They had giant gashes in their chests, exposing their bleeding hearts, which glowed faintly in the darkness. Some of them carried lamps at the ends of chains. All of them had long, black claws.

The claws were meant for snatching people away—Maggie knew that. She knew if they saw her, they'd do just that, and who knows where she'd end up then? In the Pit of Duinn? Thrown out to sea? Taken into the storm, never to be found again?

Or would they rip her to shreds there and then, all taking their pieces of her?

Maggie could not return to her human form, but she needed her claws anyway. They helped her find purchase on the rocky surface of the mountain in the steepest parts. She just tried to stay close to the wall and preferably keeping to the darkest shadows as she moved.

But it wasn't as easy as it sounded.

The lightning loved to illuminate her, and though she had dark sea-green skin, her blue and purplish translucent fins reflected a flickering shine. When the lightning arced across the sky, she held very still until she felt like she could move again, hoping for the best.

The *sluagh* were mad. They were wild, screeching things that passed around her in the sky, with no simple pattern to discern. Only the mad rush of a craving they themselves probably didn't understand.

They were the souls that sinned, judged unworthy of Tír na nÓg, though Maggie wondered how much of that part of the legend came from the Irish heart or from the influx of Christianity. Either way, she didn't want to play with any of them.

Eventually, she reached the castle walls. She saw the ghosts entering the castle via the drawbridge, but she knew that if she went that way, she may be confused for one of them or even punished for not being one of them.

Then she saw the guards: on either side of the portcullis, they watched the grounds. They were twice as tall as the average ghost as they passed by them. The guards were bipedal, but just barely as they hunched over, with their large arms hanging down in front of them. Large, bubbling humps stuck out their backs with two or three pale faces hanging from them, all with large open sockets, nostrils, and mouths. Its body had flesh, but it draped its ribs and bony hips like wet cloth, giving them a terrible skeletal look. Their heads were the hardest part to look at. Their faces were bright white like exposed bone. The cheeks were drawn wide, showing off bleeding pink gums and yellowed, broken teeth, which gave it a morbid grin that remained frozen on their faces. Its eyes were like white marble.

Both creatures carried halberds—polearms with what almost looked like double-bladed axes at the ends. One side of the axe was curved more like a hook. And they both had blood all over them and their weapons.

Don't want to be caught by one of them, she thought, noticing that her hands had begun to shake. She rubbed her hands for a moment. The joints were sore from the climb. After a few deep breaths, she started climbing the castle wall, shoving her claws between the black, shiny stone with each reach. While the castle walls were slick and the steepest part of the climb, it was the stones that made it easier. She was up and over in no time, looking along the battlement. Nearer the towers she could see more of the nightmarish guards moving around, making their way on their duties, so she looked down into the bailey. Between the buildings inside the inner wall, she could see several shadows to hide herself in.

Quickly, she jumped down, landing on all fours. Too illuminated for her tastes, she sunk back into the shadows between the buildings, pushing her back against one of the walls, looking around for where to go next.

Beside a wooden door to the building on her right, a window was warmly lit. The door opened and Maggie realized she didn't have time to move. A brunette woman came out in her white gown, which was partially transparent and blowing in the wind around her legs.

In fact, seeing the woman's immodest gown—letting her discern the breasts, the nipples and the hair between her thighs—is why she missed the worse part. Maggie saw the severed head in the woman's arms, eyes looking at her, red lipstick smeared cross her mouth. When Maggie looked to see the carrier's eyes, she saw that there was only the bloody stump of her neck.

The woman *carried* her *own head*—

Maggie looked back at the woman's eyes. The ghost's eyes shifted and found her in the shadows. Her nose wrinkled and she opened her mouth wide, crying out as her hands held onto her head tightly: "Dar'gones! Dar'GONES!"

Maggie looked across the bailey and saw the hunched giants moving for her, their twisted grins in the pale faces. They had seen her, and they were coming.

"That wasn't kind at all," she shouted at the woman, and kicked the head from her arms. The head rolled away as her body fell back. Maggie jumped her, grabbing the wall once again with her claws so that she could climb it.

The Dar'gones were too quick for her. Before she was out of reach, they grabbed her and pulled her down. One of them put the curved edge of their halberd against her neck.

"Don't kill me, please!" Maggie cried.

Blood poured from the Dar'gones' mouth as it leaned into her face. Its broken teeth opened, and blood poured out. It rasped and then sucked in a breath before it withdrew the halberd from her scrawny neck.

The Dar'gone that grabbed her pushed her forward, and she realized they meant for her to move toward the keep. She started walking, swearing under her breath at her luck, and looked for a way to escape. If she ended up imprisoned, it was going to ruin everything.

The Dar'gones were everywhere now, crawled all over the place. There was nowhere to run or hide. The only satisfaction she found was that the headless woman was still feeling the ground around her for her own head.

"Have fun, ye *right* cow!" Maggie shouted at her.

The Dar'gone Guards pushed her forward, leading her down a great hall, which stopped before two titan doors that looked like they were made of bones. Blood poured from somewhere above the doors, and it followed the carved lines in the door in small rivulets that pooled again beneath the doors.

The Dar'gones opened the door on her right and shoved her through it hard. She fell to her knees, so she looked up through her draping red hair, and saw the White King sitting on his ivory throne. Above him like trophies were two large, black avian wings. The god himself was muscular and tall. Everything of him was white—his skin, his hair, his eyes. The only thing that wasn't white was his black plate armor, which was obviously hammered carefully for a king.

"Dá Derga?" she said, hoping for the best.

Show this god that you are no lost ghost, but a woman that has the courage to meet him, she thought. After all, it was her understanding from Cuán's descriptions that the old gods cherished courage over frank subjugation.

Dá Derga looked at her as if he were confused.

"You are not dead?"

Maggie shook her head. "No. I am alive. I am a Maris. I've the blood of the *sióg* running through my veins!"

Dá Derga frowned. "Nathaira's blood, I see. Well, then, you are trespassing. Disappointing."

A Concord Above Death

1

There was a scratching sound at the door.

He didn't like it...not at all. Ever since his employer, Lord Cuinn, brought Etna McCarna into the Order, he felt something changing in the air. It was partly electrical, but the kind of electrical that just touched your nerves, raising your hairs, but showing nothing more of itself.

It was enough, however, for what the charges raised was utter, mind-numbing fear.

Damhán's grandmother said that there were supernatural forces out there—the Tuatha Dé Danann being only one of them—lurking in the fields, in the trees, in the caves and even in the hearths. Many of them had no interest in mortal affairs, but there were some that lurked because they *did* mean you harm. They had claws and teeth meant for ripping and tearing.

She even told him about her experience with them—how a goblin ate their chickens for a several weeks just before the sun rose. She would go out each morning finding one dead, its head removed and stuck on a stick. It wasn't until her ma put out a bowl of milk and surrounded it with rowan twigs that the goblin left them alone.

Foul energies were rising in the night air, and Damhán didn't like it at all.

When the scratches stopped, Damhán walked to the door and looked out its window. He couldn't see anything, so he grabbed the knob and opened the door, revealing the night outside.

There looked to be a woman with no face—it was torn away, showing a white skeletal face beneath with bloody eyes. Damhán backed up, almost letting the scream out of his throat.

"Who are you?"

The woman laughed.

She looked like Etna, but she held herself differently. More confidently. Sensually.

Where was her skeletal face? Did he imagine it?

No, this woman was a pretty version of Etna. A *provocative* doppelgänger of her. But it wasn't Etna, was it? No, it was someone else.

"C-Can I help you?"

"I am here to see Lord Cuinn," the woman said.

"I'm sorry, but he's not seeing anyone this late. You'll have to come back in the morning. Preferably around nine or ten."

Damhán then saw an old woman behind her. It was his grandmother! The sagging, wrinkled flesh of her fatty arms. The toothless gums turned purple. Her large cataract eyes.

"The goblins are watching you, Damhán!" she said with her crackling voice. "Do you feel them in the air? I do, their eyes, their claws, their teeth...Do you not feel them near?"

His grandmother—who had been dead now for more than twenty years—reached out for him with those plump, heavily calloused hands.

"No gran'ma," he said. "You can't be real."

"Oh, you can't tell me you don't feel it! That blackness that surrounds you. It's suffocating, isn't it? Ah, my Damhán! Come to gran'ma!"

"No!"

He didn't know why, but he couldn't move.

Was it the terror that ran coldly though his body?

Did he feel the dark energies?

Was his gran'ma truly back from the grave?

His gran'ma grabbed his throat and squeezed. He couldn't breathe. He tried to fight back, but she was too strong for him. It was like being a child again. Arms and legs totally useless against her might and she pushed him back against the wall, squeezing his throat with her big, plump hands.

Gran'ma laughed and her big, purple gums were the last thing he saw before the end.

2

Carman couldn't see what he was seeing, but when he went up against the wall and started suffocating—his terror visceral in his eyes—she was thrilled. Once the ghastly Eerie killed him, he slid down the wall onto the floor, slumping over. Satisfied, she made her way through the house.

When she was at the study doors, she pushed them both open. The man behind the desk jumped up, surprise all over his flush, middle-aged face. Terror was good, Carman thought. It was easier to bend people to her will if they were frightened of her.

"What the hell is going on here?!" he demanded.

"Lord Cuinn, I assume?"

"You better explain yourself right now! Where is Damhán?"

"Shut up, you mouthy kern! My name is Carman."

Lord Cuinn's eyes widened. Yes, he knew who she was.

"Wh-Where is Damhán?"

"Dead, of course. He was annoying me."

Lord Cuinn sat in his chair, looking stunned.

"Oh, I see, you didn't believe who I really was, did you? Well... Now you do."

"Aye."

"Good. Now let's move past all the horseshit and get to know one another."

Lord Cuinn sat up, summoning courage from somewhere. "Why would I help you? Hm? You are the enemy of my god."

Carman chuckled at that and went around his desk. She pushed him and his chair back and sat on his desk in front of him. He shook, terrified, but he sat there holding firm to his image as an important man who knew how to stand his ground no matter what. That was also good. She didn't need a coward right now. *Be scared, but don't be afraid to act either. Head this face on.*

Carman traced the bridge of his nose and then down his lips with a soft finger. She grabbed his bottom lip and pulled on it for a moment.

He said nothing. He didn't move.

"I'm afraid many of your history books are from foreigners. Roman trash, most of it. Christians rewriting whole stories to suit their manipulative needs. There's some truth to some of the stories, Lord Cuinn, but I am not merely a story, am I? I am true history. I am...what *you need* to learn the truth," she said. Carman leaned closer to his face, opening her mouth as if to kiss him.

His face turned up, wanting it.

"I am not your god's enemy. In fact, the Red God and I have long been allies. And if you want to raise your Red God, you'll need me to do it."

Carman licked his warm mouth.

His tongue was slow, and late.

Carman then sat up straight and smiled at Lord Cuinn, his features partially stunned and hungry for more at the same time.

"Our stories have been passed down my bloodline since before St. Albeus was even built," he said. "I do not recall anything you say to be true."

Carman sighed. "Your recollection is much to be desired. The human mind cannot store and comprehend every fact or experience. It fills in holes and gaps with loose psychic fragments, and then is twistedly told and misheard for centuries. Look, you can choose to believe me, or you can fail in your conjurings. It's really up to you."

"And what if I don't believe you and send you away?"

Carman shrugged and then got up from his desk, going around it to the other side. She walked over to the door and whispered, "Tar taibhse!"

"I find this strange conversation needs to end," Lord Cuinn said. "Will you kindly leave?"

Carman stared coldly at him.

Down the hall came steps. Slow, steady steps. *Wait until you see this*, Carman thought.

"Who is that?" Lord Cuinn pushed by her into the hallway.

Damhán walked down the halls. Blood vessels in his eyes had blown, leaving his eyes bloody. His flesh had turned gray as stone, and he already smelled like he was rotting.

"Jesus Christ!" Lord Cuinn backed up. "What have you done to him?"

Damhán reached out for him.

"My lord! I think I'm dead!" Damhán said. Blood poured out between his lips, dripping down his chin.

"Damhán!"

"I saw my gran'ma! She was here!"

Lord Cuinn looked at her.

"What have you done?"

"Maybe I should leave you two together. Maybe he can convince you where I have failed," Carman said.

Lord Cuinn quickly shook his head. "No, no! Please, no! Undo this, please!"

"Are you saying that we will work together then?"

Lord Cuinn nodded. "Please. Let his ghost go. We have a concord above death."

Carman ended the Eerie and Damhán fell as if unconscious. Only if they were to check him, they would see that he was truly dead. The man wouldn't even twitch.

"We may never be friends," Carman said as she walked through the door, "but we will be worthwhile, Lord Cuinn. I promise."

With that, she was out the door.

In the Pit

1

Maggie tried to stand up, but the Dar'gones pushed her back onto her knees. Dá Derga sat before her in his throne—not much different than a white marble statue with black plated armor. The crown on his head was made of fishbones and each spire had wedding rings slid down upon it.

"I didn't come 'ere to trespass, Lord Derga! I came 'ere because I need yer help. I look fer an undine—one who has a piece of me soul. I only seek mortality!"

Dá Derga laughed. "You have come to the right place. You will be executed by beheading, and then I will judge your soul."

"No!" Maggie cried. "No, please! I didn't come 'ere to die, just to seek...a...a cleansin'. I have fae blood runnin' in me veins, and I want to be free from the burden of life beyond the life of me fella! Can'nit ye see? I want to live a normal mortal life."

There was a long silence.

The Dar'gone grabbed her hair and pulled her face back so that she was forced to look at Dá Derga as he contemplated her words. After a long sigh, Dá Derga sat up and said: "She is to be executed on tomorrow's moon. Take her to the Pit. Upon death, she will be judged so that she may be passed on to the Crann Lár or driven on the storms with the sluagh sí."

No, Maggie thought. This can't be it. This isn't supposed to be how it ended.

Cuán. What have I done?

"No!"

The Dar'gone grabbed her and started pulling her from the throne room. Maggie fought the whole way, hoping to escape, but the thing was too big and strong. If she could only break free so that she could run, she would run to the sea and she would leave this place forever.

For Cuán.

Well, for herself as well. She didn't want to die yet, though it wasn't about that so much. It was about not living without Cuán. There was a difference.

Bloody hell, what has she done? What went wrong? Where was the other piece of her soul?

The Dar'gones took her down to the Pit. After descending a winding chasm of stairs, the went through a double set of giant doors that revealed the conical whorl of the Pit that went down deep into the bowels of the island of Duinn. The stairs laid along the walls and every few meters there was a cell. Many of them were filled with sluagh, begging to escape or screeching their horrors.

They traveled down these stairs until they came across an empty cell with a mottled white and brown goat in it. They threw Maggie into it and slammed and locked the doors behind her. Maggie went to the bars and grabbed them, looking at the Dar'gone.

"Were you once human?" she said. Her tongue flicked the bronze coin in her cheek.

The Dar'gones just looked at her, their white faces and red eyes unmoving. Emotionless.

"If ye were human once, ye'd understand," she said. "I love him, and I'd do anythin' fer him. That's why I'm 'ere."

The Dar'gone grumbled.

"I don't want to die," she said. "I want to live. I want to live fer Cuán and Oona. I just don't want to lose Cuán, either—not knowin' that he will go long before me. I can't bear the pain of it."

The Dar'gone slammed the cage with its halberd, making a terrible metallic noise that echoed across the Pit. It inspired more sluagh to scream their agonies, and terrified Maggie. She jumped back from the bars, a sob escaping her.

"Yer a bunch of useless *fecks*, anyway. Arseholes, all of ye!"

With that the Dar'gones left, climbing their way back up to the castle.

Maggie went back to the bars, checking for weaknesses in them. It was made of faerie iron—it was very much like cold iron, only it was made with glamour. Despite not hurting her, she couldn't get it to bend either.

Well, this was no good, she thought. *Feck-all death gods and their arsehole minions. They can all go to hell.*

Of course, the irony in that thought didn't escape her, but she was beyond laughing now.

2

There was grass thrown in a heap in the corner of the cell. The mottled white and brown goat chewed on it lazily.

"Name's Maggie."

Maggie looked at her dark sea-green skin, and the scars drawn on her body. Her tail was curled beside her, the spiked fins were both purple and blue. She took the bronze coin out of her mouth and flipped it in front of her.

"Seagrass Maggie," she said. "The serpent girl from Kilkee."

She had to chuckle at that. Wryly.

"You have a name?"

The goat stood up. Its front legs were now hands, and its body changed more humanoid. It looked to be a young, brunette young lady with dark horns, and golden eyes with slot-like pupils.

Maggie was shocked by the sudden change, but then not totally surprised. This was the Otherworld, even if she were in one of the darkest places.

"Fiadh is ainm dom."

"FEE-uh," Maggie enunciated, trying it out. "That is a fine name."

"I am the daughter of Dáiríne, shaman of the *púca*."

That's right. Shapeshifters. The *púca* loved to take the form of animals, and even when taking human shapes, they left animal features on their appearance somehow as a mark of who they were. Many of them took the form of goats, but over time, some would revert to other animal forms and features.

Maggie had never met a púca before.

"Why are yeh 'ere? Did the sluagh bring yeh 'ere?"

Maggie could imagine the creatures riding the storms, snatching the poor thing away from her family (herd?) when they weren't looking as they grazed green fields.

"No," Fiadh said. "I was sent 'ere to see you. Through the *Eagla*, I was able to peek into yer *cinniúint*, what my mother likes to call the Red Braid, and I found that you would be 'ere."

"So, the Red Braid is like me destiny, or somethin'?"

"Aye. No destiny or fate is a straight line. It weaves in and out of each other, and sometimes divides. The Red Braid can be changed, but it's very difficult. In a way, that was what the *Eagla* was originally for—to take control of one's own Braid and make your own way in the world."

Maggie sat beside the horned *púca* and sighed, putting the bronze coin back into her cheek.

"Well, accordin' to the Dá Derga, me fate is sealed by tomorrow's moon," Maggie said. "Not exactly a fun feelin', or even a destiny that I know how to change."

Fiadh walked to the cage on her hind legs, her hooves making a subtle clopping sound on the rock floor. She tried reaching her hand up to the lock, and then gave up, sighing.

"The locking mechanism is too strong for me. Perhaps I can be of help some other way?"

"How? You've magic in yeh?" Maggie didn't understand how this *púca* could help her at all, but she didn't mean to hurt the *púca's* feelings. "I'm sorry. I can be an arse."

"No harm," Fiadh said, squatting in front of Maggie, grabbing Maggie's cheeks. Fiadh pushed Maggie's hair out of her eyes. "You are a beautiful, strong creature of the earth. You have been changed by the Otherworld, and it frightens you because yeh think that maybe you will lose everything you love."

Maggie groaned. "Nathaira's blood, I 'ear. I really don't want to 'ear all this. It's not helpin' me."

Fiadh smiled at her. "I can't say much, but I can say this: even though you have not learned of the *Eagla*, you can use your blood to touch upon its ethereal fabrics. You can touch the Red Braid and you can reweave it to yer liking. All you need to do is expand that mind, as you've swollen yer heart, and you will be able to take control of this."

"Sounds a bit *naff*...naïve to me," Maggie said.

Fiadh frowned. "You're not making this easy on me."

"Oh. Aye. Now we've really been introduced."

"Such a sour bearing. Were you born with this?"

Maggie laughed. "Aye. Ye could say it was there since I was stolen from my parents when I was wee chisler."

Fiadh leaned in and kissed the nodule on Maggie's forehead.

"There. We can be friends."

Maggie rolled her eyes. *Great.* Friends. At least she'll have company until the Dar'gones come back for her.

She went back to the bars and tried to move them again. The door rattled, but it was heavily set into its mechanisms. It wasn't going anywhere. Maggie sighed. There had to be a way out of here. All she had to do was find it.

Maggie looked at the small cell she was in, realizing it had no restroom. *Please, no.*

"Where's one supposed to go?"

Fiadh shrugged. "Isn't that the idea? So, you don't go anywhere?"

"Oh lord." Maggie rolled her eyes again, thinking, *My eyes will roll right out of me head if this púca stays with me much longer.*

She scanned the conical chasm around the cell. From her standpoint, she couldn't see the bottom of the pit or the ceiling. She could see the sluagh moving in their cells across the pit, stupidly clawing to get out yet never succeeding.

This place was made to house the sluagh. Not Maggie. Not a Maris Demidian. Was there something she had that the sluagh didn't have? Something useful that maybe the Dá Derga could have overlooked?

"What are the sluagh? They claw at their cages and the walls, and they only remember their pain and agony. They can't think through them. Their minds were lost long ago to know only their suffering. It's part of the curse of Dá Derga—for those not pure enough for the Crann Lár," Maggie told the *púca*. "They're lost sinners."

Fiadh shook her head, looking concerned. "No. Where have ye heard that, Maggie? They are *not* sinners. Sin doesn't really exist, does it? There is right and wrong, but right and wrong has its own contexts. No one person is *purer* than another because of some unseen defilement. No person is a sinner because of defilement. People can only think bad things and/or *do* bad things. That's all. In the end, it's how you manage and what you think of yerself."

Maggie realized her head was cocked in bewilderment. "Souls cannot be purified?"

"Souls can be damaged. But they do that to themselves. It's not because they are a sinner, and they need their sins cleansed. They need to heal. No, the sluagh are *not* the sinners that Dá Derga has judged. They are the ghosts of those who haven't forgiven themselves. Sinning is a Christian invention."

"But what about those who feel purified when they cleanse their sins?"

Fiadh smiled. "Do you think relief is only something a Christian feels? People want to be heard and feel as though someone supports them. You don't need a god for that. You need humanity."

This was an epiphany. Maggie was stunned.

"The sluagh are judged and Dá Derga quiets their minds, giving them what they ask for—to dwell in the sea of their agony as punishment for what they believe they deserve. For them, it is who they are and all that they are. To me, it's what makes them the most frightful. And is also why I pity them," Fiadh said.

Maggie looked out the bars at the claws and caul-draped heads in the cells around them.

Now how could she use this?

Bloody Nothing

Fanning his hand as he moved through the smoke, he passed a drunk who accidentally elbowed him in the rib. Backing up, Cuán moved through the crowd in *The Quays*, looking from face to face, carrying the bottle of scotch with him.

A young lady with very curly, dark hair almost bumped into him as well, carrying a few empty bottles of lager.

"Oh, I'm so sorry. Excuse me," she said.

"No, I'm sorry. Hey, before you go, can yeh point me to Killian?"

The girl pointed to a corner table, walled off from most of the other tables in the joint.

Cuán gave her a nod as he popped a lemon drop in his mouth. "Thank you."

He went back to the table to see the tall, muscular figure with bright red hair. He was smoking a cigar, holding it between his teeth, as he shuffled a deck of cards. Cuán sighed and went up to the table.

"Excuse me."

The large man looked up at him, the cigar bobbing as he puffed. "*Dia dhuit*, my friend. Do I knows ye?"

Cuán shrugged and pointed to the spare seat at the table. "Do you mind?"

"Not'at'all," the man said.

"Well, it really depends. I believe we have an acquaintance. You Killian?"

"Aye."

"Names Cuán Foley. You know Maggie Connell?"

"Yer mot, I assume," Killian said, chuckling. "She's a might dote, aye?"

"Aye, she is. A wild dote, as a matter of fact. She's very important to me."

Cuán put the bottle of scotch on the table and Killian looked down at it with a grin.

Killian shuffled his deck again, saying, "Well, if yer dotey mot was seen with me, I'm sure it was completely under virtuous intentions. Name like 'Maggie' is a little bit on point for me, if you know what I mean."

"I don't," Cuán said. "And I'm sure her intentions were chaste. I've no mind to believe otherwise. No, I come 'ere because she's gone missing."

Killian looked up with his eyes. It was almost sinister to Cuán.

"Aye. You don't say."

"And I don't think she's on the island anymore, if you know my meaning."

Killian looked at his deck and then at Cuán.

"You play cards?"

"I don't like to gamble, Killian."

"Then you won't get very far, chasing after Maggie. Where she goes...Well, every minute is a new hand. A failin' hand. There's only way to make it out alive, and that's to be one fucking good bluffer."

"Aaah, feck. You ever hear them wild western stories that come out of America? There's always a third option, isn't there? A fight. That's what Maggie has."

"Then why do you worry so much about her?"

"Because—"

Cuán stopped. He wasn't sure how to answer that. It made him sort of angry, actually.

"For fucks sake, Killian. Just tell me how to find 'er."

The curly dark-haired girl returned to the table.

"Anythin' you want while you're sittin' 'ere?"

Cuán looked at the girl and then at Killian. Killian looked up at the girl. "I think he might want a pint of Guinness. The lad's goin'a need it."

The girl looked at Cuán and smiled at him. "Do you need cheerin'? I've a joke."

"A joke, is it?"

"Aye. You see a man goes up to a woman and says, 'Ma'am, I'd like to order a Guinness.' The woman frowns and says, "Well then, you must be Irish.' The man is a little miffed at this, and says, 'Oh, so ordering a Guinness makes me Irish? If I ordered a pizza, would you assume I'm Italian?'

"The woman tries to defend herself, sayin', 'I didn't...' But the man interrupts her, furious she'd try to weasel out of this, and says, 'And if I ordered a Bratwurst, would that make me German?'

"The woman doesn't think on it much. 'No, but...'

"'But! But! So *why* exactly do *you think* I'm Irish then?'"

"'Sir,' she says, 'this is a bookstore.'"

The two of them laughed together. Cuán tried not to laugh, so he sorted himself by allowing her a smile.

"I don' need jokes but thank you. At least I didn't waste my complete time comin' 'ere."

"I'll be right back with the pint," the girl said.

"**I** know you're one of them. A leprechaun, aren't you?"

Killian never failed to smile until now. He pointed a large finger in Cuán's face. "I hate that word. The only appropriate way of saying it is in the old tongue. *Leath bhrògan.* You ever use those poor choice of words again, I'll cut your fucking tongue out."

Cuán nodded, holding up his hands between them. "A'right. A'right. I get it."

"Maggie had a terrible vision," Killian said.

The girl returned with Cuán's heady black pint, smiled at him again and was off to let them talk.

Cuán took a drink of the lager, wiping the head from his nose.

"Right. Tell me then."

"She said that she wasn't aging the same as you. Ye'd grow old, and she'd have to watch ye die."

Cuán remembered her touching his face, frowning. She wasn't worried about what he'd think if she left him. Maggie was watching him age, and she didn't like it. That's why she was so worried. The poor girl...

"Ah, Jesus H and Mary," Cuán said. "Why can't she tell me these things?"

"She thought that maybe if she went to the Otherworld, there'd be a way to sever the fae nature from 'er blood, so that she could grow old and die with yeh."

Cuán let that sink in, a cold rush running through him. It was all making more sense now. He thought of Orna's funeral. "I need to go with her. She should have taken me with her."

Killian shook his head. "Ye a bloody flute? Yeh can't follow 'er. The only way I know is *thar an naoú tonn*—Beyond the Ninth Wave. I gave 'er a token that allowed 'er to slip through at the right time and the right place."

"Can you get there by boat?"

Killian laughed. "No. Not unless you want to go down with that boat."

That pissed Cuán off.

"There has to be some way for me to get to her."

Killian shook his head.

"It was in the Great Contracts written up between the Tuatha Dé and the Milesians. Our worlds would remain apart fer a reason."

"Fuck this," Cuán said, getting up from the table. He put a few coins down for the barmaid. "What if she dies and never comes back? Maybe you have sent her to her death."

Killian took a deep breath, his large chest rising and falling. "Aye. I may have. But it was her call to make."

Cuán grabbed the pint and threw it on the ground, where it shattered and splattered all over them. He wasn't sure what he'd done until he heard the crash and watched the glass shatter around his feet. "You bloody fucking spanner! You cold-blooded bastard!"

Then he stopped on the verge of crying. And he saw that the whole pub had quieted down and turned to look at him. Even the girl with the curly brown hair, eying him as if she didn't know him.

Yes, of course. Nobody knew him. Nobody here understood.

He was all alone.

"Thanks fer bloody nothin'," Cuán said. He turned from Killian and pushed his way out of the pub.

I promise you, we'll marry. I just—I sometimes worry about who I am sometimes. I don't have everythin' figured out, you know? What am I to the sióg? How will my blood affect me in my life? Will it affect our future?

Bloody feck of a fecking fuck.

It was right there in front of him.

And now he didn't have a way of getting to her.

Cuán walked Quays Lane. The city was just getting dark. His hands were stuffed in his long fisherman's jacket, and his boots clomped on the cobblestone road. From all the books he'd read, he wasn't sure any of them were helping him right now. He needed a way to the Otherworld, but in most of the stories, people were either transported there or had gotten lost, finding themselves in the fae lands without knowing it. Nobody deliberately made their way to the Otherworld, unless you were a god or demi-god.

A *Demidian*, he realized. Like Maggie.

Bloody fuck, what was he going to do?

Ah, Christ, he thought, working through everything he could remember reading on the fae. No, the books weren't helping at all. Or, at least, his memories of them.

Think outside the books. Think outside the head.

Think...*of people you may know.*

Killian was a worthless gobshite, but... Cuán knew somebody that might be able to help him. Ambrus Kárpáti. The sorcerer from London who helped Maggie and the *siofra*, Deirdre, retain their memories. By day the man masqueraded as a stage magician. He was good, too, of course. And he also belonged to an order of sorcerers called the *Lodge of Hermetic Magick*. The only problem with this plan was that Cuán had to go to London since he was certain that a wire wouldn't get him to the Otherworld.

"Fuck. I'm off to London then," he said to the dark street.

There was simply no other idea to be had.

Cuán made his way to the train station in Eyre Square and bought a ticket. He was told the next train would be arriving in an hour, and then would be heading to Dublin. From there, Cuán planned to charter a boat to Britain.

There goes your wedding and your home, he thought.

The trip would take a couple days. He had a long night ahead of him.

Maggie. Damn it. I love you. I'll find you. We'll be together. We'll figure this out.

VIII Undine

"Little girl? Can you help us?" Aedán watched, holding his sharp stick, as Bridget went up behind the girl in the fancy blue dress. Bridget reached out a hand and touched her shoulder, and the girl turned around.

She had no eyes. They were black sockets dripping black ichor.

"Have you seen my eyes?" the little girl said.

Bridget covered her mouth. Aedán could see her terror, so he moved closer to them.

"What happened to your eyes?" Bridget said.

"My father poked them out when I refused to look at the Good Book. He says if I weren't fit fer readin' the Good Book, I wasn't fit fer seein' anythin' in His World."

Bridget broke away, leaving them.

"Bridget—"

She ran through the forest as quickly as she could. Aedán didn't expect it, so it took him a while to catch up with her. By that time, she had breached through the trees and bushes to the shoreline, stumbling on the human bones in the sand.

"Aedán! This is a terrible place!" she cried.

Aedán wrapped his arms around her, thinking, *Yes, a terrible place. It was a reflection of the real world. A place of human cruelty, suffering and death.*

"I can't wake up," she added. "I try and I try, but god damn, I can't wake up from this nightmare! This is worse than the Lost Place. Have we died? Are we in Hell, Aedán?"

Aedán kissed her cheek and then held her face in his hands, looking into her glassy, soulful eyes. "I don't think we're dreaming anymore, Bridget. I think we are somewhere else, but I don't think we are dead. We've seen them. The dead. They walk as they died. Headless, diseased, old...*without eyes*. They all are drawn to the black castle at the top. None of this is true for us. I'm not dead. I feel alive, and neither of us are drawn to the castle."

Bridget, now buried into his chest, nodded with her face against him.

"What do we do? This place isn't safe. I can feel it in my bones."

They started hearing a song lifting around them. A woman's sublime voice echoed through the trees, amplified off the rocks. Gaelic, but it was the oldest Gaelic Aedán had ever heard. He barely understood any of it.

"Where is that coming from?" Bridget said, moving from him, and then she started walking along the shore toward it. Aedán followed her until they came across another cropping of rocks. The ocean crashed against them, spraying them with a fine mist. There was a bowl-shaped pit in the rocks, and it caught the water as it crashed through, but the waters were lowering. The tides were going out to sea.

A woman with very pale skin and thick black hair laid out in the water. Her upper body was very human, but she had the longest tail where her legs would normally be. It was currently curled around her, its long, fanning fins were blues and purples. Her ears were pointed like an elf, and her eyes were a dark umber.

Her flesh glistened as she laid there, her breasts slick and her nipples were hard. Laying on her chest, a silver pendant gleamed: a spiral with a triangle inset, pointing downward. Her upturned face basked in the moonlight that now peeked out from the rim of the storm clouds. She had the loveliest face Aedán had ever seen.

"Is that a mermaid?" Bridget said, sounding awed.

The girl stopped singing when Bridget said this, and then quite gracefully, she turned about and crawled up the side of the pit, the strength of her tail helping to lift and push her up without any issue. Swift on land or sea.

"Who are you?" the creature said.

Much closer, Aedán could see that he was mistaken about her skin. There was a very light tinge of blue in it.

"I'm Bridget. This is my aul fella, Aedán. Are you a mermaid?" There was so much awe in Bridget's voice.

The girl-creature seemed to relax. She grabbed her long black hair and threw it behind her. "I'm an undine. My name is Léana. You two do not look dead, so how have yeh come to Tech Duinn?"

"Tech Duinn?" Aedán said. Okay, now he understood it. Why hadn't he figured it out himself?

"This is the island of Dá Derga?"

"Aye," Léana said. She reached out and touched his face. "Ye are so warm."

"What is an undine doing here?" Bridget said. "Are you dead?"

Léana laughed. "No. I have been called by a piece of me soul. The woman who possesses it crossed over to this world, and I can feel that she is close."

"Why are you looking for her?"

Léana looked at him oddly. "She is part of me soul."

Aedán felt daft.

Bridget pushed Aedán back and got between him and the undine. "Do you know how to get out of here?"

Léana looked up at the mountain. "The only safe way fer ye is up there. In the castle. Look, I could help yeh, but I need yer help first."

"You want us to help you with finding your soulmate?" Bridget said, seeming to already understand it.

But that did not sound like a good idea at all.

"Are you daft?" Aedán shouted, perhaps rougher than he meant to. "Have you seen all those ghosts? If the stories are true, do yeh know who sits up there on a throne? The god of the dead. What if he mistakes us for his ghosts? What then? What would he do to us?"

Léana looked at him sincerely. "Oh, he will punish yeh. And it would be terrible. But it's the only way. If you do not know the way, his Dar'gone Guards will find you, or the sluagh will when they travel the storms. It's inevitable."

Bridget looked at him.

"Aedán. We have to help her. If it's the only way, then we must do it. We can't stay here."

Aedán wrapped his arms around her.

The undine regarded them.

"So, you will help me?"

Aedán nodded. "We will. Aye."

Léana crawled up onto the sands of the shoreline, and somehow her tail was gone, replaced by long, sleek legs. Aedán could see everything, since she did not cover herself up as she walked toward them. He blanched, embarrassed as his eyes wandered, when he realized it.

Not forgetting that Bridget was there, Aedán turned away from the undine. Partly ashamed of himself for having looked, even though it was unconscious and brief.

"I'm sorry," he said. "You're naked."

Léana looked down at herself. "Do I offend yer modern sensibilities, mortal?"

Not so much offended, but my mot is right here, and I think maybe she would be uncomfortable with me seeing you like this, Aedán thought. That's what he wanted to say, but he only stumbled over himself, humiliating himself further. "M-My mot, um, is…"

"Mot? Is it? Ah, aye, now I've a pet name," Bridget said.

Aedán, fighting the heat in his face, took off his shirt and tossed it to the undine, who held it up in front of her.

"What is this?"

"A shirt."

"Oh, I don't need yer shirt, Aedán." The undine tossed it back, and then out of nowhere she was covered in a simple blue dress. "I have me glamour."

"Dear God, you have to teach me that. What a wonderful power to have for a lady!" Bridget said, smiling for the first time since they'd found themselves on Tech Duinn.

Léana walked toward the woods. "I have caught word with the sprites in the area that there is a secret path to the castle that only Dá Derga uses. There will be fewer Dar'gone Guards, so it will be safer."

Aedán sighed. He knew that this was going to be dangerous, and he didn't like it all, but what choice did they have?

None, that's the truth of it.

They made their way through the woods until they came across a smaller path. The creatures flying through the clouds were gone when the clouds dispersed. The moon was out now, full and bright over the small island.

The way had more stairs along the rock cliffs, and they went through a few low tunnels, but they climbed their way up the mountain. As they got closer to the castle, they saw the large, hulking creatures with their hunched backs and all the white faces on them. The things conveyed themselves across the steep grounds, between the rocks, keeping a careful eye around them. They held long polearms with axe-like heads. They could easily chop your head clean off with a single swing.

"What the fuck are those things?" Bridget said, as they ducked behind rocks.

"Those are the Dar'gone Guards. When Dá Derga finds the right souls, he changes them into these monsters to guard his House. They guide the ghosts to his throne and walk the grounds to capture any interlopers that dare defy him."

"Oh, like us," Aedán said.

Bridget punched him in the arm. "Not helping, Aedán."

"Then how do we get by them if they are all over the bloody place?"

"I say we go slow and be very quiet." Léana regarded him, looking as though she might be worried about them. She then grabbed his pointed stick and tossed it aside. "And that won't help us at all."

"Aye. Sounds like a plan to me." Could she read his sarcasm? Bridget didn't seem to, which was a shame. "I think."

Hungry

The sun pierced the canopy of the forest while strange creatures could be heard crying, whooping, or singing. These weren't your normal forest sounds. Extravagant and colorful, and most of them Brogan couldn't even recognize.

But the sun was a good thing. It meant that the forest wasn't always so dense and hard to travel. Maybe they were even coming up on a grassy plain?

The varga-spirit trotted alongside him. In the material world, nobody could see Fáelad but himself. Here, though, every time they passed by a semi-intelligent creature, the creatures always studied them both from a safe distance.

And they saw some strange creatures. Many of them were hybrids between humanoids and animals. Little monkeys with childlike eyes and hands, almost naked but the fur on their backs. Their faces were far more humanoid, but their noses were often black or brown, and had whiskers.

There was also a large woman with bird legs and taloned feet with hummingbird-like wings on her back. Her arms and hands were humanoid, but she had the black talon-claws that she opened and closed inattentively as she glared back at them.

Brogan and Fáelad didn't approach the creatures. But if they came close, the creatures would scurry or fly away.

Brogan's stomach growled. "I'm hungry."

Maybe we should hunt, Fáelad said. *Or maybe I should hunt.*

Brogan gave the wolf a severe look. "And lose control? No thank you, Wolf!"

Fáelad started panting and then looked up, stopping. Brogan followed the wolf spirit's eyes to where there was a short, naked woman standing on a branch of an elm tree. No, not a *human* woman. The thing stood six inches tall and appeared human at first glance, but she had pointed ears, long blond hair, transparent mosquito wings on her back, and a black, rhino beetle horn on her head. Humanoid, but also...*insectile*.

"Are the two of you lost?" the little insect-woman said.

Brogan smiled at her, trying to show her that he wasn't harmful. He raised his hands to show her that he held nothing that could hurt her. "Actually, yes," he said. "Very lost, I'm afraid."

The insect woman kept looking down from the branch at the wolf.

"I have never seen a varga before. I hear they are far rarer than they used to be!" she said.

"What is your name?"

The insect-woman looked at him, squatting down and spread out her wings as if she were going to take flight. But she didn't. She stayed like this, watching them carefully.

"Ní' Blátha," she said.

"Ní' Blátha! What a pretty name! Do you and your kind live around 'ere?"

The insect-woman sat down on the edge of the branch, kicking her legs.

"Forgive me, but you didn't say *your* name, did you?"

"My apologies. Brogan Kelleys," he said. "My manners are terrible, especially when I'm hungry. Can you help us?"

"I suppose so," Ní' Blátha said. "If we go to my nest, we have plenty of honey."

Honey? Brogan shook his head. Nothing but candy! That wouldn't do for long.

Be nice, he told himself. *Don't scare her*.

Brogan forced a smile.

(*That's better.*)

"That would be wonderful! We'll follow you," he said.

Fáelad looked up at him, looking curious. He knew the honey wouldn't be enough, but what else were they supposed to do?

***

Ní' Blátha took off from the branch on her wings and zipped through the trees. She was almost too fast for them. They entered a small grove of fallen oak and maple trees all about them. More of her kind appeared on tree limbs, or from their dirt mounds to watch them. Their dwellings, carved from these mounds and trees, were very intricate in design.

Most of the creatures were women, which was traditional to the myths Brogan knew of. Many fae were female for reasons he didn't understand. But there were males amongst them, all gathering around Brogan to regard them.

Ní' Blátha landed on her feet in front of Brogan, between him and her people.

"This is Brogan Kelleys," she said. "They are lost and hungry. I wondered if we may have enough honey to share with them?"

Brogan looked around at all the human-insectile creatures. Most looked like her, though their horns varied, their hair and eye colors varying as well. Some of them were far different. Some of them had insectile legs. Others had antennas instead of the horns.

When they all walked, they walked like bugs.

Did they taste like bugs?

Brogan smiled, and in his mind, he called his varga into him. The varga growled and vaulted into his body. Upon becoming one, Brogan felt the heat and agony of the changing. His skin stretched painfully over rapidly expanding muscles and bones as they re-shaped themselves.

He too was a hybrid — wolf and man. He snatched Ní' Blátha up and crushed her between the jagged teeth in his ravaging mouth. She screamed until her bones crunched and her blood spurted from the corners of his lips.

The creatures started to run, but Brogan snatched others and fed them into his hungry mouth.

No, they did not taste like insects.

They tasted wonderfully human.

Their blood poured out of his mouth as he chomped and gulped them one by one.

When he was full, he sat back like a king on a tree stump, surrounded in brambles, overgrown in green and white moss. He held two of the twergs in his hands as he looked over the creatures cowering behind or inside their hollow trees.

Both were female, and they fit nice in his clawed hands. Brogan sat there, waiting for them to see that he was no longer eating them. Yes, he was splattered with their dark blood now. The women in his hands cried and moaned, begging for him to release them.

Eventually, a few of them got brave enough to approach him at his padded feet and clawed toes.

"P-P-P-Please let them go!" one said, dropping to his knees in front of Brogan.

The varga-spirit passed out of him, and with that, Brogan reshaped into that of a man. He was still covered in their blood. And the creatures were watching it drip down his chin, his chest and down his legs.

Some of the women-creatures started to keen their sorrow for those lost.

Brogan leaned forward and bit the head off the woman creature in his left fist. He felt the salty hard head and long hair sink down his throat quickly. Her body twitched in his hand in its death throes, while the woman in his right hand gasped and became quiet in her horror.

"No," the man in front of him said. "Why do this?"

"Because I want to make myself clear here," Brogan said. "I am a hungry god. And there is only one way to satisfy me! If you do not want to feed me, then you must be rid of me."

"How?" the woman in his right fist cried.

He looked at her. She had long, hickory hair and didn't have the horns. She had grown little black antennae instead.

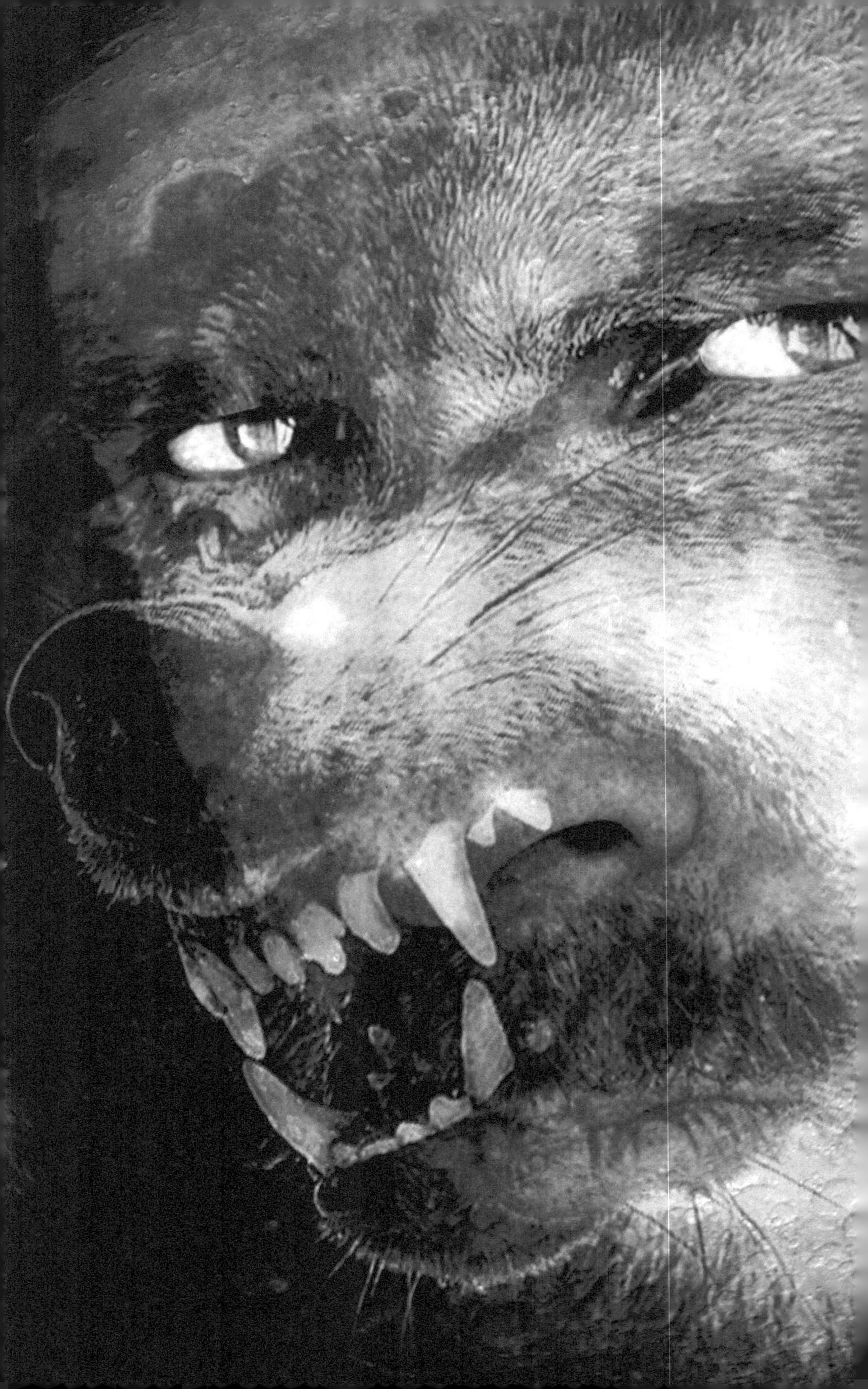

"You will gather the quickest of your kind and you will search the forest, and even beyond it, until you find me two mortal humans. Once you locate them, you will tell me where to find them. If I catch them—I won't return here again," Brogan said. "Is that clear to all of you?"

The creatures murmured amongst themselves, but none of them had to decide. The insect-woman in his hand did for them: "It is clear. We will send scouts out at once!"

Pleased to hear it, Brogan set her down on her feet in front of him. Since he still held the other insect-woman's headless body, he stuffed the rest of her in his mouth. One of her legs stuck out his lips though, and he delighted in sucking it down. He swallowed her as the twergs all watched.

It's good to finally eat, he said in his mind to Fáelad, who sat beside him on the ground, looking rather cavalier. It was good to please the wolf, so that the wolf wanted to please you.

This may be brilliant, Fáelad said. *It'll be much easier and possibly faster to find them this way.*

"That's why I'm in charge," Brogan said.

An Apparition

Just about when she was ready to give up, Maggie looked down from the cell bars of her prison and saw a piece of sharp rock on the ground. She leaned over and picked it up as Fiadh sat in the corner, eating the grass, watching her with those coin-slit eyes.

Maggie looked at where the metal edges of the door were driven with spikes in the wall. She used the sharp end of the stone, chopping away at the edge. At first, it didn't look like she did anything, but when she started using her raw, supernatural strength, the wall started chipping away.

But the rock she held crumbled in her hands as she cracked it against the wall after several good hits.

"Ah, shite," she said, looking around the cell chamber for more. Maggie found another rock and picked it up, but then she saw the bare feet of another woman standing there watching her. The other woman was semi-transparent. She had a shallow grin on her face, long caramel hair and wore a lacy white gown. "Who are you?"

The woman's grin deepened. "My name is Carman, Maggie."

"And how are ye 'ere in front of me?"

"I have one of the pieces that was made from your soul," Carman said, "that Ri Elieris took from you when you were still a babe. Let me show you."

Inside her own head, Maggie could see the fomor, Fangtooth, removing a piece of her soul. It glowed a brilliant white, and it broke into pieces. One flew from the watery chamber, but Fangtooth kept hold of enough of it so that he could forge it with a hammer.

Maggie remembered her nightmare of Elieris gutting her, and she realized they were the same event. She remembered it wrong. It was so long ago, and she had still been an infant. Her memories were powerful as her body and mind had to adapt to surviving in the dark environment with Nathaira's blood in her veins, but some of it was rather murky, especially at the very beginning.

"My soul?"

"Elieris gave me what he had. The Derdriu Shard."

"That's what he hammered from me soul?"

Carman grinned at her. "The Shard lets us see you wherever you are. Though it was much more difficult when you crossed over to Tech Duinn. Elieris was sure he'd lost you. He seems to have issues with patience. I've learned a long time ago that if you wait long enough, it eventually occurs to you."

"Well, Elieris was never a sorcerer."

"To be sure," Carman said. "Not like me."

Maggie didn't know whether to be frightened of the woman or be angry. If they could hurt her with the Derdriu Shard, Elieris would have done it already.

"What do you want, Carman? Why have you any interest in me?"

Maggie noticed that Fiadh was shivering in her corner. She shifted her shape back into her goat form. She obviously did not want Carman to see her.

Carman, however, was focused on Maggie. "I want to make a trade with you."

"Feck off."

"I will purify your blood and your soul of the fae essence if you find me three Attainments."

Maggie wasn't sure she heard that right. "Ye can make me mortal again?"

"Maggie, you are already mortal. You just have a longer lifespan from Nathaira's blood. It can be purged with the Derdriu Shard, which I will give freely back to you."

"Yeh don't say."

"*If* you find me my three Attainments."

"What if I just come and find yeh and take it?" Maggie said. That sounded like a much better plan. This woman was playing with her, and it was getting on her nerves.

"Oh, that won't happen, Maggie. Unlike Elieris, I *am* a sorcerer, and I am the wrong woman to cross."

"Aye? Is that so?"

"Maggie," Fiadh whispered, but gruffly. "Don't trust her."

Carman turned around, rolling out her hand, waving a swift gesture in the air. Fiadh rose off the ground, hovering in the air, shifting back into her hybrid form, and then her stomach started ripping apart as if by itself.

Maggie cried out in horror as Fiadh floated there, jerking in agony, her hot bowels falling to the ground beneath her, blood puddling out quickly across the floor. Maggie had to step back, trying to stay away from the blood—feeling as though touching it would taint it.

Fiadh was dead before Carman released the *púca* from the spell, letting her drop into her own gore.

Maggie didn't let herself sob. Instead, she bared her sharp teeth and pointed at the sorcerer's apparition. "That was a *hideous* thing to do!"

Carman shrugged. "I'm a hideous person, Maggie. *Don't* come and fight me. It will be your end."

Maggie looked away from the *púca*'s body. "I get yer fuckin' point."

"Good. So, do we have an agreement? You retrieve the three Attainments, and then we exchange for the Derdriu Shard and the soul purge?"

Maggie didn't look at the witch. She buried her head in the bars of her cell door. "Aye. We have a deal. What are the three Attainments?"

She could feel Carman's cruel smile behind her. "The first are Badb's Wings."

"A'right? And the next?"

"We'll see how you do obtaining the Wings before I name the other two. Good luck, Maggie. Once you have it, find a pool of water and toss the Wings into it. They will then find their way to me. Once I get the Wings, I will know and then I will seek you out for the second Attainment. Do you understand?"

"Feck off me now," Maggie said, done with the woman.

Suddenly, the bars she held onto shifted, and she realized she could push the door open.

Carman had freed her from the cell.

Maggie looked back. Carman's apparition was nowhere to be seen. Only the mess she left of the poor púca. Maggie kneeled beside the poor thing's body, and ran a hand over her eyes, closing them. It made her remember poor Róis—another innocent woman that died being too close to Maggie.

"I'm so sorry, Fiadh. Dangerous people have a way of finding me. May you find peace wherever ye are."

Carman sat in the sitting room, her legs across the couch as she held the Derdriu Shard before her. She could faintly see Maggie within it. When they finished their conversation, Carman grinned and placed the Shard onto the floor beside her.

She placed her feet on the cool wood floor and stood up, making her way to the plate that she had spilled water onto. She stirred the water up with her finger and bit her lip. There was a short sting and then she felt her teeth break skin. Carman spit the blood into the plate, stirring it into the water.

Carman whispered her incantation and then she saw the beautiful face of Elieris appear in its reflection as if he were just in front of her.

"It's done," she said.

Elieris grinned. The cunt. "Good."

"My sons?" *Give them to me!*

Elieris nodded and said, "They will be freed at once. Two of them will return to you. The other will be sent to the Otherworld."

"I wanted to see them all, Elieris."

"Life is cruel, Carman. You know that better than anyone. We must enjoy what life hands us, for it truly isn't fair, is it?"

Carman grabbed the plate, spilling the water about her, and tossed it against the wall where the porcelain exploded into powdery shards and fell to the floor.

"Bastard!"

She *will* get him one day.

Two fomori went to the watery abyss at the center of the Deep Dens, where amongst many rocky formations, a cavern wound its way into the ocean floor. It was filled with cysts that seemed made for a prison. Many cysts were driven with bars, holding onto creatures captured by the Fomorians.

The two fomori swam to one specific cell, where three brothers slept against the roof of the cave: Dub, Dother and Dain.

"Wake up!" one of the fomori said. "We have come to free you! The Ri Elieris has decided mercy is in order. Two of you will go home to your mother. One of you shall be taken to the King."

The brothers looked at the fomor, partially shocked. But inside them all, an excitement grew.

Freedom.

Mother.

"Do you know who we are?" Dub said.

The fomor hissed at him, but the brothers were not concerned.

"We are darkness," Dother said.

The brothers attacked the fomori, tearing and eating them.

The Gog-Magog Theatre

The titanic city sprawled out before him in a haze. It was a mass of buildings, horses, carriages and people. There were large crowded markets, where people kicked up dust as they selected their purchases, shops galore, banks, schools, business offices...and narrow labyrinthine streets wove between other cross streets to who-knows-where, making everything more than a little confusing to him.

Though Cuán was used to seeing Dublin, it didn't compare to the ominous expanse of London. He made his way through town, stopping to ask people for directions until finally he came across the large, stone building with the colorful banners and artwork declaring stage shows such as *The Burial Mound* by Henrik Ibsen, *The Vampire* by Dion Boucicault, and, of course, *The Magick of Ambrus Kárpáti!*

Above them, chiseled into the stone above the doors:

THE GOG-MAGOG THEATRE

Etched into the stone on either side of the wordmark were giants, crouching to lift boulders above their heads.

Cuán, wearing a paperboy hat, took it off as he went inside. Actors shifted by him. He tapped one woman on the shoulder.

"Excuse me, ma'am," he said. "I'm looking for Mister Kárpáti."

The brunette looked him over. "And who are you?"

"I'm a friend from Dublin. We met a couple years ago, and since I was in town, I thought I'd stop and see him," Cuán said, attempting good humor. "I actually worked lights in one of his shows."

The brunette stabbed a thumb behind her, returning her attention to the pile of costumes she was picking up. "He's in back. There's an apartment where he keeps all his junk."

Cuán gave her a short wave. "Thank you."

Cuán stepped out the front doors and followed the narrow alley beside the theater to the back. Behind the large theater building there was another, shorter building that almost looked like it was a small warehouse. Cuán climbed the steps to the door, knocking.

After a few moments, a pretty blond opened the door, wearing a pale blue dress and a white shawl. Cuán remembered her.

Adelynne Parish. Ambrus' stage assistant.

"Yes?" But obviously she didn't recognize him.

"Oh, sorry, my name is Cuán Foley. We—"

Adelynne beamed and threw her arms around him. "Cuán! I remember! Come on in. How are you doing? How's Maggie? It's been a couple years, hasn't it?"

Cuán stepped inside the apartment, which had a small living space and kitchen, but the large of it was filled with props, magic boxes, gears and other mechanics. A workshop, really. He recalled that Ambrus used bicycle parts in many of his illusion boxes. The man had gone to school for engineering but was drawn to performing on the stage. He was good, too.

But Cuán wasn't here because of his performance, or his engineering talents. No, Ambrus Kárpáti used all of this to disguise his true and secret ability: sorcery. The man was a master of the occult, belonging to a secret occult society that called itself the *Lodge of Hermetic Magick*. A couple years before, Maggie and Cuán were up against a sorcerer named Doran Dunn. After meeting Ambrus, the man helped them escape Dublin with their lives and even helped them deal with the sea vampyres that were sent by the fomori to capture Maggie.

"Actually, Maggie is why I'm here," Cuán said, as Adelynne picked the sprawled newspaper off the couch, tossing it aside.

"Please sit," Adelynne said. "What happened?"

Cuán took a seat on the couch and Adelynne stood back, looking at him.

"Maggie went and done a fool thing and crossed over the Otherworld alone," Cuán said, sighing. "I have to find her. She can't be doin' this alone without me."

"Ambrus is out getting parts for his machines," Adelynne said. "He'll be back soon. Would you like some tea?"

Cuán nodded at her. "Aye. Thank you."

"I found out that Maggie has been obsessing over this idea that she'll live much longer than me," Cuán admitted. "She's not aging like I am, and it was killing her, I guess. She's been talking with one of the sióg who calls himself Killian. She wants to cleanse her blood of the fae-touch that makes her the serpent. Killian showed her how to get to the Otherworld, both of them believing that she'd find her answers there."

Ambrus—a 58-year-old man with light gray in his otherwise blond hair—sat in a chair near the couch. He wore his gray tweed suit and black bowtie. He had dark rings around his eyes from his many years lacking sleep, studying the occult, running his show, and practicing sorcery.

Adelynne was on the floor, sitting on a pillow, her legs curled up under her as she looked between the two of them.

Ambrus' eyebrows shot up and then he sighed, crossing his arms in front of him. "And he couldn't help you?"

"I tried," Cuán said. "I almost punched his lights out, too. Nah, Killian said it was impossible for me to follow her. She went *Thar An Naoú Tonn*—Beyond the Ninth Wave."

Ambrus nodded, thought for a moment and shook his head.

"So, you were hoping I'd be able to get you to the Otherworld?"

"Aye."

"I'm afraid I have bad news for you," Ambrus said, leaning forward and grabbed his tea from the table beside him. He took a drink. Cuán felt impatient but waited. "I'll try to make this easy for you. Between the spirit world and the physical world is an existential yet metaphysical barrier. In most places, this barrier is very thick, keeping both worlds far apart from each other. Invoking sortilege—uh, magic—that manipulates the spirit world from the physical world is very difficult. You must penetrate that barrier in order to see ghosts or communicate with the other side.

"Now in some places the barrier is much thinner. It's because *cathexis*—emotional psychic energy—makes the barrier much more malleable. In some cases, the time of day changes the cathexis in the air. In other cases, places can thin the barrier as it sponges a lot of that cathexis up from the people who visited. Cemeteries. Some places of worship. Haunted places where tragic things have happened.

"Anyway, even with the barrier so thinned, actually walking from the physical world to the spiritual world is still pretty impossible."

Cuán blew out a long breath. "Then what about this Hollow that Maggie and Deirdre sometimes use? She mentioned once that the Hollow had doorways."

Ambrus shook his head. "The Hollow is a psychic place vibrating in the spirit worlds, but the only way you can enter it is by projecting an astral form there. And the doorways, Maggie was talking about, are people. See, the Hollow—which we mages call the Akashic Records or *agasha*—is like a psychic atmosphere that exists closer to the physical plane, binding all humans in this psychic field. The weather stirred up there is created by thoughts and ideas. Humans exude a psychic field and are doorways to their own dreams and thoughts, collectively called their mindscape. Those are the doorways Maggie talked about. None of them, from what I know, reach so far into the spirit world that you can actually travel there in a physical manner."

Why did this have to be so hard? Maggie found a way. There had to be a way! Cuán rubbed his eyes, trying to calm himself down. "I'm frightened I'll never see her again. I need to find her before something really bad happens. I have a feeling. I need there to be some way."

Ambrus set his cup down and he locked eyes with Adelynne who looked up at him from the floor.

"There has to be a way to help him, Ambrus."

Ambrus looked around the room, thinking. Then his eyes lit up, and he looked at Cuán. "Actually, I can think of one way. Maybe. Do you mind traveling a bit farther?"

Cuán nodded. "I'd travel the globe for Maggie. I'd go to Hell for her."

Ambrus got up from his chair, looking at Adelynne. "I'll have to speak with Alfred Browning. We'll need a holiday."

Adelynne looked at Cuán. "He's our boss. He owns the Gog-Magog," she explained.

Cuán looked at Ambrus. "Where are we going?"

"Wrexham. It's a small village in northern Wales. I know a woman there that might know a way to help you. She's a shaman of the Old Ways," Ambrus said. "Do you have a place to stay?"

Cuán hadn't yet thought that far.

"No."

"Well, you're welcome to stay on the couch," he said. "I'll have to perform my Thursday show, but I'm sure we can get this done before Alfred blows his top."

Cuán stood up and grabbed Ambrus' hand, shaking it. Sincerely, he said, "Thank you. I didn't know who else to go to."

Ambrus smiled and patted him on the arm. "No worries, son. I'm here to help."

Dub

1

In the Otherworld there were multiple paths that would take you from one of its planes to the next. Paths were important in any world, but in the Otherworld, they were protected places. Places of commerce, contracts and neutrality. But the paths that made their way from one spirit plane to the next were called the Argent Paths.

Dub was a skeletal being, wearing black robes and two swords crisscrossed on his back. The sheathes were red and the crimson shield banded around the sheathes marked him as one of the Red Knights of Bres. His boots splashed in the mud as he crossed the Argent Path into Tech Duinn.

Elieris promised him eternal freedom and sanctuary if he were to capture the Lovers and kill the Maris Demidian girl with red hair.

"Do this, and I will raise you amongst the fomor as a general, and you will have what you need to stand proud amongst your kin," Elieris said.

Dub grinned his skeletal grin.

I'm coming to get you, chiselers. The Darkness is coming... for you!

The Argent Path was laid out on the water and Dub walked on top of it, the swells of the spirit sea crashing about him and yet not shifting the low path in any way. In the far distance, he could see the island where the Dá Derga ruled.

Dá Derga may be his only problem, but Dub thought he could handle it.

Dub knew the *Eagla* temper of darkness, and he knew how to manipulate it. With this power, not much could penetrate and harm him. He was sure he'd be able to at least elude any gods that stood before him.

2

In the keep of Tech Duinn, they found a hallway that was unguarded. Aedán scouted ahead and waved them on. They came across bedrooms and slipped into one. Aedán was reluctant and curious at the same time.

Bridget sighed, sitting on the bed. "I can't believe we are doing this. I just can't bloody believe it."

Aedán shrugged, looking around. "Do you think anyone sleeps in these spare rooms? Who would be the occupants, aye? Ghosts? Other gods? Somehow, I don't see gods sleeping and having lives like mere mortals."

Léana went to the window and tossed the long crimson curtains aside to look. "Dá Derga's keep is the tallest structure in the castle. We have to find the staircase that takes us towards the Pit."

"The pit?" Bridget said. "What pit?"

Léana looked at her. "That's where the sluagh sleep, waiting for the next storm. It's like a dungeon that spirals into the mountain and probably deep into the bowls of the island itself. If Maggie was captured, she would have been taken there."

"What if they killed her?" Aedán said.

Léana shook her head, her eyes spacing off as she talked: "No. I would feel her die. I'd know it."

Aedán wasn't sure if he believed or trusted Léana yet, but he reminded himself that this was the only way. He and Bridget were mortals and knew nothing of this world. Léana was their only guide through it, and she would only help them if they helped her first.

He didn't like it at all, but what could he do?

"A'right then. You two stay here and I'll check for the stairs. Don't go anywhere," he said. He looked around the room for something to wield for extra safety, but there was nothing but a chamber pot. After giving up, he went to the door and cracked it open just enough to look for the Dar'gones. Unable to see them or hear them, Aedán gave another look at the girls, and then slipped out into the hallway, closing the door behind him. He moved down the hall, sticking close to the walls as he could.

He heard a *scuffing* sound behind the door. Wood squeaked repetitiously. There was a long, heavy growl inside.

At first, he thought the door would open. He was frozen still, waiting for that inevitability...and he waited...but he relaxed, realizing that while the sound continued, nothing came his way.

Aedán went to the door and slowly opened it, looking.

There were two rotting things inside. Once human, perhaps, but their flesh was barely dangling from the bloody sinew, and the woman's face was half rotted down to the very white, pearly bone underneath. She was bent over on the bed and the rotted male behind her was holding her, rutting his thick organ in and out of her, pounding her hard enough that the bed made its noises.

The male growled again as if he was coming inside of her, but then he began again. Neither noticed him nor seemed to care. They were engaged in the rotting coital act as if it was all they were there to do. Forever.

Disgusted, Aedán shut the door and moved on. At the end of the hall there was a doorway, where the stairs descended to the right of the threshold. This was it! Aedán looked around once again watching out for the Dar'gones and hurried back down the hall toward the room.

Only halfway down the hall, there was a large open window. From the dark of the outdoors, a black mist came rolling in between him and the bedroom where he left Bridget and Léana.

Out of the black mist stepped a black figure with a skeletal face, blood dripping down from his mouth. Aedán once again froze in terror as he realized that this looked just like the Red Knights in the Lost Place of their dreams. The creature withdrew two swords from the sheaths on his back and opened its bloody mouth.

"Aedán!" it said. "Don't we know one another? Beyond the Hollow doors of the Lost Place? Yes, yes. I say we do! But oh! Hey! This isn't a dream, is it? No, this is reality."

"Wh-Who are you?" Aedán tried standing tall, trying not to shake in front of the creature. This was reality. He didn't have to be a quivering mess.

Except, yes, he was certainly afraid of this dark creature.

"I am Carman's oldest son. Dub. Darkness. One of the Knights of Bres."

"Carman? Who—? What do you want with us?"

The skeletal creature laughed.

"This isn't for me, chiseler! This is for Bres and for his ally, Elieris! You know that. Surely, your father has told you this, yes?"

Aedán shook his head, not believing the creature.

"Fuck you!" Aedán tried running past Dub, through the dark mist, but the darkness wound around him and he felt it coalesce into a slimy matter that grabbed a hold of him. Dub easily moved within it, cutting the air with one of his swords, threatening him.

Only Aedán saw a chamber pot bounce off Dub's shoulder, catching his attention. Bridget stood by the open bedroom door behind her, legs apart to keep her balance. "Get away from him!" she screamed.

Dub hissed and pointed the tip of his sword at her face.

Aedán struggled with the dark matter that clung to him. No matter how hard he tried, the dark material stuck to him like a glue. Some of it came up toward his face and then slowly started wrapping itself around his neck. He could feel its cold, slimy surface slide against his skin and with it feeling so real, he became terrified.

He was going to die.

The dark matter started tightening and then Aedán couldn't breathe.

Léana came up behind Dub and wrapped her own arms around his neck. Dub reached back to grab her hair, but Léana tightened her arms. Dub stumbled backwards. He was stronger, however, and managed to grab her arm, pull it from his neck, and then he jerked his shoulders so that she lost her balance. She tried to hold on, but Aedán could see that her fingers couldn't hold and Léana fell and rolled on the ground.

Bridget was frozen in fear. Just standing there by the bedroom door. Aedán couldn't speak but he thought, *Please help me, Bridget! Please. I can't breathe!*

His body tried to suck in oxygen, but the dark matter flattened his trachea, making it impossible. His body needed air. He could feel his mind numbing. His vision dimmed.

Though in the blur, he saw something dark green move quickly down the hall. It slipped by swift enough that Aedán thought he was just seeing things until the pressure on his neck relaxed and he could swallow air again.

Breathing heavily, holding his own neck between his thumb and fingers, he looked up to see a curly, redheaded creature on Dub's back again. It was female—her dark flesh only disguised some of her hideous features. She had long, vicious teeth, spiked, purplish fins, and claws. The girl bit into Dub's neck, sinking her teeth into him, and Dub cried out in agony, losing control of his magic. The mists began dissipating.

The creature-girl's long tail whipped back and forth behind her as her legs locked around the Red Knight. One of her clawed hands found Dub's skeletal face and dragged across it, tearing more flesh and slicing into its bone.

Dub tried to shake her, throwing his back against the wall, but the girl was impervious to the pain, wrapping herself around the knight tighter, and took another, larger bite of Dub's neck.

Dub dropped to his knees and the green girl let go, stepping back, only she did it to grab Dub's head and twist his torn neck aside. A short, piercing *crack* surprised Aedán, and then the creature-girl placed a foot on Dub's back and pushed him onto his face.

Dub didn't move anymore.

While he was being suffocated by the dark mist, Aedán had fallen onto his knees. He stood up, realizing that the female creature was naked, and that she had scarification over the whole of her body. The scars were symbols, many of them he'd never seen before. There was also a small round node on her forehead between her rainbow refracted eyes.

Bridget threw herself on Aedán, wrapping her arms around him, burying her face in his chest as she wept. "I thought I lost you!"

Aedán kissed Bridget's cheek and then looked at the green, serpentine girl, who stepped back from them, hunching herself a little, the fins on her head and back standing up. Her tail whipped about behind her.

He didn't know whether to be afraid of her or not. She was frightening. Nothing about her—other than her female curves—seemed soft. Her fins, her teeth, her claws: they looked like she could tear you to pieces easily.

The serpent-girl looked over as the other woman approached her slowly. Léana held out her hands, palms up to show her that she didn't mean her harm. "Maggie. It's me. Your anam chara, Léana."

Maggie looked at Aedán and then at Bridget. She stood taller, and her fins folded down a little.

"Léana?"

"Aye." Léana nodded and smiled at her. "I'm your soul sister."

3

Once Maggie had left the Pit and climbed the stairs, she saw the skeletal creature attacking what looked like humans. They could be ghosts, she thought, but she didn't know why this thing wielded dark magic to harm them. She watched as one girl was tossed from his back and saw that the woman's tall companion was being choked by dark misty tendrils made from an Eerie, forcing him to his knees, and he looked like he didn't have long to live.

Taking the chance to surprise the dark being, she tackled it, biting into its neck until she could easily break it. Once the skeletal creature died, the dark mist magic—the strange *Eagla* that she'd never seen before—disappeared with him. The three of them looked at her, but she could immediately tell that the young lady with the white glamour gown was fae—and she smelled like the familiar sea. An undine. She even wore one of their symbols around her neck—a pendant of the spiral with a triangle in the center, pointing down.

"Yes. I'm your soul sister," Léana said.

But Maggie put her finger to her lips and shushed them. She listened. A hulking heave and light clinking of metal armor neared them.

"The Dar'gones are comin'," Maggie said. "We have to go."

Maggie waved for them to follow her, and she directed them around the corner to another hallway. In the center of that hall was a spiral staircase that went up to the next floor. They climbed it until they were on an upper floor and in yet another hallway.

Frustrated, Maggie waved for them to continue following and led them through a door into the night. They were now standing on the battlement wall. The stars shone bright and there was a cool breeze playing in Maggie's curly hair.

"Stay low," Maggie said. She gestured with her hand what she meant and then hunched down, following the wall across to a single tower. They went through its door, and Maggie closed it behind them once everyone was in. "This is a guard's tower. The Dar'gones come through them, but there aren't enough of them to stand at each tower, so they move quite a bit. From 'ere we can watch them closely."

Maggie went to the bow shaft and looked down the battlement. Not seeing the Dar'gone, she turned to the undine.

"Léana."

"Yes." Léana smiled at her again.

"But you have fata essence wound into yer soul?"

Sentient beings had three energies—what many called Essences—that made the sum of their souls: Psyche, Spirit and Vitality. But fae were never mortal. They didn't have Vitality. They had *fata* essence—an energy thread that fettered them to the Primordial and gave them Primordial power called *croí. Croí* was the very quintessence that made the *Eagla*—primal magic—possible. It was the stuff rewoven to create supernatural effects, and it was beyond mortal capability.

Maggie, being human, had been changed by *croí.* Touched by it, transforming her into a Demidian through serpent's blood, but she did not have the *fata* essence herself.

"I understand what you're getting at," Léana said. "But I'm young. My consciousness was not born—remade—until our soul was rent and lost by the Fomorian King's Soulforger, Fangtooth. I know a little, but nothing that can help us now."

Maggie wasn't sure that the undine knew what Maggie really wanted. If she was young, she might not have the magic in herself, but the undine knew the Otherworld. She would be useful, then.

"I was—" Maggie stopped and looked at the couple, holding each other. They both looked disturbed by her, maybe even frightened. She turned to them, forcing her fins on the top of her head—that also ran down the center of her back—to fold down against her body so that she would look less intimidating.

They looked up at her.

"I know," Maggie said. "I'm appalling, aye? But I was born human. The Fomorians took me from me crib and twisted my body into this form." She ran the claw of her index finger lightly along one of the spiral scars on the back of her forearm. "They scarred me with these symbols, markin' me like a slave. Luckily, I escaped them and lived as a mortal for many years. They tried to take me back a few times, but I fought them off. I won't hurt you. The only things that need to be afraid of me are the fomori."

Maggie really wished her body would respond to transformation. She wanted to look like a human, show them that she was just a young mortal woman underneath the frightening visage.

"I-I believe you," the girl said, holding out her hand. "I'm Bridget."

Maggie carefully took the hand, trying not to scratch her with the claws. She shook the woman's hand gently and smiled at her. Yes, Maggie knew that the sharp teeth came out, but she hoped that the young woman—*Bridget*—could see the intention there.

"This is my fella, Aedán," Bridget said, patting him on the shoulder.

Aedán attempted to smile at her, his eyes falling to Maggie's chest, and then his eyes shot away as he blanched.

Maggie wanted to have a little fun with him, but now wasn't the time. She went to the bow shaft and took another look at the battlement. She watched as a hulking Dar'gone came out from the keep, looked about and went back in. They were still checking the keep, looking for them.

Bloody hell, Maggie thought. She went to another bow shaft and peeked out, trying to see the battlement that led to another guard tower. Nothing there. Good.

Maggie considered Léana, who watched her with awe. It reminded Maggie of what she really wanted to talk about. "I came 'ere to cleanse myself of the fae-touch. I want to be mortal. I don't want to be a Demidian," Maggie told her. "Is there anythin' ye can do?"

Because, really, Maggie hated the idea of working with Carman—someone who just slaughtered a gentle *púca* only several moments before to show how powerful she was. The woman took a life to make a fucking presentation.

"I honestly do not have this sort of power," Léana said, holding out her hands. "I wouldn't lie to you, Maggie."

Maggie shook her head. "Léana. I *need* a path that will cleanse my soul. Feckin' help me!"

Maggie knew that she was being overly harsh, but there had to be another way. Some direction she can travel down that won't put her in Carman's hands. What was the use of a soul sister otherwise?

Léana sighed and rolled her eyes. "Look, Maggie. We can work together, a'right? We can search the Otherworld until we find what we are looking for. We will help you."

But Maggie didn't have time to search the Otherworld, did she? She couldn't keep Cuán forever. If she didn't find some way now, this would all be for nothing. Maggie again remembered her vision with Cuán, old and wrinkled, lying in bed. Dying.

No, no that wasn't going to happen to her.

If Carman was the only way to make this happen, then she'd have to follow through with it.

Maggie once again looked at the human couple. Bridget held onto Aedán's shoulder with one hand, while simultaneously leaning the side of her head on it. Aedán merely waited, listening, eyes slightly averted.

"Why are you two 'ere?"

Bridget straightened and took her head off Aedán's shoulder. "Something just caught us. We were out at these ruins near Wexford. Saint Albeus monastery. There was a standing stone nearby. Somehow, we were just here on the island."

"Are yeh tryin' to get home?"

Bridget nodded at the undine. "Léana promised to help us leave Tech Duinn if we helped you escape Dá Derga's dungeon."

Léana gestured to them. "And I will. We'll go the way of the doves."

"The doves?" Maggie said.

"One of the windows in Dá Derga's court, at the center of the keep, is an Argent Path—it takes the doves from Tech Duinn to the lands of Tír na nÓg," Léana said. "It's going to be the easiest way out of here."

Maggie was slightly horrified by this idea. "What of Dá Derga himself? Won't he be in there?"

Léana nodded and then smiled at Maggie. It was a weak smile though. "Aye."

Maggie didn't like it, sighing. But what else could they do? "A'right. You three help me find Badb's Wings and we'll go together to Tír na nÓg. Agreed?"

Léana frowned at her and walked around to face Maggie directly. "Badb's Wings?"

"Yes. It's one of the three Attainments that I'm looking for. If I find the three of them, then I know a witch who might help me," Maggie said.

"A witch? Are you crazy?" the young man, Aedán, said. Maggie looked at him and could tell that he was even more terrified now.

Maggie held out her arms. "You don't have to meet 'er or any-thin'! But look at me! I look like a feckin' demon, aye? I'd like to look like meself again. Do yeh want my help or not?"

Aedán looked away from her again, not saying anything.

"That's what I bloody thought," Maggie said. She turned to look at Léana. "And you. What do yeh say? Can ye help me with the Attainments?"

Léana appeared reluctant, but she nodded her head, sighing. "Okay."

Maggie went to the bow shafts again, checking the battlements. She was just in time. Dar'gones were leaving the keep, making their way to the tower.

"Jaysus H Christ," she said. "They're comin'."

Maggie went to the other bow shaft and saw nothing there. If they could make it to the second tower, they'd have more time to—

"How about down here?" Bridget squatted in the center of the room, where there was a wooden hatch.

"Well, aye, that might do it," Maggie said. She leaned down, grabbed the fae-iron handle and pulled it open. "Make it quick. We don't want to be caught now. I've seen the Pit. It's not a fun place to be."

The hatch revealed a spiral staircase that would take them to the base of the tower. She'd be back in the bailey again, but it was bet-ter than being trapped in a tower. Surrounded.

Once they had all descended the stairs, Maggie shut the hatch above her and followed the others down. The staircase was dark, except where there were bow shafts, which let in little slivers of moonlight. Dust motes glowed in the beams. They passed by two other chambered levels until they ended up in a chamber full of shelves holding bits and pieces of armor, sharpening stones and other materials.

Maggie looked briefly over it all, not seeing any weapons.

A pity. Maggie flicked her tongue over the bronze coin in her cheek for a moment.

Aedán poked his head out the door and then looked back at them. "I don't see anyone."

"Right. Well, the bailey isn't safe out in the open. Stick to the walls. Keep a look out for ghosts and Dar'gones. They're both out there and they can both out you. A'right?"

Aedán nodded at her and then led the way. Maggie followed behind, making sure the tower door was shut. The Dar'gones were on the battlements above, spreading out. They needed to move quickly and stay quiet. Hopefully, the Dar'gones would miss them.

'*Hopefully*,' Maggie thought. *What a fantasy.*

Suddenly, Maggie saw a hulking Dar'gone appear out of a door to a storage building, making its way to the stables. They all stilled, watching the creature make its way and then disappear through the stable doors.

"What sort of horses do ghosts collect?" Aedán whispered to Léana.

Maggie gave him the quietest hush she could make, holding a stiff index finger to her lips. Aedán saw her face and nodded at her.

They continued on, Maggie looking up at the battlements, hoping beyond hope that the Dar'gones would not look right at them in the worst possible moment. They seemed occupied with what was on the outside of the wall and in the battlement towers.

The Dar'gones may be making their way down to the bailey.

Maggie sighed.

In many ways, Maggie wished that she had Cherry Fox's *Bod Mór*. The imbued shillelagh that had Fox's power within it, and it made it easier for Maggie to take care of the vampyres that threatened her when she was trapped in their cave. It was as if whatever fae-touched ability she had was somehow amplified by the *Bod Mór*, and she could use that now. Unfortunately, after Deirdre had died, the shillelagh sank into the ground as if it melded with the island. Maggie had dug for it, almost four feet, but when she'd gotten that far, she realized that it was gone forever.

It only ever belonged to Cherry Fox anyway.

4

Bridget didn't know what to think of Maggie. She didn't know what to think about soul sisters or the fae, or even the creature that almost smothered them with its black mists. Throughout her life exploring the Lost Place, she could not have ever imagined any of this.

Maggie walked in front of them, leading the way through the haunted keep. Somewhere in this place was a doorway—an Argent Path—that would lead them to a fairyland: *Tír na nÓg*. Land of Immortal Youth. A realm she only heard about in fairy stories.

Wasn't it supposed to be a paradise, like an Irish heaven before the Christians came?

Bridget faintly remembered stories she heard about how souls crossed over as doves to live in the branches of a great tree in the center of the land. The undine, Léana, told them that the Argent Path was where the doves made their way to Tír na nÓg.

Were these doves the ghosts she saw earlier? Like the little girl who was missing her eyes because her da poked them out of her head? Would that girl become a dove in the court of Dá Derga and go to live in the great tree at the center of paradise?

It sounded quite beautiful, but Bridget was also certain she wasn't ready to die. She was sad...born feeling guilty for something she didn't understand. Hated herself sometimes. But she was not ready to die.

And she felt woefully inadequate here. Léana was an undine and apparently had her own power, being able to at least shape-shift. Aedán was a young man who seemed to be strong and very capable. Even though the creature that called itself Dub frightened them, Aedán was courageous enough to try to escape. Bridget was sure she would have frozen in fright and would have died in its black mists.

Maggie. *Oh*, she seemed *special*. She was wild and oozed an air of strength out of every pore. Long teeth made her mouth a lethal weapon. Claws. Spiked fins. Bridget had no doubt that Maggie was possibly one of the most dangerous creatures in the keep. Maggie was everything Bridget was not. In the Lost Place, Bridget felt like she could at least control herself, but here, in the real world—spirit or not—she was mortal and powerless.

Born powerless. And she let others control her. Even she knew it wasn't right, but Bridget often felt as though it was too late for her to change.

How would Bridget be able to help anyone?

She wanted to go home. Her legs were killing her with all this walking and running. She didn't know how much more she could take.

Bridget leaned against the wall. "Wait. I need a bit of a rest."

Her companions all looked back at her, and that's when she realized that she was sinking into the wall— No, not *sinking*. The stone on the wall was sinking in, and she was leaning into it. She quickly withdrew her hand, but then part of the wall made a large, rocky *clunking* sound and it opened on a hidden hinge.

They were now all looking at a secret tunnel.

Aedán and Léana smiled at her.

Maggie took the lead, peering into the tunnel. It was dark. Maggie looked at Léana: "Do you have fire? There's torches."

Léana nodded, so Maggie went in. Bridget followed behind them. Léana spoke some ancient Irish and the torches in the sconces along the length of the tunnel all sparked and flared to life. Maggie moved beside Bridget and pulled the secret door closed.

Maggie looked at her. "Good job, Bridget. We can rest in 'ere."

They went farther down the tunnel, and it opened into a secret chamber. It was empty and unused, which was perfect. Bridget smiled and took a seat on the floor, resting her back against the cold, stone wall. "Just what the doctor ordered, aye?" she said.

***

Aedán couldn't believe their luck when he turned around to see Bridget leaning against the wall, opening a secret portal in the wall. He had heard the Dar'gones coming, so it was a perfect way to get out of sight.

After finding the larger chamber, Bridget was glad to take a seat while Maggie and Léana whispered to each other. He couldn't quite make out what they were saying, but he was sure it wasn't any of their business.

He didn't know if he liked either of them.

If there was any other way, he would lead Bridget far away from them.

He didn't particularly like the untamed nature Maggie seemed to have. Sure, the young woman saved him, but that didn't mean she didn't have a hidden reason for doing so.

Aedán put his hands in his pockets, leaning against the wall, thinking about how many so-called 'allies' his father, Lord Cuinn had, who plotted behind his back, and used Lord Cuinn for their own gains.

Aedán really didn't want to trust anybody, and he was certainly not going to trust this monstrous creature who 'says' she's human underneath it all.

He felt the cool, smooth surface of the Macalla Shell in his pocket and took it out, holding it to his ears. Aedán slid down the wall, listening to his father speak. It calmed him.

Bridget then crawled across the floor on all fours until she could turn and sit beside him. Aedán put the shell in his pocket as her hand felt up his arm and her face went to his neck, kissing him there. It felt good, and it aroused him. Her warm breath. Her soft lips pressing against the sensitive area next to his ear.

Aedán turned and kissed her mouth, and she kissed him back harder. When she broke from his lips, she gave him a smile.

"It isn't like the Lost Place, is it?"

Aedán shook his head. "No."

Bridget saw his eyes turn on the fae creatures in front of them, and when he noticed Bridget regarding him, he shrugged. "I'm sorry. I just don't know if we can trust them yet."

Bridget shrugged at him and sat flat against the stone wall at her back. "We've no one else to trust, Aedán."

Aedán sighed. Yeah, he knew that already.

But it didn't ease him a bit.

The Stones of Modron

1

They took a five-hour train to Wrexham General station, chugging along at an easy pace. Cuán sat across from Ambrus in the carriage, mostly looking out the window at the English and then Welsh countryside. Ambrus read the paper, enjoying it while he could. Cuán noticed that Ambrus had become much more of a reserved man over the last couple years. He wondered if Ambrus' age was catching up with him.

At Wrexham General, they stepped off the train and Cuán followed Ambrus down the road, where carriages awaited to taxi them wherever they wanted to go. Ambrus politely paid for the two of them and the coachman drove them across town until they came across a large cottage-style house set into a wild, overgrown estate. Ambrus again led Cuán through the wrought-iron gate and up to the steps, where Ambrus knocked.

"How do you know these people?" Cuán said.

Ambrus cleared his throat. "Say nothing about this until they are ready to trust you, but the women we are about to meet are Hen Fenywod Cymru—the Old Welsh Women. They still secretly practice the Old Ways."

HEN FEN-Owed Kim-ROO. Cuán tried to remember the pronunciation in his head, though he didn't know if he would remember it at all. It was alien even for an Irish Gaelic speaker.

The door opened and there was a young woman looking up at them with glowing blonde hair and big blue eyes that shined like brilliant pools of water. She wore a blue dress with white laces and a pearl necklace around her neck. If Cuán wasn't so smitten with Maggie, he would be falling in love at first sight with her.

When she saw Ambrus she smiled. "Ambrus! Come on in, you two! Have a sit, will you?"

"Aye. Thanks, Llewella. We shall."

"Tea?" The girl looked at him.

Cuán forgot his hat and took it off, nodding. "Aye. Please and thank you, Miss."

"This is Cuán Foley. As you can probably tell from his accent, he's Irish," Ambrus said, taking a seat in the sitting room.

"Nice to meet you, Cuán. Llewella Powys." She shook his hand, and he smiled at her, already taken by her charm.

As Llewella went into their kitchen to pour them tea, Cuán looked around and saw a normal house really. He expected to see pagan relics and symbols of gods and goddesses. Maybe even Rune stones laying on the table. Stuff Cuán only read about in books.

Cuán sat beside Ambrus on the couch.

"We got your wire, but Seren had to go out for some groceries. She couldn't wait all day for you. She should be back soon."

"Llewella. Now you know, we have come with intentions to speak with her in regard to the Hen Fenywod Cymru?"

Llewella brought each of them a cup of tea at a time, saying, "Yes, oh, of course. Seren figured. You are, after all, Ambrus Kárpáti." She beamed down at the old man, and he smiled back up at her. He was obviously smitten with her charms, too.

"Do you mind at least filling me in on what's going on?" Llewella said, sitting in a divan across from them.

Ambrus nodded, sitting up on the couch. "What do you know of Otherworld travel?"

Llewella looked at them, a more serious demeanor coming over her.

"Oh well, I suppose nothing myself. I know it's possible, though it isn't done as much as it once was in the past. It's harder because the barrier, even at its thinnest, is far thicker than it once was all those centuries ago when the fae still freely walked the land. Before the last Recant. You would have to know of a special place—a threshold into the Otherworld."

"The Lodge believes most thresholds only slip into Copula Rifts—pocket realms of the spirit world that only work in conjunction with physical elements of the world. A house in London and a tree in a park just down the road could be thresholds and simultaneously landscapes together in the Copula Rift," Ambrus said.

Cuán was confused and held out a hand to stop them. "A tree and a house—What?"

Ambrus looked at him. "Well, I'll try again. There are certain places that are attuned more toward one of the Essences of the Sentient World: psyche, spirit, vitality, cathexis, fata, empyrean and malice. These places—*haintes*—thin the barrier until they become a threshold to a Copula Rift. Each threshold becomes bound to other thresholds, creating a metaphysical construction of themselves within the Rift. So, these places become the landscape of the Rift itself while simultaneously existing as haintes in the physical world, separate from each other. The haintes, or thresholds, are physically separate from each other and exist in both places, but in the Rift, they are all that exists, and they exist together. Does that make more sense?"

Cuán got the gist and nodded, though it was still a little beyond his understanding.

"The point I'm making," Ambrus said, "is that most thresholds only lead to these Rifts in the different parts of the world, and do not have doorways to other Otherworld planes. I'm assuming you do want to go to Tír na nÓg?"

Cuán shook his head. "How do you know this?"

Ambrus shrugged. "Well, if Maggie doesn't exactly know where she's going, Tír na nÓg would be the most common destination in Ireland."

Cuán sipped at his tea. "I suppose that makes sense."

Llewella, watching both of them, took the opportunity to come into the conversation: "Well, I believe I understand what you mean by Copula Rift, but…there *are* thresholds to the Otherworld. Ones that penetrate the spirit world just deep enough. But you can only find them in only some of the most ancient of places. And as I assumed you've already guessed, being as how you came all this way Ambrus, the Stones of Modron can lead you there."

Cuán looked at Ambrus. "Who's Modron?"

"Our moon goddess. The only thing left of her are the Stones. They're up in the Northern Mountain Gate."

Cuán fell into her eyes, and he didn't realize he stared until her eyes darted away. She was clearly a nervous sort, he thought. Cuán looked at Ambrus, who was clearly thinking.

"But the only way to use the Stones of Modron as a threshold, you must know the ban that opens the way…and the secrets of the ban have only been passed to my sister. Seren."

As if by fate itself, the door opened, and a brunette came in. Though her hair was darker, she had the same crystal blue eyes. The woman was a few years older than Llewella and wore more earth tone clothes: an emerald dress with umbra fringe. She wore a dark teardrop hat fixed to that dark head of hers.

Ambrus stood to greet her and Seren smiled at him, shaking his hand.

"It's been a long time, Ambrus."

"It has," Ambrus said. "I'm happy to see you."

Seren looked at Cuán, who also stood and walked over.

Seren smiled at him too, and then turned to her blood sister, saying, "Llewella, my dear, will you please bring in the groceries? I want to walk with the gentleman here, find out what these good men want."

Llewella nodded and waved at Cuán and Ambrus before she disappeared out the door.

Seren held a hand out to Cuán and Cuán took it, giving it a light shake.

"This is Cuán Foley," Ambrus said.

"Nice to meet you, Miss," Cuán said.

"Nice to meet you as well, Mister Foley."

"You can call me Cuán."

Seren nodded at him. "Okay. Cuán. Come with me. We'll walk in the garden."

Cuán let Ambrus explain everything, staying quiet as he walked behind them in the garden. The garden was both vegetables and flowering plants, which was overgrown and verdant. Healthy, too. Was there magic in these plants? Was Seren that powerful?

Once Ambrus explained that he hoped Seren would share the threshold of the Stones of Modron, there was a long moment of silence. Seren stopped them near the fountain, where there were small, white statues of nude women standing out on one leg, the other out behind them in the air, reaching out with their arms, and water poured out of their mouths, trickling into the fountain pool. Nymphs in ballet.

Seren looked at Cuán and moved toward him. She smelled of cinnamon. She touched his face and lifted his chin with one finger, looking into his eyes. He was happy to look back into hers.

"Do you know the danger you are setting yourself up for? The Otherworld has strange laws, and it's terribly dangerous. I haven't even dared to go there," she said.

Cuán looked into her eyes, and he hardened himself. "I have no choice. Maggie is all I have."

"You ever hear of the myth of the Dream of Alcyone? It's actually Greek in origin," she said. "But her husband goes on a long journey out to sea and the ship is struck by lightning, and sinks. Of course, she's on the shore and doesn't know this, waiting for his return. Morpheus brings her a dream where her husband's ghost, Ceyx, can explain to her that he has died and that she must move on with her life. Upon waking, though, Alcyone flings her body in the ocean, killing herself."

Seren let go of his chin. "It's the Greek way—isn't it?—to dramatize affection to a degree where someone becomes so desperate in love that they cannot live without them, fating them to a sorrowful end."

"Much theater has been produced by this framework," Ambrus said, smiling at Seren.

This woman just didn't understand him, Cuán thought. He shrugged. His heart was already beating fast. "I'm not Greek, but I am in love. And Maggie isn't dead. I'm risking my life to make sure of it."

Seren shook her head. "I don't know. It's too dangerous. And I'm not prone to manipulate Modron's will for the sake of a foreigner."

Ambrus took Seren's arm and turned her toward him. When he had her eyes, he said, "Modron is the only way this kid is getting into the Otherworld. It will be a chance to honor the Moon and celebrate the power of this love."

Seren scowled. "It's not love. It's fear of loss. It doesn't honor Modron."

That's when Cuán had it. This woman couldn't possibly know. "I won't honor her with fear then," Cuán said. "I will honor her with a contract."

Seren looked surprised. "A contract?"

"In Ireland, the Tuatha Dé left the Milesians to Ireland after fashioning Great Contracts—metaphysical, binding words between the fae and the Irish people. I will make a contract with Modron, and it will be binding. I will offer my service to her."

Seren nodded her head and grinned at him.

"How daring, Cuán. Would you really do this?"

"For Maggie, Seren, I'd do anything."

Seren, still smiling, waved toward the cottage. "Then let's prepare for the dance."

2

At dusk, Cuán followed Ambrus and the twelve women of the *Hen Fenywod Cymru*, who were all in turn led by Seren Powys. They all piled into wagons and made their way to the Northern Mountain Gate, only to stop as the woods became thicker and the paths became so narrow that no wagon could go any farther.

They all hopped down and made their way along the path as it got darker and darker. Luckily, the moon was waxing, filling the forest with some of its light. A few of the women also carried lanterns, lighting the way.

Ambrus walked beside him for a short while, pulling from his pocket a wooden box. He flipped it open, showing Cuán the contents of the box. It was a compass, the needle spinning all around as if it was unable to find true north.

"I think it's broken," Cuán said.

Ambrus shut the compass and put it into Cuán's hand. "It's not broken. It's said to be a talisman, and it only points to the Crann Lár in the center of Tír na nÓg. Follow it. All things in Tír na nÓg eventually seek the Crann Lár. Or so I'm told. It could help you."

Cuán stuffed it into his pocket, feeling overwhelmed. "Thank you, Ambrus. You've been a big help."

Ambrus chuckled, seeing his gratitude. "Don't let it get to you, kid."

They continued through the darkening forest, following the women.

Cuán had the jitters and caught himself multiple times rubbing his hands together as if he were cold. He wasn't really. It was a nice summer night, which would be unusual for them in Ireland. Especially the west coast.

They passed an old cottage. It was a small thing, and it crouched there in the creeping woods, keeping inside it a darkness. Cuán didn't like it. It felt somehow evil and cruel, though he couldn't say why he felt that way. For a moment, he thought he saw red eyes peering out of the window—glowing, loathing. But as soon as he saw them, they were gone.

Ambrus saw him looking at the cottage and whispered, "There was a witch that lived there. They called her Creirwy Mochyn Coch. She used several locks of hair from the village girls and wove a dark tapestry there. They caught her eventually—the townsfolk. It's why the Hen Fenywod Cymru worships in this forest in secret. The villagers would be terrified of them if they really knew who these women were."

Cuán found it all creepy himself, so he could understand it.

Eventually, the woods parted into a glade. It was a slight mound with large standing stones of different sizes forming a circle. Cuán could feel the bluestones vibrating, and could feel Modron there, even though he couldn't see her.

In the center of the circle, as the women all gathered around, Cuán could see the moon. Somehow, it was full and bright and much bigger than he'd ever seen it. It loomed over them, filling the glade with its light and its power. Cuán wondered if somehow this place pulled the moon closer or projected it over the glade in such a way that made it seem titanic.

In either case, Cuán understood it all.

The women started helping him remove his clothes. They tossed the articles aside in the grass and then stepped back and started removing their gowns. Seren and Lewella did the same. And even though they were all doing it, Cuán felt a little sheepish to be naked in front of so many women. None of them looked at him as far as he could tell, but it still felt imposing.

Don't think about it, he told himself. *This is for Maggie.*

Seren, completely bare so that her flesh soaked the moon's illuminance, grabbed his hand and pulled him to the direct center of the Stones of Modron. When he was centered, she backed up and raised up her arms in supplication to the moon.

Cuán tried not to look at her breasts, but her skin was erotically aglow with the moonlight. Her dark hair even seemed to glow to some degree. She let arms down and she peered at Cuán, saying, "Lift your arms to Modron and ask her for the contract. We'll do the rest."

Cuán looked over at Llewella, who stood with the others in a circle around him. Ambrus held hands with others in the circle as well. At first, he thought that they were all there for him, but no, they were there to celebrate the power of Modron. He shouldn't forget that.

All naked, the twelve women and Ambrus started dancing around him. They danced *deosil*—the direction that the sun and moon crossed in the sky when you faced the south. It was the direction of the cosmos.

Cuán looked up at the giant moon above him and he raised his arms.

The women began to sing in harmony. It vibrated in sync with the surrounding stones.

"Modron! I offer a contract of myself in your service! I only ask for a path to the other world. The Argent Path."

He tried looking around at the women dancing around him, but the moonlight had filled his eyes and they were blurry. The women were now only formless bodies moving around the stones that seemed to now go beyond the boundaries of the original circle.

Cuán followed the formless bodies, glowing like the moon themselves, and found himself winding through the stones.

They formed a pathway and eventually the vertigo became difficult, and Cuán fell to his knees, exhausted. He rubbed his eyes, trying to clear them, and then looked around.

Even though it was night, the colors of the forest around him were much more vivid. Ambrus and the twelve women were gone. Their harmony was faint and slowly disappearing from his hearing.

Then there were only the sounds of the forest. Birds. Chattering mammals. Insects chirping away. Cuán saw his clothes in a pile in the grass. He gathered them up and dressed, looking around.

There was a beautiful woman there who didn't look too much different than Seren, except she had long, curly blond hair like

Llewella's. She wore a long white gown, almost transparent, showing off a soft, female body that glowed like the moon underneath. Her ears were pointed and stuck up out of her yellow hair on the sides of her head. Her eyes were also blue, but they shimmered even brighter than he'd ever seen a woman's eyes, making them feel as though they roiled like waves.

"Who are you?" Cuán said, walking over to her.

She sat back on a shorter standing stone. "Here, I am Modron. But your people call me Niamh."

Cuán couldn't believe it. "Niamh? As is Oisín and Niamh?"

"Aye. But please do not mention Oisín. His name breaks my heart still."

Cuán felt his pocket, feeling the compass Ambrus gave him there. It was good he didn't lose it.

"You mentioned a contract with me, Cuán Foley?"

"Aye. I did…uh, Your Heinous." He didn't know what else to call her and he felt like a fool for it.

"Shall we discuss it?"

Cuán nodded and took a seat on the grass amongst the giant stones. "Aye. I'm ready."

A few hours later—contract blessed—Niamh took her leave, disappearing in a blink. Cuán pulled out the compass, and the needle pointed down a path that he already saw going into the wood. It was supposed to be an Argent Path with the needle pointed toward the Crann Lár. Hopefully, it would work as Ambrus described.

The Prodigal Sons

For a few days, Carman spent time in Kilkee. She put on a cheap common dress, pulled her long dark hair back in a bun and knocked on Oona's door. The older woman looked at her curiously.

"May I help you?"

"Aye. My name is Carman. I was told in the village that you might have a spare room for me for just a few days. I'm passing by and I need a rest. I'd be able to help you around the house and I'm good at washing."

Oona thought it over for a moment and then nodded, smiling at Carman. "Come on in. I'll make yeh some tea and you can tell me a little bit about yerself."

Carman smiled back. "Wonderful."

Later that evening, Oona showed her to a room that obviously belonged to a young woman: the makeup on a cheap little vanity, the costume jewelry she saw hanging up by the mirror...

"This belongs to my Maggie. She's off in Dublin with her fella, so I sees no reason fer you not to use it while she's away," Oona said.

Carman thanked her and when she was left alone, Carman laid in the bed and drove her nose into the coverlets, taking a deep whiff. Yes, she could smell Maggie alright. The stink of a girl and the stink of the sea, all mingled together as a whole.

Carman spent the next couple of days doing chores around the farm for Oona, but in her free time, Carman would slip out and look for the other people in Maggie's life: Colum, the widowed man who worked his farm, looking somber and slow. He looked twice his age and his spirit was broken, having lost his wife recently. Maggie's lover—Cuán, if Elieris was correct—had both his parents, Brian and Orna. Brian was out most days on the dogger named after his wife. Orna cared for the homestead and went around helping the vicar with churchly duties, or she visited Oona for their daily tea.

Carman watched all of them, got to know their routines and even conversed with them, trying to subtly learn more about Maggie and Cuán.

On the fourth night, she went to the cliffs and found the spot where Elieris said Cuán found Maggie, taking her away from him.

"Why did you not take her back?" Carman had asked.

Elieris had moved his head side to side. "The Cailleach was protecting her. As soon as the Queen of Winter was done with her, she placed sigils at the shorelines. It took me awhile to destroy them."

"If the Cailleach had the girl taken, why did the girl end up with you?"

"An old debt. I won't speak of those matters with you."

"And yet you still didn't take her when you had the chance?"

Elieris gave her a big grin then. "Oh, I suppose, it's because I found her so damn fascinating to watch. She entertained me."

"And now that she has found her way into the Otherworld?"

"It's time to take her back... or kill her."

Carman thought about those words as she stood at the cliffs, feeling his presence and he made his way to her. Eventually, he rose naked from the sea—a dark haired, muscular, beautiful man. He was hung, too, she noticed. Her sons rose behind the Fomorian King, following him, treading through the waters to the shore. They were clad in the armor she last saw them in all those centuries ago.

"My sons!"

Dother and Dain. The Red Knights of Bres, the sons she brought with her from Athens shortly after killing her own family. Dother's skin was a deep red, and he had black horns, lips and fingertips. His armor was black, Brigandine leather. Dain, on the other hand, was thinner, but far more graceful. He moved like a cat and had long black claws and savage canine teeth above and below.

Their original Greek names were Skotádi (Dub), Kakó and Vía, but she quite enjoyed their Irish names far better. It made them one of the people.

Speaking of Skotádi—

"Where is my First Born? Dub?"

"As I explained to you Carman, I had use for him," Elieris said. "Only, he failed."

Carman looked shocked, already angry with Elieris. "What do you mean, he *failed*?"

Elieris walked over to a pool of sea water trapped in a small bowl in the sand. He touched it and Carman came over to look to see what he was doing. In it, she saw Dub's reflection as he fought with the savage looking redhead creature. She had dark sea-green skin, scarred with ancient symbols, and her teeth were lethal. The serpent-girl bit into Dub's neck, tearing it open. When Dub fell to his knees, the girl twisted his head, breaking his neck.

And then she pushed him with her foot onto his face as he died.

Rage filled Carman like she'd never felt before. "That bitch!"

"Seagrass Maggie is quite the fetch, isn't she?"

Carman snapped a deadly look at Elieris. Carman was ready to kill that bitch, having many ideas brewing in her head already. This would *not* stand! The abomination had to die!

As if reading her mind, Elieris grabbed her shoulders as Carman started to weep. "She will get hers, Carman, but you have to have patience. She seeks your Attainments, which you will need."

Elieris—as if pulling it right out of thin air—held out a bottle of light purple perfume.

Carman took it. "What is this?"

Elieris took her hand and led her up the path, which took them to the top of the cliffs. He pointed out at the green fields around them.

"This area used to be covered in the Spring Squill. I had my fellow Fomorians gather it all up, and we extracted it into this perfume," Elieris said. "It's a gift for you."

Carman couldn't believe this monster. "You think this will replace my son?"

"No. But it is a gift. The Spring Squill is an angry little bitch, too. She might come in useful."

"What is her name?"

"Aisling."

Carman opened the bottle and held it up to her nose, smelling it. It was a beautiful scent. But it didn't take away the hurt in her heart.

"I know what may help. You know Maggie's lover?" Elieris said.

"Cuán Foley."

"Aye. Cuán Foley. Why don't you...*hit* them where it really hurts."

At that thought, Carman's chest filled with butterflies, and she took a deep breath. She could smile again—her pain had somewhere to go now. "I'll take that into consideration, Ri Elieris. Thank you." She grabbed the King's organ hanging between his legs and gave it a squeeze. Carman felt the thing react to her gesture, throbbing in her hand. And then she let it go. "I'll see you soon?"

Elieris nodded and then turned to go back to the sea.

Dother and Dain came up to her.

"We have missed you mother," Dain said. "We miss your plots."

Dother grinned. "Yes, we have. Do you have any plots for us?"

Carman smiled at her sons, touching each of them on the face.

"Oh yes. Do you two remember how Lugh was able to stop us? With his children, Bé Chuille and Aoi?"

Dain nodded and held up a clawed hand. "Yes. Bé Chuille was the sorceress. Aoi Mac Ollamain was the poet that could stir the sprites of the air with his voice. I recall Aoi used his power to know where we'd be and saw our plans and Bé Chuille used the knowledge to design an illusion that tricked us into that pit of spikes. Oh, yes, mother. We remember them well."

"The sióg are very hard to kill. If they do die, they tend to reincarnate into another life. They now live, living in mortal form," Carman said.

Dother looked shocked. "Who are they?"

Carman looked into her largest son's black eyes. "Aedán Ó Cuinn and Bridget Rose MacCailín. They found each other and became lovers. Somehow, they slipped into the Otherworld, and are now with a Maris Demidian named Maggie Connell. I want you two to find an Argent Path and make your way to them. You cannot touch the Maris...for now, but I do want you to kill the lovers that are with her."

Dother and Dain looked happy at the news. "Oh, yes, that explains why Dub was so connected with those two," Dother said. "He spoke of them and their dreams. Elieris gave him a means into their minds and instructed him to watch them."

"Consider them dead, Mother," Dain said.

"Oh, and one more thing: the Order of Bres has sent a werewolf named Brogan Kelleys. He plans to do the opposite. He wants to kill Maggie and capture the lovers for the Order, so Bres can be risen once again. We can't let that happen. The fucker will ruin everything. If you have to, kill Brogan and make sure Maggie does what she needs to do."

Dother and Dain nodded at her.

"We are no longer the Knights of Bres, Mother," Dother said. "We are yours."

"Perhaps we will use the same Argent Path as Bé Chuille and Aoi?" Dain said.

"Saint Albeus, in Wexford." Carman looked at her sons, full of pride and love for them. She placed an illusion over them so that they appeared as normal mortal men. Once this was done, they left her to follow through with her own plots. Carman, seething still, made her way back to Oona's house.

Carman went into the kitchen and grabbed a kitchen knife, holding it tight in her hand behind her back. She saw the old woman knitting in a chair, and the woman smiled up and Carman.

"Tea dear?"

Carman looked into the woman's blue eyes and frowned.

"Is everything okay, Carman?"

Carman relaxed.

No, Oona could not die now. She might be useful. No, Elieris was right. If Carman wanted her revenge, it was best done through Cuán Foley.

Carman smiled. "I'm just tired, I guess. I would love some tea, if you do not mind."

Oona smiled at her, got up and patted her on the shoulder.

"We all have our days, don't we?"

Carman stuffed the kitchen knife between the cushions of the couch.

"Aye. That we do," she said.

Crow's Wings

1

While sitting and resting in the secret chamber Bridget found behind the stone wall, Maggie pulled her soul sister—the undine, Léana—aside, wanting to talk to her in private as Aedán and Bridget rested, cuddling up with each other. Maggie took the bronze coin out of her mouth to make it easier to speak, holding it fast in her left fist.

Maggie whispered, "I'm not goin' to pretend to understand any of this. Somehow, we're created from the same soul, but ye look nothin' like me."

Léana shrugged. "While you did share your soul with me, it's not yours anymore. This piece belongs to me now. And I have to say, Maggie Connell, I do appreciate this new consciousness you have given me. I am no more a mere sprite."

Maggie bit her lip, looking away for a moment. She had to think: What were the odds here? Getting the wings and getting out before Dá Derga got a hold of them?

While the idea that her soul could give another spirit consciousness was marvelous, Léana seemed as though she wouldn't be that much help after all. Maggie needed real magic, and she absolutely hated the idea of working for Carman. Maggie was still upset about how the witch tore the *púca* to pieces before her.

Be useful, Maggie thought, looking at Léana.

"So where do I find the Crow's Wings—*Badb's Wings*—and then how do we get out of 'ere?"

Léana looked up at the ceiling and then back at Maggie. "The easy part is that there's only one place we have to go: the throne room, the seat of Dá Derga's court. That is where the ghosts go before him and are judged. The Dar'gones take the lost souls to the Pits, which transforms them into the sluagh. The rest become doves and leave through the window—the Argent Door to Tír na nÓg. Above the throne is a pair of large, black wings. He keeps them there as a trophy."

Maggie grabbed Léana's cheeks with a hand and squeezed them, squishing her lips together and shook her little face. "Oh! That's beautiful!"

Léana grabbed Maggie's hand and pulled Maggie's fingers from her cheeks, wiping her mouth with the back of her own arm. "You're welcome."

But Maggie knew that this was going to be tough. She didn't know how many Dar'gones were going to be in the court, or just how powerful Dá Derga really was. For all she knew, he'd freeze them in place with magic and snap his fingers, exploding them into gross bits all over his chamber.

Léana reached around her waist and pulled through her glamour dress an umber leather sheath hooked on a belt with a couple of useful pockets on it. A shiny, silver stake with a bone handle was also sheathed in it.

"Even though I'm finding you a bit annoying," Léana said, "I have a gift fer you."

Léana held the belt out to her, and Maggie took it.

"What is it?"

Léana pointed at the bone handle and Maggie withdrew it. There was a metal shaft and a sharp, pointed tip.

"I had it made in Cathair Aigéin—home of the merrow. I took a piece of our soul—our *píos anam*—and had it fashioned into a weapon with silver and bone. The merrow smith called it the Airgid Hook."

"Hook?"

Léana nodded. "Fling it with your wrist, but away from you."

Maggie turned so that she had plenty of room and snapped her wrist outwards, grasping the bone handle tightly. The silver extended and curved into a sharp hook.

"The Airgid Hook, Maggie. It's yer weapon."

Maggie whipped it back and forth through the air. The hook looked like it could cut through anything. It was light and well balanced, but it also felt strong, and its tip was sharp.

"By the gods, Léana, thank you! I never thought I'd have such a thing! It's amazin'!

Léana smiled at her. "I'm glad you like it. When we get to Dá Derga's court, you're going to need it."

"Aye." Maggie flipped her wrist again and the metal hook slipped back into a short, pointed shaft. She stuck it back in the sheath, and slid the belt around her hip, buckling it tight around her. The sheath hung just over her left thigh, where she could easily grab it when she needed it.

"Are we ready to go?" It was Bridget, looking up at them.

Maggie looked at Léana, and Léana gave them all a nod.

"Let's go. It's now or never, as they say," Léana said.

Maggie was about to put the bronze coin back in her mouth, when she remembered the pockets on the belt Léana gave her. Maggie put the coin in a pocket and snapped it shut.

"Do they really say that?" Maggie asked.

Léana sighed and groaned a little. "Didn't I just say you annoyed me? I mean, I'm sure I did."

Maggie and her companions dodged guards by weaving in and out of chambers as they heard them coming, making their way toward the court. Through the portcullis, the ghosts made their way through the bailey to the front doors of the keep. After entering the keep, the Dar'gones shuffled the ghosts through the large, ominous black doors of the throne room where Dá Derga sat upon his throne.

When they got to these halls that ran along the side of the throne room, Léana showed them a servant's entrance.

"The servants are required to go through these doors so that they do not disturb the process of transcendence," Léana explained in a hushed voice.

Maggie looked at Aedán and Bridget. "Look, yeh lovers, the only way this is goin' to work is if we do this fast. One screwup gets us all in trouble. Does everyone remember their part of the plan?"

Aedán and Bridget both nodded. Léana, too.

Maggie grinned, showing off the rows of her sharp eel-teeth. She grabbed the bone handle of the Airgid Hook.

"Ready?"

More nods.

Maggie sighed heavily and flipped her wrist, causing the Airgid Hook to form itself.

2

The white, pearly death god, Dá Derga of Tech Duinn, looked down on the man who stepped before him. The ghost. She walked with a broken leg, dragging it along and wincing with each step. Even in death, there was pain. The woman stopped and looked up at Dá Derga and he reached out a giant hand.

The woman looked into Dá Derga's eyes and the pain in her face went away, and her ghost started lifting off the ground, to float a few feet in the air. She reached out and touched Dá Derga's hand and her body shrank into itself, reformed and grew white feathers. In only a moment, the ghost was a dove, flapping its wings. The dove flew over to a grand window, just right of this throne, and flew through it.

The next ghost was a man with a bullet hole in his head. A black ichor dripped out of it instead of blood. In his right hand, the man held a pistol. Standing before Dá Derga, he looked up into the god's eyes, and then started to weep. He pointed the gun at his head and fired the gun off.

Brain and skull exploded in a cloud as the bullet flew through his head. But Dá Derga caught the matter and folded it into a caul, placing it over him. The man screeched as his body shook. The Dar'gone grabbed him and dragged him from the court.

Maggie couldn't believe what she saw, but she knew that she didn't really have time to think about it now. She rushed into the room, her tail flipping back and forth behind her, and jammed the hook into one of the Dar'gone's backs.

The ghosts didn't react, as if they couldn't see or hear a thing.

The next woman was old and pale...and Maggie's eyes widened when she saw her. Mona! *Her mother!* Maggie wanted to cry out to her, but when Mona saw the White God, she rose in the air. Before Maggie's eyes, she watched as Mona's ghost transformed into a dove. And in a moment, Maggie saw her turn and look at her. Her eyes were filled with tears before she was completely changed.

Ma!

Mona flew out the window, now off to *Tír na nÓg*.

Two other Dar'gones were readying their halberds and started charging for her—Maggie dragged the hook down the flesh of the guard that she surprised, and the Dar'gone screamed as the hook cut open its flesh, pouring its black innards onto the floor behind it.

Maggie then charged the next one, except she moved quickly as it swung the halberd around to catch her. Dodging under its blow, she was able to jam her hook into its underarm and yank, opening the side of its torso clean open.

Though she knew they couldn't hear her, Maggie thought, *Move, damn it. Move!* to her companions who were waiting to act...

Maggie looked up above Dá Derga's throne—where the god now started to stand—and she saw the large, black Crow Wings. His mounted trophy from the Morrígu herself.

3

As Maggie swung her Airgid Hook at the Dar'gones, Léana raced over to the great doors, swinging them shut as the Dar'gones heard the commotion, making their way to see what was happening. Afraid for her life, and the life of the others, she knew she couldn't let any of these creatures in.

Léana shoved ghosts aside, slamming the doors shut and then she went for the bar to lock the doors tight. Before the full bar dropped into place, however, a Dar'gone got his hands in the door and pushed it open.

Léana bit the hand, but it did no good. These things couldn't feel pain.

She saw a ghost beside her that continued to ignore her as usual. He had a knife in his back. Léana grabbed the knife, pulling it free and then went over and started chopping at the Dar'gone's hand.

More power started pushing on the door as more Dar'gones grabbed a hold of it, and she knew that she was failing.

They were going to get in…

"Bags!"

Only one choice left.

Léana stepped back and pulled from her *fata* essence the *croí*, reformed it with her will into an *Eagla* she knew from the waters. *Sruth*. It was like creating a watery current in the air, allowing the croí energy to push and pull at her will. Léana directed the *sruth* to grab the door and pull it back into place. Its strength was far beyond the Dar'gone's might, and so the doors came closed, slamming fully shut, severing hands and fingers from the creatures.

Léana moved the bar and pulled it down into its setting. From the other side, the Dar'gones slammed their bodies into the door with a loud bang. It came again. BANG. The door barely moved.

Was it going to stay in place for long enough?

Léana hoped so…

4

Once Léana was off, Bridget shut the servant's door and put its bar in place, locking it shut. Out of the two doors, the servant's door was the weakest, and the Dar'gones would be coming to use it, but hopefully, it would be too late.

Aedán watched Maggie attacking the three Dar'gones. The girl made herself clear: she was the most dangerous one, and the Dar'gones fell for it. When Léana got to the doors and started shutting them, Dá Derga stood and began walking over to Maggie to stop the fighting himself.

It was their turn.

Bridget saw it in Aedán's eyes.

Aedán went first and Bridget followed quickly behind him. They rushed for the empty throne. Aedán climbed onto it and tried reaching the Crow's Wings, but they were mounted too high. Aedán held out his hands to her.

"Come on. You'll have to climb!" Aedán said.

Bridget saw Maggie climbing on top of the second Dar'gone's back after slashing his underarm. She bit and clawed into the Dar'gone's neck, and then rammed the hook-thing she had into its head. The Dar'gone collapsed dead, but the third one grabbed a hold of her hair and yanked her back.

Maggie screamed out and Dá Derga grabbed Maggie's head with one giant hand.

"You've been a problem for me, *chiseler*!" Dá Derga shouted. "I don't think I could be more *mad* right now! Maybe I should kill you all so I can send you on your final journey! Bash your skulls with rocks!"

Maggie, even though her face was twisted with pain, screamed back: "Get your *rocks off* elsewhere!"

"Bridget! Come on!"

Bridget looked back up at Aedán, still holding his hands out. She grabbed them and he pulled her up. Bridget quickly climbed onto his shoulders and then he lifted her higher. Bridget reached out, feeling the fluff of the feathers in her hands, and unhooked them from the stone wall. Aedán started helping her down as she held the Crow's Wings closely to her chest. Once they were down, Bridget saw Léana running across the court, charging Dá Derga—

5

When Dá Derga grabbed her head and threatened her, Maggie wasn't sure what she was going to do. She was frightened. Maggie didn't want to go back into the dungeon. She didn't want to be killed. And everyone here counted on her.

But Dá Derga was a god—one of the many aspects of one of the most powerful Tuath Dé Danann, the Dagda. It would not go well for her...

Maggie struggled as the Dar'gone held her fast by her hair and Dá Derga held her head in his hand like all he had to do was squeeze her brains right out her ears. If Dá Derga saw the others before they could escape, it would be the end of it. If she was going to suffer, Dá Derga wasn't going to win everyone.

Keep his attention here! she thought.

"I only asked fer yer help! You're a *right* ARSE, if yeh ask me! A right, stupid ARSE!" Maggie shouted.

"I hold dominion of transcendence. That was my contract, chiseler! I follow my purview because it flows through my very veins."

"Oh, feck off," Maggie said. "You're a bloody useless sod!"

They both heard screaming and suddenly Dá Derga let go over her head. He looked over, and they both saw Léana running at them, wielding one of the fallen Dar'gone's halberds. She held it over her head, ready to swing it down on the god's back.

Dá Derga swung around and grabbed Léana around the waist, picking her up. His size had increased as if he had always been bigger. Maggie didn't even see the change herself. The Dar'gone, who had her hair, watched, distracted, so Maggie wrapped her tail around his legs and yanked it so that the spikes tore into the back of the creature's leg. Surprised, the Dar'gone was not ready for Maggie to twist around, slamming the Airgid Hook into the side of its head.

Maggie pulled her hair free from the Dar'gone's grip, slid her hook into its sheath, and then watched as Aedán and Bridget made it through the window, disappearing on the Argent Path. Bridget held onto the Crow's Wings as she went.

But Léana cried out in pain as Dá Derga started crushing her ribs in his massive hand.

"Léana!"

Léana looked at Maggie—her face broken in agony—and shouted down: "Maggie! *Go!*"

"No."

"GO!"

Maggie started running for the window and then climbed it. She looked back just in time to see Léana's form become water and splash out between Dá Derga's fingers, falling into a small puddle at his feet.

I lost another one, she thought. *Damn.*

Dá Derga turned to look at her. His face was twisted with rage.

"*Maggie!*"

"Another time, Dá Derga!"

Maggie jumped through the window and found herself in a verdant forest—a pristine, untouched wilderness of vegetation, moss and fungi. The trees loomed well overhead, and its canopy was lush and full. The sun was bright in the sky and the animals in the forest cried their verve.

While she felt relieved that she made it through, the pang of losing Léana struck her hard. She barely knew the undine, but Maggie had to ask herself why she had to lose so many people.

I'm fuckin' dangerous, she thought. It wasn't right.

"Maggie?"

Maggie looked up to see Bridget walking toward her. She still held the large, black wings to herself. The girl grabbed them up and held it out to her in her hands. Maggie took them.

"Thank you, Bridget. I couldn't do this without ye or yer fella," Maggie said.

Did she hear crashing waves of a sea?

Maggie walked past Bridget to the cliff where Aedán now stood at, looking out over the silver ocean. Maggie stood beside him.

"I know yeh don't exactly like me," Maggie said. "But we are of some use to each other. Let's try to make it as pleasant as possible."

Aedán sighed and then looked at her, nodding. "Aye. I agree."

The Ax

1

Orna and Brian heard tapping on their windows, but whenever one of them went to look, they saw nothing. Brian groaned and grabbed a lantern, lighting it with a match.

"I'll go see what it is. Probably some stupid seagull," Brian said.

Orna nodded, feeling a little nervous about it. She didn't know why. In all her years in Kilkee, she never once felt like she was in danger.

It was just something in the air, is all, she thought. "Just be careful while you're out there. It's pretty dark."

"Aye. That's why I'm taking a lantern," Brian said.

"Smart arse."

She watched Brian go out.

Not goin'na let this get to me. No. I'll make some warm tea for Brian, so he has something when he comes back in out of the cold.

That's it.

Orna went into the kitchen and put on a pot, still worried about Maggie and Cuán. She hoped her son would find Maggie and bring her home. They still had heard nothing from either of them, and it concerned her deeply. She was tired of crying about it all.

Dipping the tea infuser in the pot, she heard Brian scream. Orna wasn't young or healthy, really, but she made her way as fast as she could. She swung the door open, and Brian fell into the house at her feet, moaning, an ax stuck in his back.

Orna cried, worried for Brian and got down on her hands and feet. She shook him.

Don't be dead. Damn it, Brian...Don't be dead.

But Brian wasn't moving. Where the ax was buried into his back, there was a lot of blood coming out, pooling around his body.

It all started to sink in, and she screamed.

Looking up, she saw the woman she saw around the village from time to time—the woman Orna knew stayed with Oona while Maggie was away: *Carman.* The woman grinned and grabbed the ax, pulling it out of her husband with one swift tug.

Orna cried, horrified. "Please. Why would yeh do this?"

Carman shook her head. "It's really not yer fault, but a woman has to do what a woman has to do!"

Carman held the ax up to hit Orna with it, but suddenly Carman cried out.

As Orna sobbed over her husband, Carman bent over, bellowing out her pain. Her body twisted and jerked violently. A mad throe.

What was wrong with this woman?

Carman tore at her gown and Orna thought she saw black bird-like wings unfolding from Carman's back. Her flesh darkened around her joints, and talon-black claws started jutting from the tips of her fingers.

Carman wasn't natural. Was she one of the *aos sí*? The Hidden Folk?

Orna knew what came next. The woman was going to kill her—once she was done transforming.

Though it was difficult for her, she decided that she had to leave her husband's body. It was the only way she was going to live. Orna started getting up—her old, sore bones slowed her down. But when she turned to run to the back door, there was a hard metal force that drove into the back of her head.

Things went dark quickly.

2

Once the damn transformation finished and the agony of it left her body, Carman could think again. The sad, overweight woman tried to run away, so Carman grabbed the ax and put it in the back of her head. It was the exact same way she had killed Brian Foley, as he turned to run from her. Only she missed the head and got him in the back, chopping into his spine.

The effect was the same, so she took it.

Carman looked down at her naked body. She had torn it free, so she had room to finish the transformation. Her fingertips, nipples and many joint areas trended brownish black. She now had black wings connected to each of her shoulder blades, which were reconstructed to work the wings.

Walking outside, she flapped them and held out her arms. She laughed, far giddier than she'd felt for so many centuries.

"Thank you, Maggie! Elieris was right! You *are* the one!"

Carman had a good laugh, feeling the joy tickle through her. Once she was over it, she went back into the Foley house, folding her wings against her back. She opened the coat closet and grabbed Brian's long, black naval coat and swung it on to cover herself. It was big on her, but it did its job and covered her mutations.

Carman saw a hand mirror on a coffee stand beside the couch. She grabbed it, seeing that her eyes were also less human. They looked like they came from a bird of prey.

Nobody should see her like this, she thought. Carman pulled the coat's hood up over her head and then left the Foley's home. It was time to go back to Wexford. There was nothing left here to learn, and nothing to do here for now.

Carman considered whether she'd be back. If Maggie screwed up, oh yes, Carman would return for the rest of them. And once Maggie suffered for long enough, Carman would kill her too.

It was probably a matter of time, but for now, she was happy that the first Attainment was found. Now for the second: the *Eye of Balor.*

3

All they found around them was forest. Lots of various trees, some species were alien to them. Most of them reached higher in the sky than trees did in the mundane world. Maggie led the way, thinking about losing both Léana and Fiadh, the *púca*. Aedán and Bridget were not far behind her, and she realized how tired everyone looked. They had been moving all night long, and the sun was rising, but they were all so tired.

She turned to them. "We need to rest."

Bridget sighed loudly. "Dear God, I was just going to say I can't take another step."

"Why don't we build a fire 'ere and get some sleep," Maggie said, thinking on the night in the cave when Cuán first found her, how he started a fire to warm them both. She couldn't believe how much she missed him already. Her own eyes glanced down at the ring still around her finger—the one Cuán had given her.

You're doing this fer him, she thought. *Cuán needs yeh to be strong right now.*

Right. He does.

Aedán gathered some old wood and Maggie went around collecting rocks. Contemplating having seen her own mother at Tech Duinn, she fantasized that perhaps she could go to her mother—find her at the Great Tree—and tell her the truth: *You—You are my mother!*

While she was doing so, Carman appeared as an apparition in front of her. She was changed. She had the black wings on her shoulders, her eyes were gold and her fingers had talons. She wore a large, heavy naval coat that struck Maggie as familiar, but she couldn't quite put a finger on it.

"What do you want, Carman?"

Carman smiled at her. "To tell you that you did a wonderful job! Only two Attainments left."

"Only." Maggie whistled. "Feck you."

Carman looked at her. Maggie didn't care if the woman saw through her sarcasm or not.

"The second Attainment is the Eye of Balor," Carman said. "It's found on the silver branch of the Crann Lár. Get it for me."

Maggie stared at her—not really knowing what to say.

"We'll talk about the Third Attainment more later. First, get me that eye."

"Aye. Ye'll have yer feckin' Eye," Maggie said, turning away from the apparition. "Now leave me the feck alone."

Maggie took the rocks back to camp and placed them in a circle. With Aedán's firewood, Maggie rubbed the sticks together and got a fire going. Oddly, it burned a strange green.

Of course, it did, this was the land of *Tír na nÓg*.

The Compass

1

Cuán stuck to the path. He'd read plenty in his books about people leaving the paths, and what sorts of trouble they came across. He was sure if he left it, he'd never find it again. Ever.

He held the box Ambrus gave him shortly before Cuán made the crossing into the Otherworld. It was open, and the needle pointed down the path he took through the eldritch forest around him.

Other than seeing Niamh—Modron—after crossing over to the Otherworld, he'd seen no other faerie. And Niamh was no ordinary faerie, was she? No, she was a goddess. Cuán tried not to think about the contract he made with her in order to cross over, using the Stones of Modron. He knew it would come back to bite him later.

Right now, he just wanted to find Maggie. He was close. He was sure of it.

If Ambrus was right, the compass would lead him to the Crann Lár, and there he would wait for Maggie.

All things in Tír na nÓg *eventually seek the Crann Lár*, Ambrus had said.

Maggie would find him there; he was sure of it.

At dusk, he realized that he was tired.

Jesus, did I just move all *night long?*

Cuán rubbed his eyes and rested. His legs hurt. His back hurt. Looking around, he saw a tree that was right snug with the path he traveled. Perfect! He could sleep against the tree, his legs still on the path.

He wouldn't wake up lost. Not unless something took him off the path while he slept.

They say that as long as you stick to the path, you're safe, he thought. But was it true?

Bugger it! Cuán was too tired to worry about it. He was sure he was just overthinking it anyway. He sat down with his back against the tree. The moss made it softer than he imagined. He put the compass down beside his right hip and crossed his arms, shutting his eyes.

The rest felt amazing. It wasn't long before he was out.

2

A soft, light-purple toned young woman followed him. Her ears were long and pointed and she had dark, straight but twisting horns on the top of her head. Her name was Aisling, and she was born with a connection to the Spring Squill of Kilkee.

Only the Fomorian King had his soldiers dig up her bed and extract it into a perfume for the skin of a horrid witch. And the witch had magic to use Aisling, forcing her to bend to her power.

Aisling was ashamed of herself. Terrified and full of internal rage.

The fomori betrayed her, which, of course, didn't surprise her at all.

But Carman told her to get the boy, so here she was, *getting the boy*. She followed him for several miles as he stuck to the path. According to one of the Contracts, she could not harm the boy as long as he was on the path. Otherwise, she risked binding her fate even worse than it already was.

Paths were special places; holy places—she would have to get him off the path somehow.

When she saw the boy rest against a tree and fall asleep, she knew that it was her chance. Aisling went over as quietly as she could and grabbed the compass lying beside him. The dark-haired boy stirred a bit, but he didn't wake.

Upon him, she realized how handsome the boy was. He sort of reminded her of a certain sorcerer she took as a lover a while back. It was the dark hair. The air of confidence.

The smell of his manhood.

Aisling sighed, trying to calm her hot blood. She didn't know whether to suck out his life force or suck his cock.

Maybe she would make this boy *hers*.

That sounded so much fun.

Aisling grinned. *Fun indeed!*

Aisling used her strength, crushing the box between two hands. The parts crumbled and fell to pieces at her feet.

It would now be harder for the boy to find his way to the Crann Lár. He would need help from someone. Aisling would be that help! Yes sir! Aisling would help him find his way...straight into her little trap.

As the boy slept, Aisling made her way along the path. She had a little work to do.

3

When the sun was at its highest, Cuán woke up hot and a little stiff. He slept so hard that he didn't move even a little as he laid there. He wondered if he dreamed because he couldn't remember anything of them.

He was parched, too. Cuán needed water.

Cuán rubbed his face and looked around.

"Nonononononono!" he shouted, crawling over to the broken pieces of the compass. "Ambrus is going to kill me!"

No, Cuán thought, *I'm not going to find my way to the Great Tree! Shit!*

Cuán tried collecting all the pieces hoping that he could put it together, but it was useless. All the pieces were broken, and it was unfixable.

Now what was he going to do?

Cuán's eyes fell on the path and followed it until the forest growth concealed it from his view.

The path.

Cuán sighed. The needle of the compass had led him down this one path. If he followed it, the path should take him to the Crann Lár—*yes?* Cuán dropped the pieces of the compass where he stood and then he continued his journey. He pushed through the overgrowth of branches, vines and roots that got in his way. Looking around, he waited to see a fae meandering nearby or maybe even a solitary animal being mindful of his presence. Since his arrival in the Land of Youth, he hadn't seen a single thing except forest vegetation. It was disconcerting.

There was a voice ahead of him. It sounded like a young woman, but Cuán couldn't make out what she said at first. As he continued following the path to find her, his mind registered the young woman's distress—"Help! Help! Someone, *help!*"

She was in trouble! Cuán quickened his pace over the path, coming across a tree that had fallen over in his way. It completely crossed over the path, blocking out what was ahead.

"Jesus," Cuán said. "What the bloody hell?"

"Mister!"

Cuán looked over and saw that there was a naked young woman with midnight black hair, pointed ears and two twisted horns on her head. Her skin was pale, but perhaps touched with a purple hue. She was definitely one of the *sióg*.

"What the feck happened 'ere?" he said, going to the fae girl, kneeling down beside her. The tree had landed on her, pinching her down with a large branch.

"The fecking tree landed on me!" the *sióg* said, as if he were stupid for asking it.

Cuán realized that her attitude was warranted in this case, and he decided he could help her instead of arguing. It looked like the trunk itself missed her. All he needed to do was move the branch, which wasn't just a little thing. It was quite large, and he didn't know if he was strong enough to move it.

"Are you hurt?"

"I don't think so. I think I'm just...trapped."

Cuán sighed.

"Please, boy. Help me get this off!" the *sióg* cried.

"A'right, a'right. Let me try..."

Cuán squatted and grabbed a hold of the branch. He started lifting with every muscle his body had to offer. He felt it lift, but he knew he couldn't hold it long.

"Is that enough?"

"Aye. I'm moving. Hold it!"

"I'm trying. Make it quick though!"

The young *sióg* scooted out from underneath the branch, and then turned onto all fours and crawled the rest of the way out. Cuán dropped the branch, trying to catch his breath and then saw the *sióg* on all fours—her form rather human...and *provocative*, as he figured they would be.

Cuán looked away from her when he glimpsed a little more than just her nice rump and put a hand over his eyes. The fae were not human. They didn't wear clothes on the usual, did they? They were closer akin to the trees and animals.

"Are you afraid to look at me?" the girl said.

"Aye. Well, not afraid. It's just that I've a bird of my own. She wouldn't appreciate me looking at other girls in that state," Cuán said.

"I've glamour fer it," the girl said.

Cuán looked at her again and saw that she was in a loose tan gown now that ended just above her ankles. It was sleeveless, and she had naked feet, but it was better than having all the naughty bits out on display.

"Thank you," he said.

"I'm Aisling."

"Cuán."

Aisling took his hand and sniffed him. "You smell okay for a mortal man."

"I shouldn't. I haven't showered in a while."

The girl laughed and then became serious quickly. "You saved me. I owe yeh a debt."

Cuán shook his head. "Really. It's not needed. I can find my way."

Aisling nodded as he turned toward the path, knowing the tree had fallen over it. He'd have to climb the tree to get to the other side, only—

Wait. Where was the path?

Cuán's heart beat hard in his chest. *The bloody tree fell over the feckin' path. It should be right here*, he thought. He followed the length of the tree up and down as far as he could go before the forest growth made it too difficult. The path was utterly gone.

You shouldn't have left the bloody path.

"No feckin' shit," he said to himself.

"I'm sorry?"

Cuán turned, seeing the *sióg* sitting on the tree, watching him.

"I've lost the path!"

"So, you will need my help then? It's lucky we met, aye? Why don't you climb right on over this tree 'ere, and we can see if we can find yer path?"

Cuán sighed. Yeah, right.

How was it that he could feel so dumb around women? Why did he have to do dumb things around them?

My fate's to be a dumb arse my whole life, he thought.

On the other side of the fallen tree, there was still no path. Aisling waited as he jumped down from the trunk. She grabbed a hold of him and helped him stay balanced when he almost fell back onto his arse.

"You okay?" she said.

"Ah, aye, I'm okay," Cuán said. "Maybe my pride might be a little bruised."

Aisling smiled at him. She was pretty, he had to give her that.

"Where are you off to?" she said.

"I'm trying to find the Crann Lár. You know how I can find it?"

"Of course. But…You don't look like a ghost. Only ghosts seek the Crann Lár."

Cuán shrugged. "I heard that everyone eventually meets it."

Aisling nodded and took his hand. "Let me take you."

Cuán got a good breath of her and realized that she smelled like flowers and something else that stirred something up within him. It made him hard, and he felt a little embarrassed.

Of course, she smelled this way. She was a *sióg*.

"You say yeh have a lover?"

Cuán didn't know why he became so shy, but he tried chuckling it away. It didn't come out right. "Aye. Her name is Maggie. She's a Maris Demidian, whatever that means. I'm guessing that it means she's fae-touched, and she connected with the sea. Like the merrow."

"Aye. That's what it means. The Demidians can either be born of fae blood—like a demigod—or they can be fae-touched, transformed by the fae through the Primordial *croí*," Aisling said as they walked through the forest.

While Cuán found what she said fascinating, he looked for the missing path. "How can the path just disappear?" he said.

Aisling licked her bottom lip. "This is the Otherworld, Cuán. It's not bound by the same laws as the physical world. Your world is bound to its physics and is far more static. Here things change, moving all around, changing shapes. A tree one day can be a rock the next."

"So how the bloody feck do I find my way then?"

"By not losing the path in the first place," Aisling said, laughing.

"Well, it's too late for that," Cuán said, feeling arseways. "So, if you *do* lose the path, how do you find it again?"

Aisling sighed and grabbed his hand, pulling him along. "It's not the right question. It's 'how do you find a new path.' Once you lose the old path, it's gone. It's done. The only way to move forward is by finding a new one, and see where it goes. If you're lucky, it will take ye where you want to go."

"Bloody hell," Cuán said. He felt Aisling's soft hands squeeze his own. Her eyes looked into his and he had to pull his hand away from hers. That face. Those eyes. The velvet soft, purplish skin. Cuán couldn't trust himself around her. Her body seemed to beg him to take her and a deep part of him wanted to.

It wasn't fair to Maggie, so he forced himself to look around again for the path—No, a *new* path. Cuán groaned in frustration.

"I don't understand how you fae deal with such an uncertain world," Cuán said.

"Ah!" Aisling scoffed. "If you ask me, the mortal world is just as uncertain as this one."

A Little Closer…

Despite her best friend, Catrina, begging her to go swimming with her at the river, Emera spent the day with archaeologists as they dug up around St. Albeus. Dr. Alastar Macguire had her going around gathering any pieces, recording where it was dug up and which zone, and returning the items to the tent to be cleaned. Usually, Nevan was there, but he had some hurley game to attend to with his rich friends, and so she worked with a couple others cleaning artifacts.

As she made her rounds, she thought about Nevan. He was obviously into her, and she liked it. She just didn't know what to do with it as of yet and wondered if they would marry.

She walked by the old misplaced standing stone and looked up at it. For some reason beyond her, she felt it vibrating in the air. It washed through her, making her body feel as if it were a part of the vibrations themselves.

Was it real? Was it really rippling through the air, moving though her like it seemed?

It felt electric and…*sensual*.

Emera went over to touch it and literally felt her hand vibrate as if she had been shocked. It was faint enough, but her body fluttered with the energy. It was pure energy thrusting up between her legs, entering her, passing up through her belly and spread across her breasts and arms. Her toes curled and her body gave a small shake that felt wonderful. It made her deliciously wet.

The standing stone had been charged with sexual energy somehow. It was the only explanation she had for it.

She went back to touch it again when she thought she felt something watching her. It was like knowing she had eyes on the back of her, taking in every slight movement she made.

At first, she felt ashamed that her body had reacted the way it did, and she feared someone had seen the intimate moment—her body losing control.

Emera turned and only saw the wall of the monastery.

There was a crack in the stone wall. A thin one, but it was long, reaching from the ground just to above her head. Not remembering it there before, she reached and touched the stone rim of the crack. Cold air blew through it, and she stepped back, shocked.

What the hell was this?

Why was it so cold?

It exuded a different energy, didn't it? A horrible one.

The Nevrall Gléas watched the girl touch the standing stone and watched her body quiver. It was hungry for her, wanting her.

Come, it thought. *Touch me.*

The girl turned around and looked into the crevice, laying eyes on the Nevrall Gléas, but not seeing it. Her eyes hadn't adjusted to the darkness yet.

Good, it thought. *Very good.*

The Nevrall Gléas oozed out its dark tendrils, which flexed and moved like tentacles. It reached for her, extending its hooks and barbs so that she couldn't get away.

Come a little closer, it thought.

The girl touched the crack, but she whipped her hand away. She could feel its coldness.

And yes, it was very cold.

If the Nevrall Gléas could grin, it would.

Closer, it said.

The girl looked at it and still couldn't see it.

I will eat you and it will feel so good, it said.

"Emera!"

The girl jumped. Someone had called to her. An older male.

"You mind helping in the tent?"

"No problem, Doctor Macguire. Sorry. Just looking around."

The girl left the crack in the stone wall.

"It's okay, dear. I just need your help. I wasn't sure where you were."

Come back, the Nevrall Gléas said. It was hungry. It needed release.

Part III

The
Silver
Branch

The Umber Lock

He hunted through the wood—his primal instincts perfectly married to his heightened senses. It made him lethal, and it made him hungry. Making his way through the trees and the bushes, through small silver glades and over small brooks, he followed the scent of living meat in the air. It was all around him, but the meat he wanted smelled better than the others. Redder. Stronger.

There was a stag guarding his hind. It was immaculate, and it sensed him, too. The two eyes met and Brogan—full on wolf—charged it. The stag reacted, not backing down. He needed to protect the females.

This was fight or die time.

Brogan tackled the stag as it grazed him with its pointed antlers. One spine of its horns caught Brogan under the cheek, but Brogan could recover hastily. He wrapped his sharp claws about its breast and the two stood up together. Brogan bit at its neck and the stag began pounding into his shoulders with its solid hooves.

Though the stag was strong, and the hooves clobbered him good, bruising his ribs and shoulders, the wolf in him was smarter and pushed its weight into the stag until it fell over backwards. Once it rolled onto the ground, the wolf was on top of it, clawing viciously at its stomach until it opened, and its bloody gore came scooping out in shredded chunks.

Victory!

Brogan dove his terrible maw into its warm belly and tore chunks to swallow down.

Wake up, Brogan. There is news.

Fáelad?

Wake…up.

Brogan opened his eyes. He was but a man, laying his back against the mossy stump of a once-felled tree, surrounded by insectile-human hybrid twergs that were gathering around him. Naked little beings with chitin horns and legs. Some of them even had partially transparent wings on their backs. So he wouldn't feed on them over the last couple days, they brought him rodents, which satisfied him for now.

The fae creatures tasted good and filled him well, but he knew that after showing how cruel he could be, it was also time to show them mercy. It was important that they believed he would leave them alone once they did as he asked. It made them motivated.

Brogan crawled onto the mossy stump and sat on it like a king. The twerg creatures stayed back, out of his reach, afraid of him.

Fáelad was beside him, laying in the grass. The varga-spirit said nothing, merely looking over all the insectile twergs that gathered around them.

The insectile-woman with the long, brunette hair that he threatened earlier—holding her in his hand as he was about to bite off her head—was Banríon Míolachá. She was beautiful enough that if she were appropriately sized, he would take her, emptying everything he had into her, and maybe would even leave her alive afterward.

Banríon Míolachá stepped forth, daring to get closer. "We have word for you."

"You've found them?"

Banríon Míolachá nodded slowly. "You promise to leave us in peace?"

Brogan grabbed his chin and said, "I made a promise, didn't I?"

"It wasn't a proper contract, but yes," Banríon Míolachá said.

Brogan groaned. "Just tell me already. I've only so much patience."

Banríon Míolachá looked back at her people, and then turned to him. "There seems to be three humans who came in from the Argent Path of Tech Duinn to Tír na nÓg just this morning. One of them is a Demidian. A fae-touched. She's obviously a serpent Maris, tied and akin to the people of the waters."

Brogan grinned, sticking out his tongue. "Aye! That's them, isn't it?"

"We waited until they slept, and we clipped the hair from the human woman with dark umber hair. Since you are bound to the varga, we assume you can use this?" Banríon Míolachá held out a lock of hair. Brogan leaned down and took it from her. He took a deep whiff of it, smelling the female sweat still on the fine strands. Once he let his hands fall to his knees, he sniffed the open air and could smell it far off in a westerly direction.

"If you follow the scent, it will take you to the Pale Sea. They are resting there now," Banríon Míolachá said.

Holding the umber lock tight in his fist, he looked at Fáelad. "You will strengthen my senses. She is here."

Fáelad stood up and crawled into Brogan's body. Banríon Míolachá was obviously waiting for this, gesturing for her people to climb into the trees and other dwellings. She, herself, went into the cracks of another tree stump to hide inside it.

Fáelad went into Brogan's flesh and into his muscles and skeleton. He shifted Brogan's body into the shape of a wolf, sprouting dark brown hair and rows of savage teeth.

Brogan licked and inhaled the air with his snout, curling his black lips across his teeth. And then he ran through the woods, following the scent of the female. The harder and faster he ran, the closer he got. The closer he got, the stronger her scent.

Banríon Míolachá and her people watched the werewolf tear off into the forest, heading for the Pale Sea. She gestured for the village to look for the dead carcasses of their people strewn about the mossy stump the wolf had used like a throne.

She now hated that stump.

Once the bodies were collected into a pile, they worked to uproot the stump and tore it to pieces, feeding its bits to the earth. When they were done, they joined in locked hands around their dead, their bodies transformed into green mist, and they climbed into the essence of their forest.

As essence, Banríon Míolachá thought through how they could get their revenge on the wolf.

Bloody Witch

It was a crisp night. Rain pattered at the mansion windows. Lord Cuinn handed Etna a glass of wine, unsmiling and then took a seat behind a desk with his own. Normally, his servants would get them drinks, but this was a private conversation that they didn't want anyone to know about.

Etna took a drink of the mild bitter wine, and then said, "How have you been doing?"

Lord Cuinn cleared his throat. "How am I doing? Well, my adopted son, Aedán has disappeared with the girl. I sent Brogan to get them, but I lost contact with him as well. We found Aedán's horse tethered to a tree near the ruins, but after that, the trail goes cold. It's been days, and I'm concerned. I don't know what to do.

"Carman—oh, gods—Carman! There's her. Bloody witch. She comes in with her demands. She tells me that Aedán is in the Otherworld. Otherworld! If that's true, they may be gone forever. I don' know."

Etna knew they were in the Otherworld. With her vague and subtle connection to Carman, there's some things that Etna could sense in her. Carman was telling the truth about this.

"Brogan Kelleys is with them, too," Etna said.

She wondered if she should tell Lord Cuinn about her connection with Carman, but then thought it best to keep this a secret for now. Who knew how Lord Cuinn would take it? Maybe even think *she* was the enemy.

"If true, then we may be closer to raising the Red God than we have ever been," Lord Cuinn said. "Care for another drink?"

Etna looked at her glass, not even realizing that she had drunk it all down.

"Aye. Please."

Lord Cuinn got up again, bringing the bottle over, and he poured directly into her glass and then started on his. "I'm afraid that witch will ruin everything. She says she's here to help, but I don't believe her. I think she's playing some game that she plans to win alone."

Etna looked at him, realizing how afraid Lord Cuinn really was. Should she agree with him? Was he being a coward? No, he wasn't being a coward. She was afraid of Carman, too. Being afraid only meant that they were aware of how dangerous she was. Knowing that, they would be ready for her.

Yes. Etna found that she agreed with Lord Cuinn.

"How should we take care of her?"

Lord Cuinn sighed, sitting back into his chair. He seemed to mull over her question. He sat up after a moment and put his glass of wine on his desk.

"There's a couple guys I may know. I've never used them before, but I have...friends...who have."

Etna crossed her legs and drank deeply, feeling the wine finally going to her head.

"Do you think Brogan will be able to bring them back from the Otherworld?" she said.

Lord Cuinn sighed. "He's a Saint Albeus Wolf. If he can't do it, no one can."

"And when they return, we finish the sacrifice?"

"Of course! Their souls are related to Lugh. Their deaths will please him and feed him for his return. I've already spoken to the others about it and they're all in agreement."

Etna didn't know if she liked the idea at all. If Carman was so dangerous, and she was an Ancient, then how could they trust Bres? A Fomorian! Etna wasn't sure if she trusted any godlike entity anymore. Maybe it was better just to leave them all buried.

Maybe Lord Cuinn was a mad man.

"You said you knew people who can take care of Carman?" she said.

"I'll have to talk to my friend, but he mentioned them once. Taipan and Marú. If she doesn't know they're coming, it should be an easy job for them," Lord Cuinn said. He finished his wine and ran a finger over the lip of the glass.

Why easy? Etan thought. *Because Carman was a woman?*

Etna put her glass on his desk and leaned over it toward Lord Cuinn. She noticed that he eyed her bust, so she grabbed his chin and forced him to make eye contact with her.

"Do it quickly," she pleaded.

Lord Cuinn sighed, but before he finished his drink, he said, "I think I'll put a couple of our people at the St. Albeus to watch things at night. I want to know what the hell she is really doing."

The Brook

1

Aedán and Bridget followed behind her as Maggie pushed through the foliage, sometimes snapping or twisting things out of their way—creating a makeshift path. Tír na nÓg seemed to be like many other dense forests: thick, loud with animal and bird chatter, and difficult to navigate when you didn't know your way. Maggie hoped that they wouldn't ask her how she knew where she was going. They trusted her and she didn't want to ruin what trust they had in her.

When they took breaks, Maggie found that her quick reflexes and her claws came in handy when hunting. She snatched squirrels within no time, and the couple seemed to appreciate it when she brought them back food.

Aedán was good at starting fires and cooking them on little spits, which he made from long sticks. Once they were full and had rested their legs awhile, Maggie would once again lead them onward.

Maggie took them up the tallest hill she could find in the area, which helped as they came across a drop off overlooking the vast woods around them. In the distance, she could see the largest oak tree she'd ever seen—easily eight hundred to a thousand feet in the air. It overlooked even the tallest hill and looked incredible with all its various colored flowers intermixed with its abundant green foliage.

The Crann Lár.

Aedán and Bridget joined her at the edge of the cliff and they all looked at it.

"*Jay*sus, I've never seen anything like it," Aedán said.

"That's the Crann Lár?" Bridget said. "It's immense!"

"Now how do we get to it without losing it again?" Maggie wondered aloud. "It looks miles, and it's easy to get turned around in all of this."

Nobody seemed to have an answer, saying nothing. Maggie sighed and was about to walk away, but Aedán surprised her and pointed near the Crann Lár. "Look. You see that large lake near the Great Tree?"

Maggie and Bridget looked.

"Aye, I do," Bridget said.

"That's the Lake Dulcinea. It's said to be surrounded by a large grove of hazel trees," Aedán said. He looked at Maggie. "If you're connected with the waters, can you find your way to the lake? If we get there, then there's nowhere that we can't see the Crann Lár."

Maggie thought about it for a moment. Maybe he was right. She was a Maris. Most of what she learned was about reaching into the Hollow to find her way. Did the Hollow also exist within Tír na nÓg?

It wouldn't hurt to try, would it?

"Stay 'ere," Maggie said.

She closed her eyes and reached out for the Hollow. She could feel its psychic atmosphere all around here. It *did* exist in the Otherworld. *Good.* Maggie reached out in it, letting herself feel everything around her. Sounds became louder. The air was no longer just the wind. It was particles of elements flying around them. Her mind followed the elements, feeling out for the waters in the air. Eventually, she could feel the invisible mists and its air became cooler.

When Maggie opened her eyes, she stood at the edge of a brook that ran down the hill. She crouched down, her toes digging into the muddy embankment, and she touched the water with her hands.

Closing her eyes again, she felt the river through the Hollow, and followed it through the woods. The brook was a path to a large body of water. Not a sea. It was stiller, though it had strong currents deep underneath it. Maggie opened her eyes and saw that the brook went in the same direction as the Lake Dulcinea. The brook was the path to the lake.

Delighted, she was about to get up and go back through the woods to the cliff to find Aedán and Bridget, but then she heard a splashing sound and she looked across the brook at Léana. The undine had a long fish tail with multi-colored fins and her silver flesh shined like rainbows as it refracted the sunlight that breached the forest canopy.

Her surprise turned to gladness. "Léana! I thought you were dead!"

Léana smiled at her. "No."

Maggie's feet splashed in the cold water as she crossed the brook and she wrapped her arms around the undine, giving her a hug. It was brief, but it mattered, and she could see it on Léana's face.

"How did yeh survive? How are you 'ere?" Maggie said, wanting to know everything.

"We fae creatures draw in *croí* naturally, and through our fata essence, we can reweave it to create the Eagla," Léana said. I spent all the *croí* I had within me to form myself into water. And once Dá Derga left the throne to rest, I crawled through the window."

"I'm glad you're back," Maggie said.

"I'm too weak to move as you do yet," Léana said. "But if you plan to follow the brook, then I will follow close behind. When I get my strength back, I will join you again."

Maggie thought she understood and nodded. "A'right. Yes. We'll follow the brook to Lake Dulcinea, and from there to the Crann Lár."

Léana laid herself out in the brook. The brook wasn't deep enough for it to cover over her totally, but it looked like it felt good for her. Maggie almost wanted to crawl in with her but didn't want to be seen as an aper.

"Can yeh tell me what a Demidian is?" Maggie said.

Léana interwove her hands and put them behind her head as she laid in the water. She looked up at the forest canopy.

"A Demidian is a general term the fae call those with fae blood. Really fae blood is blood touched by the Primordial through its energy—*croí*. You can come by it either of two ways. You can be born from one who has Primordial blood—the fae or the gods themselves, so like demigods—or they can be transformed by the Primordial itself. This occurs when the fae or the Otherworld itself invests a person with *croí*. In your case, the Fomorians changed you with Nathaira's *croí* blood and made you who you are now."

Maggie thought about this. "The *croí* in Nathaira's blood."

"Nathaira's blood was the *form* of the *croí*," Léana corrected.

"So, can yeh get the *croí* out of me blood? Change me back?"

"It's easier to pollute things than it is to cleanse them," Léana said, shrugging. "If anyone can do it, they'd have to be pretty powerful."

Léana sat up, holding herself up with her arms in the water behind her. She cocked her head to the side, looking Maggie over.

"I have to tell you something else." Léana bit her lip.

Maggie sat back into the embankment, regretting it once she felt the cold, soft mud squeeze into every crevice. Maggie slid herself down so that she sat in the water.

"Tell me," Maggie said.

"When Elieris had you abducted, and you were taken to the Deep Dens, they took a piece of your soul. A soul shard called a *píos anam*. When soul shards are withdrawn from the rest of itself, it doesn't easily obey magic and parts of it found me and gave me... consciousness. It was a gift for me. The part the Fomorian Soul-forger kept, they called the Derdriu Shard. It was named after your true name, the one your mother gave you originally," Léana said.

Deirdre, Maggie thought. Though now when she said that name, it reminded her of Cherry Fox instead of herself. The name better suited Cherry Fox than her anyway.

"The fomori still have it and that's how they reach out to you," Léana said. "With it, they will always be able to find you."

"I'll have to get it back if I want to have real peace," Maggie said. She thought of Carman coming to her as an astral projection, knowing where she was. A candle flame suddenly sparked to life inside her head. "Carman has our Shard right now! That's how she found me! She showed it to me herself and I'm a blithering idiot. I just have to get to her."

Léana cocked her head again. "That does make sense, Maggie. I need you to be careful. That's why I had the Airgid Hook made for you in Cathair Aigéin—the city of the merrow. Remember that it is also a part of us."

Maggie nodded. "I will. I promise." She grabbed the Hook's handle, checking to make sure that it still hung in the leather sheath of the belt. The Airgid Hook hummed in her hand, and she could feel it deep inside herself. She may not have Cherry Fox's *Bod Mór*, but she had something now that she could call her own.

"It's been a long day. You three have been traveling the whole of it. You should rest tonight, and get started nice and early," Léana said. "I'll be with you. I promise."

Léana became water and fell into the brook, seemingly gone.

The sun was low in the gloaming, darkening sky. It would be night soon.

Maggie sighed and then looked between her legs. Blood was flowing out of her like a tendril that reached out from between her legs and down the brook.

"Shite. Not right now," she said, mortified.

2

It was dark by the time she made it back to the hill's drop-off. Aedán had started another fire, and he and Bridget were laying together on a soft part of the ground. He was on top of her, his head buried in her neck, and she was softly cooing as his hands massaged her breast.

Maggie ignored them and crawled into a soft spot near a tree, far enough away that she didn't feel like she intruded on their lovemaking. The cramps started in her back, and she rubbed them. There was menstrual blood on the inside of her right thigh.

What was she going to do about it? She was naked and there wasn't anything around her that she'd want to cram between her legs. Imagine *that*—the chaffing.

Maggie groaned and scooted down so that she could lay back.

I'll just have to deal with it, she told herself as she closed her eyes.

Maggie heard them making love. The panting. The low murmurs. And she thought of Cuán, craving him. It wasn't long before the craving turned her mind toward a fear that she didn't want to admit to: would she ever be with him again? Was this all a mistake?

Maggie re-lived her vision of Cuán in his bed, old and dying as she fingered the ring that he gave her.

No, she was doing the right thing. Cuán would understand.

She had to keep telling herself that, or she would stop believing it. If she stopped believing in it, she would give up. And Maggie couldn't give up.

Another cramp hit her back, and it tipped her over the edge—she started sobbing softly, not wanting to be heard.

The lovers were gasping with their climax.

She wept because Cuán wasn't there, and she regretted not having him there. It would be far less lonely. And he always rubbed her back when she was wracked with cramps and whispered into her ear how much he loved her. It was the most soothing thing she'd ever known.

Only a few miles left, she told herself. *The Crann Lár is close. Just keep your mind on the prize. You'll be together again soon.*

Though the cramps never really gave up, she was so exhausted that she did eventually fall asleep.

Twergs

1

There were many round, timber-stilted houses like islands across a lakeside. They had conical roofs made from brush and stone walls holding them up. From all the books Cuán had read, he realized they were crannogs. Aisling led the way over the first bridge—her body draped in her white gown, her horns standing up through her dark, curly hair.

When she got to the open door, they both saw the ogham etched into a piece of timber, dangling from a rope near the door.

Aisling turned to him. "Yeh always knock to drive away spirits that may be clingin' to yer bones before ye enter."

Cuán nodded and knocked on the wood after Aisling. Once it was done, they both stepped into the empty abode. Hides were draped over chairs and along the wall. Some of them were painted, showing hunting trips with creatures Cuán had never seen.

"Nobody is 'ere," Aisling said. "It's a twerg village without twergs."

"Twergs. What does that mean?" Cuán said, looking around the floor to see if he could find anything interesting.

Aisling shrugged. "The fae are pure. The aos sí, for example, are pureblood children of the Erus like the Tuatha Dé Danann. The leaders of the aos sí. They are closer to the Primordial like me."

Erus? Cuán heard the term before, thinking it was another word for 'gods.' "So...you're aos sí?"

"Aye. An aos sí. One of the many earlkings found around the world."

"Who are the Tuatha Dé?"

"The direct Children of Mother Goddess, Danu. Our ancestors and our gods."

"So, a twerg isn't one of the aos sí?"

"They were, but they have changed into what they become in their stillness. It's difficult to explain, but as Primordial Beings we live within the Primordial and through its connection with the earth. This connection is the fata essence itself. As an earlking, we are closer to the Primordial and are far more malleable to its influence. Through adaptations we change ourselves constantly, ever in flux. Earlkings can become twergs if they stop changing. They choose adaptations and then refuse to change for too long, the earlking discovers that the adaptation permanently becomes a part of themselves. When one stops changing, they become twergs. Twergs mate with other twergs and before you know it, there is a bloodline of Unchangeables."

"Things that don't change. Like a dwarf or a goblin?" Cuán said.

Aisling nodded. "Yes. Though those examples are foreigners to *our* land."

They followed the bridges around to the different crannogs, checking every one of them, finding the small village abandoned.

"Abandoned things return to the Primordial," Aisling said. "But tonight, it gives a roof over our heads."

Cuán agreed. It was getting dark. The moon above him was full, and it reminded him of Modron—of Niamh. He hoped that he would find Maggie soon. He hoped she was still alive. Cuán begged the moon goddess, *Keep her safe*. But the moon goddess remained quiet.

Choosing the first crannog they investigated earlier, Cuán laid down, pulling dusty hide over himself with warmth. Aisling surprised him, pulling up the same hide and crawling underneath it with him. Her hand rested on his belly, and she buried her face into his neck, kissing him just underneath the ear.

"I love your scent," Aisling said.

"You're too close, Aisling," he said.

Aisling's hand ran down his stomach, her fingers wrapping around the bulge between his legs, squeezing gently. It felt good. It aroused him, even though he didn't want to be. He loved her scent too. Flowers. A field of them. And female sex. Woven together like a cocktail made just to heat and churn his blood.

Maggie—his lover. This fae girl was not.

Cuán grabbed her hand and removed it from his erection.

"Please. Don't touch me. I've a fiancé, remember?" he said.

"Really? I don't see a ring," Aisling said. "Nothing binding you. Here, if nothing binds you, you are free."

"I'm spoken for," Cuán said, inserting more gravity into his voice.

Aisling looked at him as if hurt. "You find me attractive?"

"You're sexy, Aisling. And that makes you a problem for me," Cuán said. "Maggie is sexy, too. She's also the one I love. She's all I really want."

"Yeh lie!" Aisling said. "I felt yer hardness. Yeh need to relieve yerself and yeh can *do it* inside me!"

Cuán got up from the floor, doubling the hide over Aisling. This girl was trouble, and it made him furious that she would tempt him like this. How would Maggie feel about this?

She'd kick her ass, he thought.

"I'm spoken for, Aisling! Can't you understand this?"

He grabbed another hide from a corner and wrapped himself in it. Yes, he was hard as a rock and he craved release, but he was positive that all he wanted was Maggie. She was the only reason he came here in the first place—so they would never be a part. The last thing he needed was for this fae girl to drive him further away from Maggie.

"Fine," Aisling said, rolling her eyes. "I thought you were a man with needs. Didn't know yeh were such a cuck."

Cuán filled with rage and was about to yell at her, and then realized it wasn't worth it. She was trying to upset him. He rolled over with his back to her, deciding to ignore her for the rest of the night.

After a few moments, he fell asleep.

2

Aisling was infuriated. He was hard, throbbing in her hand, and she knew that he could sense her desire. He wouldn't let her natural musk overcome him though, and he was able to deny her. Cuán's love *must* be strong for Maggie.

It was disgusting.

If he'd only become her lover, she would be able to lead him anywhere she wanted. He would be hers to control.

What could she do if not seduce him?

Aisling mulled it over and realized the only other way.

She waited until the young man fell asleep and then left the crannog. After crossing the wood bridge to land, she went into the woods, whistling.

An insectile twerg fae appeared, the wings on her back making a high-pitched humming noise. Her legs were chitinous, and she had two antennae sticking out through her blond, curly hair.

Aisling gestured for the twerg to come closer.

"A feithidí. I have known of yer kind," Aisling whispered.

The feithidí flew nearer to her face but stayed just out of her reach.

"We watch and listen to everything in these woods," the feithidí said. "We have been watching you. You lie! You say you are an earlking, but you have been the Spring Squill for centuries. You yourself are a twerg."

Aisling wanted to grab her and crush her. "You *gick!*"

The feithidí flew back a few feet, giggling. "What have you come for, darlin' Aisling?"

Aisling composed herself a little. "I need something from you," Aisling admitted. "I need yer blessing."

"Are you proposing a contract?"

"Aye," Aisling said.

"It so happens that our Queen, Banríon Míolachá, is in need of someone of your services. There's a certain wolf that terrorized one of our villages. We want the wolf to pay."

Aisling nodded and grinned, happy to hear it so easily. She reached out one hand, palm up.

"I declare this contract," Aisling said. "For Elieris."

The feithidí flew close and placed her smaller hand onto Aisling's palm.

"I bond this contract, for the feithidí and Queen Banríon."

Aisling slept that night, but she didn't need much. She was up long before Cuán even stirred. He looked over at her and she could see his bitter expression. He was still upset with her.

Aisling had gathered berries in a piece of cloth and went over to sit beside him.

"I offer peace," she said and held the berries out in her palms, showing him.

"Are they good?"

Aisling smiled, lying: "Everything in Tír na nÓg is good."

Cuán looked at her and his scowl disappeared. He took a few berries with his fingers and stuffed them into his mouth, chewing on them and swallowed. Nodding, he beamed up at her.

"They are delicious," he said.

"Aren't they?"

The Handesome Gentleman

1

A few days later, Emera ran her hand over the cool stone of the inner wall at St. Albeus monastery ruins beside the strange standing stone there. After having touched the standing stone for its sensual vibrations, realizing that the energy was now pale compared to her first experience, she looked for the crack in the wall that felt cold and dark.

Only it was no longer there.

Emera remembered the embarrassing orgasm from the stone, and then turned to see the crack. It felt as though something had been watching her through it and she wanted to know what it was.

Funny, she thought. 'What' was it? Why didn't she think 'who'? Who was it that stared at her behind the cracked wall?

Her best friend Catrina followed behind her, talking her ear off about her parents, when Emera told her to be quiet. Catrina looked offended for a moment, but then Emera grabbed her hand and pulled her over to the standing stone.

Emera put Catrina's hand on the surface of the cool stone. She waited to see Catrina's reaction, but Catrina just looked at her funny.

"Do you feel it?" Emera said.

"Feel what? It's cold, isn't it? It's stone, for God's sake."

Emera rolled her eyes, sighing. "I know that—" She stopped herself. If she told Catrina how she felt, she knew that Catrina would laugh at her fancy. They were best friends, but Emera knew Catrina very well. There's nothing she wouldn't laugh at. Like a Puck.

"Never mind," Emera said. "Will you go inside with me?"

She wanted to see if the crack was on the other side of the wall. Maybe whatever (whoever) stared at her through the crack had been hiding inside. She didn't know what she'd find, but she was curious to look anyway.

"The monastery? What the feck, Emera?"

"You being a right cringeling, Catrina? Come on."

Catrina rolled her eyes, but followed Emera into the creepy ruins of the refectory building. The sun was out in full and beamed through the windows and the other cracks of the building, so it wasn't exactly dark. It *was* creepy though. It felt like the ancient people left their energies in this place. Some of them were really *bad* energies.

At least, that's how Emera felt. Especially in the refectory.

She wished Nevan was here, but she realized that he could only make it out to the dig sight a couple days out of the week. It was fine, really, but having a man with them would feel a bit better. Feel safer.

When they were on the other side of the wall that would now be between them and the standing stone, Emera once again touched the cool surface of it, feeling for any cracks.

There was nothing there.

"You done groping at the walls now?" Catrina said.

Emera laughed. "I suppose so."

"Then let's get out of 'ere, a'right?"

A couple hours later, Catrina kept Emera company as Emera cleaned artifacts in the bath waters in the archaeologist's tent. Catrina sat in a chair, fanning herself, once again going on about whatever ran through her mind at the moment. Mostly town gossip.

Dr. Alastar Macguire ducked into the tent and saw Catrina there, frowning for only a moment and then smiled when he saw Emera hard at work.

"I'm sorry," Emera said. "She's only keeping me company. Filling me in on what friends are doing and all. I know you don't want people 'ere who aren't working, but she's been some help and—"

Dr. Alastar Macguire started gesturing with his hands for her to bring it down. "Th-Th-That's fine, my dear, but I've more important news. We're going to have some tourists come through to take a look around, and I heard some of them were into funding excavations of this nature. I'm thinking—"

"Doctor Macguire!" a digger called from outside. "A carriage is coming up the road."

Dr. Alastar Macguire looked excited and yet unprepared.

"They're here, so maybe join me, and we'll give them a tour. Yes? I want to show them that even the youth find this exciting, and it would be most helpful."

Emera looked at Catrina. "You comin'?"

Catrina threw up her hands. "Why not."

"God, do you see that man? He's some eye candy," Catrina whispered, leaning closer to Emera's ear.

They had walked six men through the ruins of St. Albeus, through the buildings that were still standing, and past the six zones being excavated around the grounds. One gentleman was very dark and handsome. There was a youthful yet rugged masculinity that Emera could feel in him, and Catrina stared at him as if she too were smitten.

He was dressed in an expensive cashmere suit and had a naval peaked cap. There was a pipe between his teeth that he puffed on, or relit with the matches he took out of his jacket pocket and struck at the ends of the box.

The men mostly spoke between themselves, giving them very little attention after Dr. Alastar Macguire introduced them and explained how the youth had been involved, all excited for the artifacts and knowledge of the old world.

As they walked over to one of the last zones, the handsome man fell back and walked with the girls. "I'm happy to see the youth so interested in the past," he said in a slick, deep voice. The sound of it was beautiful. Emera thought about how it would be like if they heard him sing.

"My name's Catrina. This is Emera," her friend said, all giggly and Emera thought it was a little embarrassing.

"Most people just call me Captain, but I suppose you can call me Vladiv." The man stopped and took Catrina's hand, kissing it. "And it's my pleasure to meet the both of you."

Emera held out her hand and Vladiv kissed it while Catrina's mouth grew wide and smiley.

"Vladiv! I knew you were a foreigner," Catrina said. "And where is the accent from?"

"Do I have an accent?" Vladiv said. "Oh. Well, possibly Romania. It's the country of my birth."

"You live there?" Catrina said.

"I live on my ship. I travel all over the world," Vladiv said.

Catrina gave Emera 'the look' with her big green eyes. Playfully. *This guy's delicious.*

Vladiv didn't seem to notice.

"I like boats," Catrina said. "It must be huge, if you travel the world in it."

Vladiv smiled at her. "It's a monster."

Emera was flustered and felt warm around the collar. His presence tickled something inside her and she liked it.

"Could we see your boat?" Catrina said. She coyly bit her lip for Vladiv. "I've never been on one."

"Perhaps after we see the rest of the monastery?" Vladiv said. "Yes?"

Catrina nodded maybe too quickly.

Emera took a bated breath, noticing what she and Catrina were doing: *flirting* with this man. At once, Emera thought of Nevan and started feeling guilty.

Emera slowed her pace even more so that Catrina walked with Vladiv in front of her. Removing herself from them brought clarity. He was handsome. Electric, even. But she couldn't let herself ruin her chances with Nevan.

She loved Nevan after all. She didn't want to hurt him.

2

At the end of the day, Emera was exhausted. Catrina had left her to work, which turned out to be for the better. Without her distractions, Emera got more work done.

Sadly, she couldn't stop thinking about how beautiful Vladiv was. How she craved him. It was disgusting, and she silently chided herself for it ever since. It even brought her to tears, thinking about how it was so easy to forget who you really love for that dark sexual appetite. How could she do this to Nevan?

Ugh! She felt so *dirty*.

And you like being dirty.

No, she thought. She wanted to be respectable. Loyal.

Now. But when that feeling *rises* between *your legs, it's all you can* think *about.*

Putting herself into her work helped relieve her feelings, but when she left the tent for home, she couldn't help thinking about Vladiv again.

On the road up ahead, she heard the four-beat canter of horse's hooves. She looked up and saw that it drew a carriage behind it, and it approached swiftly. Emera walked off the road as it started slowing. It didn't stop until the door was beside her. The curtains in the window were pulled open and Catrina stuck her head out.

"Emera! Look at this! Vladiv picked me up in a carriage and we want you to join us."

"Where to?"

"His ship, of course," Catrina laughed. "He's going to show it to us."

This wasn't a good idea, she thought. What if Nevan found out?

How could Catrina put her into this situation? It made her angry, but then his face joined Catrina's in the window. That dark, handsome face that made her knees weak. Catrina realized how close he was, and her eyes slowly closed. Even Emera could sense her arousal.

"You coming?" Vladiv said. "I've wine."

Emera smiled. She didn't know why she said it, but she did. *May God have mercy on my soul*, she thought. "I'd be happy to join you."

Catrina opened the carriage and Emera joined them, sitting beside her friend on the bench across from Vladiv. He held out a glass of red wine to her.

"Careful. The carriage can be bumpy," Vladiv said, and then he drank from his own glass.

His eyes danced between them, and Emera couldn't believe how nice it was to have him looking at her. A part of her wanted to open herself to him and let him in completely. Emera squeezed her thighs shut, knowing full well she couldn't control herself around him. Catrina's legs took advantage of the room on the floor, doing the opposite—her legs opened.

"I have many wonderful things on my ship," Vladiv said. "Many things from many of the countries I've been to. All of it is history. By touching them, you feel one with the past. The past moves inside you and you use it to make your future. It's what life seems to tend for us all."

When they got to the Wexford pier, the teamster stopped the carriage and Vladiv led them down to his ship. It was a large sailing schooner with a black-washed hull, two masts and the words *Madeline Leigh* written across the fore on both the port and starboard sides.

A boarding plank had already been lowered with wooden cross beams across its length so one could get their footing as they walked up it and onto the deck. Vladiv grabbed Catrina's hand and helped her up, turning back to help Emera up next.

As they stood on the deck, Emera could feel the waves under them slowly rocking the schooner side to side. There were men playing cards on the main deck or looking out at St. George's Channel at the starboard side, puffing on their pipes. The men all stopped for a moment to look at them, but none approached them.

Something was off, Emera thought.

The men all looked tired. Their skin was ashen gray, and they had deep rings around their eyes.

There was something definitely haunting about this ship. The men.

Emera didn't like it.

"Can we see your cabin?" Catrina said.

"Sure, Catrina. You coming, Emera?" Vladiv said.

Emera grabbed Catrina's hand and pulled her toward her, leaning to whisper, "Let's go."

"Go?" Catrina laughed. "Are you kidding me? I've always wanted to be on a ship like this! And this man is gorgeous!"

Emera looked at her, weighing her look with as much solemnity as she dared. "I'm getting a bad feeling. I don't like this. Let's go home."

"Is there anything wrong, Emera?" Vladiv said.

Emera didn't want to look into his eyes, feeling like maybe they would mesmerize her or something. They would make her *want* to stay.

Catrina smiled at her and grabbed her hand back. "Come on, Emera. Don't be such a lily. Let's go have some fun. We'll never have this chance again."

Emera shook her head and pulled away from her friend. "No. I can't."

Catrina groaned, frustrated. "Fine. Leave then."

"Would you like my driver to take you home, Emera?" Vladiv said, looking at her with what seemed like genuine concern.

But something still wasn't right.

"Aye. If you don't mind."

"Head on down the plank. I'll have someone fetch the driver," Vladiv said. He then looked at Catrina. "Coming?"

Catrina giggled. "Hopefully soon."

Catrina gave her a beaming smile and waved goodbye as Vladiv led her into the cabin of the ship. Into its darkness, Emera thought.

Emera made her way back to the plank as the crew continued to stare at her. Wanting nothing more than to be out of their vision, she attempted the plank too quickly, slipped and almost fell down the slick boards. Luckily, she caught onto the rope along its edge and saved herself from a bad tumble.

Emera righted herself, hearing Catrina laughing flirtatiously inside the *Madeline Leigh*.

What a terrible ship, she thought. Emera knew she would never want to come back here again. If demons could manifest on earth, she was certain that the *Madeline Leigh* was one of them.

Emera waited for several minutes before the carriage came back around for her to take her from the pier. When she got further away, she started fearing for Catrina. Did she just leave her friend in the arms of a monster? Would she ever see her friend again?

Emera covered her face in shame.

Oh no, what had she done? How could she do that?

Emera also felt more relief when she could no longer see the ship.

In bed, later that night, she had a strange moment of clarity. The cold, watchful crack in the stone wall at St. Albeus that somehow disappeared before she could return to it and get a good look. And then the cold, stark fear she had on the *Madeline Leigh*. Could she be going insane? Was she finding evil everywhere because she was becoming a paranoid loon?

Emera's stomach turned.

It didn't matter. She just hoped she saw Catrina again. Hoped that she would be okay.

If she's not, it would be my fault, she told herself. *You left her with that man.*

Being Rawny

They followed the brook, Maggie leading the way she always had. Bridget still glowed from making love with Aedán the night before, using the memory to endure the biting insects and the unnamable sounds of the forest that made her a little nervous.

Maggie spent some of the morning walk talking about the brook and how it led them directly to the Lake Dulcinea. From there they would go through the hazel trees until they reached the foot of the Crann Lár—the Great Tree.

"One of its branches is called the Silver Branch. I'll probably have to climb to it, whichever branch that is. I know it's high, so yeh both can wait at the base of the trunk for me. I should be able to climb it okay, I'm sure," Maggie said. "Do yeh think you can fend fer yerself a little while?"

Aedán wiped drops of sweat off his face. "We've yet to see anything that would harm us, really. Except maybe falling off some ridiculous cliff."

"I think we'll be fine," Bridget said, though she wondered about some of the weird animal calls that she heard. They were nothing like what she'd heard on earth, and some of them seemed like they could be malignant.

For some reason it reminded her of part of her dreams—the standing stones, the woman in white, cutting a man's throat whilst others watched. She shook her head, feeling as though she needed to shake the bad thoughts out of it before they got the best of her.

Instead, she wondered about how they transported themselves from the physical world to the Otherworld. Was the standing stone they were making love next to have fairy power, making them accidently slid from one world to the next? She asked Aedán but all he could do was shrug.

"I have no idea how or why we're here," he said.

After some quiet walking, Bridget noticed that Maggie bent over to grab a branch and twist it out of the way. Aedán looked at Maggie's backside when she did this and his eyes ogled longer than Bridget liked.

Why would he look at her? Hadn't she helped him the night before with his needs?

Bridget didn't like it and it made her gut turn. Especially when she saw the erection between Aedán's legs. What if he liked Maggie more than her? But how could he? Look at her! Dark green skin with scars all over her. Fins. A tail. She almost seemed more like an animal than human. It was disgusting.

Bridget looked at Aedán again and he was still gawking, so she elbowed his ribs.

"Ouch!"

"The feck you looking at?" Bridget whispered at him, seething between her teeth.

Maggie looked back at them, and Bridget smiled at her. Maggie nodded and continued, ignoring them. Aedán looked at Bridget, holding his hands up in defense.

"I'm sorry. She's weird. I just don't understand it."

"What? You don't understand that she's got woman parts?"

Aedán sighed. "Jaysus, Bridget. I'm not meaning to look. I guess I'm curious."

It didn't help. Beneath it all, he was just being a man gawking at lady parts because he could. There was no excuse.

And it hurt her. He was *supposed* to look at her.

"It's disgusting. It's perverse. Keep your eyes off the poor girl!" Bridget said.

"Monster, you mean," Aedán said. "You see those teeth? She'll feckin' eat us alive, I'll bet. She's probably saving us for when the hunting goes bad."

Even though Bridget considered Maggie's otherness—the poor creature—it sounded awful coming out of Aedán's mouth that way. She hit him in the arm again, giving him a severe look.

"Right now, you disgust me," Bridget said, and started walking faster, leaving Aedán behind her.

"Bridget—" Aedán said, but she didn't turn around.

Fuck you, Aedán, she thought.

Aedán sighed as Bridget stormed ahead, ignoring him as he tried to apologize to her.

Truth was, he didn't know who to trust. Lord Cuinn had always made it clear that the fae were trouble. Those who looked like monsters were usually monsters.

And yes, Aedán had a look at Maggie's nice round ass because he was curious and enjoyed the sight of her. He knew it was wrong, and he did it anyway, and Bridget had a right to be angry. He just hoped that she would eventually forgive him.

I've got to do better, he told himself. *Stop being rawny.*

Up ahead, Maggie cried out: "Now we're gettin' somewhere!"

Aedán could see them. The shaggy green hazel trees and the peaking of a large lake in the distance.

Lake Dulcinea.

They still had a way to go and Aedán didn't want to think about Maggie or Bridget for a moment. He took out the Macalla Shell and put it to his ear, listening to his father speaking.

VII
Dead Spots

Carman sometimes stood staring at what she had become in the mirror. The wings, the dark ring around the golden eyes, and the black talons that poked out of her fingers and her toes. Her skin became mottled, too. She had dark fingertips and toe tips and joints. Even the skin of her groin and buttocks became darker.

She looked like an angel of death or maybe like the Morrígan—the goddess of war and death herself. It frightened her, but she embraced it. Power never came without its price, and she knew she was made more beautiful in a way. Just not the way one would normally expect.

And that was fine with Carman.

She threw on a black robe and then a dark, hooded cloak over that. It was designed to hide her malformations. Her face.

Etna would look at her, scared of her and it was fine. Though they shared the same essence, they were now two different souls. Etna was where she had come from and was nothing to Carman now—nothing but a servant. Sometimes Carman wondered if Etna thought to plot against her, but the scrawny, docile woman came off as a pathetic excuse for a human. A coward at best. Nothing to worry about.

Etna knitted in the corner of the den, which is how she relaxed in the evening before bedtime, looking up only to see how Carman stood in front of her.

"What is it?"

"I'm going to be up late," Carman said. "I need to do some scrying."

Etna sighed loudly. "A'right."

"I'm going for a walk."

This time Etna just looked at her, saying nothing.

"This place is getting rather manky, woman. Clean it up."

Carman left Etna alone in the house and started walking down the street, needing to breathe the fresh air. It was a usual routine now. She found that the sprites in the world were shut out of the houses, compelled out of the cities by the heavy populous' psychic interference. When she needed to get ready for casting her magic, it was easier to do so after she communed with the sprites.

In the air—the element which Carman felt most connected to—the sprites danced and whipped around her, speaking her name in their ancient tongue. She remembered being in the forests around Athens, breathing in that Greek air. The god's true ambrosia. Sometimes she missed Greece and wondered what became of it in the modern era. Did it still exist? If it did, she should visit when all this was over.

For now, she needed to concentrate. She had two more Attainments to find and while that Maris girl could find the Crow's Wings, it wasn't assured she would find the other. Besides, Elieris chose not to relay the whereabouts of the third Attainment and it bothered her. Sometimes, she thought maybe he was just using her and wouldn't follow through on his promises. It would be just like a Fomorian.

The neighborhood opened into the Wexford main street, which unburdened itself of mortals as it got darker. Carman realized some of the sprites were following her, but the air started feeling bad.

The sprites were getting upset—that's what it was.

Carman looked about, trying to see anyone sneaking around.

Nothing.

"What are you trying to tell me?" she whispered to the sprites.

A couple loud reports echoed down the empty street, and she felt something hit her in the chest and one in the leg. The agony overcame her, and she realized it became hard to breathe. Carman opened her cloak and touched her chest with her hand, feeling a wetness.

Someone *shot* her.

Another report rang out, and the bullet hit her left bicep, tore through it, and flew on through her to ricochet off the cobblestone street.

Frightened there'd be more fire, Carman called her magic and created an invisible shield of magical energy around her. The guns went off again, and the shield rebounded the rounds onto the street around her. Once she felt safer, she put a hand to the bloody wound on her chest and called the magic to reweave her flesh. When she could breathe again, she used her gold, predator eyes and looked around her. She spotted movement just around the corner of a dark alleyway.

As a few folks started coming out of the buildings to see who was firing a gun, Carman was already moving. Screaming angrily, she charged toward the alley and rounded the corner. The man who hid in the alley was already running. She saw that he wore a paperboy's cap and held a rifle tight in his hands. He threw the rifle aside, but she ignored it and continued after him.

Once she rounded another corner, she saw that another man with a bushy mustache looked shocked to see her and turned and started running as well. He dodged into a pub.

But the one who *shot* her tried running by the door, and she grabbed him with her talons, driving him to his knees. He cried out in pain and surprise as her talons sunk into his shoulders and then tried to turn and punch her. The hood fell from her face, and she snarled, raking the claws of her right hand down his chest. She reached into him with her magic and twisted her fist, gesturing for the magic to do the same to his spine. The man jerked as she heard his bones crack.

The man laid dead.

Now for the other one.

Only I can't kill him, she thought. These were people that were unknown to her. They were assassins, and they were hired to kill her. They had a boss and she needed to know who it was.

Seared with rage and embarrassment, she kicked the man repeatedly just to get it out of her system. These two were mere mortals, and they shouldn't have been able to take her by surprise this way. Utterly mortified by her own lack of judgement, she hoped he felt each kick in Hell.

After she was done, she went back to the door at the back of the building. She went in, realizing that she stepped into a busy pub. People looked at her, so she put the hood up over her face and backed out the door.

It wasn't a good idea.

And she didn't get a good look at the second man.

Frustrated, she went back to the body she left in the alleyway and kneeled beside it. Casting all her magic tired her out, so she knew she'd have to go home exhausted.

One more time, she told herself.

Carman held a hand out over the thug's body and then over his face. She reached into him with her magic, deep into his brain and started pulling the surface thoughts. There wasn't much because the brain was already mostly dead. However, there was a name of a partner: Taipan. They were hired by someone, though Carman couldn't get past the 'dead spots' where the memories were lost.

Before she knew it, the whole brain was dead and there was nothing else she could do.

Taipan.

"You're dead, Taipan," Carman said. "I'll find you. Don't worry."

VIII

The Craving

1

The Brogan-Wolf climbed into an oak tree on the outskirts of the hazel forest. He watched as the redheaded looking serpent-girl led Aedán and Bridget along a brook. The hazel forest had less vegetation, and the trees weren't quite as tall. From the oak tree, Brogan could see the large lake in the distance.

Fáelad climbed out of him, leaving Brogan to change back into his human form. Now he sat crouched, naked in the oak's branches. The varga-spirit floated down to the ground, looking back up at him.

What are you waiting for? the varga said.

"Do you see that creature with them? The redheaded one? I wasn't expecting her. Who is she?"

The varga looked in their direction and then up at him. *Who cares, Brogan? She smells like* meat *to me.*

Brogan could smell her in the air. She did smell of meat like the other two. Menstruating, too.

"Look at her. She doesn't look human. She could be dangerous," Brogan said, unsure of what to think.

The varga laughed in his head. *You! YOU FEAR the girl? Ha haaa!*

Brogan climbed down from the tree and ducked down behind some bushes. "We'll kill them all."

Fáelad climbed back into him, and he shifted back into his large wolf form. He looked at his humanlike hands with his long, curled claws. Hopefully, they would be enough together to kill the serpent-girl. The Brogan-Wolf followed the three of them as they made their way toward the lake. The boy hung behind the women, his head pendulant as if moping. *Aedán,* Brogan thought.

The girl Lord Cuinn called Bridget MacCailín walked closer behind the serpent-girl, looking upset. She didn't once look back at the boy.

They must be fighting, Brogan thought.

The serpent-girl, on the other hand, looked cheerful. Her tail swished back and forth behind her as she ran, splashing through the brook.

"We're so close!" the serpent-girl cried. "Bless the *feckin'* moon!"

Once the serpent-girl stopped at the edge of the lake, she turned around and pointed up at the Great Oak at the center of the world. "There it is. Only a few more hours, maybe."

"Can we rest? It's midday and I'm famished," Bridget said.

"Aye. Famished," Aedán said.

Maggie nodded at them. "I'll go hunt somethin'."

Bridget looked at Aedán and said, "I'll get the firewood. You can collect the rocks."

"Why don't I go with yeh?" Aedán said.

Bridget shook her head. "No. You can go feck yourself for now."

Yep, Brogan thought. *Fighting.*

The serpent-girl went off in one direction and Bridget went off in another, bending over every so often to pick up a stick and put it in her other arm. Aedán checked the lake for the rocks.

They're splitting up, Brogan thought. This couldn't be better. He could pick them off one by one. Brogan-Wolf started following Bridget as she went back into the hazel forest on her own, collecting her wood.

Bridget smelled delicious. Maybe he should fuck her *before* he eats her.

2

Bridget started sobbing. She was tired of being angry with Aedán. She wanted to work things out with him, but a part of her was still resentful for catching him gawking at Maggie. She gathered wood bitterly until she heard something moving nearby in the woods. The sounds of vegetation moving. Crackling steps.

Her heart stopped.

"Aedán?"

No answer.

There was a rush up her spine, raising the hairs on the back of her neck.

"Aedán. You've already done pissed me off, I wouldn't—"

There was a low growl.

Bridget stood very still, waiting to see whatever it was emerge.

"Aedán?"

Was he fucking with her? Could he make that sort of sound in the throat?

No, surely not. It had to be something else. A wolf, maybe.

Retreat slowly. Make your way back to the lake...

Another deep growl rose.

Bridget's heel hit a root, and she almost stumbled backwards, but she caught herself. As she stood up tall, a large brown wolf stepped out between the bushes, lips peeled back over savage looking teeth.

No, this wasn't a normal wolf. It was *much* bigger. Two or three times larger. Its teeth were all hooked like canines. It was a death's maw. Its pink, salivating tongue curled back in its black-rimmed mouth. Its yellow eyes were glued to her every movement.

Shit.

Bridget looked behind her, looking for a tree to climb. The problem with hazels was that they weren't particularly tall trees or had the most stable branches. There was nowhere to go unless she ran through them.

She looked at its powerful legs, knowing full well that it would be faster than her. It would catch her before she even turned fully around. Its *feet*...they were different. His back paws appeared to be the back paws of a wolf, but the front ones looked more like furred human hands with long, black claws.

Bridget bent over, holding out her hands with her palms towards the beast. It stepped closer, moving with slow, careful ease. Its throat rumbled out another growl and Bridget thought her heart was going to burst in her chest.

Fuck, Aedán, where are you? Where was Maggie?

The wolf then stood up on its hind legs, pulling back its arms beside its chest, and took another step.

No...This wasn't any ordinary wolf. It was...a *werewolf*. And Bridget didn't care that she didn't believe in werewolves, because it obviously didn't give a shit. The thing was hungry, and it wanted to eat her. She could see the drool dangling from its lips, dripping in anticipation.

Bridget looked for something to protect herself with. A sharp stick. A rock.

There was nothing at her feet that could help her.

Shit. What the hell was she going to do?

The wolf charged for her, and she screamed. Its massive body piled on top of her, and they fell back together onto her back. Its *clawed hands* were now on her chest and its wet mouth breathed its hot stink in her face. It made her puke stomach acid into her mouth, but that wasn't all. Its mouth opened wide, teeth stretching apart, and it snapped shut in her face, splattering her with its stringy spit. The mouth opened again, and she knew this time it was going to snap around her frail neck.

Bridget screamed and screamed with all her might, and as the wolf was about to take another bite, she felt another weight plow into the beast. The creature's weight tumbled off her and after a short struggle to set up, she saw that it was Aedán. He had tackled the werewolf, and they rolled just a few feet away from her.

Get up! she thought. *Run.*

Bridget scooted back, trying to push herself against a tree to support herself while pushing her legs to get up off the ground. The wolf jerked itself to twist back, rolling back over Aedán, and then it raised an arm, slashing Aedán's face with its vicious claws.

His blood splattered Bridget.

"Aedán! *Aedán!* Run!" she screamed, even though she knew the beast was on him. He couldn't escape its weight.

What else could she do?

From her right, Maggie burst out of the foliage with great speed, holding up her silver hook. A battle cry rose in the serpent-girl's throat and the werewolf looked surprised. It tried to turn to attack Maggie, but Maggie drove her hook down into his side, drawing blood in its matted brown fur.

Aedán pushed the wolf off and rolled away and onto his feet.

The werewolf snapped at Maggie, missing, but Maggie was caught off guard as the beast also twisted its body, rolling her to the ground. The hook came free of its hide, where more blood poured out.

Bridget couldn't move. She watched everything in horror, not knowing what she could do.

The werewolf kept snapping and swinging its claws at Maggie, but she scooted back and then turned and started running. The werewolf, in its rage, ignored Bridget and Aedán and went after Maggie.

Bridget followed them and she heard Aedán shortly behind her.

What was Maggie going to do? Could she fight the wolf? Kill it?

Bridget screamed when she saw the werewolf's jaws snap down on Maggie's tail. Maggie cried out and then twisted her own body around, slashing at its snout with her hook. The werewolf let go to avoid the weapon and then tried snapping at her arm, missing, as it went by.

The werewolf then leapt onto Maggie, and she fell backwards onto the ground. Its large teeth sunk into Maggie's shoulder, and she cried out. Blood poured down her arm. Ignoring the pain, Maggie pushed up on its chest with her hands and feet, lifting the silver werewolf off the ground long enough that Maggie could roll. The two collapsed again side by side, the creature losing its bite on her shoulder.

Maggie was quicker to her feet and then waded out a little way into Dulcinea's waters until it was almost up to her knees.

Aedán grabbed Bridget into his arms and pulled her back into his body.

"Bridget," he said. "God."

The werewolf seemed to grin at Maggie. Its hands opened, extending its claws as it hunched down. Another growl rumbled from its throat and then it struck: its body lurched forward to tackle Maggie again.

Bridget squeezed her eyes shut, unable to see what was coming next.

"Shit," Aedán said.

There was a splash.

Bridget opened her eyes again and saw that as the wolf attacked Maggie, she swung her hook into the side of its throat. As she swung her arms around, she pulled the wolf's body around until it fell into the water beside her.

As Maggie turned her body to meet the wolf again, raising her hook, the werewolf reached up with its claws...

And then Léana came out of the water, wrapping her arms around the wolf, and dragged him back under the water with her. The waters churned violently as Maggie backed out to the shallows and then started to still. Léana's long tail came up for a moment and then went back down into the waters with another splash.

From where they stood on the shore, they couldn't see what was happening. Bridget covered her mouth with both her hands. Aedán squeezed Bridget tighter, letting her know that he was there. Maggie just stood there, watching the surface of the lake carefully. Ready. Holding her hook tight in her right fist.

Jaysus, Maggie saved them! Bridget thought. The girl didn't have to, but she came out of nowhere and saved her from the beast's cravings. Her chest felt achy with gratefulness and Bridget started sobbing.

Léana then came up to the surface, crawling onto the shore and rolled over on her back to rest, huffing air. She didn't look like the beast hurt her at all.

"Léana?"

"I...dr-drowned...him," Léana said between breaths. "He's dead... and his corpse is...at the bottom of...the lake."

Maggie put her hook into its sheath and fell to her knees, wrapping her arms around the undine, hugging her tightly. Then she too rolled onto her back to rest, grabbing her bleeding shoulder.

"I didn't know if we were goin' to make it," Maggie said. She then turned to look at them. "You a'right, you two? Oh...*gods*, Aedán. You're fucked up."

Bridget remembered the beast slashing at Aedán's face, so Bridget turned to him. There were three long, deep scratches across his face. They bled heavily. It looked like the beast's claws missed his eyes, which was good, but he looked like he needed help.

"Oh, *Aedán!* Oh, honey! We've gotta clean this and stop the bleedin'."

Aedán looked at her and she realized that he had tears running down his face. It was hard to tell because of all the blood.

"I'm so sorry for what I did to you, Bridget. Please don't be mad at me."

Bridget ran her fingers through his soft, brown hair.

"Don't worry about that, a'right. Not right now."

Laying side by side, Maggie and the undine laughed.

"Did the Airgid Hook come in handy?" Léana said.

"Aye. Did I thank you yet?"

"I don't remember. But you can thank me as many times as you want."

Maggie laughed. "Great."

3

Fáelad crawled out of the lake. As a spirit, the water didn't affect him or make him wet. It didn't drown him like it drowned his host. Fáelad had been around for a long time. He was the first Irish varga and was the king on the island. Brogan Kelleys was a remarkable host to be bound too, but, as with anything, it was time to move on.

It was okay, Fáelad thought. There was another person out there worthy of his power. Though Fáelad didn't know who it was yet, he was sure he'd find him. The varga always did.

Fáelad felt the pull of Ériu and he returned to her.

4

Banríon Míolachá watched from the top of a hazel tree as the Maris Demidian led the wolf to water, watched them fight until the undine surprised her and took the wolf down to never come up again. She was overjoyed by Brogan's death. It was justice for her people. She was only sad it couldn't be more horrific.

One of her people had made a pact with the Spring Squill, Aisling, but the contract was nullified when Brogan died. Still, she wondered if Aisling would be useful. Maybe she should have her people watch her, too.

Banríon Míolachá whistled and her people responded by whistling through the trees. It was a harmony of words passed down by the feithidí.

The Aos Sí

1

The trees began to whistle. Bridget looked up and saw hordes of birds flying overhead and the hazel trees began to shimmer. Léana shaped her tail into human legs and covered herself with a gossamer white glamour dress. She had even given Maggie a matching glamour dress, which made Maggie happy to have some modesty.

"I didn't know you could do that," Maggie had said just before the whistling started. While her cramps still pained her, it as more of a relief that she didn't bleed in front of everybody.

They all now stood together, looking up at the shimmering trees and the large flock of birds flying overhead, all in one direction.

From out of the trees, women in similar white, delicate gowns came out to gather around them. They were all young and beautiful. The only way one could really tell them apart was from their hair styles and colors. Their ears were all longer, sticking up out of their hair into points. A few of them had antlers or horns on their heads.

One young woman stood out wearing a golden torc. She had silver eyes and long, flowing blood red hair.

"The feithidí sing," the woman said. "They sing for the glory of the Maris Demidian over a beast."

Bridget pushed in front of everyone.

"My fella 'ere. He's hurt badly. He was hit in the face. Maggie, too. She was bitten on the shoulder," Bridget said. "Can you help us?"

The young woman smiled at her and waved them closer.

"We will help."

***

The women were the aos sí. They led them around the Lake Dulcinea to their conical-roofed crannogs that stood over the waters on tall stilts. The women put soothing ointments on Aedán and Maggie's wounds. They even stitched Aedán's face with horsehair.

"He will have some scarring," the young woman replied, "but it won't be so bad with the flesh pulled together like so."

Their leader, who wore the golden torc, introduced herself as Fianna. She said she was named after the Irish warriors and heroes of the Old Times.

"I thought you were immortal," Bridget said.

"We are Primordial, Bridget. We are ever-changing."

"So, you had another name before?"

Fianna smiled at her. "Perhaps."

"Forgive me for saying so..." Aedán said, touching the stitched wounds on his face. "Where are your men?"

Fianna cocked her head and then shook it. "Most of the aos sí are women, Aedán. There are men, but they endeavor in their own lives until spring. We have special celebrations for our congress."

"And by congress..." another aos sí woman said, "she means love-making."

Bridget went up to Aedán and grabbed his chin between her fingers, looking into his eyes. "Thank you for what you did for me."

"Tackling a wolf? Ah, that was nothing!"

Bridget grinned. "Aye. Nothing, is it?"

Aedán leaned in to kiss her, but she wasn't ready and drew back. She was still a little hurt with him. When he noticed that she wasn't going to respond to it, he sighed.

"I'm sorry," he said. "Will you forgive me?"

"I'm trying to," Bridget offered. "Don't piss me off. A'right?"

Aedán nodded.

2

Bridget sat outside on the bridge to the crannog, letting her feet dangle off the boardwalk just over the silver waters of Lake Dulcinea. She swung her legs slightly, looking up at the hordes of birds still making their way into the branches of the Crann Lár.

"It's beautiful, isn't it?"

Bridget looked over and saw an aos sí with very straight, midnight black hair and short two-pointed antlers sticking out of the top of her head. The aos sí sat beside her, mimicking how she pitched her legs back and forth, toes just brushing the cold water.

Bridget laughed.

"What is your name?"

"Luí Na'Gréine," the woman said. "You will have to forgive me. You look so...familiar. You remind me of a friend I had many eaons ago."

"Really? What was her name?"

Luí Na'Gréine gazed up at the sky, sighing. Kicking her feet. Bridget gazed up with her.

"Bé Chuille. She was the White Sorceress of Lugh. His favored sorceress. She entrapped witches and even trapped Bres in eternal sleep with the aid of Lugh. Her fate was...sorrowful."

"How do you mean?"

"She had to do the unthinkable. She had to sacrifice her lover in order for him to become a guardian. She never recovered, no matter who consoled her. I think it's what led up to her death."

That made Bridget remember some of her dreams in the Lost Place—the sacrifice amongst the standing stones. The two men gathered to watch the woman cut another man's neck wide open, so that his blood gushed onto the ground at the center of the circle.

Bridget didn't want to think about it. How could she imagine cutting her lovers throat to the stones?

They both saw the birds passing across the stars.

"Are those...?"

"Souls. Yes. From the halls of Dá Derga to the branches of the Crann Lár. It's a regular thing here, you know. But it is beautiful, isn't it?"

They sat quietly for a few minutes, but then Luí Na'Gréine looked at her. "You love the fella?"

"Aye. He's an arse, though."

"Aye. They *all* are," Luí Na'Gréine said, laughing. "Sometimes you just want to beat some sense into them. Ah, but you have to love them, too. Good ones will always be there for you."

Bridget looked at Luí Na'Gréine. "Aye. But how do you know when they're a good one?"

Luí Na'Gréine shrugged. "I guess you don't until you see what they're willing to do for you."

Bridget nodded. Like when Aedán attacked the murderous wolf to save her life, knowing full well that he wouldn't be able to handle the creature by himself. Ah, he was so stupid! But he saved her life, and now what was she going to do with that?

She looked at Luí Na'Gréine. "Thank you."

"Our Lady, Fianna, tells us that you will be leaving for the Crann Lár in the morning?"

Bridget looked down at the rippling silver water of the lake. It reflected the stars and the birds. "Maggie. Our Maris, I guess you'd call her...she's on a mission to find a few things. If we help 'er, she promises to help us get back to Ireland. The physical world."

Luí Na'Gréine leaned over and kissed her on the cheek. "Good luck."

Bridget nodded and Luí Na'Gréine left her to be with her thoughts.

Bridget appreciated it.

3

Aedán laid in a corner of Luí Na'Gréine's crannog, covered in blankets. His back was against the wall, and he listened to the shell he held to his ear. Maggie watched him, still unsure of him or the girl, Bridget. They were almost useless to her, but they kept her company and she felt bad for them.

When the aos sí continued with their own tasks, it quieted down, so when Aedán put the shell to his ear, he didn't know Maggie's hearing was heightened. The shell had voices, and they were saying something.

Maggie stepped a few feet closer, hoping he wouldn't stop, so that she could make out what was being said.

I won't see my son grow, will I? I'll be dead any minute now. Dead, and my son will never really know.

No! NO! Put that away!

Maggie crouched beside Aedán and he jolted in surprise, putting the shell under his blanket with him.

"That shell is special, isn't it?"

Aedán gave her a look she couldn't quite read.

"Was that your da? The one who said he was dying?"

Aedán looked confused, and she gestured at one of her pointed ears. He nodded and looked down.

"It was his," he said. "Before he died. He knew the Macalla shell could capture voices, and he used it all the time. Especially on his travels. He said that he used to capture my voice so that when he went on his travels, he could always listen to me and know what he was working hard for. The last thing the shell captured was my da's death."

"I don't know anyone in the physical world who really believes in the supernatural," Maggie said. "This side of me is...secret from them. That's why I have to ask yeh this, Aedán. How did yer da come across somethin' that uses magic?"

Aedán shrugged. "He was good friends with the Order of Bres. They're an order of Irishman my adopted da belongs to. After my da died, they took me in. Some of the artifacts they have...they are talismanic. I'm sure my da got it from him."

"Who, him?"

"My adopted da. Lord Cuinn."

Maggie moved from her crouching position to sit down on her bum beside him, trying to ignore the cramps in her back. She leaned closer to Aedán and saw that he didn't move away from her anymore.

"You're not scared of me anymore?" she said.

"You saved our lives. I've never felt safer around anyone in my life," Aedán said. He smiled at her.

Maggie was glad to hear it and smiled back.

"I'm afraid of losing me fella," Maggie said. "I lost me ma not too long ago, and it got me thinking about how I have this serpent blood runnin' through me. It'll keep me alive for a long time. Who knows how long? But I won't be able to take me fella with me. He'll die long before me."

Aedán shifted uncomfortably. "I'm sorry, Maggie."

"If I can get these other two Attainments, I'll have a way to get it out of my blood and I won't have to lose people I love over and over again. Who knows, maybe I'll go before me auld fella."

Aedán looked at her, looking as if he didn't know what to say.

"I'm not a monster, Aedán. I'm not."

4

Early the next morning, the sky filled with red and oranges, Maggie found Fianna on the boardwalk, leaning on the wooden rails and looking out at Lake Dulcinea, which reflected the sky like a great painting before them.

"How is the menses? The wounds?"

Maggie smiled at her, relieved. The wounds had healed. Her menses had ended. "I wish periods were so short in the mortal world."

Fianna smiled back at her.

"You didn't come to me for healing, though," Fianna said. "Am I right?"

Maggie bobbed her head. "No. I came 'ere because Balor's Eye hangs on the Silver Branch. I need to make sure I reach it."

Fianna stood and took both of Maggie's clawed hands. "If Balor's Eye is in the Great Tree, then you must remove it and take it from there. It's a blight. I will send a retinue along with you to make sure you reach it safely."

Maggie didn't know how to express her gratitude in any special way. "Thank you."

"I fear that you are hunted by something very dangerous. You will need the protection," was all Fianna said.

Emotions

1

Anxious and not feeling so hot, Emera made her way across town to Catrina's house. The morning sun was up, bright and yellow. The azure sky seemed to push the night off into a sliver on the western horizon. It was perhaps too early for visitations, but she didn't care. She had to know Catrina was alive.

Catrina lived in a small cottage house on the north side of Wexford. Emera knocked on the door and straightened out her dress and waited.

The door opened and a hunched, middle aged woman with graying hair tied back, looked out. "Emera Ó Damháin! Good grief, colleen. What you doing out 'ere so early?"

"I won't be long," Emera said. "Is Catrina in?"

"Of course, she is!"

"Can I speak with her?"

Catrina's ma gave her a look and then sighed, pushing the door open further. "Come in. We're about to have some breakfast. You want a bite?"

"I couldn't impose."

"You're never imposing, Emera. Come on then."

Emera stepped into the humble home. Humble or not, Catrina's ma kept it well maintained. Catrina came out of her room, still wearing her white nightgown, stretching and yawning.

"Emera!"

Emera ran over to her and wrapped her arms around her friend. She whispered into her ear: "I'm so glad you're alive."

Emera saw the purplish hickey on Catrina's otherwise milky neck and what looked like teeth punctures. Strangely enough, they looked as if they were already closed.

"What do you mean, 'alive'?" Catrina said. "Don't you trust me?"

Emera pulled Catrina back into her room and closed the door.

"I trust you. It was Vladiv and that ship. It didn't sit right with me," Emera said. "Did he hurt you? Did he—?"

"Emera! Nothing bad happened."

Emera went to Catrina's vanity and grabbed her hand mirror and showed it to Catrina.

"Look Catrina! What happened to your neck?"

When Catrina saw the bite marks in the mirror, her eyes widened, and her hand flew to her mouth.

"How did that happen?"

"Did he do that to you?" Emera demanded.

"No. No, of course not," Catrina said, but her wild blank eyes said it all.

"Well, you can't go to your ma's table looking like that. You have something that will cover your neck?"

Catrina found a wide collared dress and Emera helped her get into it. Then Emera sat Catrina down at her vanity and started brushing her friend's hair.

"What *did* happen?"

Catrina shrugged and then shook her head. "I don't know. We had a few drinks and then I remember getting a little sick, and he had his driver take me home after. That's all I remember."

"You don't remember him biting you at all?"

Catrina remained silent for a moment. "No. Not at all."

Emera loved her friend, but she was too eager to become an adult. She did stupid things. Emera knew that she was right. Even if Catrina couldn't remember, she was sure Vladiv did this to her. Or maybe one of his creepy lackeys.

"You have to promise you have to stay away from him," Emera said.

Catrina looked at her own eyes in the vanity mirror.

"I don't know if I want to. He's...magnificent."

"Catrina. Be smart about this."

Catrina looked at her, severely. "Don't act like that. Don't act like you're smarter than me. Where is the mind anyway when one is in love? On the other. Only God truly understands it."

"Catrina."

The door opened and Catrina's ma poked her head in.

"You two ready for breakfast?"

2

After school, Emera made her way to the standing stone and touched it. It felt sensual. The energies were fading. Soon they would be gone.

So, if the stones could be charged with energies, then what charged it with sexual energy? she wondered. Did some random couple come here and make love against the stone? Did it collect their passion? Their eagerness? Their...orgasm?

Emera thought about how Vladiv made her feel. How he made Catrina feel. It was as though emotions were psychic in nature, reverberating out from everyone as an energy that standing stones could collect.

Was there a way to control those energies?

Maybe that's what the ancients were trying to do with the stones... collect and control these energies.

Emera sighed, and leaned back against the bluestone, feeling its essence running through her. In her mind, she could see two lovers making love nearby. And then they were gone.

There was also a handsome man standing there. It was but a moment, but she saw that he wore ancient golden armor, and he gazed at her with a stillness she had never felt before. Before she could get a grasp on what she was seeing, he was gone.

The energy faded and Emera turned, pressed her face and chest against its cool surface, wrapping her arms around it as if she were hugging it. She wanted to hold her whole body against it, savor what was left of all that sexual power.

It was gone though.

Emera thought about Nevan, and feeling guilty, decided that she would have to make it up to him. Even if she couldn't quite be honest with him about her sudden desire for Vladiv.

How could someone love someone and yet crave another? The idea was cruel and dishonest and miserable. It was no wonder that being an adult bided so painfully. To Emera, adulthood was about deciding who you were going to be and live honestly by that code. But with so much confusion running around in your own heart, let alone the world around you, how do you make this decision?

"I'm sorry, Nevan," Emera said. "I was weak."

Horrible Pigs

1

A gentleman's club for Wexford elites, *Conner's*, was a rather large building on the west edge of town, near a hurling field. Taipan, who she recognized by his large mustache, had paid for his room that night after picking up his payment there, and headed for the pier to get a ship out of Wexford.

Carman watched him in the Hollow, where her physical body—having completely recovered from her bullet wounds at supernatural speed—waited at the pier in a carriage. Once her astral form returned to her body, she broke herself out of the trance and climbed out of the carriage, throwing her hood over her head. She watched as Taipan started moving down the docks and then she made her move. Carman rushed over and pushed him off the dock into the water. When he came up again for air, she slashed his face with her claws.

He screamed, grabbing at his bleeding face.

Carman hushed him with a spell that would put him into a short sleep. The man went limp, and she pulled him from the water. She looked around with her heightened eyes and saw only the movements of rats.

Good.

Carman pulled Taipan to the carriage, dragging his body along the way. At the carriage, she lifted him and tossed him in. She whistled at Etna, the carriage driver, and they started for Lord Cuinn's estate.

***

Etna drove the carriage along the back road of the estate to a small cropping of standing stones as Carman instructed. There were two rings of bluestones, though there was obviously one missing, creating a gap. Carman had plans in the future to have the stone at St. Albeus put back, so the circle would be complete. In the center, there were two stones that leaned toward one another, their tops resting against each other, forming a triangular arch.

The stones honored Bres, according to Lord Cuinn. Completing the circle and charging it with energies, the power of the Old Ways would return, and she would harness it to control even the Red God.

Carman pulled Taipan's body from the carriage and tossed him to the ground. She also grabbed rope from the trunk space in the back of the carriage.

"Wait for me at the house," she told Etna. "It might be a while."

As Etna drove the carriage away between the trees, Carman tied Taipan's feet together. Taking a dagger from a sheath on her belt, she cut the rope and used the longer length of it to throw it up over a stone, lifting his body off the ground so that he'd hang upside-down against the bluestone itself. She then tied the rope to a post she drove in the ground earlier.

Over the next few minutes, she started cutting his skin with the dagger, carving the flesh open just enough for it to bleed. She traced symbols into his skin, some of them trickling blood down his body as she worked.

Through the process, Taipin started to wake up and realized what was happening. He tried wriggling free and looked around in horror.

"Help! HELP!"

"Oh, stop your cryin' now. Nobody can hear you out here," Carman said. "There isn't a single soul in miles in every direction."

Carman didn't really know if that was true, but he wanted the man to know he wasn't going to scream his way out of this. In fact, he wasn't getting out of it at all.

"What do you want?"

"I want to know the name of your employer. Who hired you to kill me?" Carman said.

"Fuck off!"

Carman shook her head. "No. I don't think so."

Taipan tried to spit on her, but it missed, landing near her feet.

Okay, he wasn't going to play nice...

"There was a sorceress in my homeland named Circe," Carman said. She walked to the standing stone on his right. There, she had another set up that replicated Taipan's situation: a pig was strung up against the stone, hanging upside down beside him just as Taipan was. She lifted its sleep with her magic and the pig woke up, snorting in terror and frantically wriggling its own body. "She used to turn men into pigs. Maybe...I should do that to you. Aye? Turn you into a horrible pig."

"Let me go," Taipan shouted over the pig's terrible squeals.

Carman showed him the dagger she held in her right hand and then punched the pig in the abdomen with it. The pig hollered louder as she yanked the dagger up, cutting the wound wider. Blood poured down as it kicked and bucked, and then its entrails fell out in a pile on the ground at her feet.

Carman stepped back, soaked in pig blood and she licked the dripping dagger.

"Oh God!" Taipan said. Now his face showed the proper horror she expected out of him.

Carman smiled at him, blood trickling down her chin.

"Your turn?"

"It was a man named Elathra. He hired us. We only spoke with him one time," Taipan said, starting to weep. "Please. Don't kill me. I—I'll leave you alone."

Carman closed her eyes as she walked around the bluestone that the gutted pig hung from. The stone filled with psychic energy: pure, delicious terror and agony. *Maleficia.*

Imagine how much energy they're getting from Taipan, Carman thought, gleefully.

Elathra. One of the other names of Ri Elieris—the Fomorian King. Would he really move against her? What was his plan? It didn't make sense, but then, one couldn't trust the fomori. It must have been in the guise of one of his avatars.

Carman looked at the dagger and then back at Taipan.

"No, no, no, no...!" he cried as she walked over to him and drove the dagger into his stomach. He was quiet by the time his guts fell to the ground. Carman wiped her dagger off onto Taipan's shirt and then started walking back toward the house. Etna slept, laying across the driver's seat of the carriage, but Carman decided to let her rest.

She needed the fresh air anyway.

2

A gardener found it that morning. Lord Cuinn looked up at the mess on the Stones of Bres. The gutted man was one of the hired killers. Etna watched him, standing back.

Did Carman know it was Lord Cuinn who hired them? She tried to discern in the night before when Carman gathered her aid to nab Taipan, but Etna didn't dare question her about anything. She feared Carman would think it was her.

When Cuinn hired the men, he specifically told them he was Elathra, hoping that if they were caught, she'd be fooled for at least a brief while. At least, that's what Cuinn told Etna.

But Carman did it *here*.

What did that mean?

"Clean this up and bury the bodies," Lord Cuinn said to one of his servants. "There's no sense in bringing the police into this."

Etna uncrossed her arms.

"Does she know it was us?" Lord Cuinn said. "If she does, we're next."

Etna went over and touched the stone while Lord Cuinn's servants started lowering the assassin to the ground. She could feel that it was full of energy. She sensed the terror and pain, soaked up by the bluestones as the man was viciously murdered.

Etna sighed and went back over to Lord Cuinn.

"I think she chose the place to charge the stones. She's getting ready for Bres' return."

"So, she is helping us?"

Etna shook her head. "Unless she's preparing the stones for something else."

Lord Cuinn walked over to her and whispered, "She stays with you. Do some digging. See if you subtly get anything out of her."

"I'm scared of her," Etna said. "She's...just *evil*."

By the look on Lord Cuinn's face, he was terrified as well.

Naked Feet

1

A great waterfall fell into a large river from the rocks above. The trees were thick and overgrown with vines and other vegetation. Green moss clung to the trees and rocks. Fruiting fungi with red caps dotted the shorelines around where they walked. There were two great statues on either side of the fall, their forms softly present in the white mists. On the left side was a nude woman with a crown with four crests, holding up stones in her hands above her head. On the right side was a nude man with a king's crown and a cloak that appeared to be made of ocean waves.

"Who are they?" Cuán asked. "They look important."

"Mother Danu and Father Allód," Aisling said. "Those whose union gave birth to the Tuatha Dé Danann."

All this majesty and all Cuán could really think about was Maggie. She would have been awed by this site, and he wanted to share it with her.

His stomach growled and Aisling shifted behind him, opening her cloth of berries.

"More?"

Cuán eagerly grabbed some berries from the cloth and put them in his mouth. They were sweet and did a great job of filling his stomach without eating too many of them.

"Too bad we don't have berries like that where I come from," Cuán said. "Mealtime would be so simple."

Aisling laughed. "For us, eating is pure pleasure. There is no hunger for nourishment like in humans." She plopped a few into her own mouth and closed her eyes, obviously enjoying the sensations in her mouth.

After a short walk on the lakeside, Cuán looked around.

"This is one huge lake. Do you think we'll find a path around here?"

Aisling licked a finger for the berry juice.

"We're already on the path," she said. The lakeside will take us to where we want to be. I'm sure of it."

Cuán nodded, not sure if he could trust her. She oozed sensuality and could be too flirty. Cuán had known girls like her in school and most of them couldn't be trusted as far as you could spit. She was helpful, however, so he didn't have a choice—he wasn't going to worry about it for now. Instead, he thought of Maggie while hoping Aisling was right. If the path took him to her, what was he going to say to her? He really didn't know, to tell the truth. Hadn't they already talked? Did they really need to regurgitate the same feelings until it sunk in?

That sounded not only arrogant, but futile. If Maggie didn't understand him, she would never understand him.

Cuán rubbed his eyes. He didn't know why but he felt sleepy. It was getting harder to concentrate. Was it all the walking? Maybe this world did strange things to his mind, and it needed rest.

Cuán blew out a breath and then rubbed his forehead. "I might need a bit of a rest?"

"Are you sure? You do look tired. I know mortals need their sleep, but I didn't realize how much you really spent doing it. How much time do you need?"

Cuán laughed it off. "I'm not falling asleep," he said. "I—I just need to sit down a bit and catch my breath. Give me about fifteen minutes."

"Fifteen minutes?"

"A quarter hour."

Aisling shrugged. "I'm assuming you mean that you don't want to—"

"Aisling. Please."

Cuán sat on a moss-covered rock and looked out at the lake. He couldn't believe how large it was. Behind them, the statues of Danu and Allód looked over them and the land before them. Majestic trees and plants, cold lake water as clear as the day, and a giant tree reaching its branches far into the azure sky—it was all stunning.

Aisling walked over to him and gazed at him for a moment. After a while, he looked up at her and realized that she looked worried.

"What is it?" he said.

"I'm being Called," she said. "I have to go."

"Called? I don't hear anything," Cuán said.

"It's not for you. It's for me."

Cuán sighed. "You're leaving me."

"Aye. But yer on yer path, right? You can find yer way so long as you don't leave it again."

Cuán nodded and then reached out a hand, meaning to shake hers. Aisling only looked at it, not knowing what to do with it. Cuán took his hand back and said, "Thanks for helping me."

Aisling licked her top lip. "My pleasure. Slán a fhágáil."

"Slán."

Aisling turned back and was gone around the bend of rocks along the lakeside in only a few moments.

Maybe I will take a nap, he thought. He was tired enough that it was hard to think let alone watch for trip hazards and feral animals. Wishing Aisling could stay to watch over him, he slid down the mossy rock and laid his head back.

Trying not to fall completely out, he tried forcing his eyes open.

But the weight of them won out and Cuán fell asleep.

2

Aisling watched from the rocks above. Cuán struggled with it, but the spell of the berries finally took him. She smiled and looked up at a fruit tree near her. Quick enough, she climbed up to its red and purple fruit and took one free, biting into it. The sweet juices went down her throat easily, dribbling down her lips and chin.

Once she finished the fruit, she spread out on the tree's largest branch and wrapped her arms around it, letting herself go deep into her own mind until she was able to leave her body through the Hollow.

Down across the rocks, she found Cuán laying there. In the Hollow, his mouth yawned extremely wide. His jaw fluttered as a psychic vortex spun inside it. It was large enough to swallow her whole.

Aisling crawled through his doorway into his fertile dreams and tangent memories.

She walked through the moment he found Maggie tangled up in the seaweed, lying unconscious at the cliffs of Kilkee. She walked through a room where Cuán and Maggie had their first kiss. When their hands first started roaming each other's bodies that ached for touch. She watched as Maggie looked at Cuán in terror as he fell into the darkness of some deep, dark cave.

Aisling watched as Maggie crawled out of the cave waters to Cuán, holding the head of a dark-haired woman with vampyric teeth.

Aisling absorbed all of it, and when she was done, she felt ready for the next part of her plan.

The vortex was closing. He was waking up—

Aisling crawled out of his mouth and then started the climb back to her physical body.

3

Cuán wasn't sure how long he slept. The sun didn't move across the sky like in the physical world. It was as if it just chose places to be in the sky and moved about on its own accord.

After waking, he got to his feet, feeling his bones aching a bit from how he slept. Trying to shake out the stiffness, he started walking along the lakeside again.

Every rock was an obstacle. They varied in sizes. Some were slippery; some were dry. Some were sharp and pointed and others were wide and blunt. But each took a thought before he stepped so that he wouldn't hurt his ankle or slip and fall into the lake.

After a few hours of working his way, he came across an old man who rubbed his red, naked feet as it sat on the rocks. He was short and had a long, white beard. His clothes were disheveled, and it didn't look like he had shoes anywhere around him.

When Cuán got closer, he realized the poor man's feet were worn down and bleeding.

"Jaysus, Mister. You a'right?"

"Aye. I came down to get some fish, but these rocks are very hard on me feet," the old man said.

"Aye. I can see that. Where do you live?"

"About a mile up those rocks towards the Carraig Ard," the old man said. He looked down at Cuán's feet and they both looked at his shoes. "Those are mighty fine shoes, you have 'ere, boyo."

"Aye. Though I'm sure they'll be ruined by the time I get where I'm going."

"Where are you heading?"

"I'm following the path, hoping it'll take me to my Maggie," Cuán said. "You wouldn't happen to have seen a redhead bird walking about these parts? She sometimes has green skin."

"She gets sick, does she?"

"Well—" Cuán wasn't sure what to say.

"Actually, I may have seen her," the old man said.

"You have?"

"Maybe."

Cuán laughed. "You've seen a redhead then?"

"Aye. She was with three others." The old man stroked his chin, considering this.

"And?"

The old man shrugged. Cuán looked at his feet and then at the rocks ahead of him. This frustrating little man had seen her! Maybe she was close—

"Will you tell me?"

"Oh, I don't know," the old man said, rubbing his bleeding foot. "How do I know the likes of yeh mean no harm to a pretty thing like that?"

Cuán slapped his forehead. "A'right. How about this? You tell me where you've seen her, and I'll give you my shoes."

The old man beamed at him. "That's a wonderful contract, my boy! The coppertop you mentioned joined the aos sí at one of their villages on the other side of this very lake. Can I have my wonderful shoes now?"

Cuán groaned, but he sat down and took off his shoes, giving them both to the old man. The old man, laughing with joy, put his shoes on. Somehow, they seemed to fit him perfectly. As if this was supposed to happen.

"You fine now?" Cuán said.

"Fine and happy, Cuán. How about this? Since you so kindly gave me your shoes, I'll also give you something else you don't know. I can either tell you some good news about Maggie and how you may come across her sooner, or... you can hear the bad news about your parents."

At first, Cuán didn't understand what he said. It didn't click. And then his eyes opened, and his heart felt like it seized in his chest for a moment.

"What about my parents?"

The old man looked sadly at him. "I'm afraid that a witch wanted revenge on Maggie, so she went to your house, and she murdered them in cold blood. They are now in the Halls of Tech Duinn."

"You're having me on, you arsehole!"

The old man cocked his head, as if he didn't care what Cuán thought. "I told you what you wanted to 'ear, Cuán. Our contract is done. You can choose to believe me, or you can choose not to. That's all on you, my boy."

The old man went down to the lake, taking a fishing wire out of his pocket, carefully unwinding the hook on its end. He tossed the hook into the water and started whistling.

Cuán broke into tears.

He couldn't be telling me the truth, Cuán thought. Could he?

Rolling it around in his head, he knew that the faerie were great liars, but they had a contract. They didn't break their contracts.

Cuán was horrified.

Mom? Dad? No...No, he *had* to be lying.

"Good luck finding your Maggie!" the old man called from the distance as Cuán walked across the lakeside rocks with his cold, naked feet.

XIII
To the Deep

Ensorcelled to protect herself from the pressures and coldness of the waters, Carman went deep into the sea. Beyond the Ninth Wave, to the Pillars of Faoi Dhorchadas. Through the long, yonic crevices that went deep into the ocean floor, through its thulian tunnels that started to shape into spiraling pits and towers. At its center, a colossal man with crustaceous claws, octopoid arms and barbed tentacles, half hid in the darkness of his own spiraling madness that he made around himself.

Humanoid sized creatures, with faces mimicking vicious sea creatures and other malformations, went about their businesses in his court, swimming or floating about. Here, in the lair of the Fomorian King, an ominous air was its own oceanic pressure.

Carman flew through the waters of the Deep Dens to his colossal face, and he bared his pearly teeth, peeling back his large lips as his giant blue eyes focused upon her.

"Carman."

"Ri Elieris!" She expected to come across his avatar but seeing him in person was much better. He didn't seem to expect her to visit him in her own mortal form.

"Have you news for me?"

Carman shook her head. She was enraged, not knowing fully what to say, but she was here to find out if it were true…

"Did you send men to murder me?"

Elieris gave a laugh and the fomori around her stilled.

"Why would I do that, Witch? Do we not have a contract?"

"Aye. So says you. A king of a tribe driven off Ireland for bringing such terrors and manipulations, causing all to suffer," Carman said. "I thought we knew each other enough! But you are fucking *worthless* god! A *cheater*!"

"Watch your words with me," Elieris said. "I won't have this disrespect in MY court!"

"Cheater! You lied about our contract, didn't you? Is our contract even true?"

"Carman. Enough! I did not lie. The contract of the order makes it...*impossible* for me to lie. If assassins caught you out, it was not I who sent them."

Carman pointed a finger at him.

"Then tell me who!"

"I do not know 'who'," Elieris said. "My sight upon Ireland is severely limited here in the Deep. The Tuatha Dé Danann made sure of that."

"Then prove to me our contract still stands! I demand that you show me that your words are true! Where is the Golden Wheel of Taranis?"

"You are a FOOL if you believe I would give you the location of the last Attainment before you even have the second. You must prove to ME that you have what it takes to follow through," Elieris said. "Now, *leave* my court before I immure you for your blasphemy."

Carman couldn't control herself. She was too angry. How dare he ignore her? Without her, there was nothing he could do, trapped here himself until the earth passed away.

Threaten her?

He was an arrogant fool! A pig!

"Irish pigs! All of you! Irish fucking pigs!"

The Beacán Cnámh

1

Cuán pushed brush aside as he walked around Lake Dulcinea. His bare feet were sore, yet numb to every pebble and thorn, and his mind spun at the thought of his parents being dead. He still wondered if the old man lied, but he also felt as though their contract should have protected him from any lie. But he wasn't sure about how contracts were written or how they worked. Could the fae have used some supernatural loophole he didn't know about?

His stomach turned. He had a deep, cold feeling that maybe they were dead and he started to think that it was his fault.

I'm afraid that a witch wanted revenge on Maggie...

A witch? Cuán had been too confused, too distraught, to ask for the witch's name. He was infuriated at himself for thinking of it only now.

Warm tears escaped his eyes and ran down his cheeks. What had Maggie gotten herself into? Was this all for nothing? Cuán didn't know. All he could do was move forward, hope that he found Maggie, and hope that the old fae man lied.

Dear God, please let it be a lie.

As the embankment became steeper, he had to walk out into the cold lake, which climbed to just above his knees. He waded, looking around for any dangers around him, and when he came to the other side, he saw someone sleeping naked on the shoreline as it flattened out again. The shore was made of fine white sand. For a moment, he remembered finding Maggie long ago near the cliffs of Kilkee. She looked about nine or ten and was wrapped in seaweed from her head to her toes. The ocean waters had dumped her along the shores. Lake Dulcinea was large and had its own wake crashing up against the rocks, but it didn't reach the body he saw on the sand.

It was a redheaded young woman with soft, alabaster skin. *Maggie?* She slept naked in the sun, curled up and unaware of him.

Cuán couldn't believe his eyes and he started running through the water to the beach. He dropped to his knees beside her, and she opened her eyes. For a moment Maggie jumped, frightened and then her face changed into a beaming smile.

God, her smile always warmed his heart.

"Cuán!"

She jumped on him, wrapping her arms around him.

"I'm so glad you're 'ere! H-How did you get 'ere?"

Cuán smiled, holding her warm body against him, enjoying every minute.

"I had to come for you. You left me," he said. And saying it, made it hurt again. It made him angry. He pushed her back lightly with one hand so that he could look her in the eye. "How could you leave me?"

Maggie frowned. "I'm sorry. I know it was wrong of me. I just had, too, Cuán. I have to save us both from the Fomorians."

"I thought you came here to shed your serpent's blood?"

Maggie frowned deeper. "Yes, that too. You know I don't want to be this thing. I need to be free of it."

She still didn't mention her worries for him dying of old age while she herself remained young. Cuán wondered about this and then thought that maybe Maggie had changed her mind about what was important to her.

"What are you doin' out here naked?"

Maggie looked down at her body.

"I went fer a swim. I had to think. I was missing yeh, of course," Maggie said. "Swimmin' helps me clear me mind."

Cuán nodded. He knew that.

"I'm sorry fer everythin'. I should have brought ye with me."

Cuán couldn't take her frowning anymore and leaned in and kissed her mouth. She kissed him back, wrapping her arms around his neck. It had been so long, the kiss made him hard, and he wanted to take her now—only his stomach felt sick. He only disengaged from her in order to keep from throwing up in her mouth.

"What is it?"

Cuán groaned. "Sorry. I'm not feeling well. An old man took my shoes, and I haven't had much to eat or drink for a while." Maybe those berries weren't so good for his stomach after all.

"Let's rest 'ere, shall we? I'll catch us some fish. Ye remember how to start a fire?"

Cuán grinned at her.

Maggie dove into the water and returned with a fish flopping around in her tight grip. He'd just made the fire with sticks he collected up the hill a short way after surrounding a pit with small stones next to the water's edge. That way it'd be easier to kick water up on the fire, putting it out.

They speared the fish down the middle and cooked it. Afterwards, Maggie picked the meat off the bones and Cuán drank from the lake. He scooped the water up in his palms when she told him that she'd picked the fish clean.

They ate, chewing on the meat and Cuán watched Maggie the whole time, unable to believe he finally found her.

"Up the river is a clan of fae women. They've been helpin' me look fer the cure fer me fae-blood," she said. "Over this ridge is a cave with a very rare mushroom in it called the beacán cnámh. They said that if I eat it, it will purify me blood and I will be left a human. The fomori won't have a use fer me anymore. I'll be free and we can move on with our lives."

"The beacán cnámh? I've never heard of a mushroom like that," Cuán said. "They said it was in the cave? How deep?"

Maggie shrugged, holding more fish meat between her fingers and sinking her teeth into it. Juice dripped down her lips.

"Yeh want to go with me? Once we have the mushroom, we can go back to the clan. Maybe they will have shoes ye can wear fer our return trip to Kilkee."

Cuán sighed. He knew Maggie's head would be on what she came for, but he hoped she'd be more excited having him there. Was she angry with him? He couldn't tell. Cuán did remind himself that it was Maggie who ran off without him. She *better not* be angry with him for looking for her.

"You know I'm always with you, Maggie. Always."

Maggie looked at him, looking almost sad.

"What?" Cuán wasn't sure where that face came from.

Maggie forced a smile. "Nothin'. I'm fine."

"Are you, now?"

"Aye."

Cuán thought she was lying again, but he didn't want to fight with her.

"You know you're nekkid, right?"

Maggie looked at herself again.

"With your titties out and everything. I mean they're nice titties. Distracting, really."

Maggie cocked her head and rolled her eyes.

"Shut up, Cuán."

Cuán grinned. "Okay."

2

Cuán followed Maggie up the hill into the woods, leaving Lake Dulcinea behind them. He felt much better and after thinking about it, he realized that Maggie's journey was close to being over. Once she had this *beacán cnámh*, some fae mushroom, she'd be cured, and they could go home together.

Home to his parents, if they were still alive.

Cuán thought about telling her about what he learned from the old fae man, but he decided to wait. He didn't want Maggie thinking about anything else but getting her cure so they could move on with their lives. Get the hell out of here. College even briefly came back to mind.

After over an hour of walking through the woods, they came across a sunny glade. It was mossy and filled with ancient stones and fallen ruins of a castle long forgotten.

Cuán was in awe.

Maggie walked past the stones, working herself between them and Cuán followed her cute little butt as her legs shifted with her nimble gait through the grass. They came across an arch that looked like it had fallen over onto the rocky, mossy ground and just over a cavern. Cuán knew that it hadn't fallen over, though. The arch was built into the stone entrance of the cavern, where old stone steps descended into darkness.

As they closed in on the archway, thousands of lightning bugs rose into the air, lighting up around them. They looked around the glade, watching them fly like a pulsing cloud about the lush green meadow of grass and stone.

Maggie had a huge smile on her face, her crystal blue eyes all lit up.

"It's amazing," she said.

Cuán investigated the darkness of the cavern. "It looks old. I thought everything in Tír na nÓg was old."

Maggie shrugged as she walked up beside him. "Like in the human world, if the fae don't keep it up, things fall apart to be recycled again for other endeavors. What isn't recycled..."

"...goes to rot," Cuán finished.

Maggie nodded. "And the land recycles it."

Maggie froze and was incredibly still. Cuán had never seen her do that before. She was like a statue for a short moment and Cuán couldn't tell if she even breathed. And then suddenly, she smiled at him.

"Shall we?"

Cuán didn't know why, but it chilled him.

Looking down into the cavern, following the stairs as they disappeared into the shadows, Cuán snapped out of it. They were so close to finishing this, they had no choice but to keep going. He didn't like the dark caverns. He heard horror stories about mines collapsing and wondered how dangerous it was, moving around in the darkness of the caverns without being able to see.

"I should go first," Cuán said.

Maggie shook her head. "I'm not goin' to argue with you."

Cuán tested the first stone step and then the next. Before he considered that it was unlike Maggie to hold back, always pushing ahead into danger without thinking sometimes, he felt her hands push against his back. The strength of the push sent him flying forward, and he fell into the darkness, hit the stone steps and started rolling down each one. He tried to stop himself, but each step crashed into his body, beating him on all sides before he came crashing to a halt at the bottom. Cuán was splayed out in the darkness on his back and his whole body was in shock from the agony of the beating he took. He was sure he had broken bones.

"Sorry, Cuán. I had my objective, and I had to complete it, you understand? May your fortune change, Luv." The voice wasn't right. It didn't sound like Maggie. His mind tried sorting out what had just happened, and then he realized that he was being tricked. That's why there were several moments that felt wrong. The whole time, it was Aisling.

"Aisling! How could you do this? Aisling! Help!"

There was no answer. Cuán yelled for her for a long time, his voice giving out. There was only darkness at first. After a while, he started hearing things tapping around him. There was chittering. Something gathering around him. As his eyes grew more accustomed to the dark, he made out hundreds of legs and antennae. Big black bodies and claws.

"No," he said.

Something sprayed his hand, leaving it gluey on the stone. He tried moving it, but the white fluid held his hand down tight. It was...a *webbing* of some sort. They sprayed him across his legs and another spray landed on his chest and arm. They were...*covering him* in this gluey silk.

"No, *no*," he said, scared now more than he'd been for a long time—since waking in the icy cave waters with a vampyre clinging to his face, perhaps.

They continued to spray his body down and he could feel its chemicals saturating him, oozing into his pours. He was tired and the last thing he thought was, *Maggie. Help me. Wherever you are. Please help.* After that, there was only complete darkness.

3

Aisling removed her glamour, glad to feel her own body again. Maggie's glamour form was uncomfortable for her. It always was when she had to take a glamour form of someone who made her jealous.

Yes! *Jealous*, damn it all.

Aisling could remember taking Maggie from the Ó Fionnáins when she was just a babe, leaving behind the *siofra* in her crib. If she would have known Maggie would grow up to be such a pain in her ass, she might have rung the infant's neck until she was dead instead of giving her over.

But it was done. She could go to sleep again and rest.

By the gods, she hoped that this time she'd be forgotten. She wouldn't mind sleeping an eternity away. It was what she deserved.

As Cuán called for her in his terror, Aisling walked back into the forest to find her path home to the Spring Squill. If she couldn't have Cuán, Maggie couldn't either. And that worked for her.

The Apples, The Eyes

1

Fianna charged Luí Na'Gréine with leading Maggie, Aedán and Bridget, with a small company of the aos sí to the Crann Lár. Léana had stayed behind at the crannogs, saying she'd be no good in a tree, and would wait for them to return. Maggie was grateful for Luí Na'Gréine, following her as the others walked behind them. They felt well-protected, and Maggie knew that Fianna was good at her word.

Luí Na'Gréine was wrapped in a glamour gown of diaphanous white, as were the other women of the company, her midnight hair like a waterfall around her shoulders. She had two-points on her antlers and stood proud and tall. Maggie could feel that she was a strong leader and an accomplished warrior. The feeling emanated from her.

Maggie had no problem following her.

The aos sí were quiet, which is why Maggie could hear Aedán and Bridget whispering to each other as they walked through the hazel trees. She couldn't make out everything, but they were being terribly romantic and cheesy. Stuff Maggie didn't really want to hear at that moment. It made her think of Cuán and how guilty she felt.

Ahead of them, rising above the hazel canopy, was the titan of all oaks. Its branches spread out for miles above them and its trunk was like a mountain. Birds of every species flew in large clouds around the great limbs and leaves, making the Crann Lár feel so much more than just a tree. The thing breathed and pumped like the very heart of Tír na nÓg.

When they came across the base of the massive trunk, Maggie could see that her claws would fit nicely into the bark of the tree and that it would be an easy climb for her—easier than climbing the castle wall of Tech Duinn. The first branches were hundreds of feet above her, but she felt refreshed and ready to go.

Maggie turned to Luí Na'Gréine, saying, "Thank you. I will never forget this."

Luí Na'Gréine nodded, cocking her head a little as her eyes went to look up at the Great Tree. "You will be rising to the heavens, and you will touch the very heart of the land. Be respectful, Maggie. It makes us and it unmakes us. Its branches are the paths of fate we all must follow toward our destinies."

Maggie didn't know why she did it, but she bowed to Luí Na'Gréine and then turned to Aedán and Bridget, who stood behind her, surrounded by the graceful aos sí. The aos sí were standing back but enfolded the group as if they were all together on this.

Aedán had his arm wrapped around Bridget's shoulder, holding her tight, and smiling at Maggie.

"I'll have to go up on my own," Maggie told them.

"Be safe," Aedán said. "We'll be right 'ere."

Bridget took Maggie's clawed hand, rubbing it with her soft fingers.

"I'm scared," Bridget said. "But I know you can do this, so I'll wait, knowing in my heart that you will come back safely."

"If you want to make the climb before nightfall, you must go now," Luí Na'Gréine said behind her.

Maggie nodded and squeezed Bridget's hand before letting it go. Maggie walked up to the tree, her spike-finned tail swaying back and forth behind her. She rubbed her hands together, took a deep breath and then extracted her claws on her hands and feet. She started the climb. At first, she dug her claws in too deeply, making extracting them from the bark a little difficult, but she learned to ease up and it made the climb swifter for her. Before she knew it, she was forty feet in the air, looking back down and seeing that her company was already looking so small beneath her.

I can't believe I'm doing this, she thought and continued.

The first few branches she came across were sparse and skinny. The higher she climbed the thicker and fuller they became. Maggie thought she'd be tired, but her body surprised her. It was like swimming in the deep for her. The more she used her muscles, the stronger she sometimes felt. It made it feel as though she were light as a feather and could almost float in the air.

The truth was, and she knew it, if she let go, she'd fall to her death. Maggie wasn't going to let go, and she wasn't going to let her feathery movements get her all cocky and careless.

Maggie worried about the Silver Branch. She didn't know what it looked like. Was it really silver? The bark, the leaves, the nuts or fruit? How was she really supposed to know what it looked like, and she'd found what she was looking for? Maggie wished she'd asked more questions when she had her chance with Fianna, or even Luí Na'Gréine.

The girth of the branches she started coming across were as big around as roads. Some even bigger. They went off in their own directions, covered in leaves and birds. When she started seeing these larger branches, she came across one with silver veins and snowy white leaves. Maggie climbed upon it and started following the branch. It was like its own ecosystem. Birds were flying about, making nests in branches that spread out from the main one. There were white apples amongst the silvery oak leaves. There were even silvery eyes trying to hide in the shadows of thick billows of leaves.

The eyes didn't look friendly, so she watched them from the corner of her vision and didn't approach them to see what they were.

Surprising her, Maggie stepped back when she saw Mona's silvery hair and big blue eyes. She wore a simple white gown and her skin looked radiant for her age. Maggie's heart lifted, never happier to see anyone in her life.

"Mother?"

Mona smiled at her, holding out her arms. Maggie flew into them and hugged her tight. Feeling her warmth. Her love. Maggie even forgot that she herself looked like a monster. Unable to control herself any longer, knowing she had to tell Mona now before she never had the chance again.

"I'm so—so sorry for everythin'," she said. "I never told you. I'm Deirdre, Mam, I'm your real daughter. I—"

Mona was shushing her, stroking her hair. "I know, darlin'. I know you're my daughter."

How? "Who told you?"

"Once I became one with the Great Tree, its branches touch everything. My life is here: my family, the moments I had with them, and the truth behind things showed themselves. Deirdre was my daughter, too, and I love her more than anything, but I know who you really are, Maggie."

Maggie was filled with so much delight, she wrapped her arms around Mona again, not wanting to let go.

"Know that I don't regret anything. I blame you for nothing, and I'm glad you could move past our obstacles and still make your way back to us and to our arms," Mona said. "I'm proud of you."

"I wish Da were 'ere," Maggie said. "I want to tell him the truth, too. I want everyone to know."

Mona beamed at her. "Don't worry. If you come to the Great Tree, he will know. And we will be connected to your life until you, too, join us. We are all a part of the Crann Lár."

"If that is true, why do I feel like I'm so alone right now?"

Mona stroked Maggie's red, curly hair. "Because you are not focused on life, Maggie. You are too focused on what may or may not happen. Do me a favor, Maggie. For your Mam. Live life. Endure love. Be free. Do these things, and I cannot ask you to do anything else."

Maggie wrapped her arms into her mother and held her tight again. "I will try."

Before she knew it, Mona was no longer in her arms. She didn't feel sad. She felt relieved, and it made her feel stronger. And though she couldn't see Mona's ghost, she heard her one last time:

"Always remember that time...is very important. The time we have. If you let it slip by, then you'll lose more than you ever know."

Maggie stood in silence for a moment until she realized the silver eyes were still watching her from the shadows. Her mother seemed to be gone. Whether she wanted to or not, it was time to find that Eye. As she located more of the white apples, she began to touch them and turn them in her hands without pulling them free from their stalks.

Where are you? she thought. *Show yourself to me.*

She turned more apples, seeing nothing. Feeling nothing. Maggie found gold apples and pewter like ones. Unlike fruit on the Éire, none of these fruits looked appetizing. Maybe they only looked tasteful when you were a ghostly bird, hanging out here for the rest of eternity.

Maggie found a more bulbous apple, grabbed it and found it slick and soft. It dripped with some clear fluid, and when she turned it, she almost gasped in shock. Its cataract pupil bored right into her being.

Balor's Eye. She found it.

Maggie plucked it from the stalk, and everything started to get blurry. Dizzy.

What the hell was going on?

She heard a scream from somewhere below her. It felt miles away, but she was sure it was Bridget. Maggie rubbed her eyes, trying to clear her vision, but she stumbled and fell to her knees, holding the Eye of Balor as tight as she could. She didn't want it rolling away, losing it forever.

She heard more screams below her. More women. The aos sí!

Unable to shake her dizziness or blurry vision, she tried to stand, but she found it difficult to find which way was up or down. She rolled onto her back, starting to believe she'd roll right out of the Crann Lár's great branches and fall miles down to her death amongst the screaming aos sí.

2

When Maggie opened her eyes, she stood in a dark cave. She didn't know how she got there, but she could see an enormous naked man, bearded, with white hair sleeping with his back against the earthen walls. He held himself with one hand, half hard and his tongue licked his lips back and forth as if he was having an erotic dream. His eyes were closed, except the white one that sat in between the others, a little higher on the forehead. It was larger, milkier, with a gory pit bored into it. The hole where Lugh shot his sling-stone, Maggie thought.

How did she get here? Balor had perished during the Battle of Mag Tuired. Could she have walked through time, and been taken to the moment Balor breathed his last? It sounded crazy, but she knew what she was seeing here. She would know a fomor from anywhere.

Maggie turned, hearing strange noises in the caverns behind her. She ducked down behind some large rocks, hoping to keep cover as whoever it was, walked by her. If it were the fomori, they may be coming to claim the dying Balor.

But it wasn't. Maggie's eyes opened wide as she peered just over the rocks she hid behind. There was another woman here. She had a full head of red hair and deep green eyes. She had horns on her head, which turned back along the sides of her skull and ended in two points. Her ears were long and pointed and her divine form was armored in a soft, green-dyed leather. As the young woman made her way over the cavern's rocky floor, she leaned on her black shillelagh with a gold head, ancient symbols written down its shaft.

Maggie knew who this was.

Sionnach Silín—Cherry Fox—with her Bod Mór. Maggie had never seen her in this form, only knowing her inside a siofra's body-copy of Maggie's own likeness. Maggie had once hated her, wanting to take her head as a trophy for stealing her life from her, but Maggie learned that they were both being victimized by a sorcerer named Doran Dunn, who attempted to use them as pawns for his own ambitions. They had worked together to save a village from Dunn's dealings with the fomori, where brine vampyres awaited to trap them, but Cherry Fox—Deirdre to her family—was killed before it was over.

This was one of Cherry Fox's past lives. When she dared face the most twisted of gods.

Maggie simply couldn't believe it.

Balor opened his eyes when he heard Cherry Fox enter the cave. The large, white bulbous one in the middle even rolled around, dripping mucus over the crest of his nose and around his other two eyes.

Cherry Fox saw his nakedness and then looked up only at the fomor's face. Balor regarded her as well.

"I have heard legends of you. Have you come to please me?" he said.

Cherry Fox looked disgusted and wrinkled her nose. She pointed her cudgel-staff at him.

"I have come to finish the job Lugh should have finished long ago. The Morrígan has sent me," she said.

Balor sat up, anger brewing up in his face. His shadow fell across the cave, though Maggie couldn't even see where the light came from.

"I AM DEATH TO ALL. I AM... *eternal fire*. I may not have my soul-burning eye, but I am still Balor!"

Balor began reaching for her, but Cherry Fox saw it coming. She jumped over his hand, ran over his right thigh, jumping over his sex, and then swung the Bod Mór at his face. Balor didn't react in time, too slow as the golden bulbed-head of her staff crashed into the side of his middle eye. The globular thing popped out with a thick, wet plop and flew across the cavern. The skull on that side of Balor's face shattered and started bruising over even before Cherry Fox could jump off Balor's lap and back onto solid ground.

Balor roared in rage and pain, grabbing his wounded face.

Cherry Fox wasted no time, turning back and swung the cudgel-staff again at his chest. It smacked into him with a loud, hollow thud—and he grabbed his chest, crying out, "My heart!"

He began gasping for breath and then fell back, unmoving.

Maggie was appalled and astonished at the same time. Did Cherry Fox just kill a titan by stopping its heart with one blow?

Maggie stood up as Cherry Fox went to where Balor's Eye landed in the cave. She picked it up and looked at it, looking revolted by it. Maggie started toward her, but then the scene changed, and she saw Cherry Fox hanging Balor's Eye on a stock on the Silver Branch of the Crann Lár.

The mighty tree took hold of the Eye and held onto it for this whole time amongst its white apples. Cherry Fox faded away and Maggie was left standing there, disappointed that she couldn't say anything to the fae woman who, in the end, became like her sister.

Her mind once again got a little dizzy, and she shook it, suddenly hearing the screaming again.

Maggie's heart started racing.

That's right. The aos sí were in trouble.

3

Bridget watched as Luí Na'Gréine and her company of aos sí found places to rest in the grass below the Crann Lár. Aedán sat beside her, apologizing for his behavior.

"I know I've been a complete moron," he said. "I want you to know, I only want to be with you. Nobody else. Maggie is helping us, yes, and I thought she was a monster. She's not. Is she? No, not a monster. But she or any other woman... not even amongst these women here, could compare to you. I don't know if you believe me, but it's true. If you're done with me, I understand it. I was horrible to you, and I get it. I really do."

Bridget sighed. She believed him deep in her heart, even though it still hurt her a bit. She wasn't going to stay mad though. She kissed him and he gratefully accepted it and kissed her back with equal intensity.

"If Maggie comes back with the Second Attainment, we'll be almost done. One more to go. And then we're home. What do we do when we get there? Knowing what we know now?"

Aedán smiled at her. "We go on with our lives and tell our families to fuck off if they don't understand us. We live a good life, knowing that one day you and I will be up in this great tree, free and together. It's our destiny."

Bridget pushed out her lips. "So cheesy."

"Don't I know it," Aedán said, laughing.

It was then that Bridget saw the darkness come out from behind the bushes and hazel trees. A creature rose, pushing a spear through one of the aos sí, who screamed before gagging on her own blood.

Bridget stood up.

"The Red Knights! They're here!"

Aedán turned to see, his face twisted in horror.

"No..."

"It's Dother and Dain!" Luí Na'Gréine cried.

All their lives they had been haunted by the shadows of the Red Knights of Bres in a Lost Forest, deep in their own subconscious realms when they slept. Though it had brought her and Aedán together, it also traumatized them for life. They were, literally, their very nightmares.

When Bridget asked Fianna about the Lost Place, asking about whether she knew about the Red Knights, Fianna told her about the sons of Athens witch, Carman. She knew now that Dother was the one with the devilish red flesh, black horns and lips, covered in black leather armor. His brother, Dain, was the black creature with the spear. Gaunt and fanged like a large cat.

Dain withdrew his spear from the first aos sí as the other women cried their despair and rage at him. Dother came out of the trees nearby, pulling swords from the scabbards on his back.

"Ah! The aos sí! May you all die!" Dother bellowed.

The company of aos sí drew glamour swords that seemed to appear out of nowhere and they rushed the Red Knights of Bres. Both sides hungered for death, and Bridget knew that if she lived through any of this, it would be out of pure luck. She grabbed Aedán's hand, trying to pull him away from the fray. At first, he struggled, not wanting to leave, but then he relented and went with her.

The aos sí descended on the monstrous brothers. Swords slashed through the air and clattered off each other. Right away, Bridget could see that Dother and Dain had an advantage with their skill. They swiftly cut through a few others in the company, drawing blood and severing limbs. Some of the women screamed as they were cut down, while others went quietly.

It was a bloodbath.

Bridget and Aedán slipped behind some bushes, not knowing if they were noticed or not. Neither of them knew how to fight like this...this was an ancient skill on display here, and it frightened Bridget. She didn't know what to do, or how she could help. Watching seasoned warriors being murdered before her eyes was enough to hold her still and freeze her mind.

"What are we going to do?" she asked Aedán, who now looked frantically around them.

"We run."

"We can't leave them!" Bridget said, shocked Aedán would even say that.

"Bridget. We are nothing to the Red Knights. These women are dying trying to protect us. Getting ourselves killed only disrespects what they're trying to do!"

"I can't," Bridget cried, feeling the tears down her cheeks. "I won't do it, Aedán."

Dother drove Luí Na'Gréine to her knees and held her down with the edge of one of his great swords. Bridget wanted to run to her, help her, but she didn't have a weapon.

"You have failed," Dother said.

Luí Na'Gréine cried. "I don't see how my death helps you. I am not your enemy."

"Ah, but you are."

"No." Luí Na'Gréine held her hand up to him, her eyes watering up. "I can heal you."

Dother's lips closed around his teeth. His face softened.

"How do you mean? How do I need help, girl?"

Luí Na'Gréine nodded. "You need a wife."

Dother grinned.

"You would please me?" he said.

Bridget couldn't stop herself, shouting, "No!"

Dother's head snapped to the side to look at her and he bared his teeth again. "You!"

And then his face twisted in shock and agony as someone dropped from the Crann Lár. It took a moment for Bridget to realize that it was Seagrass Maggie. Tail flip-flopping behind her, she came falling in, landing on Dother, swinging down her Airgid Hook. The hook went into Dother's back and Maggie pulled him down with her to the ground.

Letting go of the Airgid Hook, Maggie opened her lethal-toothed maw and bit into the back of his neck, tearing and ripping with her jagged teeth. Dother's body spasmed until she grabbed her hook again, freed it from the monster's flesh and re-drove it into his skull.

Dain cried when he turned from the sí woman he felled with his spear, having driven it through her skull. He withdrew the spear.

"You have killed my brother!"

Dain charged through the women, pointing his spear as he ran toward Maggie. Maggie crouched and hissed, holding her silver hook ready and Luí Na'Gréine swung for Dain's legs as he raced by.

Luí Na'Gréine's sword went quickly through Dain's leg, and Dain tumbled forward onto the ground in front of Maggie, his severed leg left behind, pouring blood all over the ground.

Maggie stood up and stomped on Dain's head and the monster's skull smashed under her clawed foot.

Without saying anything, Maggie went over toward the towering trunk of the Crann Lár, stooped and picked up the globular white eye. As she did, Bridget watched her and Aedán followed her out of the bushes.

Luí Na'Gréine and only two others of the aos sí survived. They were trying to catch their breath, their glamour swords already returned to wherever they were made. Luí Na'Gréine kneeled to make sure that Dain wasn't moving. But it was obvious that his crushed skull did him in.

"Dear God, I thought we were all dead," Bridget said.

"We almost were," Luí Na'Gréine replied.

Aedán pointed at the eye in Maggie's hand. "The Eye of Balor?"

Maggie nodded but considered Luí Na'Gréine. "How would yeh like to honor the dead?"

After several hours burying the dead under the roots of the Crann Lár, Luí Na'Gréine led them back toward Lake Dulcinea. Everyone followed her through the hazel trees. It seemed like it took longer to return to the lake than it did to get to the Crann Lár itself. When they finally reached its silver waters, Maggie twisted herself, rolling her arm back, and then pitched the Eye of Balor as far as she could muster. In a subtle arch, it finally splashed out deep into the waters.

Bridget dared put a hand on Maggie's back, just below her neck under her curly red hair. She meant it to comfort her, knowing how much Maggie must be going through.

"So, where are we going next?"

Maggie turned her face to look at her. Bridget looked over the deep curves and scars in Maggie's dark green face that drew out the ancient symbols. She looked at the small node on her forehead, as if she had a third eye herself. Like Balor.

"I don't know," Maggie said. "Carman is supposed to tell me where to find the Third Attainment, but I haven't heard from her in a while. Hopefully soon. I want to go home."

Bridget sighed. "I'm with you there."

"Come. Let us go back to the village," Luí Na'Gréine said, leading the way along the shoreline of Lake Dulcinea.

Aedán, looking worried, pushed through the group and grabbed Maggie's shoulder, stopping all of them.

"Carman?" he said. "Is that the witch you have been talkin' about?"

"Aye," Maggie said. "Why?"

"Well, my father told me about this witch from Athens. Her name was Carman. Her three sons were the Red Knights of Bres. Those demons. They could be her sons. But she's supposed to have died thousands of years ago. Could she back?"

That got Luí Na'Gréine's attention and she and Maggie both looked at Aedán in surprise.

"If it is her, in no way should we be helping her," Aedán said. "Not that bitch."

"Why would she send her sons to kill us...?" Maggie stopped, thinking. Bridget wondered what was on her mind, but it wasn't long before Maggie finished. "She wasn't trying to kill *all* of us."

As they made their way through the hazel trees, back towards the village, Bridget pushed forward to walk with Luí Na'Gréine. She didn't know why, but she trusted Luí Na'Gréine and couldn't get something off her mind. She didn't know who else to approach.

"We shared dreams, Aedán and I," she said. "Do you know how that is possible? I keep thinking I'm still dreaming... and that we're lost in that shared place, but this is very different. It feels...more... *real*. You're one of the fae. You know the answer, yes?"

Luí Na'Gréine continued to walk with purpose, the deaths of her people still visibly on her mind yet she seemed to think on what Bridget said. After a moment, she sighed. "If the two of you shared dreams, it was because those Red Demons bound your mindscapes together in the Hollow. It would be the only way. It's quite difficult to do...it takes a lot of essence and skill. It might be easier of you and Aedán had some sort of past connection, otherwise, I don't know how those demons would have the power to do this."

Bridget shook her head. "There's no connection I'm aware of."

Luí Na'Gréine shrugged. "Then maybe it was their mother."

"But didn't Aedán say that their witch mother was imprisoned for thousands of years?" She knew Luí Na'Gréine wouldn't have all the answers, so she was speaking more to herself than anyone else.

XVI
Subjugation

Elieris disappeared before her and she floated alone in the Deep Dens, everything shimmering around her. Carman rubbed her eyes, thinking something was wrong and then a splitting headache blew up in her head. She cried out, seeing Lugh toss the sling-stone toward her, nailing her in the forehead. Cherry Fox swung her cudgel-staff at her head, knocking his powerful eye out of his head.

She was Balor. Before he could kill the fae girl, she was able to swing about again, hitting him in the chest.

Her chest wretched with an agony not even Carman felt before.

Carman could feel the Eye of Balor growing between her own, centered high on her forehead. Instead of cataract, the eye blazed a bright saffron. And with it she could see Seagrass Maggie killing both Dother and Dain at the base of the Crann Lár with the help of the sí.

She found herself back at St. Albeus monastery, and she held Maggie down, jabbing a sharp dagger into her head, killing her.

Now the Fomorians were tearing her limb from limb, feeding on her. Elieris watched, laughing. She gradually died, hearing his snickering.

The bastard.

Balor's Eye showed her possibilities where her fate might lay. It was Elieris—holding all the strings, *manipulating* her. Rage boiled deep in her veins. She shut Balor's Eye and spread out her dark wings.

Now she saw Elieris' titan form before her in the waters of the Deep Dens. He looked shocked and ignorant of what she'd seen—a good thing. Carman started gesturing in the waters, almost like a full body water dance, and the sprites of the earth began to get agitated. The earth made the floor of the ocean, so when she shook them, the Dens shook. The earth pushed and pulled against each other, cracking, tearing at Elieris' titan form and he screamed as the caverns turned against his body.

Her rage gave her extra strength, making the earth shake around them longer than she thought possible. In all her desire, she wished for the earth to grind and cleave the Fomorian King to pieces, destroying him utterly.

Eventually, however, her power faded, and the sprites calmed. The Fomorians who'd looked for shelter began coming out of their hiding spots, looking about them. The rocks of the caverns had been displaced, some of them falling in slides to the floor. The whole kingdom looked as if it were all but torn down.

At first, she didn't see Elieris, as the shaking ocean floor kicked up a huge cloud of dense, impenetrable flotsam. Carman knew that if he wasn't dead, she was to be punished. Executed. She started swimming out of the Deep Dens, but the fomori were on her, grabbing her arms and legs. They were strong, yanking her back toward the Fomorian court.

By this time, most of the flotsam had settled again and she could see the wounded titan still holding strong in his bed of logarithmic spirals of stone, pale calcite and glinting pink aragonite. The Fomorians dragged her before Elieris, who opened his eyes. His lips curled back.

"Do you really think a witch like you could harm me?" he said.

Carman broke down, her hope completely decayed away.

"You killed my sons!"

Elieris' face softened. "Seagrass Maggie—that serpent girl—*killed* your sons."

"You pulled the strings!" she cried, burning with hatred.

"You are weak. Your sons have fallen, and you let yourself fall with them. Do you not seek glory? Subjugation of the Gaels and their ancient gods?"

"Yes, I do," Carman said. "But I have very little left!"

"You have found Badb's Wings and Balor's Eye. You are so close," Elieris said, "*to greatness.*"

"But I need the Third Attainment and you will not give it to me! Why? Why, you bastard!?"

She waited for his answer, and then it came slow.

"You seek the Golden Wheel," Elieris said.

"Yes. Tell me where it is!"

Elieris manifested a human avatar before her. She'd seen this form of his before. The avatar grabbed her by the throat as the Fomorians holding her let her go and drew back from their king.

"First, you will *suffer* for your *insolence!*"

A Recharge

1

The night was damson on the horizon, the sun going down not too long ago. The breeze was cool, but they were wrapped in a blanket, wrapped around each other, kissing deeply. Making their own heat. Nevan couldn't believe this luck, his mouth engaged with Emera's, and she reacted like she enjoyed it every bit as him.

The ruins of St. Albeus were all around them. She had taken him to this spot and wanted to make out near the standing stone. *It would be romantic*, she'd said. And it was. They seemed to be alone, rubbing each other's bodies, petting heavily. Breathing heavily.

Could this be the night she let him have her? They had made out a few times before, but she reminded him that there were expectations of her, and she couldn't lose the reputation she had worked so hard to garner over her young lifetime. Emera wanted to be a lady, not some girl he had a fling with and got bored with before moving on. Of course, Nevan tried defending himself, saying he'd never leave her. *I've found who I want to be with.*

Emera went for his belt and released the tension on the front of his slacks, pushing her other hand into his warm slacks, grabbing him. Nevan was surprised, diving hungrily into her neck, kissing and sucking on her ears. His body didn't take long, as excited as he was, and he came.

Emera removed her hand, and he looked into her big brown eyes. "I'm sorry. I—"

Emera giggled and put a finger to his lips. "Sh. It's okay."

She kissed him and he grabbed one of her soft breasts through her blouse. After a moment, Emera put her hands on his.

"It's time for me to go. My parents will be worried if I'm much longer," she said.

Nevan sighed and nodded. "Okay. Emera?"

"Hm?"

"Thank you, Luv."

Emera gave him another grin as he rolled over, sitting beside her as she gathered herself up. After a moment he got up and gave her a hand. Once she was on her feet, she was leaving, waving with a smile.

Nevan waved back and then realized that his trousers were still undone. He refastened them and then reached down to grab the blanket. When he looked up, he saw a crack in the side wall of the monastery. At first, he thought someone gazed at him through the crack, unwavering.

It occurred to him that the crack hadn't always been there. Or he had never noticed it before. He walked over to it and looked inside. It was dark, but he could make out something sitting there. Wondering why nobody had seen it and removed the item, he reached in and pulled out to objects. A golden wheel landed on the ground at his feet, but he was able to hold onto a small amulet in the shape of a round flask. It seemed to be made of some stone, almost like bluish marble with bands of gold around it.

He didn't know how or why, but he knew it was called the Nevrall Gléas. Nevan held it up, trying to get more moonlight on it so that he could see the ancient symbols written over its smooth, cold surface.

Nevan looked around for Emera, knowing she'd love to see this thing, but she was already gone. Possibly halfway down the road by now.

Looking at it, the Nevrall Gléas cracked. It happened so quickly, it surprised him, and its black ichor started dripping out of it in strings around his hand.

What the hell was this?

He didn't have time to consider it further. Once the ichor touched his hand, it burned, and he tried shaking it off. The Nevrall Gléas fell from his hands in pieces and was mostly dust before it landed on the ground. The ichor felt as though it were tearing open his pores, pushing into his flesh.

"Help!" He shouted because it was the only thing he could think to do. "Jaysus! Somebody! HELP!"

He shook his hand as hard as he could, even tried grabbing it with his other hand to pull it free, but that made it worse as some of the ichor separated and started tearing into his other hand.

It spread, entering his flesh. He could feel it work through him like a burning poison.

What had he done?

2

Nearby, watching over the site, two druids sat outside a tent, hearing the screaming. Lord Cuinn had called them to watch over the ruins at night, and neither expected anything to really happen. But they couldn't ignore this. They wondered who it could be and decided to check, leaving their tent with gas lanterns and separated to comb the monastery grounds. The screaming continued, so both ended up converging on the old cloister. Near the misplaced standing stone, they saw a bloated man with tallow flesh, mottled with large purple bruises all over his body. Especially around the joints and groin. It looked oddly like Lord Cuinn's son, but they weren't sure. He tore out of its clothes as muscles grew and pushed out his stretched skin. His black hair started falling out, leaving greasy tufts about his skull.

They knew the stories of Bres and had heard tales of the Bresquinn Arrachtaigh. They assumed that this was the creature they were seeing, knowing how close they were to summoning their eldritch god.

The druids, frightened, hid themselves behind the old, broken pillars and waited for the thing to leave. It didn't. It had seen them.

It stalked them through the old stones of the ruins, hunted each one down and caught them. It choked them and broke their bones.

Having killed them, the Bresquinn Arrachtaigh left the two broken druid bodies in the cloister and headed for town.

3

Emera walked down the road, thinking about what she'd hopefully accomplished: recharging the standing stone. She remembered seeing the man in stone age armor the last time, watching her before disappearing as the erotic charge from the stone danced through her. Would she see him again? Nevan might have spilled his seed too soon, but she didn't know if that mattered or not. It was a test, anyway. Though she'd like to check on it and see, she knew that she'd have to wait until Nevan left St. Albeus.

Emera was proud of herself for pleasing Nevan. It was her way of getting rid of the guilt she felt lusting after Vladiv. Doing it made her feel as though she repaid her transgressions against his trust in her, even if he'd never know it himself.

She also thought about going back early in the morning, before anyone else started showing up for work. It would give her time to look for the crack in the wall and the watcher behind it.

Catrina seemed safe. For that, Emera thanked God. To Emera, the feeling she had with Vladiv seemed to resemble the instinct she got when being watched by whatever lurked behind that cloister wall. Emera thought it could be a supernatural energy or power, something that gave them an uncanny presence that stirred the air around them. Sexual energy seemed to boost whatever power was there and she couldn't wait to see if it worked—like a child waiting for Christmas as it came around the corner.

She just didn't understand how it all came together yet.

Part IV
Cathair Aigéin

Kintráth

1

In Fianna's crannog, on the wooden stilts of the Lake Dulcinea village, a few of the aos sí shaman council gathered around with Fianna, Luí Na'Gréine, Maggie, Aedán and Bridget.

Luí Na'Gréine described what had happened with the Red Knights of Bres, the last two sons of Carman. Maggie added that she had already killed the first son on Tech Duinn. Dub. And she was glad of it, knowing that if they had all been together, defeating them would have probably been another story all together. A bad path with a terrible ending.

Léana soon joined them to hear out the story and Maggie warmed to see her spiritual sister. It made her feel more at ease, but inwardly, she wondered how Fianna was taking any of this.

After about an hour and half they'd gone over much of it.

Fianna's face remained still and unreadable.

Maggie wondered if she should tell them that Carman had tricked her into finding the first two Attainments, and Maggie wasn't sure if 'tricked' was the right word. She wanted to cleanse her body of the fae blood to retain her mortality for Cuán, and she allowed herself to ignore what Carman could be capable of. She still remembered the morbid fate of the *púca*, Fiadh. If she were to stop now, would she find her cure? Would she be able to return to Cuán at all?

This terrified her.

Fianna looked at the two aos sí, who survived the encounter with the deadly Dother and Dain, and returned with Luí Na'Gréine, Maggie, and her mortal companions.

"You agree with Luí Na'Gréine and Maggie?" Fianna said, her eyes flitting between them. "This is what has occurred?"

The aos sí warrior women nodded and remained silent.

Fianna took a deep breath and sighed. "Then I decree the story true and Luí Na'Gréine's party will fear no consequences. It was beyond their control, and they did what they had to do."

Maggie sighed in relief.

"Fianna," she said, "I'm not sure what to do. I was seekin' the Eye of Balor in order to cleanse myself of the fae blood. I was made into *this*—" she gestured at her serpentine form, "unjustly and—"

Fianna scowled suddenly. "*Cleanse* your blood?"

Maggie wasn't sure what she'd done. "The Fomorians. They changed me, taking my human body and tainted it with serpent's blood, turning me into this...*monster*."

Fianna looked shocked at her. "Twisted you into *this monster*? They twisted *your soul*? Made you do *dark things*?"

"Well...I'm talkin' about this...body. *Look* at me!"

Fianna shot to her feet, looking disgusted. "How *dare* you, Lass!"

Something clicked in Maggie's head and now she understood why Fianna was disgusted with her. Some women in the room had horns, others had hooved feet and all of them had long, pointed ears. Maggie insulted the fae by calling their blood tainted, the blood that affected them all and made them all who they were. Maggie didn't mean it that way, but she could see how it would be disgraceful.

"I didn't mean—"

"Get *out!* This instant!"

Léana had already got to her feet, pulling Maggie out of the crannog by the arm. "What do you think you're doing?"

Maggie placed her hands over her face. "I didn't mean to say it like that. I'm just...*lost*, Léana."

Léana sighed, still holding her arm, pulling her down the board-walk away from the nearest crannog. "You've offended her. Any help you might have gotten from her, you've now destroyed."

Maggie stared at the docile lake waters around them.

"There's nothin' I can do?"

"We better be off soon. The aos sí—well, the fae in general—are easily insulted. When they have been offended, you never know what they might do."

"Great."

Léana smiled. "But...Luckily, you have your *anam chara*."

Maggie looked at her, wondering what Léana could be thinking. "I'm not followin'."

Léana started walking down the boardwalk toward the shoreline. Maggie followed her, wanting to know what Léana wasn't saying.

"Don't make me throttle you, Léana."

"Well, while you were away looking for Balor's Eye, I took the time to question Fianna to learn about reversing contracts."

"Reversing contracts? Can you do that?"

Léana nodded. "Whatever has been done to you can be reversed along the proper *kintráth*—or...road, so long as the contract is reversed. It's not a cleansing, so much as it's about removing what has been done."

"There's a difference? And what the hell is a kintráth?"

Léana turned back to her, saying, "Stay here. I don't want to upset the aos sí more than we already have. I will gather the other travelers and then we'll set off for Cathair Aigéin. When we're there, I'll explain it all more to you."

Maggie didn't like to wait, but she understood.

"Aye. A'right. I'll be waitin' 'ere."

2

A few days later they were standing on the shorelines, overlook-ing the shimmering turquoise waters of the Eternal Sea. They had to climb down from cliffs. The heat almost felt tropical here, and they were all sweating copiously. They had reached the waters by midday and Léana left them on the shores, diving into the waters after reshaping her legs into her powerful tail. She was gone maybe another hour and after returning, she reformed her legs.

Maggie, Bridget and Aedán gathered around her.

Léana turned her fist over and unwrapped her fingers, revealing two white pearls.

"What are these for?" Aedán said.

"Cathair Aigéin is the city of the merrows," Léana said.

Aedán still looked confused, and Maggie watched Bridget tap him in the arm, saying, "It's *under* the Eternal Sea."

Léana grinned. "Bridget understands. Maggie and I are accustomed to breathing the waters. You two will drown, unless, of course, you have some help."

Léana grabbed one pearl and pressed it against Bridget's chest just above her breasts. The pearl seemed to sink into her skin and disappear within Bridget.

"How do you feel?"

"I can't feel anything," Bridget said.

"Good. These pearls are sea charms, enabling you to breathe the waters as we do," Léana said to Aedán, who looked back at her with some concern. "You will also be able to hear Maggie and I speaking through the Hollow. You may be able to do so as well, so long as you think in short communications and give some time between each projection."

Bridget touched Aedán's hand. "It's okay."

Aedán nodded and Léana pushed a pearl into his chest next.

Léana then looked at Maggie, who watched all of this with great interest. She thought it would be great to give one of those to Cuán so that he could see the ocean through her eyes. It would be romantic. Magical. She would have to remember to ask Léana where to find them later before they returned to Ireland.

"Maggie. They will breathe after some adjustments when they're in the water. They'll be able to withstand the pressures as we do as we go deeper, but they won't have the strength to swim as we do. They won't have the speed or endurance to make the nine waves. We'll have to hold onto them."

Maggie nodded. "Aye. It makes sense. I'll hold onto Aedán."

They all walked into the waters, the waves lapping at their legs, almost strong enough to tug them out to sea already. Maggie held Aedán's hand. Léana held Bridget's.

"On three," Bridget said, nodding.

Maggie could tell that the two of them were a little nervous.

"Don't worry. We have you," Maggie told them.

They waded out farther. Léana's legs shifted back into a tail and then she drew Bridget under. Maggie looked at Aedán, nodded and then they both dove in. Maggie's free arm, legs and tail started sweeping through the waters, propelling them forward. Holding onto Aedán dragged her down a little, but with her strong tail, she was able to get them up to a good speed so that she didn't lose Léana.

It felt good to be back in her environment. Soaring through the azure depths, feeling her body moving through the fluidic pressures that wrapped around her like being in a womb again—a euphoric pleasure, almost like the headiness one gets when inhaling their lover's breath while coupled.

They seemed to be diving deeper and deeper. On occasion, she would look back at Aedán to make sure he still lived but he would look back at her with wide-open eyes. At first, he seemed to spasm, almost as if he had difficulty breathing in liquid. It didn't last long as he grew accustomed to it and then he seemed to be enjoying the dive.

They swam past the corals and island of Tír na nÓg into the deep. They passed large humpback whales and went through a school of glistening tuna. The deeper they went, the fewer animals they came across, though they did find a field of glowing jellyfish that Léana was smart enough to stay clear of.

In the oceans of the physical world, the deeper you went, the darker it got. Light did not penetrate past a hundred meters—a little over a half mile—but in the Otherworld, the waters themselves seemed to glow.

After a few hours of diving, they came across a leviathan rock of caves and corals, floating like a sunken iceberg. There were large disc-shaped and globular-shaped polyps surrounded by colorful tentacles, which connected to the other surrounding polyps or the strange, floating steel-blue stone that they grew upon. Between the tentacles there were cracks and crevices, or other arched entryways.

We're here. Cathair Aigéin, Léana said through the Hollow into Maggie's mind. Léana slowed, and they gathered together to look at it, once in a while seeing figures move about the colorful, organic city.

It's gorgeous, Bridget said.

Maggie thought that if she had ever needed to leave Cuán or her life on the land, this is where she would seek a home. She didn't know why, but it spoke to her in ways that awakened how much she loved the sea and how powerful it made her feel.

Will we be safe 'ere? Maggie said.

Léana shrugged. *We should be. While the merrow can be vicious, like the aos sí, they have a code of honor.*

That was enough for Maggie. *Then we follow you.*

Léana nodded and started swimming forward, holding Bridget in tow as they made their way closer to the floating coral city.

The only thing to be aware of is the tentacles. Stay clear of them. Many of them have stinging cells that would kill most, Léana said.

They swam carefully by the stubby, languidly fluttering tentacles and made their way towards the hidden arches of Cathair Aigéin. Maggie could see the hairy white cells dangling from the tentacles, reminding her of the web-like tongues of the brine vampyres she met in Séala Bán—a village north of Kilkee. She remembered how the cells penetrated into her flesh like branching roots, injecting venom that burned like fire.

Entering the tunnels, they found the walls lined with bioluminescent algae that seemed to be worked into the stone like a splotchy mosaic of crystalline marble.

I can't get over how shockingly beautiful this is, Bridget said. *But there's also an ominous feeling here. Like everything here is watching you. Even the walls.*

Léana gestured with her hand across her vision before her. *It's possible. The whole city is living.*

They continued in through the tunnels. Léana, meanwhile, explained *croí* and the *kintráth*: croí *is the basic essence of the Primordial itself. The* fata *essence of the fae is constructed from it at its most microscopic level, allowing the fae to manipulate* croí *itself.* Croí *is also the lifeblood of the Primordial and weaves throughout every part of Creation. It's not the life-force of mortals, but the energy of Creation itself. With it, the cosmos is created, driven along the* kintráth, *and will eventually be destroyed in order to be recreated into something else.*

Maggie contemplated this.

So, when you say kintráth, *you are saying it's 'our progression along our own timelines of fate'? It's our destiny.*

Léana stopped and looked back at her. She and Maggie were still clasping Bridget and Aedán's hands, keeping them close. They merely watched Maggie and Léana in wonder.

Aye. Personal threads of fate that weave through time, woven by fata. *Kintráth are threads only woven for the Rowan. Mortal threads are woven by their Vitality Essence, connecting them with life and their destinies but ultimately have an ending. Though mortal humans do not have the ability to shift their fate through magic like the fae, they can still do so by making decisions on their journey through life,* Léana said.

Maggie thought she understood. *Mortals do not have a* kintráth. *So, I don't have one. I'm only...touched.* A Demidian. Her heart sank, but then she noticed that Léana shook her head.

The Demidians have been touched and when they are, a kintráth is also forged for them through their blood.

Maggie looked at her fae-sister's eyes. You're suggesting I can move along my own kintráth and have my contract annulled?

Léana put her free hand on Maggie's shoulder. And I'm hoping the merrow themselves know how to travel the kintráth through the Hollow. Not many know how to do this, but the merrow have some of the most ancient fae in the world. Maybe they will show us how... for a price.

Why hadn't Maggie thought of that? Of course, they would ask for a contract, a barter of conditions, significance or expense. But what did she have to give? Maggie didn't have anything save the Airgid Hook Léana gifted to her. And she would never sell the mortals beside them, knowing that she could never be that cruel.

Maggie hated the feeling of letting others have some power over her, even if the power is in the act of the negotiations. Deals were the most dangerous. If one didn't have the wit, the world could make a slave of them without ever realizing it. Doubly true in the fae worlds.

The Hidden Tomb

1

Emera's mother shook her awake, looking concerned. She bit her lip like she did when she was afraid her da had come home with a little too much booze in him. Coming out of her sleep was like climbing out of quick-drying cement.

"What is it, ma? I'm tired and—"

"I believe Nevan Ó Cuinn has died last night."

Emera was stunned, and a coldness washed over her chest.

Not Nevan, please.

"Are you sure you're not confusing—?" But she saw it in her ma's eyes.

"I 'eard it right away this morning. I went to the well, and we saw the wagon go by. They had a cloth over a couple men. Rumors are going about that Nevan and a friend of his perished last night. I mean, who else could it be if they're sayin' that? Why would people lie?"

"Perished! You make it sound as if they 'just died'."

Her ma clapped a hand to her mouth. "I believe they were murdered."

Emera had been with Nevan the night before. If she weren't in such a hurry to flee her guilt—using Nevan to charge the standing stone—she might have walked with him and then...

...And then you could be dead, too. But who knows what really happened?

Surely, her ma must have gotten some wrong information. Emera couldn't even believe that Nevan could be dead. No, she wasn't going to believe it until she saw it for herself.

Emera crawled out of her bed and started pulling her nightgown off from around her head.

"I have to go," she said.

"Of course," her ma replied. "Let me know if I can help you in any way."

Emera looked at her ma and saw her tears.

"Ma. I'll be okay."

Her ma shook her head. "No, you're not. It just hasn't hit you yet."

2

The ruins of the 7th century monastery, St. Albeus, stood there in the grassy green valley of the countryside in the early morning sunlight. The early morning sun rose behind her, making the ruins glow.

Emera ran down the road, holding up her skirts, and passed over fields, seeing many of the diggers coming to work early. She asked one of them why they were there so early, and he told her that Doctor Alastar Macguire had sent for them. Something had happened, and he wanted to speak with them.

As others gathered around, Emera recognized *Gardaí*—the Irish police—there as well. They were letting people gather around. Doctor Macguire himself stood before them with the Gardaí, telling the workers to hurry and gather as quietly as possible.

Emera wanted to hear what the doctor said, but she also wanted to know about the standing stone. Had her encounter with Nevan the night before charged them? And what would she do if they were? Would the wall be 'opened' to her so that she could see beyond them?

Her mouth dropped open.

The wall.

What if after she left Nevan there, the crack opened? What if what they did the night before caused his death?

Emera's hands started shaking.

"Please quiet down!" Doctor Macguire shouted. "I called you all here early because a couple of townsfolk were found dead last night here at the monastery. None of our workers, I'm glad to say, but the Garda have questions for all of you. Go ahead and line up and the Garda will gather you into the tent, so they can ask you a few questions in private. Once they're done, we'll get back to work, digging. You all understand?"

A few diggers called out. Emera heard one of them clearly: "I heard it was Lord Cuinn's son, Nevan. Any truth to that, boss?"

When others heard this, the diggers started a commotion, but Doctor Macguire was on it, gesturing with his hands to bring it down. "Don't be jumping to any conclusions. The Garda aren't saying who it is yet, and they want to keep it that way for the time being. Please now. You all have some patience and work with these Gardai so they can do their jobs and we can get back to work."

Emera snuck away, making her way around to the cloister and around to the standing stone. She went to the wall, seeing the cracks again. There were more of them, reaching along the whole of the wall like a spiderweb. As she walked past the stone, she let her fingertips brush its cool surface. Her body felt the erotic energies discover all the right places, stirring up her heart and the tingles. Had she held on for a moment longer, she was sure she'd have another orgasm.

However, a gold glint caught her eye, and she looked down, seeing a gold medallion there. It had a chain and the medallion itself was shaped like an old chariot wheel. She stooped to pick it up and looked at her carefully. When she looked back down to see if anything else remained, she saw the broken pieces of some blue stone. Emera crouched, leaning over her knees, and picked up some of the pieces. There were engravings and paint on some of the pieces, though most of it had turned to dust so that it'd be impossible to read. It didn't look modern, either.

Without thinking about it, Emera put the medallion around her neck, feeling its weight lay against her chest, and put her hands on the rim of the cracks on the wall. The hole at its center breathed cold air and she could smell something foul in it.

What could this be? What about the standing stone opened this crack in the wall? And why? What was its purpose?

Emera grabbed the stone around the black hole, and she found that the pieces crumbled easily. She started pulling on the rock, but before the rocks fell to the ground, they somehow faded into nothing as if they never existed. Awed by this, Emera's curiosity consumed her, and she continued pulling at the stones, making the hole bigger until she knew she had something big enough to crawl into.

It was as if it were opening itself to her, beckoning her forward.

Creepy, yet mysterious and...*tantalizing*.

Emera raised a knee and set it on the stones of the wall and pushed herself into it. Crawling on her hands and legs, she pushed forward into the darkness. The light got smaller and smaller behind her.

Didn't this wall go into the refectory? She seemed to be submerging herself into a deep cave rather than through a refectory wall... *Magic*, Emera thought. *This is all magic.*

Maybe demonic magic. That thought scared her. What if she made her way into the perilous den of some demonic figure? Maybe this is what Vladiv was looking for? Was the Captain of the *Madeline Leigh* searching for a doorway to Hell?

Don't be ridiculous, she told herself.

It was too late, though. It was now at the back of her mind, like a goblin clawing at the back door of her hovel, whispering to let it back in.

Before she knew it, she crawled into a larger chamber. There were lit torches all round her. At her knees, an old inscription had been engraved into the stone floor:

Εδώ βρίσκεται ο Κάρμαν
*A thyng of unnatyral evyl. A dymon of
womnh'd. It shakes its mylky brests and
scratchys thee walls wyth its clahs late
into thee nyte.*

From her amateur studies in archaeology and world myth and history, she knew the first part was Greek, but she couldn't read it. On the opposite wall of the chamber, Emera could see a naked woman splayed out on her back over a short, flat stone like an altar. There were lit candles around her body. And chains.

What was this woman doing here?

Emera started to walk over to it, taking it slow, trying to make out more of it as she got closer.

The woman had bird wings attached to her shoulder blades. She had something viscous and bulbous on her forehead. A dagger sat fully into her chest, right where her heart would usually be, and black ichor dripping from the wound, pooling around the altar on the floor.

Emera, not sure where she got her courage, pushed the woman's dark hair aside and saw what was on her face. It moved and Emera screamed, backing away. The body jerked.

And then all at once the woman was a mangled mess on the floor, as if hacked to pieces and left on the ground to rot. Whatever vision of the woman that was there was now gone, replaced by a rotting pile of hair, feathers and flesh.

Afraid now for her life, Emera ran back to the tunnel that led her to this chamber and crawled back into it. Going as fast as she could, she sprawled until she saw the light again and let herself fall onto the grass outside. Trying to catch her breath, she crab-walked backwards away from the cracking hole in the refectory, expecting that horrible bird-witch to come after her, jumping at her from the darkness, even though she'd been mangled.

But nothing came.

"Emera?"

Emera screamed, not expecting to hear anyone.

It was Doctor Macguire. After a startled moment, he held out a hand.

"I'm sorry. I didn't mean to scare you. Did you fall?"

Emera sighed and took his hand. He pulled her to her feet.

"No. I was just looking at this hole…"

Only when she looked back at the wall, the hole had disappeared. Doctor Macguire looked where her gaze rested and then gaped back at her with concern. "Are you feeling okay? Perhaps the news of what happened has brought you to a weakened state? Maybe you should go home for the day. Come back tomorrow."

Emera nodded. "Perhaps you're right. Before I go, I wonder, do you know any legends around the area about a bird woman from Greece?"

Doctor Macguire looked at her funny.

"I don't know about bird woman. But there's the legend of Carman. She was from Athens, if I remember correctly. She tried to conquer Ireland with her three sons. Lugh and his small band of witches and bards were able to stop them, however. Why?"

"Are they associated with these parts?"

Doctor Macguire shook his head. "Further north, I believe."

Emera wiped her brow.

"Go home, Emera. Get some rest," Doctor Macguire said.

Emera sighed again and nodded. "Aye. A'right, Doctor Macguire. I will."

3

Emera walked down the road. The day had already been so heavy, and she could feel the tears coming. Her chest heaved, and she sobbed, hating it all the while.

Was Nevan really dead?

Had he gone into that chamber without her?

Was she at fault?

Black magic, she thought. *Dark sorcery.* She was certain. Somehow, she'd done something and Nevan might have paid for it. If that were true, she would never be able to forgive herself again. She damned her ignorance. Hated herself for thinking that wanting to know more was enough of a reason to tempt the fates. Tempt... dare she *think* it*?...God?*

Now frightened of the standing stone and the ruins, she realized that what she needed to do was find Nevan and make sure that he was okay.

And if he isn't?

Emera's chest beat with an agony she had never felt before, thinking *I'll just die, if that's the case; die and suffer for it.*

This Head

1

In the Hollow, the misplaced standing stone in the St. Albeus cloister, began to project a well-muscled man with long black hair, a golden torc around his neck and scars along his face. He held a spear with divine beads made from bone, hanging on leather straps around the base of the spearhead.

With the energy left in the bluestone, Cridhinbheal's ghost now had power to free himself from the stone itself.

He grinned.

It is now time to find his companions. *In the name of Lugh.*

And then the energy faded. His disappointment burdened him as his projection lost its power.

It wasn't enough.

2

He closed his large, indigo window curtains against the morning sun, not feeling like breakfast. Lord Grady Ó Cuinn's grief laid heavy on him, and the sunlight felt like a hellish radiance, making him feel sickened. He also closed his study doors and then planted himself behind his immaculate desk.

In his locked drawers, there were papers and logs of his businesses and his works within the Order of Bres. The Order had been passed down from father to son for more generations than he knew, and his dream was to pass it all to his son, Nevan, when he could no longer fit for the job of High Priest.

Once the lad grew up, figured out who he was making himself to be, after he became more responsible—all those things little boys were supposed to do to grow up and become men.

Grady wept. Of course, he worried about losing his children. All parents at some point reluctantly imagined their child's death and pondered it in horror, hoping at the core of their soul that they would never have to endure it. Some were lucky. Others weren't.

Grady had seen what the Bresquinn Arrachtaigh had done to the two druids he'd directed to watch the dig at St. Albeus. So, when it came into his home and sat in his office without saying anything, he knew this was bad.

Grady was not only mourning, but he was terrified.

His hands shook, trying to pour himself a whiskey into a glass on his desk in front of him.

The thing that his son turned into—a tallow, morbid-looking giant—stared at him, frowning. His greasy hair had mostly fallen out, leaving only scattered tufts behind, and pustulant cysts had grown and consumed the poor kid's head. His yellowed eyes languidly watched Grady. The pupils narrowed, never leaving him.

Grady had tried to talk to his 'son', but after some effort, he realized that Nevan was no longer there. The creature was a living shell for some demon that inhabited him. Grady simply didn't know what to do.

"Who are you? Do you come to stop me from calling Bres from his *Codail*? His Sleep?"

The monster said nothing.

Grady winced, taking in more of this creature's rotten smell. "Why won't you speak?"

The Bresquinn Arrachtaigh peeled back his lips, showing his large, flat teeth.

Grady thought about calling in his druids, have them shoot the creature down right there. Would bullets harm the thing? He wondered. He'd heard of his family curse before and knew that Lugh once created a poison for Bres, which had been like landmines hiding in the area for their family since the beginning. A tale or two had been spoken in whispered voices about the family becoming monsters.

The stories he'd heard were so old, Grady hadn't believed he would see it happen to his own son.

"Please. I beg you. Give him back to me," he said, even though he knew it was hopeless.

The creature smelled of decaying flesh. The sharp odor twisted in his gut.

"If you've come here to kill me, do it! You bastard!"

At that, the creature languidly leaned toward him, its eyes rolling in its skull with no agenda.

"Why didn't you tell me, Father, how powerful we could become? Why didn't you show me the way?"

"Nevan? No, you're tricking me. Nevan is dead," Grady said.

The Bresquinn Arrachtaigh cocked his head. "Am I, Father? I am still finding my way through this new head. It shows me things. Things from the past. Dark things. They puzzle me. But do I do it to trick you?"

Could his son still be in there? He thought his own father had told him that when the Lugh's poison worked in the veins, it took over the body, banishing the soul to the sky storms with the other *sluagh*. If there was a chance his son was still in there, then he had to use it. If not, the Arrachtaigh would kill him. He was sure of it.

"Nevan! By the gods, I'm happy you're still in there. I didn't know you could survive the process. I wouldn't wish the Bresquinn Arrachtaigh on anyone! You do believe me, don't you?"

The Bresquinn Arrachtaigh licked his lips, his eyes rolling back in his head for a moment. "I don't know what to believe. I see you as you are, Father. I see you when you were fifteen. You hated your mam and when she fell ill, you went into her room into the night, and you got her to swallow enough pills to stop her breathing. When the sun came up, nobody even guessed at what happened. At least you got her water to *slick her throat*."

Grady hadn't thought about that for a long time. As the High Priest of the Order of Bres, he'd had to do things for the good of the Order. Some of them heinous. He knew it. But matricide. That was purely personal. Oh, how he hated her bickering and of her ridiculous demands. And his cowardly father never put the woman in her place. Grady had learned a valuable lesson from it. *If you wanted others to obey you, you had to show them you could be a lion.*

But hearing this from his morbid son made him feel ashamed, and he hated it. He found his rage to hide his humiliation. He jutted a finger at what used to be his son.

"You know nothing! I had to do what I had to do," he shouted.

The Bresquinn Arrachtaigh grinned. "Did you now, Father?"

"STOP CALLING ME THAT!" Shouting this burned at his throat and he realized that losing his temper wasn't going to help him here.

"And then there's Aedán Deasún's father. You murdered him so you could keep Aedán close for the return of the Red God."

Grady sighed, holding his head.

The Bresquinn Arrachtaigh suddenly reached over and grabbed him, pulling him close. Grady couldn't believe the size of his son. His large hands could cover his head, crushing his skull to a pulp without much effort.

The creature didn't do that, though. Instead, it leaned forward and bit into his shoulder, tearing his arm from its socket joint. The Bresquinn Arrachtaigh spat the arm aside and shoved his father back onto the floor.

Grady cried out, not believing the pain and was surprised when he landed on the hardwood floor behind him.

Grady knew he was in trouble, and he could see no way to save himself. "Don't do this, Nevan! I beg you!"

"I thought I was nothing but a trick, Father?" The Bresquinn Arrachtaigh leaned over him, holding up a fist over his shoulder.

Feeling sick, Grady saw his shoulder bleeding out. He was going to die soon. He wished he had someone to relay a message to his council, telling them that they must go on, but there wasn't hope of that.

Would his plans fail to come to fruition now?

He had no idea.

"Have mercy on me, Nevan. I am a... a *foolish* man."

"Yes. A foolish man," the Arrachtaigh said, and brought down his fist hard onto Grady's head. Grady felt the impact for less than a second.

3

Climbing the stairs of the Ó Cuinn estate home, Emera wiped her watery eyes and took a deep breath. She knocked on the door and waited a moment. Emera couldn't hear anything, wondering why nobody answered. She tried again.

Still nothing.

Emera, wanting to know what happened with Nevan, trying the doorknob and found it unlocked. She decided to slip in.

"Hello? Hello! I've been knocking!"

With nobody answering, she didn't like it. Were they trying to hide something from her? Upset, she decided to walk through the house, looking for someone to answer her.

Then she heard a scream, coming from Lord Ó Cuinn's study. Emera raced over to it and threw open the doors, seeing a giant man with buttery yellow skin and tufts of black hair. The giant held his fist up above Lord Ó Cuinn, who laid on the floor, his shoulder bleeding out into a large pool around them.

"Yes. A stupid, foolish man," the creature said—its voice deep and controlled.

The monster brought his fist down, and with such force, Lord Ó Cuinn's head disappeared into a fractured mush.

Lord Ó Cuinn's arm sat on the floor near the wall. It dripped blood onto the floor as well. When Emera took in the whole gruesome scene, she felt like she'd fallen and plunged into icy water. She screamed, and the Arrachtaigh turned around to look at her.

It was Nevan, she thought. Sure, the deformed head had large, pussy cysts and his body was swollen with muscle and fluids that turned his skin sickly, but through all of that, she could still see her dear Nevan Ó Cuinn.

"What have you done?" she said.

The creature's hands dripped with blood and brain matter. He just looked at her for a moment.

"Nevan. Please. What happened to you?"

She thought about the monstrous witch in the ruins. Could the witch have done this? But she wasn't sure. Emera could see her cursing Nevan, transforming him into this thing. Could this be what happened when he had found the witch in her tomb?

"I know you."

"Aye. You know me, Nevan." Emera tried not to cry, overwhelmed by everything. What was going to happen now? Was her life over? "Can we talk? Please."

Nevan cocked his head, his eyes rolling over her. "I know you. This head. I'm still trying to understand what it shows me. Even reconcile some of them."

"What does it show you?" Emera said.

Nevan's eyes shot to her, and he lifted a finger, pointing it at her. "I see the urge between your legs for another. A Captain."

Emera was shocked. "I've no such—"

"Don't lie to me," Nevan said, growling. "The Bresquinn sees everything."

Emera didn't understand any of it. Somehow Nevan knew. Could the witch have told him? She didn't know. The only thing that was real for her now, however, was how threatening Nevan looked as he started moving toward her.

4

Through the Hollow, Etna stood back and watched as the Bresquinn Arrachtaigh smashed Lord Ó Cuinn's head into a pulp on the floor.

She had felt the disturbance once the Lord's son, Nevan, transformed, and the part of her that she shared with Carman, knew what happened. Etna stepped into the Hollow and followed the vibrations to where the Arrachtaigh faced his father.

Etna saw the son's girlfriend enter the estate home, looking for someone to help her. From what Doctor Macquire had told Etna, Emera had been a hard worker at the dig site, helping cover many functions. She didn't care to see what the Arrachtaigh would do to her, leaving the girl screaming as she started running from the study—the girl was surely dead, and Etna could do nothing for her.

No, instead, Etna decided things were getting out of hand. With Lord Cuinn's death, the Order of Bres had failed, only letting loose a monster to destroy what was left. And where had Carman gone? Etna figured that Carman would be psychically aware of what was happening, knowing that being here would be dangerous. That cowardly witch hid elsewhere.

There wasn't a point in any of this anymore. Carman didn't need her. The Order didn't need her.

She needed to get the hell away from this before she ended up dead, too. But if she wasn't careful about it, Carman would make a mess of things. Etna needed to make sure that Carman wasn't going to look for her. The trouble was, Etna didn't know Carman's thoughts and couldn't determine her true intentions. Carman said she wanted the Order to succeed, but Etna had her doubts.

Reaching out into the Hollow, she followed her mystical connection to Carman. It drew her to the ocean and down into its dark depths. Surprised, Etna found her in the Deep Dens, in a prison of sorts, weeping.

Etna reached into Carman's mind for information. She saw how Carman manipulated a girl with serpent's blood, in the Otherworld, to locate the Three Attainments. *Seagrass Maggie*. The serpent girl had been successful with two of the Attainments, each transforming Carman, giving her more power. But when she challenged the Fomorian King for the Third Attainment and the death of her three sons, Elieris had the Fomorians beat her to inches of her life and imprisoned once they decided they were done.

Etna found some gratification—even delight—in knowing how the witch suffered.

But this was a good thing, Etna thought. Etna could escape, knowing that Carman was too distracted to care about her right now.

Leaving Carman and the Hollow, Etna woke up in her own bed, crawled out of it and started packing. She didn't know where she'd go, but she knew deep down that Hell would have to freeze over and become ice-cream before she returned to Wexford.

She caught a coach to the train station, and she bought her first ticket out of there: Galway. Would that be far enough? Etna didn't know, but she held on tight to that ticket, begging the gods to bless her journey from the horrors she left behind.

A part of her started feeling guilty for not helping Nevan's girlfriend, Emera. But could she really do anything? Probably not. She'd only get herself killed, too. It was better this way. With Carman in a Fomorian prison, hopefully forever, Etna thought maybe the rest of her life could be good.

Boarding the train, she didn't even look out at the countryside one last time. She shut the curtains and tried resting her head.

The Cloch Chroí

1

Somewhere deep within Cathair Aigéin, they came across a star-shaped chamber with tunnels leading off at all of its points. As with the tunnels, the walls of the chamber seemed splattered with bioluminescent algae, lighting the chamber.

Léana and Maggie let go of Aedán and Bridget's hands. Aedán looked about, full of awe and couldn't help feeling unsettled in such an alien place. He watched as Léana turned to all of them.

Maggie. Come with me. You two will wait for us. Be sure to stay in this chamber. Do not stray, she said.

Aedán took Bridget's hand and squeezed, and he could see that it made Bridget feel a little less wary.

We'll be here, he said.

Léana started for another tunnel. Maggie waved at them and then swam after Léana to keep up with her. Once they were gone, Aedán felt less certain, though he saw the smile on Bridget's face.

Why are you smiling? he said.

Because, look *where we are. We dreamed together in a Lost Forest, traveled from Tech Duinn to Tír na nÓg. And now we are here. Deep under water...in a fantastical city. It's the stuff you only read about in myth,* Bridget said.

We made love for the first time in our dreams together, Aedán said, recalling some of it with pleasure.

We did. Bridget looked at him and he swam up to her, pressing his body into hers as they floated in the center of the star chamber. They wrapped their arms around each other and Aedán was glad that they were able to get past his previous behavior.

He felt very guilty about being a part of the Order of Bres. He hoped she would understand what had to happen when they returned to Ireland. She was all that mattered to him, but he also knew that Lord Cuinn's mission was also important for the Order and the future of Ireland. Inside, it made him feel a little divided. Should he protect what they had for each other, betraying his father's trust for love? Or should he follow through with his father's mission, possibly betraying Bridget's trust?

Aedán didn't know. But he was raised with Lord Cuinn's insistence that the mission became everything. The Order must be successful to end England's hold on Ireland and to set the Irish people free. Maybe it was more important than Aedán's selfish needs.

He grabbed the shell inside his pocket, wanting to feel its reality, thinking about how he got there. What it all meant for him.

And then Aedán kissed Bridget, happy and hungry for her.

2

As they went down the tunnels, Léana started filling Maggie in.

There is a council of shamans amongst the merrow. They go into this state of Codail and become one with each other. Combining their fata essences, they become a singular entity with enough power to reach out into the Hollow anywhere in the world and bring back sacred knowledge with them. By joining the circle, you can reach out yourself for the answers you need. There is, however, one danger. If you reach out into the Hollow, going beyond the Merrow's Call, the power of it has the ability to strip you of your essences and shred them out into the cosmos.

It is very dangerous, Maggie. So, this is where you choose now whether stripping yourself of the fae-blood is worth the inherent dangers.

They came across a giant central chamber. Floating in the middle was a colossal standing stone. It looked like a hundred merrow—with their red tendril like *cohuleen druith* draping about their heads—joined hands around it, eyes closed, all singing like the whales into the cosmos. All joined in hands and song together, reaching into the psychic atmosphere.

This is the Heart of Cathair Aigéin, Léana said, holding back near the arched entrance tunnel.

Maggie noticed, turning around to look at her fae sister.

Why have yeh stopped? Maggie said.

Léana pointed toward the circle of shamans. Maggie looked and saw the fish-tailed creatures—some looking like mermaids, others looking much like the fomori in all their ugliness—as they held hands, heads rolled back, circling the sacred Heart Stone.

I can't do this. It must be you. You must now make your choice. Do you go back to Cuán safely and live as much of his life with him as you possibly can? Or do you dare reach out into the Hollow on the Merrow's Call for your answers?

Maggie mentally sighed and remembered how Cuán looked on his death bed as she sat there on the edge of his bed, helpless and weeping. A black cat watching all. She could see Cuán dying and how she would live afterwards, her heartache reverberating forever. And what was worse? Forgetting him as time went on. The most despairing idea she could think of. Forgetting the very person who made her feel alive.

There really wasn't a choice for her.

Maggie left Léana at the arched tunnel entrance and swam toward the merrow's circle. She slipped between two of them and undid their hands with hers, joining it. The circle expanded slightly, and she felt the merrow's song fill her. Maggie could feel it in every bone in her body, so mimicking it was the easiest thing she'd ever done.

Once she joined the Merrow's Call, she projected out into the Hollow with such power and finesse, she found moving through the worlds swiftly. She could travel much faster though the minds of men and make her own doorways through the multiple netherworlds that existed beyond Ireland itself.

Focus, she told herself. *What are you looking for?*

And don't reach beyond the Merrow's Call.

Maggie could see the yellow and green energies of the Primordial enter the world, filling it with water and earth. From the waters, it started life, which progressed over the land—

Too far back. Much too far…

Focus.

Maggie could see the energies and realized that it was *croí*—the heart of creation itself. As creation formed, time began. As living entities were created, they formed their own lines of fate through time and creation. First amongst them were the fae, and their *kintráth* were formed from these Primordial energies, linking them strongly with the cosmos itself. If the stars changed, so did the fae. With this essence—*fata*—binding their souls, they could manipulate *croí* into the *Eagla*—the Eeries.

Maggie reached out and touched it and she suddenly started to realize how it all worked. The ancient secrets of how *croí* formed the mystical forces. She knew that she didn't have the *fata* to work the purest magics, but there were Accordances that she found that she could use. Reformed from the water elements, she was connected with the waters in ways no human would ever understand. Not just physically, but spiritually and magically.

She wanted to go farther, but the farther she went, she could hear the Merrow's Calling fading away. At the seams of this Calling, she could see a serpent crawling around the magical ether. She was a dark blue with scales, tentacles and large teeth. She had black hair that fell in tendrils and giant claws for hands and feet. Barnacles clung to her body and her long, lashing tail had three points. Along her massive body, from her head to the tips of her tail, were spiked purplish fins, some of them ragged and torn, giving away how ancient she was.

Nathaira. The Queen of the Depths. Maggie could feel her blood boiling inside her now.

I WILL COME, Nathaira said. Her voice pounded inside Maggie's head, filling her with dread. YOU WILL BE MY VESSEL.

Terrified, not wanting to risk losing herself, she pulled back from the edges of the Merrow's Call. Maggie hadn't come here to learn the Accordances of the Maris Demidian—and she would be damned if she would get closer to Nathaira herself to do so—but to find a way to purify her blood from the fae essences. From Nathaira's blood.

Focus on what you came for, she told herself.

Yes. *Cuán.*

But then she is within her own body, being forced away from the merrow's circle. Merrow, not connected by the circle, grabbed her arms, yanking her toward an arched tunnel. The sudden break from the Hollow left her with a headache and when she realized what happened, the merrows were forcing her up against the wall of the giant chamber of the Heart Stone.

How dare you join the Sacred Call? one shouted into her head. For this blasphemy, you will be our chum.

No, please, Maggie shouted back. *I only seek answers. I don't mean any harm.*

The other merrow, her face leaning in so close to Maggie's own, bared her teeth and her big, wild eyes bore into her. *We said... you're CHUM.*

Wait!

It was Léana, swimming up from behind the other merrow.

This girl, Maggie, is with me, she said. Do not harm her. She has been given the privilege to join the circle by Coiréil Réalta, your queen. We didn't have time to let the council know. Please. I have Coiréil's seal.

The merrow turned to look at Léana and glanced at the seal she had on her necklace around her neck—a spiral around a triangle, pointing downward. After a moment, their eyes met again.

Then we will all go see the queen, the merrow said.

They pushed Maggie ahead of them and Léana followed behind.

Great, Maggie thought. So close. How could this happen? She wanted to blame Léana for this, but she didn't know why Léana knowingly violated their rules for her.

Several tunnels later, they came across a chamber filled with pearls and other merrows, lounging about the room between organic, oblong pillars. Some merrows were making out, not acknowledging their presence, while others watched them with great caution.

Maggie could feel the merrow beginning to pry at her mind through the Hollow, and she created a psychic block to stop them. Or...she *hoped* to stop them.

Coiréil was very humanoid. She had a grayish blue complexion with a lagoon blue chest and stomach. She had fins on her fore-arms and on the back of her calves that were of similar coloration. Her long hair, which fell just past her backside, was turquoise and she wore a band of colorful calcite polyps and pearls around the cap of her petite skull. Her hair was partially tangled with her red *cohuleen druith*.

Maggie noticed that her ears were longer, pointed and subtly fanned out like her fins, though they remained the same complexion as the rest of her body.

The merrow that led Maggie and Léana to this chamber from the Heart Stone, approached their queen, who rested on her side, running a hand over a large, colorful polyp in front of her. Its tentacles touched her, but they didn't seem to sting her.

This Undine and the Demidian were both found in the Chamber of the Heart Stone—the Cloch Chroí. *The Demidian joined the Sacred Circle and reached out with the Merrow's Call.*

Léana swam up beside the merrow who escorted them, bowing before Coiréil as she climbed up in the waters to her feet, and then Léana took off her seal. Maggie watched all this, hoping Léana knew what she was doing. She wished to have one more time within the Merrow's Call.

I meant no disrespect, Léana said

Coiréil touched the seal and smiled at Léana.

Léana has my seal and therefore my voice, Coiréil said, but then she turned and looked at Maggie, cocking her head. After a moment, she looked back at Léana. *But why did you bring this stranger, Léana? She stinks of the serpent's blood.*

She is my anam chara, Léana said. *She needs to use the Merrow's Call in order to learn about her kintráth and how to use it. The Fomorians have twisted her body, making her something other than who she feels she is.*

Feeling humiliated with her ugly form, Maggie couldn't wait any longer and swam forward, pushing in front of her escorts. *They made me into this, and I only seek to purify my blood. Wash it clean. I only seek knowledge so that I can be free from what those monsters did to me.*

Coiréil frowned. *You despise this form?*

Maggie didn't want to offend her as she offended Fianna and the other aos sí.

I only wish to return to my true *self*, Maggie said.

<h1 style="text-align:center">3</h1>

Coiréil reached forward and touched Maggie's face.

You are beautiful, Maggie. The Fomorians may be monsters, but they know the arts of creation—the Eagla—as certain as the merrow and the aos sí. They have made a physical form that represents your soul and your connections to the oceans of the world. This, Maggie, is your true self. To remove your form only makes you mortal.

Maggie sighed. Frustrated. None of them got it. *Being mortal is the only part of me that I wish to retain, Your Highness.*

Coiréil nodded and then let herself softly float back until her buttocks landed on the floor. She patted the floor in front of her. *Sit Maggie. Everyone else must leave us for now.*

The merrow followed her bidding, but Léana became reluctant until Coiréil told her that she would be fine. *I wish only to speak to her alone,* she said.

Léana nodded and swam from the queen's chamber.

Maggie sat in front of the queen, who took her hands in hers. That's when Maggie realized Coiréil had bright yellow eyes, almost bioluminescent themselves.

Coiréil closed her eyes, saying, *Give me a moment. Let me hear the Merrow's Call.*

They sat in silence. Maggie could only think about how close she was to going home and gathering Cuán up in her arms. She smiled, enjoying how it made her feel. What she wanted so badly was to be locked in his arms, being crushed into his body with his need to have her close. The comfort. The safety. The love. Maggie wanted to embrace it and never let it go again.

Coiréil opened her eyes, almost surprising Maggie.

In order to use the Accordances, you will have to put yourself back together. You're missing a part of yourself.

Maggie nodded. Yes, she remembered. *The Derdriu Shard.*

Yes. Carman has it. She has used it to make connections with you before, Coiréil said. *You will have to take it from her and free your spiritual essence from the shard before you can use the Accordances with the Wheel of Taranis to walk through time on your kintráth. There you may rewrite the contract, ending the fomori's influences over you.*

Maggie was shocked. *Walk the* kintráth? *Is that like traveling through time? I don't—*

Coiréil squeezed her hands. *Yes, but only on an astral level and no farther than your birth.*

What is The Wheel of Taranis?

The Wheel is a symbol of time and space moving together. It is a doorway through time and space, but only as it pertains to one's fate, Coiréil said.

Lost and Found

1

Aedán decided that he wanted to share more of himself with Bridget. Maybe if he could explain it to her, she would understand his duty to the Order of Bres. He reached into his pocket and removed the Macalla Shell.

I would like you to listen to this, Bridget, he said.

Bridget still held onto him, but she let go to take the shell. She put it to her ear and listened to it. Her face changed to shock when she realized what happened and then changed to pure horror. She looked at Aedán, looking sorry.

I won't see my son grow, will I? I'll be dead any minute now. Dead, and my son will never really know.

No! NO! Put that away!

Who is this? Bridget said.

My real father. Before Lord Cuinn took me in, Aedán replied. *I don't know who murdered him, but the shell itself somehow recorded his last moments. I think the shell was a talisman from Beyond the Ninth Wave. Thar An Naoú Tonn. Coming here, the shell helps me feel like I'm home.*

You think this is the key to finding out who murdered him? Bridget said, handing it back to him.

I do, Aedán said.

Suddenly, Aedán felt something large hit him, throwing him back across the star chamber until he hit his back against the rough, calcite wall. Something swiped the shell from him, and he saw that a large, male merrow held onto it. He growled at Aedán, bubbles furiously rolling out of the creature's mouth.

Aedán couldn't lose the shell. Almost trembling, he reached for the Macalla Shell and tried kicking in the water at the creature. The merrow snapped back—its fist hit the side of his jaw with a swift crunch. Undeterred, Aedán grabbed the merrow's arm and tried twisting it, but the beast managed to punch him with his other hand. And then Aedán was wrenched away from the merrow by others of his kind.

No! Bridget cried, but they began dragging him quickly away from her. He saw that she tried to swim after them to keep up, but the merrow were just too fast. They left her behind, pulling Aedán through the winding tunnels.

Great. Now what have I done? he thought. He couldn't lose the shell, but he didn't want to lose his life either.

He wondered where Maggie and Léana were.

Dear God, he hoped they'd be able to get him out of this.

2

Carman hurt. She felt terrified and every inch of flesh on her bones ached from the beating the fomori gave her. Trying to sleep in the depths was different, but her body acclimated, and she spent most of her time dreaming about her revenge. For the sake of her sons. For the sake of her conquest.

She only had to play Elieris' game a little longer. When she had the Three Attainments, she would spend the rest of her life finding ways to destroy the Fomorian King.

Carman huddled inside her wings and used the Eye of Balor to see beyond the cages of the Fomorian prison. She watched Maggie enter Cathair Aigéin. Lord Cuinn was claimed by his son after turning into the Bresquinn Arrachtaigh. The creature also hunted down Nevan's girlfriend, Emera.

Oh, what a mess we make, she thought.

With Lord Cuinn out of the way, she could take full control over the Order of Bres. Doing that would give her connections to the modern occult world, which may help her find ways of getting what she ultimately wanted now. But could Bres be trusted? He was half fomor. Was there a way to turn Bres against Elieris, his own father?

Carman wondered.

When a voice interrupted her—*Carman*—, it startled her. *The Ri is setting you free.*

Carman unfolded her wings and stretched out her body, seeing the fomor Soulforger, Fangtooth, open her cage.

It's about time, Carman said.

Leave here and never return, Fangtooth warned. *But Elieris does send you with a parting gift. He says that if you want the Golden Wheel, you must find the girl, Emera.*

Carman had just seen Emera die by the hands of that mutant beast in Balor's Eye. If the humans had discovered the Golden Wheel of Taranis on her body, they'd remove it. Maybe she could get there first.

Carman didn't thank the fomor, feeling humiliated and resentful. Instead, she left the Deep Dens in silence, and as she road along the Argent Path over the Ninth Wave, she rewove what *croí* she had left, and followed it back until it portaled out at the Ó Cuinn estate.

Carman tried the manor door and found it open. She went in. She could tell the police had been there. All the bodies had been removed. Carman recalled Emera running from Lord Cuinn's, dropping the Wheel of Taranis at her feet as she went.

Carma moved to the where she'd seen it in her scrying and picked it off the floor, a wide grin forming on her face as the metal glinted before her eyes.

Too easy, she thought.

Walking down the path toward the estate gates that evening, she looked up to see the large man who had visited her before. His hands were stuffed in his mariner's long coat—his peaked cap slightly askew just above his gorgeous yet powerful face. The Dominion.

"I have been waiting for your return," he said. "Care to join me?"

Carman sighed. *Great.* "Sure, my Lord. Where to?"

"Let's go back to my Maddy. We may discuss things," he said. "Besides, my dear, I'm hungry."

Carman felt terrified of this man. She could feel his barbarity in the stink of the blood left from the innumerable pile of corpses he left in his wake through the centuries.

They went by coach to the Wexford pier, and they boarded his ship, the *Madeline Leigh*. In the Captain's berth, he wrapped his arms around her and kissed her neck until his teeth sank in. He swallowed the blood he sucked from her until she felt weak.

She fell into his arms, feeling an orgasm ripple through her body.

The Dominion laid her back onto his bed, parting her legs, tearing at her clothes until she was exposed before him. His face sunk between her legs, and he began lapping at her sex, which felt grotesque and wonderful at the same time. When she had another orgasm, he kissed up her body, over the Wheel of Taranis now dangling around her neck and nestled between her breasts, and to her lips.

There was something about being so close to death and having sex. It was its own allure.

They kissed with her taste on his lips, but she didn't care.

"We join together, Carman. We destroy Elieris once and for all. Destroying the Fomorian threat, once and for all. And afterwards, we make Ireland ours," the Dominion said. "Do you believe me?"

He looked into her eyes. Carman grabbed his head, digging her fingers into his skull, and kissed his forehead.

It was nice having someone on her side for a change, though she was sure he only used her for his own hidden purposes. At least, she knew she could use him in return.

"It's time for the Fomorian King to die," she said. "I'm with you."

The Dominion grinned. "Good. But we need Maggie."

Carman pulled out of her hemline pocket a bottle of perfume, which she now always kept with her. Suddenly, a nude young woman stood there with dark, curly hair and tall, twisty horns on her head. One of the *sióg*. The girl licked the air, hissing.

"I have a little help in that department," Carman said.

The Dominion grabbed the bottle of purplish perfume from Carman and smiled.

Carman returned the smile. "Spring Squill. Feminine. Wild. Magnificent. And she has a secret that will make things...much easier."

 Trouble

1

The merrow shoved Aedán into a small chamber off one corridor. It wasn't well lit, and he knew that the merrow were planning to kill him. The merrow snapped at his face and then placed a hand over Aedán's chest. He started feeling the pearl coming out, making its way out of him, drawn to the merrow's hand.

There was nothing more agonizing than drowning, he thought. This wasn't supposed to be how it ended. He thought about how Lord Ó Cuinn had raised him in the arms of the Order of Bres, showing him the path toward the Great Summoning of the Red God Bres.

"You fall in love and that love must be sacrificed for the greater good," Lord Ó Cuinn told him. "It will be hard. Terrible for you. But that's what sacrifice is. Letting go of the things you cherish the most for the greater good. Do you think you can do that, me lad?"

"Yes, Father," he'd said. "I can."

It escaped him at the time—what he really said. Finding love meant making a deep connection to someone: two powerful magnets slowly coming together, refusing to let go once they were fully joined.

Aedán was supposed to pull them apart from each other and use the power to draw down the Red God.

This journey would end there, inevitably. Bridget at the Stones of Bres. The Rising of the Red God.

But the pearl came out of his chest and the merrow collected it up in his grasp. Just before the pearl was removed, Aedán took a deep breath, but he didn't know how long he could hold it. The merrow pushed him back against the wall of the chamber, showing him its terrible sharp teeth. Its large fisheyes narrowed on him. Its tongue slithered around and flicked across its own teeth.

A message: the merrow planned to make a meal of him once he had drowned.

Aedán couldn't do it any longer. His lungs threatened to give and draw…He sealed his lips shut as hard as he could, but his lungs burned. Just before he took a deep breath of water, the merrow cried out and was pulled away from him. Aedán saw Maggie's powerful tail sweeping back and forth through the waters.

Léana put the pearl into his chest, and he took a breath, and the waters filled him with breathable oxygen. As he gasped to get as much of it as he could, he saw Maggie scratching and biting at the merrow until he swam away, bleeding.

My Macalla Shell! Aedán cried.

Maggie swam up to him and opened her hand. In her palm, the shell sat safe.

Oh, Maggie. Thank you, he said.

Maggie smiled at him. *The merrow, by and large, don't want us 'ere.*

I noticed, Aedán said. He wanted to tell Maggie about the Order, but he loved his father too much, and he couldn't bring himself to ruin his father's hope for the future. Then he remembered Bridget. *We've got to get back to that star shaped chamber!*

Léana led the way. When they returned, however, Bridget was gone.

Shit, Aedán said. *Where did she go?*

Léana put a hand on his chest. *We'll find her. Remain calm, Aedán.*

Easy for her to say, Aedán thought.

2

Maggie was exhausted, and she hadn't been able to return to the Heart Stone yet. All she could think about was getting back to the stone, so when she realized that Aedán and Bridget were in trouble, her frustrations heated to a boil.

Maggie told Léana that they should split up to look for Bridget. They left Aedán in the chamber with the Macalla Shell and started off into the tunnels.

When she was alone—as if the witch knew somehow—Carman projected before her, startling her. Maggie, disgusted and furious, growled at her.

Leave me now, you witch! I never want to see you again, Maggie seethed, feeling her face burning.

But I've one more Attainment, Maggie. You swore you'd help me, Carman said.

I did no such thing. We had an agreement, but I'm breakin' it on account of you bein' a right slag!

Maggie swam past her, using her tail to speed herself down the winding tunnels.

Carman projected herself in front of her again.

I thought you might be difficult, Carman said, *so I decided you might need extra incentive.*

Maggie stopped. She could hear something cruel in her tone and Maggie knew how clever and dangerous the witch actually was.

What are yeh talkin' 'bout?

Carman smiled. *Cuán Foley. I have 'em.*

No. Maggie's heart skipped a beat. Her blood burned in her veins. *Where is he?*

Don'na worry your pretty head, Carman said. *You'll get him back.*

Fer the Third Attainment? Maggie said, already knowing her game.

No, actually. I need another favor from you. I would like you to bring me the two mortals you're ploddin' around with. Bridget Rose MacCailín and her boyfriend, Aedán Ó Deasún. If you bring them to me, I will return your beloved.

Fuck you, you slag, Maggie said. *I don't trade in lives.*

I'm na' joking, Maggie dear. Bring them to me, and I will honor the deal, Carman said, half-grinning. With nothing more to be said,

Carman's astral form disappeared. If she'd really been there, Maggie would have clawed out her throat.

Maggie didn't know what she was going to do with that, but she decided that finding Bridget was more important right now. She swam on, using her tail and the spiny fins down her back to sleekly move through the waters as swiftly as she could.

Down the tunnel, she saw another merrow holding onto Bridget, towing her along to who-knows-where. Maggie opened her hands, extending her long, black claws and then she raked at the back of the merrow's neck, drawing blood. The merrow screamed in surprise and pain, letting Bridget go.

Crying out in anger, Maggie slashed and snapped at the merrow until it gave in and retreated quickly down another tunnel.

Thank you, Bridget said. Her face was twisted in terror and Maggie felt bad for her. These two really needed to get home, and she needed to get them there before she went back for Cuán.

Without them, she wondered how she would free her lover. Maggie knew she couldn't give Bridget and Aedán to Carman. That was like Maggie turning her back on the fact that she herself had also been a slave. She would never do that. An individual's freedom exceeded a person's personal desire no matter the cost.

You're welcome, Maggie said. *Let's get back to Léana and Aedán. There's one more thing I have to do before we go home.*

Home?

Aye, Maggie said. *I think it's time fer us to go home.*

VII
Undoing Knots

1

Carman waited in Lord Ó Cuinn's study at the Ó Cuinn estates. Having reached Lady Reagan Leary, she promised to be there that evening. Carman didn't know much about the Leary family, only that they were titled and had an estate in Blackwater, a little over nine miles north along the Muir Éireann, the Irish Sea. From what she gathered from Lord Cuinn's journals, Lady Leary worked through her father to secure resources for the Order of Bres. If Lord Cuinn were to pass—and he had—Lady Leary would be the next in line to run the Order of Bres.

Carman sent her a letter, expelling who she was and how Lord Cuinn met his fate. Carman asked her if she still wanted her position in the Order. If so, they should meet, and have supper together.

Early that morning, Lady Leary responded via a messenger, who came by horse.

"Lady Reagan Leary would like to take you up on your offer and will be here before supper this day," the messenger said.

Carman happily approved. If Lady Leary played her cards right, they would make great allies until she wasn't in need of the Order any longer. In fact, Carman was excited that she would be working with a woman. Thoroughly disgusted with men at the moment, she felt it would be nice not to worry about sexual perplexity that plagued most men's interactions.

While she waited, she set to work, guising herself with an illusion. Unlike glamour, illusions only tricked a certain number of senses and couldn't manipulate physical reality; that is, change the natural laws of physics. Nevertheless, Carman made herself appear as Lord Cuinn and spoke with the solicitor to change the will so that Carman would own the bank accounts and the estate would fall to her. After all the paperwork was done, she allowed the man to return and file the paperwork with his offices. Before bed, she planned to cast a curse that would leave the solicitor def and dumb, unable to communicate with others that he'd seen Lord Cuinn after his death.

If it all worked—and it wasn't a perfect plan—she would be able to continue to run the Order with Lord Cuinn's money and estates. Besides, the Stones of Bres sat on the estate grounds. They would come in handy for raising Bres from the grave. If she couldn't get them by tricking the legal department, she would have to find another trick to own them.

They hadn't found Nevan yet. Or Aedán. If she had to, she'd use them to get what she wanted. So far, the hired staff had no problem serving her—mostly because they feared her and knew some of her power. She was sure that they knew she was a witch and feared telling anyone.

Sitting back in *her* desk, Carman ran her fingers along the edges of the Golden Wheel of Taranis. She could feel its power and she had already scryed out its effects. With it, one could travel through the timeline of another's fate. Or *kintráth*, as they fae called it. Hell, maybe with the Golden Wheel, she could follow Lord Cuinn's fateline back to before he died, force him to sign over his money and estates after his death.

The power opened so many possibilities.

2

The *Madeline Leigh* lightly rocked on the waves of the Irish Sea as it sat in the pier where he had docked for weeks. Catrina sobbed, having just left Emera's—her best friend's—funeral. She was dressed in black and held a parasol tight, trying to dry her tears.

Catrina scoffed at the idea. No body had been found. Her death was assumed because she had seemed to just disappear. While Catrina knew it was unlike her, it was too hard to believe that Emera was really dead.

She came here because she needed comfort. While Vladiv felt a little dangerous—it was what excited her a little about him—she hoped him capable of giving her comfort.

And if not comfort, she'd gladly enjoy having sex with him, which would take her mind off losing her best friend. She'd come here many times for his passion. What he could do with her body, she would have never dreamed of such torrid pleasurable.

Wiping her eyes, she boarded Vladiv's ship and knocked on the cabin. He opened it, naked and hard.

"I knew you'd come," he said. "Would you like to come in?"

She couldn't take her eyes off his excitement and threw her parasol aside. Catrina frowned though, not knowing what to say to him.

Vladiv grabbed her hand, pulled her inside and shut the door behind her—all before she realized what was happening.

"Her loss has given you such forlorn thoughts, haven't they?" Vladiv said.

"Yes."

Vladiv started tugging on her dress, breaking buttons, tearing through all the knots.

"Together we will forget such mournful, unfortunate things," Vladiv said, revealing her naked flesh and tossing the dress aside. "We will revel in life after death."

He lifted her up and took her to the bed, laying her back onto it. He entered her and hungrily kissed and sucked on her neck and ears. One hand grabbed her buttocks and shoved a finger deep into her backside, making her squeal. His mouth found hers and Catrina accepted him in every orifice—her body deeply immersed in his eagerness.

"I'll never forget her," Catrina said, losing a tear down her blushed right cheek.

"Then use her memories to elevate yourself," Vladiv whispered into her ear.

Vladiv then bit into her neck.

Her body shook, losing control with his thrusting and sucking, riding his pleasures until her mind went soft and death took her.

The Alastríona

1

Out on the azure Irish Sea, the fishing dogger, the *Alastríona*, rode on the ocean waters, making its way out to capture its first haul of the day. Ulick, the Chief Mate, took the time to check over the crew's jobs as they all prepped the ship. The white-bearded Captain stood at the wheel; his blue eyes fixed on the horizon.

The starboard hull sounded as though it had brushed up against something. Suddenly, the ship jolted and rocked. Ulick went to look overboard and saw some of the largest black seals he'd ever seen.

"Whoah! Whoah!" he called to the captain, using one hand to gesture a full stop.

The captain started slowing the *Alastríona* down as the seals continued to slam up against the sides of the boat.

"Why are they doing that, Ulick?" one of the crew asked. A boy who'd just started with them only the week before.

"There's a lot of them, all clustered here," Ulick said, smiling. "They're hunting for fish."

The boy smiled back, and Ulick turned to the crew.

"Lower the nets!"

2

They broke to the surface Beyond the Ninth Wave, Léana leading them from the depths of Cathair Aigéin. They had passed out of the Otherworld and found themselves back in the physical world.

Maggie could feel the difference in the ocean waters. It was colder. Maybe even brinier.

They were all treading water, bobbing up and down as they rode light but consistent waves.

"We are home!" Bridget said, with a huge smile that they all probably shared in common.

"At least, closer to home," Aedán said, gesturing around them. "I don't see the shores."

Léana pointed west. "Ireland is just over there. I've called the seals. They'll help us."

"Are we to ride them?" Aedán said, but Maggie could see his facetiousness all over his face.

"I have to leave you," Léana said. "I'm an undine and a creature of the Otherworld. My power here is severely limited by the Recanting and I've done what I've come to do. Return you to your homes. Keep you safe."

"And for that, we thank you dearly," Bridget said.

Léana swam over to Bridget and gave her a hug. She then went to Maggie, who tried not to cry herself.

"I don't want to lose you," Maggie told her.

"You won't, Maggie. We're sisters. We'll see each other again."

With that, large, dark seals swam around them. Bridget screamed and then laughed when she realized what they were.

"Are they dangerous?"

Maggie nodded. "They can be."

"But I've summoned these to help you. Stay with them and you'll be safe," Léana said. She waved at them and then she submerged herself beneath the surface waves. When she didn't come back up again, Maggie knew Léana was truly gone.

She wasn't sure how the seals could help them either. Maggie knew that she could swim for the shores easily, but Aedán and Bridget would never be able make it. They didn't have nearly the strength or endurance to go that far.

Riding seals: a ridiculous notion.

"Maggie?" It was Bridget. Aedán turned in the waters, looking surprised himself when he looked at her.

"What?"

"Is that really you?" Bridget added.

At first, Maggie didn't understand what they were saying, but then she brought up an arm and looked at her pale skin. She had transformed back into her humanoid form! Maggie checked for her tail, but it was gone. There were no claws on her hands. The only thing that remained was the Airgid Hook and its belt, still wrapped around her waist.

"You're gorgeous," Bridget said.

Maggie blushed. "I am not. But I'm not a monster either."

Maggie started hearing the engines of a ship. The engines were slowing down and then she saw it coming over the horizon. It wasn't far away, so she started shouting: "HEY! OVER HERE! STOP! OVER HERE!" Bridget and Aedán saw the ship, and they all started shouting as loudly as they could together.

The ship seemed to be following the seals.

Because, Maggie thought, *the seals know where the fish are*. A fishing vessel, bellowing out steam from a great pipe that stood at its center, started letting down its anchor. Maggie had never seen such a ship in her life, and she knew what was on and under the waters in Ireland. The vessel must be new and state-of-the-art.

As it got closer, Maggie could read the side of the ship. The *Alastríona*. There are men pointing down at them. She could hear them talking and shouting, but she couldn't quite make out everything they were saying.

Maggie and her companions waved back at them, making sure that the men didn't lose sight of them. They were throwing ropes overboard with tubular safety floats. Bridget and Aedán were able to get the first two. Maggie almost thought to disappear then, knowing full well she was naked, since she could swim to shore herself, but she couldn't abandon her friends. She decided to deal with the humiliation of it.

It's not like you weren't naked as the sea serpent through the whole trip in the Otherworld, she thought. Only her thick, scarred green skin almost seemed like it was its own sort of clothing. With her pale skin, she felt fragile and exposed.

Maggie grabbed her float and then put it around herself. The men hauled them up the side of the boat. One man took off his coat and wrapped her in it as soon as her naked feet were onboard.

"How the 'ell you all get out 'ere?" the man said.

Maggie didn't know what to say to them, so she just acted as if she didn't understand or that she was in shock. They'd probably fill them full of questions before the day ended. If they thought her mind was soft, they may let it go.

One man attempted to inspect the belt around Maggie's hip, but she swiped his hand away. Luckily, the First Mate glared at his crewmate.

"Ulick," the Captain said to his First Mate, who lit himself a cigar with a flaming match, "we'll have to take them back to the docks right away. They may need medical treatment."

"No chance to catch a haul before we go?"

"I don'na' think that's a good idea, do you?"

Ulick looked at Maggie.

"Perhaps not. A'right."

Puffing on his cigar, he started commanding the crew to turn the *Alastríona* around. Maggie huddled next to Bridget and Aedán, partially for warmth but also because she wanted to talk to them.

"They're goin' to ask us questions," Maggie said. "We've got to answer as few of them as possible."

"Maggie," Aedán said. "There's something going on."

"What is it?"

"I don't know. I just feel funny. Something has changed and I can't put my finger on it yet," Aedán said.

There was a roar of something overhead. They looked up and saw a small object flying through the sky like a wooden bird soaring with wings spread wide. It flew by overhead in the same direction they were heading.

ALASTRIONA

"What the fuck was that?" Bridget said.

Maggie didn't know either. Where the hell were they?

Maggie leaned over the edge of the *Alastríona* and watched the seals dispersing, having done what they had come to do. Maggie tried not to show how scared she was. Many things raced through her mind. Where was Cuán? Was he okay? Were they really home? In Ireland? What were they going to do if they'd found another world? How would they find their way home without Léana?

Suddenly, Maggie wished Léana hadn't left them.

Part V

The

Order

of

Bres

Her Life's Work

September—1922

Eileen McCarna took a deep whiff of the bread in front of her at the *Kilkee's Bakery*, the small shop near where she lived in Kilkee. She had been taking care of her grandmother for so long, she hadn't been out much and had almost forgotten how wonderful fresh produce smelled. She grabbed a loaf of bread, thinking that her grandmother would like it.

After she'd paid for the small amount of food she had, she started down the road, whistling as she went, enjoying the warm weather they were having. It wouldn't last long when the night came, and the colder air came off the western sea. For now, though, it was an utter delight.

When she'd gotten back to her home, going in through the door, she heard a noise in her grandmother's room. Eileen, worried, crossed the distance and swung the door open, hoping she hadn't hurt herself again.

Her grandma's hair was much lighter than it used to be. The old woman had always had sad eyes and had told her about things that happened to her long ago—horrible things that Eileen thought she might be making up. Eileen had never seen ghosts or demons and didn't know if she believed in them anymore. Though she would never think to dismiss everything. Some of her grandmother's stories were about bad people doing bad things. Eileen had seen her fair share of people hurting others, so she knew her grandmother had seen something that had twisted her worldview into shambles.

Eileen's eyes fell on the water basin, saturating the wood floor. It had toppled over. Her grandmother wept as she sat on the side of her bed, her nightgown crumpled around her thighs, revealing a leg mottled with liver spots.

"Grandma?"

Her grandmother's watery eyes shot on her as she pulled her hand away from her face. "They've returned from the Otherworld. Carman is going to make her move."

"What were you doin' with the basin?" Eileen asked.

"I felt them. I thought I felt them, so I scryed them out. The sea serpent and Lugh's champions. I saw them surface after all these years."

"Grandma. You're scarin' me, 'ere. You're not makin' any sense."

Eileen went to her to help her into bed, but her grandmother grabbed her wrist, squeezing it tight. "We're not going to play these games! You'll listen to your grams, do you 'ear me?"

She'd never seen her grandmother so clear and direct before. Most of the time she mumbled and appeared as though she spent time somewhere else. In her own dreams, perhaps.

"Grandma. You're hurting me."

Her grandmother let go of her arm and then grabbed Eileen's face. She gazed right into Eileen's eyes.

"Oh, poor Eileen." Her voice suddenly changed to an older woman's confusion and fright. "I don't know how I can help you. If your ma was still alive, she'd go with yeh, but she isn't 'ere no more. You have to go yourself and find her."

Eileen gaped at her, confused. She tried putting everything together in her head, but nothing came of it.

"Find who?"

"The sea serpent. Seagrass Maggie. She's the only one who'll understand what's really going on. She can stop that Greek witch. Keep her from raising the Red God."

Eileen was about to pull away from her, but her grandmother caught her arm again. She didn't know why her grandmother talked like this. Eileen knew she needed help. She needed to find the town doctor.

"Let go, Grams!"

"No! There's no time. I've to tell you the story and I need you to listen. Only I know you won't believe me if I do it the normal way, so forgive me for this!"

"Grams?"

Her grandmother revealed her hidden hand, which grasped a long needle. She stuck into Eileen's arm. It stung and Eileen cried out. The pain inspired more tears to pour down her cheeks.

"Grams! Why?"

Her grandmother wiped the blood with her other hand and smeared it over Eileen's face, saying words Eileen had never heard before.

Eileen had trouble keeping her eyes open. Before she knew it, she could see her grandmother Etna's life racing through her mind. Eileen could feel every emotional experience sharply and vividly. Every physical pain that she'd ever had to endure. When her grandmother let go of her arm, Eileen woke from the spell and could feel the blood drying on her face.

"Do you see now, Child? Did you feel the witch in your blood?"

Eileen cried. "Yes."

"I'm dying. I don't have the strength to do it myself. You're the only one I can count on. I know. It'll be dangerous. I wouldn't ask this of you, if it weren't so important," her grandmother said.

Eileen nodded and wiped her tears with the side of her fist.

"Grandma. I saw it. I understand," Eileen said, feeling the blood in her veins starting to course through her like an icy stream.

Her grandmother stood up and took her hand again, this time rather gently.

"I've some old papers and other research I did on the witch."

"Carman," Eileen said.

"Aye. Carman. You need to get this to Seagrass Maggie."

"But if the witch shares our blood, can she not see us whenever she likes?"

Her grandmother led her into the kitchen.

"I've one last spell for you, Eileen. If it works correctly, it will hide you from her."

Eileen packed her things, getting ready for her trip. Her grandmother had saved money for her train ticket, which Eileen put into her purse. They didn't have a motorcar, but Eileen knew a man in town who would take her to Galway. She hugged her grandmother one last time and stepped out into the nippy day, feeling the ocean winds blowing about her.

It wasn't until she climbed into the motorcar that she started feeling a horrible sense of disparity. When Eileen concentrated on it, she saw that it was in her grandmother's spell that had given her all of her grandmother's memories. Grandma Etna was frightened, and she knew she'd be a weakness to her granddaughter. Eileen suddenly realized what she planned to do and ran back inside her home, hoping it wasn't too late. As she swung open the door, she heard it go off: a loud POP, and then a numbing silence.

Fresh tears fell. Eileen pushed open her grandmother's door and saw her grandmother laying out on her bed. The gun in her right hand laying aside her. The bedspreads and the wall above the headboard were painted with the old woman's blood, pieces of skull and brain bits.

"No," she said, and covered her face as she fell back into a chair beside the wall. It was a chair she usually sat in when she read to her grandmother—the newspaper, the daily letters, and the memoirs of archaeologists and anthropologists that were expanding the science over the years.

Eileen's heart broke and she didn't think she could leave anymore. It all seemed so hard...so *impossible.*

Only, in sitting there, sobbing, she remembered Etna's experiences with Carman and how dangerous the woman was. She also remembered some of the research that she'd collected about the witch's deeds, based on myths and some history records that alluded to her existence.

The woman needed to be stopped.

After a few more moments, Eileen was ready to finish her grandmother's life work.

Eileen just hoped she wouldn't be Carman's next victim.

New Wexford

1

Over the years, Carman used her magic to create a tattoo. Something that the sailors and fisherman would all want—something that made them all part of the Big Boys Club. She would haunt the Wexford docks for the best fisherman and award them a tattoo, which would give her access to their minds whenever they saw certain repetitive items: three people; a girl with red, curly hair; ocean waves; and an inexplicable finding of any sorts. Once these ideas were all seen together, the fisherman would subconsciously project what they saw to her, and she could see it for herself.

Once the information was gathered, Carman could ease into their minds through the Hollow, and take control of them for herself. For a little while.

The Chief Mate, Ulick, saw the three rescued survivors huddling for warmth on the deck as they headed back to the Wexford docks. He was a little upset that they would ruin several hours of good fishing over this, but he knew they had to follow the law. Because of the British oversight, punishment would often be steep and life shattering for businessmen who thwarted British rule.

He looked over and saw the cabin open, and the Captain waved him in. Ulick went in to speak privately with the white-bearded man. Ulick figured he wanted a report.

The Captain shut the door behind Ulick and then grabbed his right shoulder.

"Do you have the tattoo?" the Captain said.

It took Ulick a moment for him to remember the tattoo and then he pulled his sleeve back, showing the back of his wrist. There was a simple ink drawing of a withered man. It was haunting, but to the men, it meant they toiled against the Famine. A way of saying 'Never Again'. All the sailors and fishermen, who were anyone and made their money off the sea, had the tattoo.

"Aye. I figured," the Captain said, smiling. He went to the rear window and pulled the curtains aside. He looked at the huddled survivors. "Those are The Three."

"Excuse me, Sir?"

The Captain looked at him. For some reason, Ulick thought his Captain's eyes were blue, but they were now a golden yellow. Were they always yellow? Ulick didn't think so.

"Never mind. I need you to do something for me once we dock, can you do that?"

"Certainly," Ulick said, now wondering. "You want us to call in the survivors we found?"

"No. No, I don't want you to do that. We shouldn't do that. Instead, I would like it if you'd keep this all quiet. We'll take the day as a loss," the Captain said.

"Sir? Really? I mean we could—"

The Captain shook his head. "I don't want to argue, Ulick."

Ulick sighed, exasperated. "Aye, Sir."

"I want you to head over to the Dolphin's Crown. There's a man who patronizes the pub most of the day named Rowan Flynn. I want you to tell him about The Three and how we found them. Give him a full description of each of them."

Ulick nodded. "Aye, Sir. I can do that."

"Good," the Captain said, smiling at him again.

His eyes were blue again. Weren't they just yellow? Maybe Ulick could use a day off. His own mind played tricks on him.

After leaving the Captain's quarters, Ulick started stewing. He knew if they didn't make the quota, the Captain would also dock him pay as well as the rest of the crew. He'd have to not only ease the crew's tempers, but he'd have to keep his pockets tight for the next week.

It was enough to make him hate the Captain sometimes.

2

Bridget sighed in awe as she saw the other large steam vessels leaving or approaching the docks. As they began to turn starboard to meet port, Bridget could see some of the Wexford roads. There were carriages running around without horses, making little sputtering-grumbling noises. There were great stretches of cable running along the streets, crisscrossing above people's heads. The buildings seemed taller.

"I don't understand any of this," Bridget said, wrapping an arm around Aedán. "If this is Wexford, it's not the Wexford we left behind!"

Aedán shook his head. "It's not. This was my home. It's different. I can see some of the old town in pieces, but it's like someone came along and changed most of it. How can this be? What happened?"

Maggie wasn't saying anything, so Bridget looked over at her pale face. Could pale faces get whiter? The girl looked sick. Her watery blue eyes were wide. Her mouth was in a small 'o'.

"Maggie? What is it? *Maggie!?*"

Maggie broke out of her trance and looked at her. Bridget thought she looked sick, but the freckly-nosed redhead looked terrified.

"We have to see the papers," Maggie said.

"Why?"

"I want to know what date is on the paper."

"Can't we just ask someone?"

Maggie nodded. "Aye. We could, but I want to see it in ink. I want to see its reality."

"I don't understand," Bridget said. "Why would—" And then she did understand. The wooden bird with the stiff wings flying overhead. The innumerable changes all around them. When it dawned on her, she clutched Aedán much tighter. "We lost more than a few days or weeks, haven't we?"

Maggie nodded.

"Possibly more than a few feckin' years," Maggie sighed.

How many?

Bridget had to know the number. She thought about her parents. Her friends. She walked up to a fisherman and grabbed his arm.

"I'm sorry, Sir, but what is the date today?"

The short, stocky man's face screwed up, looking confused and seriously agitated.

"September Twelfth, Nineteen Twenty-two. You okay, ma'am?"

When she heard it, she knew why Maggie wanted to see it. She couldn't believe it, even though deep down she knew it was true.

67 years. Bridget quickly did the math in her head. If her ma was still alive, she'd be a hundred and three. Her da, a hundred and five. No.

"Ah, fuck," she said, wanting to weep. Had anyone ever lived that long? Ever?

The only stories she remembered hearing were in the Old Testament. Biblical level stuff.

Bridget looked to see how Aedán grasped it and she saw that his eyes were red. He looked upset.

"That can't be possible, can it?"

Maggie looked away.

"Have you ever read any of the myths?" Maggie said.

"Some of them," Aedán said.

Maggie sighed and told her story. About how when she was little, only a few days old, the Cailleach took her from her parent's. After ending up in the hands of the Fomorians, the creatures reared her in the Deep Dens for eighteen years before the Cailleach returned to free her.

"I thought only eight years had passed," Maggie said, "But I lost eighteen of them. I still looked like a child while the *siofra* that took my life and remained in the mortal world had aged normally with the rest of the world."

Maggie also told them the story of Oisín and Niamh. Niamh was from the Otherworld, and when they became lovers, Oisín returned with her to Tír na nÓg. When he returned to Ireland, he had aged three hundred years.

"You knew about this?" Aedán growled.

Bridget held onto him tighter, hoping he wouldn't attack Maggie. Though she understood why he'd be angry, even if Maggie wasn't the reason they ended up in the Otherworld. She could have warned them—prepared them—for what would happen. No, Bridget realized, they couldn't really blame her, could they?

"I—I didn't know," Maggie said. "I thought if I was only in for a few days rather than a few years, we wouldn't lose that much time."

Well, obviously you don't fucking know anything," Aedán shouted.

Bridget held him tight, feeling Aedán's heart race. Feeling his muscles constricting. Hardening.

"Aedán. It wasn't her fault. She's not at fault," Bridget said softly. "Please."

Aedán relaxed. "Well, what the feck are we goin'na do?"

Once the Chief Mate gave them directions to the hospital, he bade them well. Bridget thought it was strange that he didn't send men to accompany them or call upon the authorities for a statement. Maybe things have changed over the last 67 years.

Hell...Was this even Ireland anymore?

As they walked the roads, they saw many things were still the same. People still used bicycles and horses, even though many loud, self-moving carriages went this way and that. More people kept to the sidewalks, leaving the roads to these odd carriages.

Bridget was surprised to see photographs on paper in shop windows, advertising sales, or scheduled shows. Inside one shop, a man winded up a metal box on the wall, holding a bell-shaped cup to his right ear and talked into it.

The world had moved on. It both awed and shocked her and made her feel very strange. Maybe even a little scared.

This wasn't the world she came from. It had moved on without them.

"I have to go home," Aedán said matter-of-factly. "Will you come with me?"

Bridget didn't know. Shouldn't she go home as well? See what had changed? See if there was anyone alive who remembered her?

"I don't know. What about my parents? My friends?"

Maggie took a paper from a paperboy's hands.

"Hey! Ma'am! You have to pay for that!"

Maggie looked at them with shock. She showed it to Bridget.

September 12th, 1922. Just as the fisherman told them.

Maggie gave the paper back to the boy. It was then that Bridget realized that Maggie was still only wearing the coat the Chief Mate gave her to cover her nakedness.

"You'll need clothes," Bridget said. "And you've no shoes."

Maggie looked down at herself and nodded. "Aye. But I can take care of myself."

"Maggie—"

"No. You two go home. We've done come back now, haven't we? We all have our own lives. Ye go back to yers, and I'll go back to mine."

"Maggie—I—"

Maggie smiled at her, putting a hand on Bridget's shoulder.

"I'll be fine, Bridget," she said.

Bridget didn't think so. She didn't think any of them would be fine. And what would Bridget do once she inevitably discovered that her life no longer existed? It was too much to bear.

"I'm not sure if I can do this alone," Bridget said. "I didn't mean to be alone."

"You could come with me. Once we drop by the estate, we could go to Dublin, see your folks," Aedán said.

Bridget didn't know. "Are they still alive, Aedán?"

She didn't think she could wait.

When she looked back at Maggie, she was already down the road, head hanging, hands stuffed in her coat pockets, disappearing into the crowd.

What she really wanted was Maggie to stay with her. She had a sneaking suspicion inside of her that only Maggie would be able to keep herself in this new world.

3

Maggie was terrified, confused and angry. She hated herself. She knew it had been a risk—the time fluctuations between Tír na nÓg and the mortal world were at best untrustworthy. She dared mess with the supernatural world to free herself of the fae blood, and where had this gotten her? Through all of it, she wanted to do this to live her life with Cuán and not have to deal with living without him. And what did she do? Maggie surpassed his lifetime, leaving him...alone.

It *mortified* her. The ache that it caused her, wrenched and tore at her heart. It cut through her without mercy, oozing frigid blackness into the pores of her spirit. All she could think about was Cuán's face. That adorable, youthful, spirited, beautiful face with all that messy, dark chocolate hair.

He would be gone, wouldn't he?

Carman knew, too. Maggie was certain of it.

Unless Carman told her the truth and that Carman was the only chance Maggie had to save him. Maybe the witch kept him alive somewhere? Or maybe Maggie should return to Kilkee to make sure there wasn't a grave for him there.

Gods, please, no...

This cannot be happening, she thought. There had to be a way to fix all of this.

Maggie's feet were hurting. Without her serpent-skin to protect her from the elements, her flesh was soft tissue, fragile and easily torn.

"Feck," she said, sitting on the sidewalk to rub her toes. One toe bled, having caught a wood sliver deep into the flesh.

Yeah, she needed clothes. Shoes.

Maggie looked at the shops around her and saw a pub.

She had no money or food, and she didn't know how she was going to get anything she needed. Until she remembered Cuán's ma, Orna, bringing her a box of clothes from the church soon after she'd been found. She'd just come from the sea, having escaped the Fomorians, and when Oona and Orna discovered her, they made sure to dress and feed her properly. It was a kindness that Maggie would never forget, and she would always remain grateful to them for it.

I've got to find a Church then, she thought.

Maybe someone in the pub could direct her to the nearest one.

Before going in, she removed the bronze coin token from the belt Léana gave her under the peacoat. Hoping to increase her luck, she closed her eyes, and she rewove the *croí* from the token Killian had helped her find and sent it out into the world. Tied to her life-force, it should bring good things to her. It was what the *Cloch Chroí*—the Heart Stone of Cathair Aigéin—showed her when she reached out through the Merrow's Call.

She also interwove these words to it: *Lead me on my way toward good fortune*. Not an Argent Path, but an essential one.

Once she opened her eyes, she went into the pub.

The pub was full of men having a drink for their lunch, maybe some of them doing business at one of the tables, and so Maggie found it crowded. She already realized that it wasn't typical for a woman to walk into the pubs, especially one as ill-dressed as she was.

She tightened the fisherman's coat around her nakedness so nothing accidentally slipped out and stepped carefully so the gentlemen wouldn't step on her small feet. Many of the men gawked at her out of the corners of their eyes, if not straight at her.

"Ooooo, what a weee sight we have 'ere," a large man said behind the counter, filling another's man's mug full of Guinness. "You get loss, Lass?"

"Aye. I was wonderin'—"

"Look at that little bird," someone said amongst the men, possibly louder than he intended.

A few laughed at this, but the large man working the pub waved her over.

"Sophie! You mind helpin' out the Lass 'ere?"

A young woman pushed her way through the crowd, wearing an apron and her hair all tied up. "Dear God! Look at the state of yeh! Come 'ere. We'll take yeh in the back and get you somethin'. You can't be trodden around like town like that!"

Sophie blew on the stray hair that kept landing on her nose and put a graceful hand on her back, leading her to the back out of everyone's eyeshot. She closed the door as Maggie looked around, seeing a small kitchen, a shower and a small bedroom where clothes hung on a steel bar in one corner.

"It's not much, I know. Most of the money that comes in feeds the mouths and keeps the pub goin'. But enough of that! What about you? What is yer name?"

Maggie looked at Sophie and scratched her nose, just thinking about the loose strand of hair on Sophie's.

"Me name is Maggie. I'm from Kilkee, but I fell in the water. A fisherman gave me his coat," Maggie said. It was an easy lie to tell. Not far from the truth.

"Ah! You must be cold. How about I get some water from the well? We'll warm it up so you can have a nice bath. You look to be the same size as me, so I can probably part with one of my old dresses," Sophie said, and gave her a big smile.

"I appreciate it, but I don't want to put yeh out. I was just comin' in to see if ye knew the way to the closest church. Sometimes they have clothes they can offer," Maggie said.

"Aye. I can do that, but I can help you, too. I'm not beyond helpin' those who need help when they need it."

Maggie gave her a small smile. "I do appreciate it. I thank yeh."

Sophie nodded toward the back door with her head, blowing on her loose strand of hair. "Follow me. I have to get back there and help my husband, but I can get the water started for yeh. Show you what you need to do."

Maggie didn't know how tired she was. After taking the warm bath, she pulled on the simple cream-colored dress over her head, her body agonizing over every movement she made, and thought she'd only lay for a moment on the floor. Before she knew it, she woke to a raucous in the pub. Laughter. Shouts.

"Do you know why God created whiskey? He didn't want the Irish taking over the world!"

More laughter.

Maggie looked out the window, seeing the hours had taken her into nightfall.

She peeked through the door, watching the men talk loudly, clinking frothing dark mugs together, laughing, and occasionally, push and shove on one another. Usually in jest. She couldn't believe how much clothing had changed. She was used to seeing men wearing frock coats that fell as far down as the knees and were rather drab over contrasting trousers. These men tended toward more trim jackets and cuffed pant sleeves. Most of them were clean shaven, which was different from the indulgent beards and mustaches that men used to wear. She was also intrigued with the sleek short-brimmed hats some of them wore, which she'd never seen before. An odd composite between a bowler hat and western Stetson-style, pinched near the front on both sides.

A part of her wanted to go in there and join the men and ask them all kinds of questions. She wanted to know how much had changed and wanted to have fun, let herself forget her current nightmare.

A handsome young man caught Maggie's eye, who looked a lot like Cuán but wasn't—he shook each of his mate's hands and waved at the Sophie's husband. "I'll see myself out, Patrick! Oíche mhaith." He put on his felt hat and went out the door.

Maggie saw that another gentleman with fairer hair watched him, putting on a bolder hat and followed him out. The first young gentleman—the one who looked like Cuán—didn't seem to be aware of the other in the bolder hat. Feeling that the second man was up to no good, Maggie decided to slip out the back and go around to the front. Maggie grabbed the Airgid Hook and belt and wrapped it around her waist before starting out. She still didn't have shoes, and the night was chilly, but she was certain that the young man was in trouble.

She watched Bowler Hat follow Felt Hat down the road, but he stuck to the shadows. Felt Hat whistled an Irish tune, just as unaware as Maggie thought. Maggie made sure she trailed both gentlemen closely, keeping them in sight.

Felt Hat made a dangerous mistake, dipping into an alleyway. Maggie saw the smile on Bowler Hat's face, and he removed a revolver from a holster on his hip. Maggie didn't want to destroy the dress she wore, so she only extended her claws, making her skin turn slightly blue. Her human teeth were replaced by her sharp rows of long, hook-shaped teeth.

Maggie attended both men in the alleyway, keeping to her own shadows. Felt Hat continued to whistle away, oblivious to either of them. Maggie kept her head low and tried to close in on both as quickly as she could.

"Barry! Stop right there!" Bowler Hat shouted, pointing the revolver at Felt Hat. "Or I'll shoot."

Felt Hat—Barry, apparently—whipped around, holding up his shaking hands.

"Alton?"

"You made a fucking mistake," Alton said. "I told you it was a bloody mistake. You should have listened to me."

Barry pushed his felt hat back a little on his head.

"Now, we can talk about this," he said. "Don't shoot."

Alton closed one eye, aiming. Maggie wasn't going to wait any longer. She moved behind Alton and jumped on his back. He fell forward, and they toppled to the ground. The gun went off, a loud report echoing off the brick buildings around them.

As Maggie realized the agony in her shoulder, seeing the blood pouring down and ruining the dress Sophie gave her, Barry kicked Alton's head, knocking him out.

"Thanks for that," Barry said, extending a hand to her. "But we've better go. It'll be like flies on horseshit with that gawdawful noise."

Since she was shot in the right shoulder, Maggie held out her left hand and Barry helped her to her feet. He then grabbed her hand and started pulling her from the alley along with him.

The Returned

1

Rowan Flynn stabbed a cigarette in an ashtray, blowing the smoke out as the girl next to him rubbed his inner thigh. There were several fishermen coming in for their evening drinks after finishing their jobs on their boats, making it loud. He was used to ignoring most of them, and the woman beside him happily did the same.

"You buy me a drink, boyo?"

Rowan grinned.

"I'd love to. What will it be, Cookie?"

"A pint would do me," the woman said, biting her bottom lip.

"*I'd* do you, Cookie," Rowan said.

The girl laughed, but it was fake enough that Rowan was already bored with her.

When he looked up, one fisherman stood next to the table, looking at him. He was tall and had on a thick white wool sweater.

"Who are you?"

The girl rolled her eyes. "Who cares who he is. What about me drink?"

"Feck off," Rowans said to her and then looked back at the fisherman standing there. "Well?"

"My name's Ulick," the fisherman said. "My Captain sent me to talk to you."

"Aye? He did now?"

"He also told me to show you this," Ulick said, pulling back the sleeve of his sweater.

The withered man.

Rowan knew that Carman had a number of fishermen pledge themselves to her, marking this pledge with the withered man tattoo. Her sign: the famine. If Ulick was showing him the tattoo like this, it meant that Lugh's companions had been found. In all his years as the High Priest of the Order of Bres—a duty given to him after his father passed away twenty-six years before by Carman herself—he didn't think that it would happen during his time.

The Order had protocol.

Rowan removed the woman's hand from his thigh and put his arm around the fisherman in the white sweater.

"Let's go to a more private place, shall we? You can tell me everything about them," he said.

"Feckin' arsehole!" the woman behind them shouted. "You promised me a pint!"

In the sea-frosted air of the late night, Ulick explained how they were led there by seals. There were three people found in the waters. All about their twenties. Two women. One male. The redhead was naked, so he'd given her his peacoat to keep warm and later let her keep it when she got off the boat.

Rowan couldn't believe his luck and gave Ulick a cigar and twenty pounds. The price for their information.

"I can't believe this!" Ulick said, excited. "I didn't know I was going to be paid so much, I—"

Rowan snapped an index finger to his lips. "Sh. This is for your silence. You understand?"

Ulick nodded ecstatically. Smiling. "Aye. I understand very well, Sir."

"Good day then," Rowan said.

Laughing gleefully, Ulick left Rowan alone outside the pub. He walked down the road to his red Nash Touring and got in, starting it up and made his way back to the estate. It was once owned by Lord Cuinn's family before Carman purchased it and gifted it to the Order of Bres. It made the Order more public, but most thought of the Order as a gentlemen's club more than anything else, so it wasn't a problem. Instead of parking in the garage he had built four years prior, he parked in front of the front doors, so that he could hurry as hastily as possible. He made his way up the stairs and knocked on Carman's door.

"If you're looking for Madam Carman," the butler behind him said, "she went out earlier. She did tell me to remind you that *Cellar Boy* needs your attention."

Rowan shook his head. Where was she off to? And why did it always seem that she was not only one step ahead of him but also liked to leave him in the dark? "I'll need you to make some calls for me. I'll make you a list. Will you come with me, Brendan?"

"As you wish, Sir," Brendan said, following Rowan to his study.

2

A few hours earlier, while Rowan drank at the *Dolphin's Crown*, Carman shed her disguising magic and donned a black robe over her lithe, curvy form. She went outside and stood at the doorsteps just as Aedán walked up the roadway.

Come here, boy, she thought, *and tell me what you have learned.*

To many, the last 67 years had been a lifetime ago. Many things had already changed. For Carman, it seemed a little more than a blink of an eye. She was used to waiting centuries, so a little more than half of one was nothing. She had merely used her time wisely to put things into place so that she would not fail.

"Aedán, my boy. You've come home...to us," she said, when he came within hearing distance. He looked cold and sad.

"Who are you?"

"The High Priestess of the Order of Bres," Carman said. "Your father foretold your return. The time of the Red God is now."

Carman smiled. And when she *destroyed the Red God*, his power would feed her apotheosis and sovereignty over all Ireland. She had sacrificed much over the centuries and now was her time. She was sure of it.

"You look like a monster," Aedán said, wiping his mouth. "Are you here to kill me?"

Carman shook her head, showing him her fake concern, hoping it looked real enough for him. "I don't intend any harm. But I am a prophet of Bres and together we will finish what your father has started."

3

When Aedán saw her as he walked toward his parent's home, he started to feel as though he was in danger. The woman was robed, but she wasn't wearing anything else. She had large, black corvid wings that were now folded on her back, a large globular eye on the middle of her forehead, and a golden amulet of a wheel around her neck—its medallion laying between her breasts. She had birdlike features, too. A sharp, pointed nose. High cheekbones. Her skin had dark rings around the eyes, the nose and mouth. He also saw the dark complexion around her fingertips and around her toes.

I don't intend any harm. But I am a prophet of Bres and together we will finish what your father has started.

"Where is my father?"

The woman hung her head. "Dead. His son, Nevan, was fooled into drinking Lugh's poison—part of a curse that followed your family over the centuries—and he became a monster. The Bresquinn Arrachtaigh. He rampaged through the house soon after you left, killing your father, your young step-sisters, and a few others."

The woman didn't seem distraught about any of it. Aedán wondered if she was telling the truth. And then he recognized the black wings and the big white eye. These were the Attainments Maggie had been seeking in the Otherworld.

"Are you lying to me, Carman?"

Carman didn't look surprised. "So, you do recognize me," Carman said. "That's good. Should we take a walk?"

Carman met him at the base of the steps and started walking back towards the gardens. Aedán realized there was another building adjacent to the estate building next to the stables.

"What's that?"

"A garage. For the motorcars. Surely, you've seen them."

"That's what they're called? Motorcars?"

"Or automobiles. Yes. Times have changed since you left the mortal world."

Aedán broke down, thinking about Nevan and Lord Cuinn.

"They were everything to me. They were supposed to be here," Aedán said. And then he looked Carman over again. "I was there when you had the sea serpent find those Attainments. Now I see why they are called that."

Carman shrugged. "They have made me more powerful than you can imagine. It makes me stronger. Makes us stronger. It allows us to finish this and raise Bres from his Sleep."

"You've been watching me and Bridget all our lives, haven't you? Your sons held us prisoner in our dreams, holding us to this Lost Place." Aedán thought that maybe if he came out with the truths that he discovered on his journey, she would find it harder to lie to him about anything. He waited.

"Yes. I used magic to touch your spirit long ago."

"Spirit?"

"The one that reincarnates over lifetimes," Carman said. "Except spirits are hard to track as they make their way around the world through their different lives. When you were born here, I knew my three sons could trap you by visiting you within the Hollow. Binding your souls together was easy."

"You mean, mine with Bridget's," Aedán said. "In the Lost Place."

"Yes. Ever since, I've been struggling to get you both here in the flesh, so that we can do as your father wished—to raise Bres from his death sleep and take Ireland back from those who'd oppress us.

Since you've been gone, it has only gotten worse. The Irish Republican Army is now fighting against the Provisional Government to drive the British from Ireland. If the IRA loses the Civil War, the Provisional Government will lead us back into British subjugation. If we can bring Bres forth? We can save the Irish people from all this meaningless suffering. After all, what was the Great Famine, but the British taking advantage of Ireland ruthlessly and cruelly. Can we afford to let this happen again?"

Aedán sighed. "No."

"There's fighting in the streets. The British have made the Irish turn on each other. The Irish are killing Irish. Ireland is eating itself alive and the fat, malicious British are watching, laughing. Waiting to take advantage of what's left, if anything."

Aedán looked at Carman's big white eye, which rolled back and forth in her head, even though the other two were fixed ahead as they walked. She wasn't a demon, he told himself. This was pagan magic. Pagan sorcery. And it was once used long ago to defeat the would-be oppressors.

"Your da would be proud of you," Carman said. "I watched you as you made your way, and I saw how you grew into being a man. If he could have done the same, he'd be beaming with pride. The only thing that is left now, is to raise Bres and take back Ireland for the people."

Aedán felt her anger, but it was a righteous one. If what she said was true, then his father had been right all along. The British were only going to take and take and take until Ireland destroyed itself. It was time to fight back, and this is how he could do it.

"Where is Bridget, Aedán?"

"She wanted to go home. I gave her what little money I had left, hoping it would be enough for a train ticket," Aedán said. "I don't even know if my money will even work in this time period though."

"It will. As before, Ireland uses the British standard sterling," Carman said. "We must stop her."

"How?"

"I have a way," Carman said, smiling at him. "There is one more thing I must show you."

Carman led him to a cellar door behind the estate manor. She unlatched the door, and they went down the stone steps into the gluttinous dark. Once his eyes got used to the limited light, he saw a circular cellar with standing stones up against the walls, surrounding them on every side. There were twelve of them, all equally distanced.

In the center, chained up, a large, tallow giant laid quiet and unmoving. It was hairless and grotesque lumps grew out of its head. Though humanoid, there wasn't much in the face that was human anymore.

Nevan.

"Dear God," Aedán said, holding a hand to his mouth. "He's still alive."

"IT...has *changed*, Aedán. Don't get too close."

This is what his path demanded he sacrificed. His father, his brother, his little sisters, and now his closest lover. Could he do what needed to be done? He didn't know.

Right now, he only knew pain. Life was so damned unfair...

The Redhead

1

Bridget paid for a train ticket and took a seat at the bench. She had a few shillings left, so she put them in her socks.

She smelled. Her hair was a mess, all tangled together and filthy. It wasn't until she watched all the respectable ladies around her, all wearing their nice suits and dresses, that she noticed how terrible and revolting she looked. Bridget tried grooming herself a little. Brushing out her hair with her dirty fingers, trying to pull it straight, rubbing her face with her sleeves. Anything to make herself look just a little more presentable.

All, mostly, for not.

Bridget sighed. She ran out of tears, and it fatigued her to think about all the things that might have changed at home. 67 years. They surely assumed her death after a couple years, even before they had passed away themselves. What of her nieces and nephews? Cousins? What of the friends she missed so much?

Possibly...all of them...*gone.*

When she heard the boarding call, she stood up and started for the line of passengers, when someone grabbed her arm and pulled her back.

"Ouch you!" she cried, looking to see two Gardaí there. One had her arm. "Let go!"

"Easy now, Miss," the chubbier Garda said. "We just want to take you downtown to ask you a few questions."

"Questions? I'm getting on a bloody train," Bridget said. "I'm off to see my family. Will you kindly leave me be? I've done nothing."

"I'm sorry, Miss," the Garda said, "but we must insist."

Bridget didn't want to push her luck. If she did want to go home, and not set up in a jailhouse, she'd better cooperate. Though it brought her so close to tears again.

"Fine. Will this take long?"

"I don't see why it would, Miss."

The Gardaí put her in the back of one of those motorcars—it was painted white with black stripes that read *Ireland Garda Síochána - Guardian of the Peace* on it. Manhandled into it, she realized that the doors only had levers on the outside.

"Is there a reason for any of this? I'm not even sure why you'd have questions for me."

Neither Garda said anything, and it felt ominous to her. She didn't like it.

Not at all.

2

Barry McDermott sat back in his chair in his small apartment. The redheaded girl slept in the next room, soft snores coming from her. He spent an hour looking for his girlfriend, Líle Burke, who spent an additional hour digging the bullet out of Maggie's arm, sewing her up with thread and bandaging her shoulder. Barry watched, trying to keep them both company while Maggie cried and moaned in pain as Líle worked.

Once Maggie passed out, Líle stood over him as he sat in his chair. She was dishy. Her blond curls bouncing on each side of her head. Her full lips pursed tightly in agitation.

"She can't stay here," Líle said. "I can't trust you with her."

"Trust me? Have I ever cheated on you?"

"She can't stay, Barry! It's not so much I don't trust you, but I don't trust her. She's a messy girl, but she's also pretty. And I know you have wanderin' eyes. You can't tell me you don't. She might even try seducin' you, and you'd be willin'."

Barry laughed. "I assure you, darlin', that would never happen. You're my dishy girl and you make me dizzy like no other girl, and you know it."

Líle half-cocked her head and gave him a stare with her blue eyes. "You're all talk with that flap-trap."

Barry grinned, leaned forward and pulled her in close. He laid his head into her warm stomach, and she wrapped her arms around his head.

"I owe her," he said. "She saved my life. I don't know why. But she did, Líle. I'll see how I can help her. Pay her back. She'll be gone soon. I promise."

Líle sighed. "If she don't go soon, we'll have a bloody problem. You know the guys are plannin' something in Dublin in a few days, and we've got to be ready."

"Aye. I know."

"And she can't be around to feck it up," Líle said.

Barry tightened his grip on her and took a deep breath of her. "I know."

Speaking of the guys, he decided he better get going. He stood up, holding onto her.

"You mind staying and watching her for an hour or two? I've a few errands to run," Barry said, looking down into her eyes.

Líle rolled her eyes.

"Two hours. Then I have to go."

"I'll hurry. I promise, aye?"

Líle sighed. "Okay."

Barry kissed her warm mouth. She kissed him back. He let her go and whisked his fedora from the hat rack, twirling his body as he walked back towards the door. He left his grin on.

"I think it's cute you're jealous," he said.

"Shut the bloody feck up," Líle said, smiling back at him.

3

Líle watched him go and then frowned. Not liking this at all, she went into the kitchen and grabbed a knife.

What if she cut the girl's throat?

Líle slid into the spare room and went to the bed. The redheaded girl slept soundly. She had freckles across her nose and her lips were slightly parted as she breathed easily. She was holding on tightly to a belt with some sort of metal stake sheathed in it. It was odd, but Líle couldn't see how the stake could be that dangerous.

Líle thought about it. Killing the girl would be the best thing. Not knowing who she was bothered her. What if she were a spy for the Provisional Government? She could have saved Barry's life in order to place herself in their group to learn sensitive information. It almost made too much sense. Why else would a woman go to all the trouble—putting herself into that much danger—otherwise?

Líle put the knife to the girl's face and brushed some of the girl's red curls away. She looked at the veins in the girl's creamy cheeks and in her neck.

And she couldn't do it. The girl hadn't done anything wrong. Not yet. While she knew that she'd have to watch her carefully, she also knew that she could just be an innocent bystander. Why were they doing all this, if not to protect the Irish nation? The girl was someone she should be trying to protect—not murder.

Líle sighed, letting her knife drop to her side.

"You're a lucky dame," Líle said. "I'm a sap."

4

Barry made his way back to the pub, watching for Alton. He didn't want any sudden ambushes. It was already tough enough trying to work unseen, preparing for the next move, he didn't need Alton's shit.

Barry saw a few of his buddies in the I.R.A., who were sitting around, chatting with Rowan Flynn—a husky, dark-haired man wearing a nice suit. Barry knew he had secured his wealth though his father, who inherited Lord Cuinn's estate after his death back in 1855. He also knew that Rowan belonged to the Order of Bres, a gentlemen's club for Wexford elites. The Order was an ally, slipping funds to the I.R.A. under the table. They all agreed: the Provisional Government had to go.

"…she's got curly red hair and was last seen only wearing a peacoat. Have any of you boys seen her?" Rowan was saying.

Barry frowned. Why would Rowan Flynn be looking for the girl who saved him the night before? He decided to play it cool as he walked up to the table. She deserved at least that from him.

"Hey, boys, how y'all doin'? Mister Flynn. Nice to see you about this morning. Can I get you a drink?"

Rowan folded his jacket over his arm, holding it in front of him in a relaxed manner.

"Maybe a drink with you boys would be fine. One drink, though, I've got many things to do today," Rowan said. He looked at Barry. "You haven't seen a redhead wearing a large peacoat on her, have you?"

Barry jerked his head in a lazy way, indicating that he hadn't. No peacoat, anyway. "If I had, I would have been too fluthered to know it. What did this birdie do to yeh?"

Rowan shrugged. "Nothin' yet. Just want to find her, is all. She's important to my family."

"Future friend, perhaps?"

Rowan chuckled and shook his head. "Codding me, are yeh? Maybe she is."

Barry gestured for the barback to come over.

"Can we have a drink for this fine gentleman?" Barry said, putting his fedora on the table. "What will it be? The black stuff or cider?"

"This early, it should be a cider," Rowan said.

Barry didn't know much about Rowan, but he figured if he called himself a High Priest, he was probably both arrogant and extremist.

Not that he hadn't been called extremist a time or two himself. But religious extremism was the worst. Their only end game was to feed like leeches off the hard-working people, selling repentance to the desperate like a con artist sells air to the mouthbreathers.

But would it be worth making a deal with him?

If this redhead was trouble, maybe giving her to Rowan would be a good solution for his problem. Barry, though, couldn't get past the idea that the redhead was harmless. He wouldn't—couldn't—just give her over to get rid of her.

The barback brought Rowan his drink.

"Will you boys tell me, if you see her?" Rowan said.

Barry's men nodded.

Barry gave Rowan a smile. "I don't see why not."

Thick of Me

1

Maggie woke up and felt her arm, and noticed she was still clinging to the Airgid Hook and belt. Agony flared up when she moved her arm. Looking around, she saw that the man she had saved from the shooter—Barry—must have taken her to his apartment. It smelled like a bachelor's pit and wasn't the best kept. A curly blond with her hair in a bob and a hair pin in it sat in a chair, flipping through a *Reader's Digest*. The sun caught her hair, making it glow, and she seemed to have big, beautiful blue eyes.

For a moment, she thought she was naked, but when she pushed the blankets aside slowly, Maggie breathed some relief. She'd almost forgotten the navy blue and white gingham pullover housedress they'd given her to dress herself in. When Maggie sat up, it was enough to get the young woman's attention. She tossed the *Reader's Digest* on a table and came toward her, leaning her thin body against the door frame.

"Finally up, are we?" she said.

Maggie rubbed her arm, trying to gauge what time it was.

"How long was I out?"

"Since about six this morning. You passed out once I got the bandage on yeh," the blond said, walking into the room. She checked the bandages. "And it looks like we should change these and clean the wound while we're at it. You're still bleeding a little."

Maggie groaned when the girl pushed on her wound.

"What did yeh do that fer?"

"Just seeing how fast it bleeds. I'd worry if there was a lot, ya' know," the girl said.

Maggie realized she didn't know her name. "Who are you?"

The blond looked at her severely. "I'm Líle Burke. Like the flower. Barry's my fella, if you know what I mean."

"I do."

"Good. Then you know to leave your hands off him."

Good gods, Maggie thought.

"Of course. I wouldn't disrespect any other woman like that. I've loyalty," Maggie said. "If we're changin' the damn thing, can we get on with it?"

Líle cocked her head, tight curls jouncing, smiling at her. "Sure. And what is your name?"

"Maggie."

"Just Maggie?"

"Well, Connell."

"Maggie Connell. I wish I could say it was nice to meet ye."

She wasn't obviously grateful Maggie saved her fellas' life.

After a half an hour later, Líle had added a couple more stitches, bit the thread off and re-bandaged her arm with clean material. Maggie suffered through the pain of her arm being yanked about, but once it was done, the tightness of the bandages made her feel more comfortable about it.

"Thank you," Maggie said. "I've never been shot before."

"Neither have I," Líle said.

Maggie gave her a faint smile and grabbed Líle's hand. "No? I figured ye and yer fella might be mixed up with something where bullets were the everyday."

"Oh, please! Don't bother guessing how terrible my life is," Líle said, sitting up from the bed. "Would you like some food? We don't have much. The Brit bastards make sure of that. But, at least, there'll be something in yer belly."

If they didn't have much food, Maggie didn't want to take it but Líle seemed the kind who may take offense, having gone to the trouble to offer it.

Líle went into the kitchen and started water in a Belfast sink, which looked as though it were porcelain. Maggie had never seen running water in a home before. She went to it and put her hand under the tap.

"You've a well inside yer home?"

"It's a sink," Líle said, looking confused at her. "It goes to pipes, pulling in the water from the city water tank. What's wrong with yeh? The marbles a bit of a mess up there?"

Maggie looked at her, realizing she gave away her ignorance for the times and technology. It still amazed her, though. Maggie smiled at her and backed from the sink, trying to come up with something, but had nothing.

Líle sighed. "You're a strange one, aren't yeh?"

The door opened, and they both looked over, watching Barry enter, pulling off his fedora and setting it on his hat rack. "Ladies. We've got to talk."

Barry went to the windows and started pulling curtains shut. Then he double-checked the door.

"What's goin' on?" Líle said.

"Rowan Flynn is out looking for her," Barry said, nodding his head at Maggie.

"Maggie Connell," Líle said. "We got to know one another a bit."

Barry sighed. "Maggie. Nice to meet yeh, but can you tell me why Rowan Flynn is out looking for you?"

Maggie really didn't know.

"I—I'm just tryin' to get back to Kilkee. It's where I'm from. Originally. I have family there." *Had* a family there.

Barry shrugged. "Well, we should get you out of town as soon as possible. If Rowan is looking for yeh, it can't be good. He's part of some club that calls themselves the Order of Bres. He funds the Irish Republican Army, but I wouldn't trust him with a three and half meter pole."

Maggie understood. Rowan Flynn was Carman's new puppet. He probably already had Bridget and Aedán. Maybe leaving them was not a good idea. She had just been so blindsided by the idea she'd lost Cuán, she didn't think about how much danger they could still be in.

"Ah, I bolloxed it," Maggie said. "Oh, how bloody thick of me."

"There something you're not telling us?" Líle said, her big eyes gawking on Maggie.

"Maybe. But I don't mean to get you involved. That's fer sure."

Barry crossed in front of Líle to get Maggie's full attention and held out a hand in peace. "We're not going to fight this out, aye? Instead, I'm going to pay you back for yer kindness in taking out Alton before he chilled me off. The quicker we do that, the faster everyone moves on with their own lives. A'right?"

Líle stuck her tongue out at Maggie and then stopped just before Barry glanced at her. She just looked innocently at Maggie after that. "What he said."

Maggie, a little upset, wanted to punch the girl in the nose, but Barry stood between them, and she wasn't worth it. Maggie thought maybe *having it out* would make her feel better, but she knew she wouldn't wear the indiscretion well. Maggie sighed in frustration and looked away from Líle. "Fine."

Maggie leaned over onto the bed and grabbed her Airgid Hook and belt, wrapping it around her waist.

"A'right then. Let's figure this out," Barry said.

2

Rowan lit up a cigarette as he walked from the garage to the manor. A small Model-T pulled into his drive, so he stopped and waited for it to come around. It stopped next to him as Rowan puffed away.

Inside the car, he recognized one of Barry McDermott's boys. Rowan couldn't think of his name, but it didn't matter. The boy just wanted a quick pay day. The boy got out of the car, removing his paperboy hat and nervously pounded it with his fist.

"Mister Flynn? May I have a word with you?"

"Well, so long as it's good news," Rowan said. "Is it good news, boyo?"

"Aye. It is."

"Well, tell me then."

The nervous kid nodded hastily. "Um—Uh, well, I don't know why he didn't tell you about it, honestly, but Barry was with a woman you described late last night. I watched him help her on an account that she was hurt. She had her arm around his shoulder. I'm sure that Barry took her back to his apartment."

"And how do you know that?"

"Because that was the direction, he was helping her off to," the boy said.

Rowan thought about this. It could be true.

Now he had to deal with the boy.

"I suppose you ratted him out because you want the money," Rowan said, smiling. He started walking back toward the garage. The boy followed him.

"I wouldn't be honest if I said no. It would help."

Rowan nodded. "Money is an important commodity, isn't it? It can even make us turn on those who we are supposed to be loyal to."

The boy nodded. "How are we to get anywhere without money? Am I right?"

Rowan sighed. "Oh, I don't know. Loyalty is important, too. After all, how do we trust those who will give everything up for money? It could cause problems. Names get mentioned. Before you know it, the whole enterprise falls apart."

"Sir?"

Inside the garage, Rowan reached for the heavy monkey wrench. Before the kid understood what was going on, he turned on a foot, swinging the wrench into the boy's head. With a dull thud sound, the kid fell back on his ass, grabbing at his bleeding scalp.

"We can't have that, can we?" Rowan said. "I need to know my boys can keep their mouths shut."

He started beating on the boy's bloody head until the kid's body stopped throwing about. It exhausted him and his sore arm throbbed, but the boy wasn't going to be a problem anymore.

Now to get his butler, Brendan, to clean the mess up.

***

In his red Nash Touring, Rowan drove by Barry McDermott's apartment. As luck would have it, Barry, his little blond mot, and the curly redhead strolled out to his Model-T. They got in and they took off down the road. Trying to stay out of eyeshot, Rowan followed the Model-T as far back as he could as they made their way across Wexford.

They stopped outside a brick warehouse Rowan knew Barry's family owned. Rowan parked down the road, lighting a cigarette as he watched the three of them go around the building toward a cellar.

"So, that's where you're planning on hiding her for now," Rowan said. "That's easy enough."

He put his Nash Touring into gear and turned around for home.

It was important that he didn't get his hands messy with all of this. He had other more important duties to handle.

Alton Headly

1

They pulled Bridget out of the garda car and put her in handcuffs. She balked and complained the whole time, not understanding why they were cuffing her or why they lied about taking her to the Gardaí station.

They were parked in front of the Cuinn's manor house.

"Will you shut the *eff* up?" the heavyset garda said. The only one of them that even talked to her.

"I've never been arrested, and I don't think this is an arrest anyway. Why are we here?"

Both gardaí sighed, pushing her up the steps. The wiry guard knocked on the door and a balding butler answered the door.

"We've got her," the heavyset garda said.

The butler gestured for them to come in and then he shut the door behind her. The gardaí shoved her through the large foyer. A large, immaculate stairwell laid out before her. On either side were doors going to who-knows-where.

Bridget was frightened. She didn't know how she was going to get out of this, and she wished Maggie had stayed with her. She also wished she'd stayed with Aedán.

Shouldn't he be around here, as well? Once he saw her, he'd get her out of this mess. She was sure of it.

"I want to speak with Aedán," she said. "He won't let you do this."

"Oh?"

Bridget looked to the top of the stairs. Leaning on the banister, a slick-looking man in a fancy dark blue suit stood there, watching over them. Aedán walked up beside him. He saw her right away and his eyes widened.

"Bring her up," the well-dressed man said.

The gardaí grabbed each arm and started pushing her up the stairs. The whole time Bridget looked to Aedán for help, but he only stared back at her, his chest rising and falling heavily.

"Aedán? What's going on? Help me, Aedán. Please."

Aedán didn't say anything.

Fear seemed to jolt around inside of her, but it didn't dawn on her that Aedán wasn't on her side anymore until she was at the top of the stairs. The fear turned to anger, and she screamed. "Aedán! What are you doing?! *Aedán!*"

"Feisty, isn't she?" the well-dressed man told Aedán, who gazed away from them. "That's okay. We've got a room for you, Miss MacCailín."

They all followed her down the hall to the room at the end. They tossed her inside. Aedán went in with her, looking apologetic. "I'm sorry. I do love you, but this is important."

"Oh, *feck* off!" Bridget shouted.

Aedán started backing out of the room, but the gardaí pushed him back into it. Aedán suddenly turned and saw the well-dressed man peeking in on them.

"Sorry, Aedán. I can't really trust you either."

The door slammed shut and Aedán went to it, banging his fists on the door. "Rowan! You bastard!"

"So, I've been told..." They could hear him as he walked away.

Aedán tried the doorknob, finding it locked.

Bridget could only stare at Aedán in horror. He betrayed her, and she didn't know what to do. Who to trust. Now what was she going to do?

Her heart broke, and she found it hard to breathe. She sat back on the bed, trying to catch her breath. Aedán looked at her and then started walking over to her. She shot out her arm between them.

"Not a step closer!"

Aedán stopped. "Bridget. I—I had to do this. My father…"

"I don't care!" Bridget sobbed. "You would rather destroy us, then love me."

"That's not true! I—"

"Get the FUCK away from me, Aedán!"

Aedán sighed, tears welling up in his eyes.

Good. The bastard deserved them and more. She would beat him with her fists if she knew she had the strength. Everything they've been through, and he was *one of them*? Lies, deception and now cowardliness.

Aedán could go fuck himself.

2

There were six druids brought into the Inner Circle, indoctrinated by Carman and Lady Reagan Leary until they came of age to take their place. They were all gathered for the occasion, given rooms in the manor. Lady Reagan Leary was still alive at 88, being pushed around in a wheelchair by a short, lanky girl named Elen. While Lady Leary took care of the day-to-day finances and organized the political functions, Carman continued studying sorcery and the occult to gather what was needed for the Waking of the Red God. As Rowan came of age and risen to his place as High Priest, he started learning from Lady Leary, because they all knew one day soon, she would be gone.

Of course, Rowan had learned a thing or two from Carman as well. Once he was sure Aedán and Bridget were locked up tight in a room, he removed his clothes and stood naked in a circle of yew bark, his blood painting archaic symbols around him across the floor.

There was a metal basin of water at his feet. He let his bleeding hand, which he'd cut with a knife, dangle over the basin and bright red drops landed with a *sploop, sploop, sploop*…fanning out into a cloud as the water saturated it.

Rowan sat down with his legs crossed in front of the basin and grabbed a hold of it, lifting it. He took a deep breath and then he pushed his face into the water so that his eyes, nose and mouth were covered in the bloody water.

The spell awoke. Rowan found himself flying over Wexford until he landed in the warehouse cellar, where Barry and his mot took Maggie. She saw a heavy door, which Barry opened, and once Maggie stepped in, he shut it behind her, locking her in. Maggie pounded at the door, upset, and Barry apologized, saying he did it for her own good. His blond mot laughing all the while.

Good, Rowan thought. She would go nowhere.

Now he needed somebody expendable.

The spell seemed to hear his thoughts, and he went flying again. This time he turned up in a rat-infested apartment with a fair-haired man who sat brooding. There were tears down his eyes and he held a revolver, slowly turning the barrel around. A bowler hat sat on the coffee table beside him.

"Who is this?" Rowan asked.

The spell whispered in his ear. "Alton Headley."

He was flying again. Rowan watched things play out. A shootout took place between the British and a rebel faction of Irish a few years before, during the Irish War of Independence. Alton's older brother, Norris Headley, made the mistake of separating himself from the other British soldiers, hoping to get around a barrage. Barry stepped out of his hiding spot behind some rubble.

Barry fired, hitting Norris in the arm. Norris cried out, falling back.

"Barry! It's me! Don't shoot!"

"What are you doin' 'ere?"

"I'm 'ere to do my duty!" Norris cried.

"Me too, I suppose," Barry said, shooting Norris again in the shoulder. "Stay down, or I'll have to kill you." Barry ran after that as the British soldiers heard the gunshot and moved around to find Norris laying there.

Norris would live long enough to write a letter. The British medics could get the bullet out and bandage him up, but gangrene set in, and Norris died less than a week later.

Rowan flew again until he landed in London. Alton received his brother's letter, saying that Barry McDermott shot him. They both had known him because their fathers had been long-time friends. A few days later, Alton also hears about his brother's death.

Rowan woke, dropping the basin that splashed about him. He half-choked on the water and then spat it out. He was back at the Cuinn manor. Safe in his room.

Alton Headley didn't know where Barry was, and he wanted Barry dead. *Badly*. Maybe there was a deal to be made here. Because, in the end, Carman warned that if they let that redhead bitch live, she would ruin their plans. Rowan wanted to not only prove himself, but he wanted to be there to see the Waking.

Rowan pondered this. Should he send someone to Alton? Just to be on the safe side?

No. Someone else could possibly ruin the plan. The Waking was soon. If he didn't catch Maggie now, he didn't think he'd get another chance.

Rowan had to do this himself.

Bugger Off

1

Once the two of them tricked her into the small room filled with bags of rice, they left her as she yelled after them to set her free. The door was a heavy, thick oak wood. Even if she became the serpent, she wasn't sure if she'd have the strength to break down the door. Besides, it was banded with iron. She could *feel* it radiating its unnatural coldness.

Maggie wanted to cry. Things were getting worse. She thought she could trust Barry because she wanted to trust her destiny—the one she made for herself. She hugged herself and paced in the cell, swearing under her breath. The cellar was cold, too, and all she could think about was Bridget, Aedán, and Cuán.

"Oh, god, Cuán." She broke down and then wiped her wet eyes.

How could anything get worse? Not only did she fail to cleanse her blood from the fae-touch, but Bridget and Aedán were in trouble.

Cuán.

Could Cuán be dead? If he was alive, she had no idea where he could be. She wasn't supposed to be here. She was *supposed* to be with Cuán.

Maggie never hated herself more and it hurt so absolutely.

She could see no hope. Sixty-seven years too late to do anything. There were motorcars and telephones and Ireland itself was in a civil war that worked at eating itself. It confused her and frightened her. Especially the thought of being alone. The very thing she feared more than anything, which set her on her path that ironically twisted her back here. It was like a cosmic joke.

"Let me out," she pleaded, but she didn't think anyone could hear her.

2

From Etna's memories, Eileen could remember how her grandmother—still spry at 49—went to see an old woman named Oona. Etna knew the old woman had raised the serpent girl, but the woman was perpetually mournful for having lost her daughter, never knowing where she'd gone off to. Oona happily talked about her and told Etna everything she knew about Maggie. It was obvious, however, that she never knew that Maggie had been changed by the Fomorians and possessed supernatural abilities.

Etna put Oona to bed, telling her that she would see herself out. While Oona slept, Etna opened her vanity drawer and grabbed a lock of red hair—Maggie's hair. And took it.

As an old woman, before blowing her own head off, she'd given that lock of hair to Eileen in a small paper bag. Once Eileen was in Wexford, she knew the next step would be to find where Maggie was located. She took a few strands and placed them in the basin of water.

She incanted in the old tongue.

"Taispeáin dom cá bhfuil sí."—*Show me where she is.*

As if the water dissolved the hair, it disappeared and was replaced by an image of a warehouse. She saw its number, and she saw the street name. It was enough to find her.

3

Rowan found him seething in the back of a pub on High Street, drinking a pint, clearly drunk. He worked his way through the other patrons until he sat at the table with the younger man.

"Alton Headley."

"What the *fuck* you want?" Alton said.

"Well—"

"Can that. Bugger *off*, mate."

"I know this may surprise you—maybe even alarm you—but I have what you want," Rowan said, trying to stay focused. He wasn't going to let this mangy man pull him into his pit.

"I said bugger off."

Rowan nodded, leaning forward. "I know where Barry McDermott is."

Alton frowned at him. "I don't know what you're talkin' 'bout."

"Don't play games with me, arsehole. You want him or not?"

Alton glared at him for a long time. Rowan tried not to breathe in the man's drunken stench. "How do you—?"

Rowan shook his head, holding up a hand. "We don't need to know the whys, do we? Or the hows? How about we just make a deal to stay out of each other's business, except for one thing. We make this slight deal where I tell you where to find McDermott, and you bring me back the redhead he's holding on to?"

"How do I bloody do that?"

Rowan looked around and then dug into his pocket, revealing iron shackles. "She's quite strong, so you don't want to underestimate her. Put these on her, though, and she's piss in the wind."

Alton grabbed the shackles, looked around for anyone watching, and then stuffed it in his coat. "Well? Where's this McDermott *fuck*er?"

"You have to bring her to me alive. You understand?"

Alton nodded. "Aye. I have you. No worries."

Satisfied, Rowan whispered the location to Barry's warehouse. When he was done, he finally saw a smile on Alton's face.

"You're serious about this?"

"Aye. Deadly."

Alton sniffed. "You mind gettin' me drink? I lost me bits."

Rowan sighed, grabbing Alton's hand tightly.

"Be careful. Go in quietly, shackle the girl, and then take McDermott out as quickly as possible. If the working crew hears the noise, you'll have to move quicker, or you'll screw yourself."

Alton yanked his hand back. "Just tell me where to take the girl when it's done."

Cocoon

Cuán. Wake up, boyo.

Cuán thought he had, but he could only see darkness. His body swayed, wrapped up tight in a cottony or silky material. He wondered if it could be a soft chrysalis. He couldn't tell if he was hanging upside down or right-side up. It all felt weird, as if he were floating in the ocean, and it terrified him.

Though he didn't know where he was, he started hearing things. Whispers.

A low groan.

"Oh, are you sad?" He had never heard the woman's lustrous voice before. "I thought the Bresquinn Arrachtaigh was supposed to be a terrible creature, capable of killing Demidians. Demigods."

Cuán could tell she mocked some creature.

The creature growled this time. It almost sounded human.

Cuán tried to wriggle his arms free. If he could just get them up, he might be able to pull the surrounding material apart. The harder he struggled, though, the tighter it seemed to get.

The woman laughed.

"Oh, you are finally awake. I made the call days ago," the woman said. "Cuán, isn't it?"

Cuán tried to talk but found his voice weak. He cleared his throat and tried again. It left his throat all scratchy, but he softly worked the words he wanted: "Where...am...I?"

"You are underground, Cuán. So your precious Maggie can't find you. At least, for now."

Maggie. Oh God, it was good to hear her name...She was alive!

"Who...?" The word came out just a little more than a puff of air.

"My name is Carman. I'm the one who had you captured. The details aren't important, are they? You need to stay there like a good boyo, and when it's all said and done, I'll discard you with the rest of the trash."

"Where...is...she?" It seemed that his voice got stronger.

"Maggie? Oh, don't worry about that creature. You need to hush now. I can't have you upsetting Nevan," Carman said.

Her footsteps started walking away from him. He could hear it dissipating. Panic gripped is chest.

"No! ...Don't leave...me."

The woman laughed from across the chamber, wherever they were.

"I wouldn't fight too hard. Even if you escaped the cocoon, I'm not sure how long you've been in there. It's been keeping you alive, so I don't know what would happen if you were to come out. Could be devastating."

"What...do you...mean?"

"Oh, I forgot to tell you." He could tell by her voice that she moved a little closer to him. "You've been asleep in there for over sixty years."

Over sixty years? *How?*

"Help me," he said, not completely understanding. Fear climbed up within him. Not only could he remember that he lived, but what a fragile situation he fell into. He vaguely recalled Aisling—the fae girl who tricked him into going into those caverns, setting him up to be spun up by half-shadowed subterranean creatures.

They hadn't made him their meal. He was a gift for Carman.

She had been setting this all up for a long time. And Cuán didn't even know who the bloody hell she was. Certain that she didn't really want him, like Muirgen before her, Carman wanted to get to Maggie.

Cuán calculated his age in his head. He was 26 when he went into the Otherworld. Sixty some-odd years: that was at least 86.

I'm an old man, he thought. *Or I'm a dead man if I leave this damn cocoon.*

His whole life...gone. In a blink. What had happened all those years? And...what had he done?

Cuán had never been so upset. He started screaming, trying to tear and kick free of the web in his rage, not coming to his senses until he realized the cocoon still held him tight. He didn't have to worry about dying right now—the chrysalis wouldn't free him to the void.

Cuán broke down and sobbed his heart out.

Treachery

1

The long hours alone in the dark cellar trapped in the small room, took its toll on Maggie, and she found herself falling asleep again. It reminded her of her imprisonment in the pit of Tech Duinn back when she first started her journey. Time was strange. Even though she knew it wasn't too long ago, it felt far away. Around sixty-eight years, apparently.

When she awoke, it was because she heard a sharp click, noticeable in all the quietness. When she looked up, she realized a man stooped beside her and stood up as she regarded him. He was familiar, but it took a second.

"Who...?"

When she tried to move a hand to support herself so that she could get up, she felt the old tug on her other arm. In shock, she noticed that her hands were shackled together with cold iron.

She also recognized the man. Bowler Hat: Alton. The one who stalked Barry McDermott that night, she saved him from getting shot.

He grinned.

"Fuck is this?" Maggie said. "Let me go, now!"

She wondered how he got in there but realized the latch on the 'prison' door was a bolt lock. No key, so he could waltz right in and take advantage of her while she slept.

"Sh," he said, putting an index finger to his lips. "Rowan Flynn wants you alive. I'd love to do that for him, but it's only going to happen if yer quiet. You understand?"

Feck me, Maggie thought. Could this get any worse?

"What is this? A weapon of some sort?"

The man grabbed the Airgid Hook and belt from around her hip and slung it over his shoulder.

"You haven't heard I'm kind of dangerous, have yeh?" Maggie said, hoping to make him nervous. "If ye don't let me go, I'll have yer head as a trophy."

The man forced a smile. "You look like a pussycat now, Luv. As I said, you need to keep quiet, or this won't end well for yeh."

Alton grabbed her arm and easily shoved her out of the small room, though she tried to resist a little. Without her powers, she was a small woman with very little weight. Maggie cursed the iron and his knowledge of it. *Why was her one weakness something so fecking common?*

The man hit her hard in the head with the back of the gun.

2

Líle couldn't help but smile. She could trust her fella far more than she thought. She didn't really think that Barry could do it—put the girl in the cellar and lock her up like that. She was pretty proud of him.

The warehouse was for grain and rice. The workers were trucking the product into the warehouse and then others logged it, fulfilled orders, and dispersed it amongst the Wexford shops. Barry's father was older, almost an invalid, and Barry was slowly taking over the business. They were in his office, with some of his I.R.A pals gathered around, with the door shut tight.

"I've heard the Free State forces are getting a British guard to run a shipment of guns to Dublin from the Wexford port," Barry said. "They'll be unloading the boats at midnight, so we'll lock them in there, and we'll get the guns. I'm not going to lie. It'll be dangerous, but if we stop them from getting those guns north, it'll deadlock the Free State forces, giving our men more of a fighting chance."

"Do you know how many men there'll be?" Patrick said as he dispersed rifles to each of the men.

He handed one to Líle, who opened it up and checked the chamber.

"I'm guessing two men per truck. Maybe twelve. And at least half of them will be British guards, so they'll be armed," Barry said. "Is there anyone 'ere that wants out?"

None of the men protested.

Barry nodded, grinning. "That's right. My feckin' men stand the feck up for this country, fer their blood is the country, aye?"

"Damn straight," Patrick said. "Green blood."

The men cheered and Líle joined them, laughing.

"For the Eire!" she cried.

The men joined in: "For the EIRE!"

From the corner of her eye, she saw a man with dirty blond hair walking toward them. He leaned forward a bit; his face screwed up. She wondered at first if he was one of Barry's crew, but as he got closer, Líle got an ominous feeling about him. She didn't like it all, and before she could ask Barry who he was, she noticed the revolver in the stranger's hand.

The man pushed through the door, raising his gun and shot at Barry and the other men. Six loud pops and it was all over. Líle even forgot she held her own rifle, it happened so fast. When the man looked at her, he punched her in the face and then he went out the door. The punch sent Líle reeling across the wall and onto the floor beside Barry, who had dropped there himself, half behind his desk. She looked up at his face and saw cold staring eyes and a mouth agape in horror. There was a small, bloody cavity beside his left eye socket and nose.

Blood poured out of his lips and down his cheek, and Líle realized his face—his eyes—showed no life.

Barry was *dead*. But she wouldn't let herself believe it. Maybe he was only faking it, so he wouldn't get shot again. "Barry! *Barry*, come on, don't be dead," she said, getting on her knees, ignoring the painful sting in her jaw.

Barry didn't move, so she looked around. The other men were shot as well, but most were groaning as they checked their wounds. The assassin had been sloppy. He hit men's arms, shoulders and one grazed Patrick's rib, but only one other caught a bullet wrong. Líle couldn't remember his name, but he was on his ass, legs splayed and there was a bleeding hole in his chest, creating a pool around his legs.

How did this happen?

Líle felt rage boil up in her and she decided that she was going to run after the killer. She grabbed her rifle off the floor where she'd dropped it and pushed through the men and into the warehouse proper. There were no clues—no signs of him, but he couldn't have gotten too far yet, could he?

As she made her way to the front entrance doors, she thought about the shooter. He shot Barry's whole crew, but he didn't seem to care to kill anyone but Barry. That's why Barry was his first target and he made it count. It was smart. Create chaos and get the blood hell out of there.

Except she wasn't going to let him get away so easily, if she could help it.

Líle climbed down the stairs and lifted the muzzle of the rifle up, pointing it in front of her, waving it from doorway to doorway as she searched the halls. As she met and passed the warehouse crew, they put their hands up and backed against the wall until they were sure she was ignoring them.

Damn it, she thought. *Where the flying' feck are yeh?*

3

With Etna's research all packaged up and beside her in the Model-T, Eileen pulled up outside the warehouse just in time to see some action. A man came out of a cellar with a redheaded woman over his shoulder, looking as though he was in a hurry to escape. Eileen parked and saw the man staring at her, coming toward her.

"Oh shit," she said. The man carried a revolver, and he lifted it at her.

The man started firing and the Model-T's windows shattered all over her.

Eileen screamed, but it was the last thing she would do. And she remembered one of Etna's memories with Carman so long ago—

You are nothing but a shadow, and without me, all your efforts will be for not. Even your children will be shadows and expire early and with no importance. You...Etna...are what I choose you to be, and nothing more.

Though she was now dead, Eileen could smile. She knew that wasn't totally true.

4

Alton dropped the redhead on the ground and pulled the dark-haired woman out of her car. Once he had thrown the dead woman aside, he grabbed Maggie and put her into the back seat. Then he climbed into the front seat, leaving the dead woman on the street.

He heard someone shooting at him, but they missed.

Alton grinned, putting the pedal to the floor.

5

Bridget refused to talk, hunching herself down near the window in the corner. Aedán rambled his apologies and tried to excuse his behaviors, but she didn't hear any of it—didn't *want* to hear any of it. Screw the Order, screw his political ideals, and screw him.

"What you don't understand is we are only cogs in a giant machine. Our love is important, but so is Ireland and all its people. We have a chance to become more than ourselves. We have a chance to be the doorway to an Ireland ruled by the Irish!"

Go fuck yourself, Bridget thought. *After all, we've been through, and you preach to me? Yeah. Go fuck yourself sideways, you big arse.*

Once he stopped, he went quiet for a long time. He sobbed. His eyes were red and plump. Bridget knew he'd slid down the opposite side of the room, but she refused to even look at him.

If she got out of this, she wanted to find Maggie. The two of them would figure things out together. Bridget really wished she'd chased Maggie down and went with her. Seeing the scraps of the life she left behind was somehow now less important.

It was more than likely all gone anyway, she thought.

Men rushed the room. Druids. They had on white robes, and they grabbed their arms, pulling them to their feet and out into the hall.

"What are you doing? Let me go! Go die, you prick!" she shouted, all falling on deaf ears as they dragged them in two different directions. They shoved Bridget into a room where there were three other women. Bridget tried to fight until she became exhausted, and they let her sit on the floor for quite a while, none of them saying anything to her.

One of the men crouched down and looked her in the eyes.

"We can do this all day and all night, if we have to. It'll be easier if you cooperate. In the end, it'll be worth it, and we'll all have a nice drink afterwards. What do yeh say?"

"Go suck your lord's bollocks," she said.

The druid frowned at her and stood up, saying to the others in the room: "I guess we'll have to do it the hard way."

The men grabbed her again and started stripping her. Once they shoved her into a cold bath, the women took over, holding her down and scrubbed her raw. The women threatened her and growled at her as she tried pinching and scratching, but, in the end, there were more of them, and she couldn't stop them. The men pulled her out and one of the other women threw a towel over her to dry her off.

"Get her dressed and ready for the festival," the man said and walked out.

Once dressed in a white gown, given some makeup and perfume, and crowned with flowers, she watched Rowan Flynn walk in. Behind him Aedán and a couple other druids appeared behind him.

"Beautiful, Ladies."

Rowan looked at her.

"This is the night the Red God, Bres, returns. You both will be his doorway and an offering. For what you've done to Bres, he will return unto you."

Rowan pulled a long knife. Bridget could see it plummeting into her, cutting organs and she imagined bleeding to death right in this room. Her hands trembled, and she felt tears falling again.

"Don't. Don't do this," Bridget said.

Aedán held out a hand. "We'll be okay, Bridget. We are not like the others in this room. We don't come from the Gaels. Lugh is our chief. Our sacrifice will create a balance between the Lugh and Bres, and Tuatha Dé can renegotiate the Great Contracts with the Fomorians. It will make Ireland stronger! My father says he foresaw it!"

Bridget shook her head at him. "You've lost your *fuck*ing mind. They're going to murder us, Aedán! You betrayed me and you betray everything that you stand for with your dishonor. Ireland isn't made better by people who want to rule it. It's not made better by murder or death. It's made better by the people showing each other loyalty and courage in the face of oppression. You are what's wrong with all of us—all of humanity. Can't you see that?"

Aedán didn't say anything. He only regarded her.

It didn't matter.

If her life was lost, what did it really matter in the long run? With everyone she cared about either dead or old enough to be near death, there was nothing to live for anyway. Sure, it would have been nice to have Maggie there with her so that she didn't feel so alone, but in the end, it didn't really matter.

Aedán moved toward her, but a druid grabbed his arm. He yanked free and went to her anyway. He grabbed her bottom jaw and lifted her face to meet his.

"We're immortal. Don't you see? We are gods. We may die, but we will be reincarnated as we've done in the past. It won't be forever and it's for the good of the people. Please understand!"

"I don't understand you," Bridget said.

Carman laughed, entering the room. She studied Aedán. The witch was dressed in a white robe, almost blending in with the other druids of the Order. She looked elegant and moved sensually.

"Is that what your father told you?" she said with a huge smile on her face. She thought it funny.

Aedán frowned at her. "Of course. I once walked with Lugh as Aoi Mac Ollamain. I was a poet and could weave the imbas since my first birth. Bridget walked as the white witch, Bé Chuille. We worked with Lugh to stop you and your three sons from devastating the island with famine. You were imprisoned by Bres himself, hidden somewhere to be forgotten, only you used magic to be reborn through your bloodline. So, my question is, why do you now seek to awaken the Red God?"

"You figured a lot of it out," Carman said. "I should be stopping all of this, shouldn't I? Leave that bastard in his grave. Only I'm not. I'm helping the Order awaken him from Codail."

"Why?" Rowan said. "If what Aedán says is true, why do you help us?"

"Because what you are all forgetting, is that Bres was also betrayed by the Lugh and the Tuatha Dé. If anyone hates you more, I don't know who does. And when Bres rises, your offerings will even be sweeter! He will destroy your souls utterly until all that is left is the *croí* energy, which will be the power to awaken the Red God and its leavings recycled into the Primordial itself. You will be gone forever. And then Bres will forgive me for my past deeds, and we will come together to build the Order of Bres into a real power. Maybe even Britain will fall, and we will then put them into slavery as they have us."

Rowan grinned at Aedán, who now looked at all of them in horror. Now he truly knew how she felt: *betrayed.*

"But what about the Great Contracts and the balance?" Aedán said.

"There's no such thing as balance when it comes to power. There is only the sovereign and the whelps below them," Carman said. "And you're...a whelp."

"So, let's draw the line between the stones and complete the Waking!" Rowan shouted. The druids in the room cheered.

One of them pushed Aedán toward Bridget. She still didn't look at him. Not even to tell him she told him so, which she wanted to do with all her heart.

"I'm sorry," he heard him whisper. "I didn't know I was being lied to. By my own father."

Bridget still refused to look at him. There was a part of her that felt sorry for him, knowing how it felt, but another part of her that knew that this all could have been avoided if he'd only believed in *their* truth.

The Journal

Maggie woke, a headache blooming throughout her head, and she felt her body bouncing. She slowly opened her eyes, remembering Bowler Hat shackling her and thumping her on the head with the back of his revolver. She was in one of those motorcars, the side of her cheek wet with drool.

She didn't want to move and tip him off that she awoke. It also came to her that he would be taking her to Carman, and Maggie didn't like the idea that she'd be powerless when facing such a powerful woman. What would she do to her? The witch would only think of her as a threat and would probably kill her just as soon as she beheld her.

It wasn't going to be good, and Maggie knew it.

But what could she do?

Maggie looked at the shackles holding her hands together with a short chain, disgusted how the iron felt cold on her skin, weakening her, taking her powers away.

Carman knew exactly what she was doing.

Maggie's eyes slowly moved up the back of the seat in the Model-T. She noticed that the glass windows had been shot out. Particles of it all over the seat and all over the floor. She saw the back of Bowler Hat's head as he drove. Unless she made a noise, she didn't see how he would know she awoke.

Maggie lifted her head and looked out the back window. They were just leaving Wexford for the countryside, probably heading to Cuinn manor, where Aedán probably was right now.

Was Aedán in danger?

Maggie worried about him. She hoped Bridget made it out of town.

She didn't understand how any of this connected, but she knew she had to get out of this situation and find out. Fast.

When Maggie saw that they were far enough from the crowds of people walking to and fro, she jumped up and slid the chain of the shackles around Bowler Hat's neck, yanking back on them, strangling him. The Model-T drifted off the road as he grabbed the chain, trying to free it from around his neck, but Maggie pulled hard, steading herself with her feet against the back of his seat. Not even he was strong enough to fight, and, gagging, he finally faded and went slack. Maggie held it tight for another minute just in case he was faking it in order to escape.

By that time, the Model-T stopped in a green field, puttering silently and spitting.

Maggie let him go, figuring he'd have the key to the shackles in one of his pockets. She grabbed the handle, opened it and went around to check the man's pulse. Unable to feel any life in him, she opened his door and pulled the man out onto the ground and searched the pockets of his jacket and trousers. In his left pocket, she felt the cold metal and shape of the key and pulled it out.

"Go straight to hell fer me," Maggie seethed in his ear.

Within seconds, she was free, and she tossed the shackles aside, getting back into the Model-T, which still sputtered, alive. She had no idea how to drive the thing, but she decided an open green field would be a great place to learn. Maggie moved the moveable shaft thing in the center of the vehicle, and the thing kicked and died. She tried turning the key in the ignition, and she could hear it turning, but she didn't understand how to keep it going.

Was it because she moved the shaft?

Maggie slammed her fist into the wheel, frustrated beyond belief. How could it be so hard?

She looked over at the passenger's seat and saw her Airgid Hook and belt on the floorboard. She also saw a paper bag full of stuff. Maggie almost ignored it, but she saw that someone had written on it with ink. It was in feminine hand: *Carman the witch.*

What was Bowler Hat doing with this?

Maggie grabbed the Airgid Hook and belt, refastened it around her, and reached for the bag and dumped out its contents. Most of it was paperwork and included a journal. She started glancing over all of it, finding everything known about Carman by local historians dating back to the earliest written records.

Fate always did work in mysterious ways...

The journal told Carman's story thoroughly, piecing the records and other notes that Maggie had also found in the bag. Translating and puzzling it all out over several years, the woman even reflected on her own experiences with the witch. The archaeologist, Etna, described the moment when Carman came from her own flesh while she was lying in bed. How Dark Forces came to her and gave her Sreng's Finger, and how it took her to a Hidden Place at the St. Albeus monastery ruins. It took her to a monster that Carman would slay.

Εδώ βρίσκεται ο Κάρμαν
A thyng of unnatyral evyl. A dymon of wom-
nh'd. It shakes its mylky brests and scratchys
thee walls wyth its clahs late into thee nyte.

The notes held the translations in Greek for her and went on to describe how the witch infiltrated Lord Cuinn's *Order of Bres*. As she plotted, she abused Etna however she could. Killed people who got in her way. Etna also noted how she went to Kilkee and murdered Brian and Orna Foley as retribution for Maggie killing one of her sons.

A foreign witch, Carman had no geas until she
devoted herself to the Fomorians to gain their trust and
other occult secrets. She only looked for power, but as
always, the Fomorians have a price—a geas shaped that
she must always answer the call of her father.

It then goes on to describe what Etna found in Athens: a dialogue and written account between two men about a murder, whereupon a daughter with three sons killed her whole family so that she could abuse their resources.

So, Carman's father was dead.

What did the witch have to fear then? Maggie wondered. What sort of geas was this that fate gave such an evil woman? How did the divine not intervene in such a case?

The journal mentioned only one way to trap her...taking her back to the Hidden Place. Maggie didn't understand why at first.

Maggie wished she understood how the gods worked. It seemed that when they could step in to stop such evil from creating chaos, they only chose to watch. Didn't they have any moral sense or obligation to humans or perhaps the world at large?

She did remember Dá Derga as he spat at her: *I hold dominion of transcendence. That was my contract, chiseler! I follow my purview because it flows through my very veins.*

Maggie felt disgusted, but Etna's files cleared so many things up.

Carman wasn't going to use the druids only to raise Bres; she planned to feed Bres to an even bigger shark, whatever this Dominion was.

I would like you to bring me the two mortals you're ploddin' around with. Bridget Rose MacCailín and her boyfriend, Aedán Ó Deasún. If you bring them to me, I will return your beloved, Carman had said.

Maggie didn't have either of them anymore. She'd let them go...

And Maggie bet the witch already had both of her friends. She would have collected them for the ritual. Carman needed them to appease Bres long enough, so the god didn't foresee what came. Maggie only wished she knew what Etna meant by the Dominion, or Dark Force. Some descriptions reminded her of the *Maidí Uaimh.*

> *He kisses her on the neck and with fangs buried in the flesh, takes what he wills from her veins.*

Like a brine vampyre, Maggie thought. Only she spoke of the creature as a powerful male with dark powers. Maggie hadn't seen any *Maidí Uaimh* males. In fact, the name suggested only females were amongst their clan.

Her third-class teacher—who also taught Cuan a few years before her—told her stories about the *Abhartach*, the Irish vampyre. He was one of the *neamh-mairbh*, the walking dead.

> *In the Slaghtaverty parish in Derry, there was a dwarf named Abhartach who was a dreadful tyrant and magician. Throughout his life he existed amongst men such cruelties, both rape and murder, so that he destroyed people utterly. He was a blight that even God had turned away from. After some time, a clan chieftain, Fionn Mac Cumhail, slayed Abhartach, and the dwarf was buried unceremoniously and quickly afterward. Though he was buried in the ground, his heart no longer beating, he was still often seen in places he had once visited in life. He murdered many, drinking their blood, and sometimes ate their flesh as a wicked revenge upon the land.*
>
> *Fionn Mac Cumhail, knowing not what else to do, fetched a druid and sought their sacred knowledge. Fionn then tracked the still-walking dwarf to its lair and slayed it again, removing its head and burying it into the ground neck-first, so that it could not crawl out again. Once this was accomplished, they placed a standing stone atop his grave, so Abhartach would not be able to rise again.*
>
> *To this day, it is said the dwarf is still there, hungry for mortal blood.*

Maggie sighed. A vampyre. She was sure of it.

She mulled it all over again, and then an idea came to her.

She climbed out of the motorcar, grabbed her Airgid Hook from the passenger's floorboard, and started walking down the road, putting on the belt. Eventually, she'd come across the gates of the Cuinn estates, and she'd enter them with a plan.

XI

Shadow & Cellar

When Líle pushed through the warehouse entrance doors, she stood outside and watched as the assassin climbed into a Model-T, leaving the body of a young woman in the street. He drove off quickly, but Barry's motorcar was next to her on the street, so she shoved her rifle into the car and got in herself.

Líle started the car and punched it, following the man, but remained far enough back to make it more difficult for the shooter to notice her following him. She instinctively knew that if he looked back and saw her there'd be a car chase, and she wanted to avoid it at all costs. Ambushing him when he least expected it would be the best bet.

Trying to contain her rage so she could think through all of this, Líle stayed a few cars back and watched every turn he made. The assassin was green at this, she thought. For a few blocks, he checked his mirrors often, checking around nervously for anything unusual, but he seemed to ease the farther he got from the warehouse, thinking it safe all too soon.

He left Wexford.

When I catch you, you arsehole, I'm going to make sure your brains are all over that car, Líle growled inside her head.

Suddenly, the eejit's car started jerking side to side and then started off the road into the country fields. Confused, Líle slowed down and started pulling over. She saw the car in the distance but didn't want to get too close yet.

What the hell was going on here?

Líle's hands squeezed the wheel tight until her palms hurt.

The assassin's car came to a stop. A few moments later, Maggie crawled out of the backseat of the car.

How did—?

Líle almost forgot about her. She started having a sneaking suspicion that Maggie orchestrated the whole thing. Líle could see the British plotting to have Maggie 'save' Barry's life so that they could set up the assassination—the British government doesn't look to be involved, and Maggie then frames the assassin and leaves.

Oh, that fecking bitch!

Maggie pulled the assassin's body out of the car. She was shackled, so she searched the body and freed herself from the chains. Then she got into the front seat of the car, leaving the assassin's body on the ground in the field.

Was he dead? Líle hoped not. She wanted the pleasure of killing the bastard herself. Líle thought about taking the rifle and holding Maggie up at gunpoint, but then realized that the assassin had a gun. Maggie would have taken it and that made her deadly. No, that wasn't a good idea at all.

I'll wait and watch. She'd follow Maggie and see what she's up to, Líle thought. It was the safest route, at least for now.

It looked like Maggie tried starting the car, but knowing nothing about them, she couldn't get it to go. The redhead started walking across the green fields to a road and then started making her way along it.

Líle followed in Barry's motorcar. Slowly creeping, just barely keeping the redhead in her field of vision. After about a half-hour, they came across trees and a gate to a fancy estate. Líle parked the car as she watched Maggie grab the bars of the gate. Maggie looked around it for a bit. Líle didn't know if she were looking for help or knew the people there. Either way, Maggie seemed to be searching for something.

And then Líle's eyes opened wide in surprise.

Maggie leaped up eight feet, her feet easily landing between the iron spears, and then she hopped down onto the other side.

How the hell did she do that? And *in* a *dress?*

Líle climbed out of the car, turning back into it only to grab the rifle, and then she started jogging up the road to the gate. Maggie disappeared between the trees, probably heading to the manor that Líle could see just on the hillside.

What was she going to do? She wanted to question Maggie and find out what was going on. Another part of her wanted to go back and see if the assassin was really dead. Another part wanted to mourn Barry, burying her face into a pillow.

She told herself to be strong. Líle had to do this *for* Barry. For the I.R.A.

Líle checked her magazine to make sure it was fully loaded.

She would need to recon the place. Get the lay of the land. And then she could see about getting a hold of Maggie. If this soulless ginger so much as gave her any trouble, Líle would have no problem shooting her dead.

At the gate, she found it locked shut. She flung the rifle strap over her shoulder, so the rifle was on her back, and she climbed the gate. Not as graceful as Maggie, she finally got on top it and then jumped over. One spear caught her dress though, tearing it. Swearing to herself, she started heading for the manor, sticking to the tree line.

The sun was getting lower in the east. The day cooled, which was a regular thing in Ireland. Líle gripped her rifle tight as she made her way, trying to keep from thinking about the chill.

The closer she got to the manor, she realized that something was going on here. There were people in white robes walking around, having a craic in small clusters here and there. Not knowing where Maggie went off to, Líle decided to get closer to the manor, but wanted to avoid the white robes.

She found a truck to move around behind, and then she found a wall adjacent to the manor, which enclosed stairs into a cellar. Líle quickly made her way behind the wall, and went down the stairs, thinking that maybe there was an entrance into the manor house from the cellar.

Hearing some of the white robes walk by, she pressed herself against the wall until she heard them pass. They were talking about the Waking and how it was happening that very night. They seemed pleased and excited about it.

Líle had no idea what they were talking about and didn't care.

Once they were gone, she went to the heavy door and pushed it open. Inside, she turned around and pushed the door shut before anyone could see or hear her. Surprisingly, the cellar was lit, and it turned out much larger than she thought it would be. There were more stairs that went down into a wider chamber and there were lanterns along the walls. It formed a large circle with large blue stones every few feet around the area.

The manor was built on something ancient here—a hidden New-grange like site, being kept in secret by the druids here.

There was another set of smaller blue stones forming a ring around the center of it. In the middle looked like a large, deformed man. Líle had once read articles about a man who lived between 1862 and 1890 named Joseph Merrick. He was made into a spectacle before dying of a dislocated neck or asphyxia in the London Hospital. She had seen the pictures of the bedeviled man. The tallow man here reminded her of him, and her heart poured out to the man. He was hideous and obviously abused, chained to the center of the circle of stones, done purposefully, though she couldn't guess why.

The giant man in the center inhaled and exhaled in shallow breaths, appearing asleep. In case he was dangerous, she walked around the stones forming the center of the chamber. The lantern lights flickered on the blue stone and the raspy breaths of the giant made her feel ill-boding.

Líle's eyes shot around the room, looking for anyone who might see her, but the chamber appeared to be empty.

What the hell were these people doing? Was Maggie a part of all this?

Líle wondered if this was some sort of British black magic. Were these British druids, trying to abuse an Irish stone age site for their own purposes?

There was a white, silky coffin-shaped thing hanging in the back of the chamber from the ceiling. Líle was dismayed, looking it over in the lantern light. Like a cocoon or a ball of webs spiders made after catching insects for later feeding, it hung there as if waiting for some unknown purpose. It looked like it breathed, so she stepped back, afraid that whatever was inside might jump out at her.

That's when her butt hit a stone behind her. She turned around and found an altar. Líle looked over the flat stone, seeing an amulet with a golden wheel-shaped medallion, and there was a seashell next to it. Líle put the seashell to her ear, and she didn't hear the ocean. Instead, the shell whispered into her ear.

The cellar door Líle had come through opened. There was a flood of bright light for a moment until the door slammed shut again. She heard voices, so Líle quickly moved into the shadows behind one of the larger stones against the cellar wall.

Líle didn't recognize the man at first. He was in white robes like the others. But then she was shocked again: Rowan Flynn. The biggest I.R.A. benefactor in Wexford. Barry's 'middle-man'. Barry said he had been looking for Maggie. Why?

Was this the Cuinn estate? She'd never been out here before, though she knew stories of satanic practices and demons were widespread. She knew from the stories that Lord Cuinn had summoned a demon and put it into his son. When the son became possessed, he killed his father, his sisters, and his girlfriend. The estate then fell into the hands of a mysterious cult.

Was all of it true? She looked at the tallow giant, still slumbering in the center of the cellar.

Rowan Flynn kneeled just outside the middle stone circle and spoke in the old language. "The full moon is almost upon us, Lord Bres. Protect us in our mission and awaken for the glory of the Eire!"

Rowan then stood and took a bow before heading back up. Once he left the cellar, Líle breathed a sigh of relief just before the cocoon moved... and moaned. Líle let out a short scream, looking at the cellar door, expecting Rowan to check on the noise. After a minute, she realized he was truly gone and wasn't coming back.

Líle walked around to see the cocoon in full. It shifted again.

"Hello?"

"H-Hello?" It was a man. His voice sounded dry and cracked.

"Are you okay? H—How did you get in there?" she said.

"I, I, I—I need you to help me," the man said. "I can't get out..."

Líle held her rifle tight and realized she still held the damn seashell, too.

"How?"

"H-Help," he said. "These...aren't the only...stones."

"Should I cut you down?"

"No! No, that won't...help me," he said. "I don't know."

The Stones of Bres

1

The druids gathered together as the gold and red dusk turned plumb. The moon was full and bright overhead like a divine lantern, casting them all in its beam. Bridget wanted to cry again when they pulled Aedán and her out of the locked room, all dressed up in gowns and flowers, and led them down the path through the estate's small woodland. The path they took wasn't covered by its canopy, however, leaving them out in the glow of the moon as they went.

Aedán began pleading with her again, begging her to listen to him. "I didn't know. They tricked me. If I would have known…"

Bridget continued to ignore him, losing his words. It was like walking on death row…They were being led to their deaths, and all Aedán could think to do was clear his conscience. Well, she wasn't going to give him any satisfaction. Not while she walked to her own death by his own doing.

Only she couldn't totally ignore everything. Aedán, through tears, said some things that she knew were true. She knew it deep inside.

"You were once one of my greatest friends and allies…in a time long, long ago. We campaigned with Lugh, along with Cridhinbheal, your lover. I was always jealous of him, but we were all great friends. You— You are Lugh's sorceress, Bé Chuille. The White Sorceress. Don't you see? They want you because you imprisoned Carman with your magic so that she could never leave her tomb. You are the one who made the Stones of Bres so powerful that Bres can do nothing but sleep! Cridhinbheal…"

Cridhinbheal. The man in the stone circle. It was decided amongst them: her, reluctantly, Bé Chuille…Lugh, Aoi Mac Ollamain, and Cridhinbheal himself. The Red God, Bres, needed to stay down for good and the stones needed a guardian to make sure of it. They gathered in his circle, and she murdered her own lover with a dagger—cut his throat as he stood on his knees before her in submission—all while Lugh and Aoi Mac watched. Bridget could remember fully driving the blade into his throat and heard him whimper with the knowing that it begun. A profound coldness entered her—the horror of what she'd done so long ago.

"...and I helped you and Lugh take down our enemies so that we could stand as champions before the Tuatha Dé Danann. They all want us because we are the only ones who can break the magic. You. Bé Chuille. Are the only one who can break the magic."

"It doesn't matter who I was," she said flatly. "I am not her anymore." She needed to believe that as her horror of what she'd done ran through her.

"You are Bé Chuille. You will always be Lugh's White Sorceress. The Red God himself—Bres. He wants to awaken. His Red Braid is woven into ours probably until the end of time. You are the only one who can cut us free from him. That's what I believe!"

He should have loved her enough, she thought. Just enough to stop all of this from happening.

Aedán continued: "...and you're breaking my heart. I would have never..." But she didn't want to hear anymore and did her best to drone him out.

Rowan Flynn led the druids down the path. Carman walked behind them, barely dressed, exposing her otherworldly transformations—her dark wings, her dark, mottled skin and the hideous white globular eye on her forehead. She wanted all the druids to see not only her power, but that they were all on a mission that was more than mere myth and legend. It was reality. The Hidden Folk. The Fomorians. The gods. All irrefutable and palpable...And it was all laid out before them.

Bridget even heard the druids speak of her as a god and venerated her under their breaths. They feared and loved her for it. Bé Chuille. Their sacrifice. It disgusted her. If she could get her hands around the witch's neck, she'd kill her and enjoy every minute.

"... okay? Please? Will you please listen to me?"

She had enough. "Shut your *pie*-hole, you *right* bol*lock!* Jaysus! I don't want another word out of yeh. You done fecked yerself, now live with it! You don't have to worry. It's not much longer now, is it?"

Aedán snapped shut, and she was glad of it.

Bridget tried keeping her eyes peeled for a way to escape. If she could only find a second and at the right moment in the right spot...

She knew her chances were low, but she couldn't let herself give up. No, she'd never do that. Aedán was right: she was Bé Chuille.

"You two saw the stone at St. Albeus, yeah? It was the lost stone that completed the Stones of the Red God, Bres. Wait until you see it," Carman said behind them. "I hope you do like it. It was quite an expense moving such a large stone here."

"Why was it at the monastery?"

"To break the circle," Carman said. "But the circle always finds its way back around, doesn't it?"

Bridget sighed. Of course, it did. Like the dreams of murdering her lover...always with her even though she couldn't remember the details until now. No wonder she had always felt sad in some way. Maybe she did deserve this...

2

Maggie ducked down in the woods, watching the druids move Aedán and Bridget down the small path between the trees. She followed them, wondering where they were going, until they came across a hill with blue standing stones crowning it. The full moon seemed to hang right over it. Without thinking too much about it, she knew these were the Stones of Bres.

As the druids began grabbing the couple, forcing them into the center of the stones, Maggie almost jumped when she heard a noise behind her. She saw the moon-glow curls of hair bouncing on Líle's head before she recognized her. The girl was prone, crawling with a rifle up next to her, breathing somewhat heavily.

"What are you doin' 'ere?" Maggie whispered.

Líle put a finger to her lips, then whispered back: "You don't want them to hear us, do yeh?"

Maggie sighed and shook her head.

"I got caught up a bit," Líle said. "Back at the manor house, I bumped into this fella. He's in a cellar, wrapped up in this silky shite."

"Fella?"

"Your fella," Líle said. "He said his name was 'Cuán.'"

Cuán! He was alive?! Maggie's heavy heart seemed to ease a little, though she knew they were all still in trouble.

"He said if I helped him out of the silk, he'd be like the ocean," Líle said. "Not sure what that means, but he said it was bad. The silk is keeping him alive."

Ocean?

Then Maggie realized that she meant *Oisín*—the mythic hero who after returning to Ireland from the Otherworld, aged three hundred years after falling off a fae woman's white horse.

He was in trouble. Maggie reeled at the idea that this could be more than she could take. What was she going to do to save everyone? While she had a plan, a lot of it rested on the fact that she could get Carman back to the Hidden Place at the monastery. She was *still* trying to figure out how to get that done, however.

"You know, I was going to shoot you dead," Líle said, keeping her voice as low as she could. "I thought maybe you were a part of all this and might have had something to do with Barry's death."

"Barry?" Maggie was not only surprised, but even more furious. Why did so many people have to die? Why did people have to do this to each other? "What happened?"

"That guy who had you shackled in the back of the car. He shot him before he put you in the car," Líle explained. "But Cuán said that there wasn't anyone better who could help us all get out of this, so I'm going to put my faith in ye, if you don't mind."

Maggie didn't know if that was such a good idea.

Líle grabbed a golden necklace from around her neck with a large gold wheel medallion. Maggie took it from her, realizing it was the

Golden Wheel of Taranis—the Third Attainment. Líle also pulled a shell out of her pocket.

Maggie was excited to see the Macalla shell as well. Once she had both talismans, she realized how she might be able to pull this all off. With any luck.

"Maggie, I'm sorry. Listen. Am I the most attractive person out there? Of course not. But do I have a good personality? No. But do I wake up every day and try to be the best person I can be? Also no. But I did make a mistake and I'll own up to it."

"Thanks," Maggie said, feeling more and more grateful for her.

"I'll break up this party," Líle said, readying her rifle and she pulled its lever with a satisfying *click-click*. "You go do what you have to do. For Ireland."

"For Ireland," Maggie said.

"Scram, will yeh? They don't have much longer."

Maggie nodded but looked back up at the hill. The druids were tying Aedán and Bridget's hands up with ropes against two of the Stones of Bres. Rowan and Carman were taking their places.

"Go."

Maggie nodded and started crawling away.

Behind her, the rifle rang off, followed by the distinct *click-click*. And then another shot. Suddenly, the night erupted in more reports echoing about her. Vegetation around her were hit, and she heard one bullet zing past her head.

Shit, she thought. And crawled faster though the dirt and brush.

Maggie ran through the woods, hearing the guns firing behind her. She didn't want to get hit, but after a while she had to get up and make a break for it. The cool night seemed still as if the woodland listened to the violence unfolding behind her.

She didn't stop until she saw a wolfhound appear not too far away from her. The large, gray-blue hound looked at her and she saw that she could see partially through his body. It was Ponc, her beloved wolfhound that belonged to Cuán when they were kids.

When Ponc saw that he had her attention, he walked through the trees. Whenever Maggie had seen the dog, he would lead her on her path in ways that sometimes she didn't always understand. But she knew they were necessary. She followed Ponc until he disappeared by a large trunk of a fallen oak tree.

Maggie walked around the tree, looking at it and then around her to see if anyone searched for her.

She didn't understand why Ponc took her there, until she realized that the tree was ancient... and hollow. Maggie found the end of it, seeing that it would be a tight fit, but she crawled into it. Here, she could hide, and she could keep herself safe until she returned from the psychic Hollow.

On her back, deep in the log, she put the Golden Wheel around her neck and held the Macalla shell tight to her chest. She closed her eyes, trying to block out the gunfire. After some time, she reached into the Hollow and left her body. Since both the Wheel and the Shell were made of glamour, they remained with her as she climbed out the other side of the trunk.

As an astral projection inside the Hollow, she was able to lift her form up into the air, and she flew towards the Stones of Bres. She saw that a couple of white-robed druids Líle had killed were lying dead amongst the stones. Carman was behind a bluestone for cover, while Rowan was on the other side of the hill, holding his head down. Other various druids fired back into the woods, hoping to hit the shooter who had attacked them.

Maggie didn't have much time, so she ignored the helter-skelter and went to Carman. Her doorway was utterly dark, but Maggie knew that it was the only way to get inside the witch for what she needed.

Maggie stepped into Carman's darkness and disappeared.

Here Lies Carman

1

The druids pushed their backs against their stones and started tying up their hands. Aedán watched helplessly, ashamed and angry how badly he screwed everything up. The druids were done with Bridget first, pulling on the ropes around the stone to hold her back against it. The druid, working on the ropes on his hands, still wrestled the knot when gunfire went off around them. The druid looked at Aedán and then Aedán noticed that there was a large hole in the druid's neck, which was flooding his chest with copious amounts of blood.

He dropped on the ground at Aedán's feet.

The druids scattered as another gunshot went off. Two druids fired back, blindly, into the woods where they thought the gunfire came from. Aedán took advantage of the situation and pulled his loose ropes apart and went to Bridget.

"I'll get you out of here," he told her. He started working on her knots, finding them more proficiently made and harder to pull apart. *Great.* He struggled with them, finally loosening one and then started working another.

The gunfire was loud. He didn't know who was shooting more—the druids or whoever shot at them from the woods, and it didn't matter. They needed to take this gift and go.

A bullet whizzed past his head and hit the stone, shattering particles everywhere. Bridget screamed in surprise, but Aedán untangled the last knot, pulling on it, and set her free. She rubbed her wrists as he grabbed her elbow, leading her away as quickly as he could, hoping to descend the hill and make for the woods across from the people firing the guns.

Pain suddenly exploded through his gut and then another went through the left side of his chest. He saw blood, but tried to ignore it to concentrate on running, but his legs went weak, and he realized that it was getting hard to breathe. He choked up blood.

He didn't even know who shot him.

Bridget looked at him and cried, "*No!* No...Aedán!"

Aedán fell, trying to grasp for his breath. He got small amounts of air and then coughed out more of his blood.

Bridget grabbed his arm and started pulling him across the grass, sobbing. He tried kicking his legs to help her. Once they were a little way behind the trees, Bridget let go of him and fell to her knees, pulling him up into her arms.

He was bleeding all over her.

Aedán knew he was going to die. The agony in his lungs. His stomach. He knew vital organs were hit. He'd probably choke to death on his own vital fluids.

But Bridget had to know before he was gone. She had to understand: he was sorry for everything. He made a mistake, he was sorry, and he was happy that at least she'd be able to go on.

"R-R-R-Run," he managed, nodding. His whole body trembled.

He couldn't get any more air. His lungs were filled with liquids. A heavy consumption and tiredness pulled him away from her.

Have a beautiful life with dreams far better than we ever had.

2

It was almost like hunting, she thought. Aim, fire. Rechamber. The druids shot wildly, which happened because they didn't know where she was. Líle, however, could see them.

Aim. Fire. The druids dropped like flies until she ran out of rounds.

Líle crawled behind another set of trees, letting the druids fire wild, and she watched from between branches. There was a woman that fell, black wings fluttering violently about her body as she kicked and screamed. Something was happening to her, even though Líle was sure she didn't hit the woman herself.

Rowan Flynn, the coward, came out from behind one of the stones drawing a long dagger. He rushed the seizing woman and attempted to stab her, but other druids pulled him back.

"Don't you see! If she lives, she will take this all out on us!" he shouted desperately.

The druids continued to pull him back, and they all started making their getaway. Running into the fields from the woods around the Stones of Bres, the druids ran as fast as they could away from her.

Líle was excited to see this. She was harmless now, but they had no idea.

She watched as Rowan broke off from the main group, probably thinking that whoever was after them might follow the main group. Oh no, she thought. Rowan Flynn was going to pay for Barry McDermott's death. Líle dropped the rifle and pulled her own knife out, sneaking through the woods like her I.R.A. brothers showed her.

He had no idea what was coming to him.

3

While traveling the Merrow's Call when she was within the city of Cathair Aigéin, she learned that one could travel through time through the Hollow, but they could only travel as far back as someone's lifespan. Being born was also the birth of a person's *kintráth*, of course, so it didn't exist in time before it. But that wasn't a problem at all...

Maggie followed Carman's lifeline back through time, using the Golden Wheel of Taranis and Carman's memories as guides. Maggie found the last moments Carman had with her father before she killed him.

Maggie walked invisible through time at the house of Mihalis in Athens, long ago when Rome still stood powerful. Carman poised in her mother's room, using magic to twist her mother's body painfully until she was shaped into a rat, screaming all the while.

When Carman's magic fulfilled its purpose, the rat jumped off the bed and ran out of the room, squealing almost nauseously. These things were long ago and were unchangeable. Even if Maggie wanted to, these events wrote themselves into the stone face of time itself.

Carman gleefully left the room, following the young girl who appeared behind a column, screaming her lungs out.

"No, Carman! Carman, please!" the girl screamed.

"Oh, Irida! You make this all seem so horrible! You don't have to be a rat, after all. I could make you into a cute little bunny."

"No, sister. Please!"

"Stop pleading with me, bunny! Or I might have to break your neck just so I don't have to hear that incessant noise you make!"

"No stop! Come to me, Katerina! Please. Come to me and let us talk."

Katerina? Perhaps Carman had changed her name? And then Maggie remembered reading in Etna's journal that she was supposedly renamed by the sorceress, Hecate herself.

Maggie looked over and saw an older, handsome man with dark wavy hair and sharp Greek features. She could see that this man was Carman's father. They looked a lot alike. He came into the chamber across from them, holding up one hand in defense.

Maggie walked between Carman and the little girl, who sought refuge under a table, trembling desperately.

"You have betrayed me, and you have betrayed my mother. You have betrayed your wife, and you have betrayed your children!" Carman shouted.

"Come here, Katerina. Please..."

Maggie looked at the little girl and knew in her heart that Carman had already killed her. It didn't make it easier, watching the poor child frightened for her very life.

Carman was a monster. There was no doubt about that.

But Maggie had come for what she needed, and she started following the memories forward along her *kintráth*, where Bres and

Bé Chuille worked together to trap her in her prison. Her tomb. Maggie went beyond that and found the point where Carman stood amongst the Stones of Bres, watching someone shooting at the surrounding druids.

Maggie held out the Macalla Shell. According to what she learned while in the Merrow's Call, the shell could record voices while it was being rubbed. Like a magic lamp. Now she held it to Carman's ear, hoping to get Carman to join her in the Hollow.

The Macalla shell carried the voice of Mihalis—

No stop! Come to me, Katerina! Please. Come to me and let us talk.

Her geas demanded she listen to her father. If she denied his voice, fate would turn on her...

Come here, Katerina. Please...

Carman tried to resist, but she stepped from her body as her psychic self, letting her physical body drop to the ground behind her.

"Oh, Maggie. So clever," Carman said. "But you have made a big mistake."

Maggie cocked her head. "Have I now?"

And she flew to the monastery, following Carman's *kintráth* to the darkness of the Hidden Place. Again, Maggie held up the shell and let it call Carman to her.

Come to me, Katerina! Please. Come to me and let us talk.

"No!"

Maggie could feel her trying to resist the urge to go, but her destiny pulled stronger than ever. Quickly, she searched through Carman's memories and found what she was looking for.

As Carman appeared in the Hidden Place, Carman's kintráth warped, tossing them through time once again. As space and time warped around them, Carman tried grabbing her, but Maggie grabbed the Golden Wheel around her neck and started hitting her in the face until she let go.

"I will kill you, you *fuck*ing serpent!" Carman screamed and charged her again.

Maggie looked at the warping around her and grabbed Carman's head as she charged, pushing it over into the warping. The witch's astral face was pushed and pulled like wet clay as she screamed all the while before Maggie finally let go.

Carman started screaming in agony, so Maggie took the Golden Wheel and stuffed it into the crack of the wall of the Hidden Place. After that, she stepped back into the darkness.

The warping was done, and Carman's astral projection rippled. There was a body laying against the wall, covered in dust—somehow magically preserved for centuries. It looked just like Carman. The body started pulling her toward it like a powerful gravity well and Carman screamed.

"No. No, this is the wrong body!"

Once her body had her, the effects of the warping that affected Carman started shifting her flesh, muscles and bones...

"I believe this is where ye really belong, Carman," Maggie said.

Maggie knew Carman couldn't follow her until she was able to concentrate again, so she took the opportunity to skip back into Carman's dark doorway. She ran as fast as she could along Carman's *kintráth* until it closed.

4

Carman's original, ancient body turned into her prison, holding her spirit back from her copy that existed at the Stones of Bres. The transformation became agonizing. The wings regrew, Balor's Eye opened on her forehead. Claws extended from her fingers and toes. Her body darkened with mottled black and blue bruises. And then the warping started changing her. It tainted her psyche and now the psychic and spatial effects were working their destruction on her face. Large mounds of flesh and bone jutted about, twisting her face into an almost indescribable form.

When it was over, she spent a long moment holding her malformed head.

Carman saw the encryption on the stone on the floor, as she started pacing back and forth, trying to figure out what Maggie had done with her.

Εδώ βρίσκεται ο Κάρμαν
A thyng of unnatyral evyl. A dymon of wom-
nh'd. It shakes its mylky brests and scratchys
thee walls wyth its clahs late into thee nyte.

Εδώ βρίσκεται ο Κάρμαν—Greek. *Here is Carman.* Or, *Here Lies Carman.*

This was her original tomb that held her original body, where she was now trapped. The prison Bres designed for her.

What had Maggie done to her? She was now in some other time, trapped in her own tomb, where her old body had been waiting for centuries for her own awakening. Maybe she should have broken her *geas*? Maybe this would be much worse? Trapped in here for many more centuries to come?

What a nasty trick to steal her father's voice in a shell and drag her here. How did the little serpent know how to use her Red Braid in such a clever way?

In the front of the chamber, she heard a noise, and she backed up, uncertain of who came for her. And then she realized where in time she was. A naked woman walked in, holding a machete at her side, determination and pleasure written across her face.

"Nooooo! Stop! You don't know what you're do—" Carman shouted at the reborn version of herself, but the naked woman came at her, shouting her battle cry. Carman raised her arms to defend herself, trying to spit, *Recognize me!* But those words never reached her lips.

Having just left Etna's cottage, the new, reborn Carman was desperate to kill her and steal her power. Only she wouldn't get it, would she? Not this way— It had all been an awful trick by the Dominion himself.

Carman hacked and hacked at herself and didn't even know it. The warped, monstrous version of her landed on the ground, dead, mauled viciously by the sword—a pile of chopped meat and feathers.

The reborn Carman stuck the machete into the ground, trying to catch her breath.

"Good," the Dominion said behind her as he stepped into the chamber. Carman saw some blood on her finger and licked it off as he walked up behind her.

"You have set yourself on your path," the vampyre said. "This will benefit both of us."

Carman smiled at him before returning to Etna's cottage to plot her vengeance and locate her sons.

5

Bridget ran as fast as her legs could carry her, trying to escape all the gunfire. She heard someone behind her. Heard him breathing. Getting closer.

No!

All she could think about was Aedán's face as he died in her arms. Frightened that she would be taken down, too, she didn't have much hope. She had left the path for the woods, because it felt like a safer idea. Whoever was chasing her, she wasn't going to let them get her.

Out of the blue, someone tackled her from the bushes. They fell together, landing hard on the ground, and he quickly climbed on top of her.

"No! NO!" she cried, seeing that it was Carman's lackey, Rowan Flynn. He still held the long dagger.

"We can still raise the Red God. We'll just sacrifice you! You should be enough!" he shouted at her. "Your divine power!"

He smacked her to make her stop swatting and punching. The blow almost took her consciousness with it. For a moment, she

couldn't hear him speak as he continued shouting at her. Her ears started ringing.

This is where I die, she thought. Again.

Behind Rowan, she saw a handsome man standing there. He wore a gold torc and his face was scarred from Dain's claws. The part of her that remembered being Bé Chuille knew who it was: Cridhinbheal. Aoi's best friend and her first lover.

Rowan didn't know he was there until...Rowan's eyes went wide, and he gagged up blood, which splattered Bridget's face... and *then* he knew. He leaned back on his knees and Bridget saw Cridhinbheal's spear jutting out between his rips, through his heart. Rowan spit up more blood. It poured from his lips, down his chin and poured onto her chest.

As Rowan gagged on his own blood, Cridhinbheal leaned in toward her. "I forgive you, Bé Chuille. I will always love you. This was not only my sacrifice, but yours. I may always be a guardian of the stones, and it gives me eternal purpose. I wish you peace."

Bridget started weeping, feeling a weight lift off her—one she didn't know she had been carrying for so long. She recalled herself as Bé Chuille, cutting his throat at the site of the stones to make him their guardian. Lugh was behind her, looking mournful. Aoi Mac Ollamain—Aedán, then—watched outside the circle, almost looking triumphant. Cridhinbheal forgave her for binding him to the stones. Cridhinbheal forgave her!

"Was it you who did all this?" she asked.

"I heard the Order make their plans. I knew Carman was reborn. I only pushed you in the right direction."

"You are the one who sent us to Maggie! To the Otherworld!"

"I am the guardian...after all. The stones are within my power now."

Bridget shoved Rowan as hard as she could until he fell off her. She rolled over and climbed to her feet. She looked again for Cridhinbheal, but he was no longer there. Instead, she saw a blond-haired woman standing there with a rifle, her curls bouncing beside her ears.

Was this the same person who'd been shooting at them?

Bridget wanted to scream again. She didn't know what to do. "Please," Bridget begged her, but the blond held up a hand in defense.

"I'm not goin' to hurt yeh. I'm with Maggie," she said.

Oh Jaysus, she thought, *thank the gods*. They weren't out of danger yet, though. Bridget looked for Cridhinbheal's spear, but it wasn't running through Rowan any longer. The man was still, the wound pouring blood in a slow trickle now. He wasn't going to hurt them, but there were more druids in the area. Who knew what they were willing to still do to them?

Bridget tried to stagger to her feet. The blond woman helped her.

"Thank you, whoever you are," Bridget said.

The blond shrugged and then gestured at Rowan's body.

"What happened to him?"

"A ghost from the past," Bridget said. Bridget leaned over and grabbed the long dagger out of Rowan's already stiff fingers. "But I'll take this."

1

Maggie stepped out of Carman's doorway through the Hollow, watching Carman's body shake and kick. Carman might have been powerful, but she didn't realize that the whole time, her truest enemy was herself. Maggie watched as the younger Carman, reborn from Etna's flesh, ignorantly hacked her future self to bits.

Maggie was always a fan of letting arsehats take care of themselves.

She found her body in the hollow tree and woke herself back up in the physical world. Feeling ants crawling on her, she wriggled free of the tree and swiped them from her flesh until she was sure the little bastards were all off.

She didn't hear anyone else firing guns, so she made her way back to the Stones of Bres. Amongst some of the druids who were killed by the gunfire, Maggie found Carman's body again. An empty shell now. Maggie started pressing her hands into her flesh, searching until she found the Derdriu Shard hanging by a leather string on her rope belt.

Maggie snatched it from her. "This is mine."

Cuán—

Maggie walked down the wooded path, knowing it would take her back to Cuinn's manor. From the Merrow's Call and from Léana's own words, she knew that she could use the Derdriu Shard to cleanse Nathaira's blood from her bones forever, freeing her to live out the rest of her mortal life with Cuán. All this work, and now she could save herself!

It has wondrous magic in it, your soul. It can cleanse the darkest places and destroy the brightest lights, Léana said. If you follow your own destiny and weave it to your accord, your soul can also be the key to saving the world around you.

Right. Mushy shite, Maggie thought.

Maggie took deep breaths of the cool night air and looked up at the full moon. Dark, cotton clouds whipped across its surface, hiding a chink on its face. She didn't know why, but she was done crying, done worrying, done thinking for the time. There was a deep need inside of her to just take a deep breath and let this whole life of hers relax into itself.

Of course, her mind always went back to Cuán. Was Líle telling her the truth about Cuán being in some cocoon, unable to escape it or risk aging 68 years in a blink? Maggie did the math in her head and sighed. Cuán probably wouldn't survive the aging. He'd be 96.

Anxiety started filling her up again. Like a Guinness, except the shits were in the air.

Maggie also wondered about Líle. Was she alright? Where could she be? Hopefully, the druids hadn't found her yet.

Eventually, the wooded path opened again, and she could see the manor. Maggie picked herself up and ran as fast as her dress would allow. Following the walls of the manor around to the side, she found the encased stairway that led down into the cellar.

She pushed open the door, not expecting to see a large chamber with more standing stones. Líle stood at the bottom of the stairs, holding a dark brunette, who sobbed into Líle's chest. It was Bridget.

Maggie started down, seeing the yellowish giant corpse-looking thing shackled with chains in the center of another circle of standing stones.

"Jaysus," Maggie said, seeing the giant man-creature. "Who the bloody feck is that?"

Bridget moaned louder when she saw Maggie, and the girl started running up the stairs toward her, leaving Líle like she didn't matter anymore. Bridget threw her arms around Maggie.

"Oh my *god*, I'm so glad you're here, Maggie!"

Maggie wrapped Bridget up in her arms, feeling her wet tears dampen her chest. Bridget sobbed a bit longer and then looked at Maggie with teary red eyes.

"Aedán's dead," Bridget said.

Maggie's heart broke for her.

"Oh, Bridget. I'm sorry, Luv."

"We need to..." —*sniff*— "go get his body."

Maggie nodded. "We will. There's something I have to do first."

Maggie shrugged free of Bridget and went down the stairs. Líle pointed at the back of the chamber. With another deep sigh, Maggie started around the ominous circles and the unconscious creature until she saw the cocoon hanging upside down from the ceiling.

"Cuán. Is that you?"

The cocoon shifted.

"Maggie?!"

Dear gods, *it was him.*

Maggie tried to hold herself back, trying not to tear up again. "It looks like ye got yerself into a bit of trouble again."

"Um, yeah, I suppose you could say that," Cuán said, the silky fibers wrapping him muffled his voice some. "Look. Maggie. I'm in a situation."

"Oooooh, I know it," Maggie said. "Líle told me about the ocean."

Cuán chuckled. "The ocean, now?"

Maggie tried not to cry, so she forced herself to chuckle back.

"Aye. The one who fell off his horse and aged three hundred years."

"Probably didn't live much longer after that," Cuán said, sounding far more cheerful than Maggie would have expected. It hurt her even more. He was always such a good, fun boy. The man she loved was in a situation and Maggie couldn't think how she could face it.

In a way, it was her worst fear, wasn't it? Watching Cuán die old while she remained young. It was why she'd gone to all this trouble, even going so far as to risk her relationship with the love of her life. It wasn't fair. This was the love of her life...and they hardly had the chance to live it yet.

"God damn it," Maggie said, sobbing. "I hate meself for putting you through this. I hate meself fer bein' so feckin' daft! I should have stayed with yeh! Jaysus Christ."

"Maggie, Maggie, Maggie...Come on, now. Don't do this to yourself. You're worth dying a hundred times over for. You were doin' this all for me. I figured that out a long time ago. You were doing this for both of us. It's not your fault."

Maggie wiped her nose and sniffed again.

"God damn it," she said again. "I'm going to try cutting you out of there. Okay?"

"That would be great, actually. Am I hanging upside down?"

"Um, yes."

"Then do me a favor and cut me down first. I'd hate to land on my head."

Maggie found herself having a small laugh.

"Shut up and wait a moment." She looked at Líle and Bridget. "You two mind helping' 'ere?"

They both nodded.

Maggie extended her claws, tore the skirt of her dress to shreds to free her legs, and climbed the wall until she was near the ceiling. The girls below grabbed hold of Cuán's head and shoulders and lifted him up. Certain they had him tight, Maggie used her claws to slash at the webbing until the thing came free and dropped.

The girls held steady and pulled, so that his feet would fall toward the ground instead of his head.

"Fuck me. Ouch," Cuán shouted.

Líle and Bridget laid the cocoon down and backed away as Maggie dropped from the wall onto the ground and walked over. She crouched and clawed at the webbing around where she thought his chest might be. His arms were folded there, and once Cuán felt the webbing get pulled away, he started grabbing the sides of it, tearing and pulling to free himself. Líle and Bridget both joined in.

Maggie revealed his face and saw that he looked to be in his forties. She smiled when she could gaze into those gorgeous dark eyes of his. Once she retracted her claws, she touched his face and felt his soft skin.

"Hi," she said.

"Hi," Cuán replied with a smile.

He was already looking about fifty. His hair was graying.

"Am I dying?" he said.

Maggie bit her lip, shaking her head, trying not to cry again. "Yes."

Cuán frowned. "I don't have much time then. Fuck me. Hey, I just wanted to say, though, my aos sí—"

"I'm not an—"

"Sh. I'm dying'," Cuán said, grinning. He reached his sixties. Liver spots were forming. His skin drooped, becoming more fragile. "I want to say that I have loved you ever since I saw you wrapped in that seaweed. Everyone loved you. My folks. Oona. Hell, all of Kilkee loved yeh, and I will die loving you. I don't want you to ever ferget that."

"Cuán," Maggie said, touching his lip.

He was already reaching his seventies. His body shrank a little. His skin sagged even more. His hair turned ghost white. A couple of liver spots showed up on his cheeks.

"And I want you to find yourself someone you can be with. I don't want you wandering this world alone."

"Ah, Cuán. Shut up. I couldn't ever—"

"I love you."

Maggie bit her lip again and said, "I love you, too. But I'm not letting you die."

If you follow your own destiny and weave it to your accord, your soul can also be the key to saving the world around you.

It was worth a try, wasn't it?

Maggie swiped Líle's knife from her belt and grabbed the Derdriu Shard that she kept around her neck. She put the Shard on the ground and cut down into it with the knife.

"Hey! That's my knife!"

"I'll give it back!" Maggie shouted, frustrated.

After letting the knife drop from her hand, she pulled the Shard apart until it started glowing a brilliant white light. The light was beautiful, washing across the large cellar.

Even the tallow giant in the circle of stones groaned and lifted a large hand from the ground.

Maggie touched Cuán with the Shard, willing her soul to enter him. The light went inside his body. He was looking about ninety now, and he was grabbing his chest.

Was he having a heart attack?

"Maggie!"

Maggie ignored him and closed her eyes, focusing on her spirit through the Hollow, using it to turn back time on his flesh. His blood. Before she knew it, the light was gone, and she fell out of the Hollow, back into her body. It was like a blast, and she physically fell back herself, rolling on the floor. When she came to a stop, she placed her hands on the ground and pushed herself up to look over at Cuán.

Both Líle and Bridget were looking at her, both awed by what they had just seen. Neither of them knew what had happened, but they were amazed by it.

Maggie crawled back over to Cuán's body.

He looked as young as the day she left him for the Otherworld. It appeared to have worked, but Cuán's eyes were closed. Her heart started racing again. Was it too late? Did the heart attack kill him before she could make him young again?

Maggie put her head down on his chest to listen for his breathing. His heartbeat. *Something.*

"Whatthefeckwasthat?" Líle said, still amazed.

"Her putting everythin' into saving the boy," Bridget told her.

Maggie waited.

He was dead, wasn't he?

She couldn't hear a thing.

Then she heard it. Softly. Slowly. *Thump...thump.*

Again, faster. *Thump, thump.*

Cuán took a deep breath, and when Maggie lifted her head to look at his beautiful face, she saw him open his eyes. He saw her smiling down at him, and suddenly his face lit up, too.

"Am I still alive?"

"Oh, fuck yeh," Maggie said. "Not losing you yet."

Bridget touched her hand, getting her attention.

"But didn't Léana say that the Shard could cleanse your blood? Didn't you just lose it?"

"I don't fuckin' care," Maggie said, and she swept Cuán up in her arms when he raised himself up. She squeezed him tight and kissed him hard, not wanting to let him go ever again.

Cuán laughed when he broke free. "You chose me over your own freedom?"

Maggie grinned at him. "Of course, stupid. Always."

She kissed him again.

2

Maggie, Cuán, Bridget, and Líle rested a little before they returned to gather Aedán Ó Cuinn's body up. They took him home and laid him in his bed in his old room. Bridget stayed with him as Cuán and Líle followed Maggie back downstairs. In the foyer, Cuán sighed and said, "What are we going to do with that creature downstairs?"

Maggie shrugged.

"We'll have to get far from here before the authorities discover what's happened. Otherwise, this might all be misconstrued as being our fault," she said. She didn't want to suffer anymore for a mess that she didn't intentionally make. None of them deserved that.

"It so happens I know a few fellas that know something about explosives," Líle said. "Don't worry about it. I'll have them show up as soon as I can arrange, and they'll blow that monster downstairs to bits. The manor, too.

"Besides, this place was crawling with arseholes. I'm goin' to find the funny buggers and stuff a bomb up each of their arses once I get the chance."

"I definitely support ye and yer dreams," Maggie said, nodding.

Epilogue

1

Líle had to stay low for the next few days. There wasn't any link between her and the murders at McDermott's warehouse. His loyal men didn't even mention her as being there when the assassin, Alton Headley, stormed in with his gun, shooting up Barry's office. Líle was grateful for that, and she kept her nose down for a while just to be sure.

At the pub, however, she met with Barry's I.R.A. friends. A few of them were there that day when Mr. Headley shot the office up and were wearing bandages from being shot, but they were all healing just fine. They were here for her as they were there for Barry.

Líle quietly told them about the satanic goings-on at the old Cuinn estate. She suggested that it was a bit of Irish history that should be forgotten, and they all agreed.

A few nights later, they took a few trucks full of TNT and wired the manor up. Nobody was brave enough to go back down into the cellar, but Líle thought that when the whole place came down, surely, it'd kill the huge creature in the basement.

Surely.

They lit it up. The central part of the manor went up first, filling the night sky with such fire. The other sides of the manor and garage erupted into flames next. When Líle and her men saw it go up, they made their way toward Dublin allen in their trucks. It would be a while before they would return to make trouble for the Irish Free State on the Wexford pier. Líle wouldn't go back until after the Irish Civil War, and she only went back to find Barry McDermott's grave, so that she could finally say goodbye.

2

Cuán, Maggie, and Bridget took odd jobs around town until they were able to make enough money to purchase tickets to Kilkee.

Cuán found a job on a fisherman's boat. He struggled the first few days getting used to the steamboats, but most of the job hadn't changed in the last sixty-eight years, to his relief. Maggie and Bridget enjoyed showing him the things they had already seen. The electrical cables, the telephone, motorcars, and they even went out to a small airport to watch the planes land and take off. Even though it started out showing Cuán the new world they found themselves in, they were all still in awe about the whole thing themselves.

Bridget worked for a tailor woman in a small shop who fixed old coats for people. Because of Bridget's family, she was never prepared to work blue collar jobs, but the woman turned out to be patient and understanding, teaching her a lot about sewing.

Maggie found it harder to find a job, but she secured a job selling fruits at a stand in the market. She called and sold the fruit, sometimes coming home with nothing or a few shillings every day.

But together, they fed each other and saved up enough for their tickets. Bridget wanted to head back to Dublin and make her way. She wasn't sure what she wanted to do, and it scared her, but when she said she was ready, Maggie believed her. Besides, after they visited family in Kilkee, they planned to return to Dublin anyway. They were determined to meet up with her as soon as they were able once they returned to the city.

Once they had gathered their money in hand, ready to leave in the morning on the first train out, Maggie woke in Cuán's arms to find Ponc looking at her in the dark. His eyes glowed blue.

"Ponc. What is it, boy?"

The wolfhound panted and then turned and walked through the front door. Maggie slid out of Cuán's arms and wrapped herself in a gown, and left through the apartment door. Ponc was sitting by the staircase, waiting for her, his tongue hanging out his jowls.

When Maggie stepped closer, Ponc started down the stairs until he poised outside, in the cold, wet grass in her bare feet. Ponc sat at her feet, and Maggie saw Léana standing there. She had on a glamour dress of blues and greens.

"Maggie." She smiled and ran toward her, throwing her arms around Maggie.

Maggie was happy to see her and more than a little surprised. "H-How did ye get 'ere? I thought yeh weren't strong enough to stay long in the physical world?"

Léana laughed, squeezing her tight. "When you broke the Derdriu Shard, you strengthened both of us. While I know my place is in the Otherworld—this realm now belonging to the mortals—I had to take the chance to see you again. See if you are still okay."

Maggie smiled at her. "I'm fine, and so is me fella. And Bridget, too. She left a few days ago for Dublin."

Léana sighed. "That is really wonderful to 'ear. But how did you use the Shard? I still feel the serpent's blood in you. Didn't you use it to free yourself?"

Maggie shook her head and took a deep breath. "Honestly, it's a good thing. Cuán is more important to me. If I lose these...special *abilities*...how am I to protect the ones I love from the nightmares that I now know this world is full of? Ack. I suppose my fate is to be the serpent in my blood for a good long time, at least."

Léana grabbed her shoulder.

"If you ever come back to the Otherworld, I'll find you," Léana said. "We are sisters after all, aye?"

"Aye. We are."

"A'right then. I'll let you get your sleep," Léana said.

Maggie kneeled and stroked Ponc's blue-gray coat. "I love ye, too, boy."

Ponc barked and followed Léana toward the pier.

When Maggie crawled into bed, she wrapped her arm around Cuán as he slept soundly. They were both ready to go back to Kilkee to find out what had happened to their families, but deep down,

Maggie knew a well of pain waited for them there. She didn't think she could handle it, knowing full well that she had left a lot undone and unsaid to the people she'd known, and it was perhaps too late to say anything at all.

At least, there was Mona. Who went to the Crann Lár knowing the truth. Maybe her father was there, too, and Mona had told him everything.

It would be the best thing she could hope for.

3

Cuán was the first to jump off the carriage that brought them back to Kilkee. It was slightly overcast. They could see from the road as they came in, that the piers had changed—grown, filled with larger fishing boats. When they were downtown, they went into what was once *Gilroy's*. The old sign had fresh paint on it, now displaying *Josephine's Groceries*.

Cuán paid for a bag of lemon drops.

"You'll never change, will ye?" Maggie said.

Cuán laughed, popping one into his mouth. "Hell no, Luv. I mean, I missed you a lot when we were away, but I missed the lemons more."

"That doesn't surprise me at all."

Across the street was once the Foley's home. It was gone now, replaced by another building, simply titled *Kilkee Bakery*. They slipped inside, looking around. They looked over the baked goods beneath the glass at the counter and just breathed in the wonderful scents of all the loaves of bread and sugars.

"Oh. It's 'eaven, Cuán. We should stop back by later."

Cuán became somber, and Maggie took his hand.

"It's all gone now," Cuán said. "Like a blink of an eye, really."

Maggie nodded. "Aye. Like a blink."

They then walked out to Oona's small farmhouse. It was still standing, but another family appeared to live there.

"I wonder what happened to all my things," Maggie said. "Do ye think they were all thrown away?"

Maggie remembered her vanity, her makeup supplies, her dolls, and other souvenirs she'd collected throughout the years. She had nothing to remember Oona by either, and when that hit her, she found it much harder to contain her tears.

Cuán put a hand on her shoulder. "Come on."

"Where are we going?"

"Maybe the library has kept the papers. Maybe we can learn more."

That sounded like a good idea.

Over the rest of the day, they compiled newspapers and read through them starting in 1855. Slowly they gathered what had happened to many of the people they once knew. Of course, Cuán found the article about the heinous murder of his parents, Brian and Orna Foley, by some unknown stranger. The authorities, another paper wrote, concluded a few months later that the Foley murderer must have been a stranger passing through, as none of the clues linked the murders to anyone in Kilkee or the surrounding area. This must have put a lot of townsfolk at ease, whether it was true or not. Only Cuán knew the true story—how Carman had killed them to punish Maggie.

Colum Ó Fionnáin lived to sixty-three and was found dead in his barn of a heart attack in June of 1869. He remarried after Mona had passed, but his new wife, Sheila, found him dead and lived by herself until 1888.

Oona Connell passed away in 1899 at the ripe old age of 98. She remained a widow, but it wrote in her obituary that though she faced the loss of her only daughter, Maggie Connell, her spirit was strong, and she was known for donating her time and energy to the Church, the priest's there, and whoever needed her help.

"Sounds like Oona," Maggie said, sniffing, wiping her teary eyes. "It takes a woman like that to raise the likes of me."

Cuán chuckled and squeezed her against his side. She put her head on his chest.

They went to a flower shop and paid for some bouquets and then went to the graveyard and found each of their markers. In each grave they found—they placed a bouquet.

This is what was left of their family.

It started to rain lightly.

"So, now we're in a new world," Cuán said. "The only way to go is forward."

Maggie nodded. "Aye. Forward. To Dublin."

"Maggie."

Maggie looked at her handsome fella. "What is it?"

"We were going to get married," Cuán said. "Do you think we should reconsider this?"

"Reconsider it?"

"I mean, since everything has changed."

Maggie turned in front of him, looking confused. "My heart hasn't changed. Has yers?"

"No."

"Then why the feck wouldn't we get married? If anythin', I believe we owe it to ourselves to make this happen more than ever now," Maggie said. "Yea?"

Cuán smiled at her. "I'm happy to hear it."

They hugged again, holding each other close.

Maggie whispered into his ear. "I'll always love yeh, Cuán. The stars couldn't change that. I don't want to be anywhere else but in yer arms."

"Heard and understood," Cuán said. "In Dublin, then?"

"Well, not 'ere, that's fer sure."

"And once we're married, you're going to the University. Can't have you gettin' much older without an education. Wouldn't want the brain to fall out of use, would we?"

Cuán threw an arm around her shoulder, and they strolled out of the graveyard together, letting the rain fall on them.

"I guess all we have now is what we do with the future."

"Aye. So, let's make something of it."

4

Before the I.R.A. had the chance to blow the Cuinn estates to pieces, Elieris appeared as an avatar in the driveway in the middle of the night. He made his way around to the cellar, descended the stairs, and found the chamber of the stones that were holding the Bresquinn Arrachtaigh back. He knew Carman had gone rogue and was probably plotting against him, but he also sensed that something else seduced her. A dark, foreign evil.

Having no idea what to expect, and wanting answers, he checked the manor for any clues.

The first thing he noticed was that the Bresquinn Arrachtaigh was gone. The stones that surrounded him were pulled down, and they had broken into smaller stones that were all over the chamber floor. Something powerful destroyed them, setting the Arrachtaigh free.

Who seduced Carman and turned her from him? Who set the Arrachtaigh free?

He needed to find out, realizing that Seagrass Maggie was nowhere near the other danger that lurked just out of his sight.

Elieris left the chamber and followed the path towards the Stones of Bres. Mortals wouldn't know it, but the path had been there since ancient times before it had been forgotten and found again by mortals throughout the centuries. It was part of a ley line, and the path to the stones was always rebuilt in the exact same place every time.

Elieris walked it, feeling the stones vibrate with a power it had gathered from all the violence and death over the course of the last half-century. As he got closer to them, he could feel its power growing. He also felt something different about it. Some alien stain.

His nose wrinkled. The Commination. The infernal curse that fell across the world after the Immaculate War. It was a foreign war to him. It occurred after his own time when he had larger bouts of sleep. But it was the Commination festering into Ireland that woke him in the mid-16th century.

He should have smelled its stink right away.

But what brought it here? The thing that infested Carman?

Speaking of which, he found her body amongst the druids there. She was on her back, her body locked in a horrible pose of agony and seizure. He knelt and touched her face with an open hand. He reached past her death and found her doorway gone. Only necromancy would discover what had happened to her, but her soul was no longer here.

"Who is this?"

Elieris turned, suddenly seeing a pale young lady in a tan dress with straight, blond hair and pink eyes. Blood poured from her tear ducts, streaming down her alabaster face.

It was an empusae—the walking dead, raised by a dark, vampyric spirit, a creature that held onto the memories of its host. Empusae were very much like vampyres but served more powerful masters who created them. This girl had been an empusae for a while now.

"Don't get too close, my Queen of the Puck," a man said, slinking out of the shadows from behind the Stones of Bres. "It's the King of Fomorians."

Elieris grinned.

"At least you show your respect," Elieris said. "And who are you?"

"I go by many names. Most call me Captain."

The large man appeared powerful. He was definitely a vampyre, and old, too. Not quite as old as the strigoi, but old, nonetheless.

"This your empusae?"

The vampyre nodded. "Catrina. One of my favorite Queens."

"You took Carman from me, didn't you? Why?"

The vampyre cocked his head slowly. "Because I want your power. And the only way to do that—"

"You told Carman that if she destroyed Bres during the summoning, she could use the Wheel of Taranis to destroy me. Very clever."

The Captain nodded. "And then she could have Ireland just as she always wanted."

Elieris was furious. "Even if you had succeeded, I'm more powerful than you know!"

He watched as Catrina started to slither around him like a hunting shark.

"Tell your bitch queen to back off," Elieris said.

The Captain grinned. "Oh, you don't have to worry about her. See, when I realized that the serpent-girl used the Wheel to place Carman's soul in her original corpse inside her tomb, I realized that Badb's Wing and the Eye of Balor would wait there unguarded. I took them and I gave them to someone else."

Elieris could almost feel its hulking size in the darkness behind the vampyre. The closer it got, the more he could smell it, too.

The deformed Arrachtaigh appeared as the moon touched its horrible face. It had changed again. Now the white orb of Balor rolled around on its forehead, and big, black corvid wings sat on its shoulders, outstretched. Because of the wings, it now had claws on its hands and feet.

"You gave them to…*an Arrachtaigh?!*" Elieris was not only shocked, but worried. Most man-creatures lacked the mental ability to retain much intelligence. They were dumb brutes. And this vampyre gave two powerful Attainments to it?

It was an abomination.

"Destroy him," the Captain said, and Catrina laughed.

Elieris thought he'd be able to escape—slide sideways and use his power to return to the Deep Dens—but the Arrachtaigh was quick and snatched him with its large, robust hands.

Elieris fought back as it turned him into another fist, holding him tight, but its strength was beyond that of his avatar. He saw the Arrachtaigh bare his teeth, and the large, white globular eye stopped and focused on him. A white ball of light shot from the eye, bathing Elieris' head in its luminance.

Elieris thought that once the avatar was destroyed, it would be fine. After all, this body wasn't the true Fomorian King. His true sentience was in the Deep Dens themselves. But the bright, white light burned through him and suddenly he wasn't so sure of anything.

No, he thought. *This will put me back centuries! No—!*

He could feel the Deep Dens fill with the light and he could feel everything burning. He didn't have time to register what any of it meant as he evaporated.

5

Catrina laughed, enjoying the sight of the pagan god burning in the bright white light of Balor's eye. Once done, the god was nothing now but ash. Catrina whistled. Out of the darkness around the Stones of Bres, other empusae queens appeared. They surrounded the Arrachtaigh and put the cold iron shackles on its wrists and around its ankles.

She went beside the Captain, who kissed her mouth and then put an arm around her shoulder.

"He dead and gone? Did you just destroy a god?" she said.

The vampire gave her a half grin. "Who's to say, my Puck? We are but shards drifting to the ever-lasting whims of nature. Only the Primordial itself knows for sure."

"Still," Catrina said, coyly. "You have defeated him."

Her Captain shrugged it off, bored already of the conversation. "It's time to go back to the Madeline Leigh. We've got more work to do."

Catrina continued to smile. "Oh, yes, Captain. We have what we need 'ere."

The vampyre and his queens loaded the Bresquinn Arrachtaigh on the back of a truck. As it gazed at the moon peacefully, they all made their way back to the Wexford pier.

To Be Continued...

GLOSSARY & PRONUNCIATION

Anam chara— [*ah-nom ka-rah*] A soul twin.

Aoi Mac Ollamain— [*E mac ool-a-men*] Lugh's poet and bard companion, who could wield the imbas with his music. (Imbas are the inspiration of poets, which also made Aoi Mac a great wartime analyst for Lugh.) He has been reincarnated as Aedán Deasún.

Aos sí— [*Ehs shee*] The aos sí are the descendants of the Tuatha Dé Danann. They were all born earlkings, but many become twergs over a great amount of time. Most of the aos sí are women who live modestly in the Otherworld.

Arrachtaigh— [*AR-rock-tog*] A general term for an Irish monster.

Badb's Wings— [*Bahv*] Also called the Crow's Wings. One of Carman's Attainments. The Morrígu is a goddess with three distinct avatars: Morrígan (Macha, or Anand)), Badb and Nemain. The Crow's Wings are a token of love between Badb and the God of Bones, Dá Derga.

Balor's Eye— [*Bay-LOR*] Balor is one of the most powerful fomor ever born. Lugh struck him down with a sling-stone and Cherry Fox finished him off when he crawled off to heal. Balor's Eye is the blight that brings death to nations and to gods themselves.

Bé Chuille— [*Bay-shool*] Lugh's companion and a white sorceress. She was in love with Cridhinbheal in their first life.

Instead of dwelling immortal in the Otherworld, Bé Chuille undergoes reincarnation through lifetimes in the physical world. In her current life, she is Bridget MacCailín.

Bresquinn Arrachtaigh— [*AR-rock-tog*] Lugh created a poison to stop the fomor, Bres. Bres' mortal lineage has been haunted by Lugh's poison, which turns their children into monsters. See also Nevrall Gléas.

Cailleach— [*CAL-lee-ehk*] The Queen of Winter, one of the oldest goddesses of Ireland. Her name is often used to refer to witches. She saved Maggie from the fomori when she was still a child.

Cathair Aigéin— [*CATH-ar Ah-gen*] The coral city of the merrow, found between the Eternal Sea of the Otherworld and Beyond the Ninth Wave of the mortal world.

Cloch Chroí— [*clock cree*] The Heart Stone in the center of the Merrow's Call. The Merrow's Call sends multiple minds out into the Hollow, creating a window into knowledge across the cosmos from the beginning of time to the end of time.

Crann Lár— [*cron LAR*] The Great Tree and the very heart of the Otherworld, specifically Tír na nÓg.

Cridhinbheal— [*Krey-en-veil*] Lugh's companion and probably closest friend of the three. He was a satirist who learned quickly how to become a warrior at Lugh's side. His soul has been trapped by the Standing Stones of Bres.

Croí— [*cree*] The magical lifeblood of the Primordial, the Creator Force of the universe. The fae naturally gather croí to their fata essence, giving them the ability to cast Eeries (magic).

Dá Derga, The God of Bones— [*dah der-gah*] The Death-God aspect of the Dagda, who dwells on Tech Duinn, gathering and guiding the transformation process of souls to their places in the underworld.

Dar'gone— [*dar-gon*] The souls Dá Derga twisted into guardians of Tech Duinn.

Demidian— [*deh-mi-dee-ehn*] A mortal with divine blood. Either a demi-god (born half-blood) or gifted with divine blood. Demidians do not have fata essence, so they cannot use the Eeries, but they can learn Accordances that mimic some of these powers.

Derdriu Shard— [*der-droo*] Maggie Connell was originally born Deirdre Ó Fionnáin, so when the fomor Soulforger, Fangtooth, fashioned the Shard from a piece of Maggie's soul (her píos anam), it was called the Derdriu Shard. The shard itself is slight, but it allows anyone to connect with Maggie wherever she is.

Dullahan— A headless man in all black, carrying a whip made of spines and riding a black horse. He is Dá Derga's marshal, who seeks out ghosts who try to escape Tech Duinn.

Eagla/Eeries— [*eeg-lah*] The Eeries are natural powers that the fae may use by weaving their croí. The fae only have access to Eeries within their nature. Eeries comes from the Gaelic root Eagla, meaning fear. Mortals feared the power of the fae, and still do to this day.

Earlkings— The fae who continue to adapt and change with the cosmos, changing their whole beings over centuries. Sometimes the fae will call them True Bloods because they continue to dance along with the fluidity of the Primordial.

Elieris, the Fomorian King— [*El-ay-res*] The God-King of the fomori, who has become the dwellings for his people since they were banished from Ireland by the Tuatha Dé Danann. He seeks vengeance against the Tuatha Dé and the Gaels (Irish) for taking fomori land.

Fae— A term for any Primordial Being (including fomori, fir bulg, the aos sí, etc.). Those with the fata essence.

Fáelad— [*fay-laud*] The first varga-spirit born in Ireland, who adopted the name of his first host, Laignech Fáelad. Fáelad is Brogan Kelley's varga, who gives him the ability to assume the shape of a monstrous wolf.

Feithidí— [*fee-thee-dee*] Twergs who have adapted to the life of insects. Queen Banríon Míolachá rules these fae.

Fomor (sing.), fomori (pl.), Fomorian (nation)— The demons of the sea. Once a tribe of fae who ruled Ireland many centuries before the Gaels arrived.

Glamour— Croí can be made to manifest through the physical fundament of a place, creating a magical substance called glamour. Glamour can shape appearances and form magical materials (called glamour tokens). Magically enhanced matter, it can break the laws of physics and form powerful illusions that can manipulate all five senses. Glamour tokens can remain with an astral projection in the Hollow.

Golden Wheel of Taranis— One of the Carman's Attainments. Taranis was a Celtic god of thunder and lightning. His Golden Wheel may travel the Red Braid of anyone who finds the doorway, though it cannot extend before the creation of the Red Braid itself or its death.

Great Contracts, the— After the Milesian Battle, the Tuatha Dé gained respect for the Gaels who fought for their place in Ireland. Mother Danu forbid the Tuatha Dé from destroying the Gaels and instructed them to the Final Recant (withdrawing into the Otherworld from the physical). In order to make it so, they constructed a magical peace treaty with conditions that vibrate in the souls of both fae and the Irish.

Hollow, the— The psychic atmosphere hidden all around us, created by the sentience of all living things. Sorcerers tend to call it the agasha, or Akashic Records. The Hollow can be traveled via astral projection (a projection of their Psyche Essence), where people become doorways to their inner mindscapes.

Kintráth (the Red Braid)— [kin-roth] Mortals are born with their fate, but only fae have a kintráth. The Red Braid is created from their fata essence and runs the length of their lifespan. With the Eeries, the fae may reweave their Braid and the physical world that exists around them.

Leath bhrògan— [*lee bro-gon*] Twergs who fancied comfortable living, hiding amongst the Irish. Many became shoemakers or worked in pubs, slowly adapting themselves to the places they dwelled. For example, Killian is the leath bhrògan of The Quays— his fata essence is woven into the pub itself.

Lost Place, the— The shared dream world created when Carman linked Aoi Mac Ollamain's and Bé Chuille's mindscapes together so that her sons could keep a close eye on them as they reincarnated through their lives, despite being prisoners in the fomori dungeon.

Lughnasad— [*Loo-nah-saud*] A Gaelic festival opening the harvest season, traditionally August 1st.

Merrow— Earlkings and twergs that adapted to life at sea.

Nathaira— [*nah-thair-uh*] The Great Oilliphéist (Sea Serpent), daughter of Caoránach—the Mother of Demons.

Nevrall Gléas— [*Nev-rall Glos*] Lugh's poison; traps to curse the Ó Cuinn family so that they cannot awaken Bres from his sleep. Changes them into monsters, confusing their minds, and makes them dim.

Niamh/Modron— [*Nee-ev*] A powerful aos sí, worshipped as a moon goddess as Modron to the ancient Welsh. She was famous for choosing a mortal husband, Oisín, who left her after three years to find the world moved on 300 years and died of old age. She is, however, favored for creating the Fianna warriors. She continues to be considered the Princess of Tír na nÓg.

Óenach Carmán— Carman cursed Ireland when she was captured by Lugh and his companions, so that if she was not honored, a great blight would once again attack Ireland. The Óenach Carmán festival on Lughnasad was a contract between the Tuatha Dé and the Gaels that the Gaels would continue this tradition to keep Carman's curse from manifesting.

Píos Anam— [*pees ah-nom*] A piece or shard of one's soul.

Púca— [*poo-kah*] Considered twergs, though many of them are shapeshifters. They adapted to life as animals. Over time, they tend to choose a single animal that best fits their personality, solidifying them as a twerg.

Saint Ailbhe— [*alv*] A disciple of St Patrick, who was known to have been suckled by a she-wolf when King Cronan ordered his death when he was only a babe. He became a medium between the Irish vargas and the Irish people, and he venerated the wolves of Ireland. The vargas of Ireland respect him.

Siofra— [*SHIF-rah*] An unborn of the fae that can take the shape of others. They are often used as changelings and are protected by the Great Contracts.

Sióg— [*SHI-oG*] The Irish catchall term for the fae.

Sluagh sí— [*sloo-ah shee*] Ghosts who have chosen to dwell in their suffering and serve Dá Derga in the storms.

Sreng's Finger Bone— Sreng was a mighty Fir Bolg warrior, famous for chopping Nuada's arm off in battle (one of the Tuatha Dé). No one is certain how Sreng lost his finger bone, but it has bloated with black magic.

Stingy Jack— A jenny-burnt-tail, will-o'-the-wisp, ignis fatuus, corpse candle. Another variation of a ghost who wanders as a flame between worlds. Otherwise, they are often seen as birds (especially doves) in the Otherworld.

Tech Duinn— [*tech DOON*] The island fortress of Dá Derga, where most ghosts are drawn after they lose their lives.

Thar An Naoú Tonn— Irish Gaelic for Beyond the Ninth Wave. The old sailor's adage that the ninth wave was always killer because it existed between both the physical world and Otherworld. This border area between both worlds is where the merrow tend.

Tír na nÓg— The Land of Youth and the central realm of the Otherworld.

Tuatha Dé Danann— [*Too-ah dey DAN-nahn*] The first few generations of Mother Danu and Father Allód. The Tuatha Dé are known as the ancient gods of Ireland and also the fairies of the mounds. They are the tribes of people who fashioned the Great Contracts with the Milesians (Gaels) and the rightful heirs of Ireland.

Token, Glamour— A glamour manifestation mimicking a physical object. It can be a sword, clothes, a coin or anything else imagined. Glamour tokens are impossible to discern by most from a real physical object that it's based on. See Glamour.

Twerg— Primordial Beings were created by the Primordial to keep changing and adapting as the cosmos needs. However, over time, some Beings slow their change and refuse to adapt to being anything else. These are twergs. Those who continue to change within the cosmos are often considered earlkings.

Varga/varga-spirit— When a wolf dies rabid, there's a chance that its spirit becomes a varga—vicious, mad spirits of nature. When a varga possesses a man, they may transform that man into a werewolf.

POSTFACE

In Ireland, there are two sets of tales about travel to the Other-world or fae realms. The *echtra* were the pre-Christain tales, while an *immram* were Christian stories. I knew the second Seagrass Maggie book needed to be an *echtra* after developing her character in the first book, which was primarily set in the real world. And while there is said to be a central, sacred tree in Tír na nÓg, there wasn't any official name for it, so I turned to the Irish language and called it the *Crann Lár* (the Middle Tree), which I imagined as the fulcrum of all magic within the fae realm.

Possibly the first bishop of Ireland, St. Albeus (*Ailbe of Emly*) had an interesting life according to the *Vitae Sanctorum Hiberniae*. Unwanted by King Cronan, his father fled, and the King ordered that the infant be put to death. Left in the wilderness to die, Albeus was discovered by a she-wolf and raised by her. Later, he returned the favor by saving the she-wolf from a hunting party. He would continue to feed the wolf and her cubs throughout his life. This is why I chose him as a sort of patron saint of werewolves in Ireland, and why Brogan venerates the ruins of St. Albeus. The story reminded me of the Roman myth of Romulus and Remus, who were both suckled by a she-wolf after being left for dead.

There isn't much about Carman and her three sons, save the *Metrical Dindshenchas*. While it states that she was a witch from Athens, I took a creative route and invented her history and her motivations for wanting to conquer the Éire.

Finally, scholars have seemingly connected the Welsh goddess, Modron, as an aspect of Niahm and also of Morgan le Fay. I decided it would be pretty neat if they were all the same woman. After all, the Celtic tribes were known to share stories with each other and with the idea of the triple goddess (like the Morrígu, who consists of three—Badb, Macha, and Nemain) as a popular ideal, why not have Niamh being one aspect of a cross-cultural goddess?

I'd like to personally thank my chief development editor, Susan Russell, and my beta readers, Megn Thomason, Chase Reineke, Larcy Allen, Stacey Gallagher, Gareth Lunn, Ann Jean, Leanne Pert, Paul Allen, and PG Devlim. A huge thank you to my Irish translator, Greg Darwin, as well. Writing books really does take a team, so thank you all!

Charles Allen
Post Falls, Idaho
March 27th, 2023

Excerpt from A GRAVEYARD OF SHIPS,
The Seagrass Maggie Trilogy, Book III.

I. Tagann Nathaira Dúinn

A.D. 1075

The swells rose high in the misty dark of the Irish Sea, plunging the *MacTíre Mara* between its buoyant oceanic valleys. The crew—the *Nordmainn*, Saraid was sure—worked hard to batten down as much as they could on the knarr as others pulled in their oars. The storm came in swiftly, and every man and woman aboard the ship bore their apprehension in different ways. Some quiet. Some cried uncontrollably as the ship rocked, rose, and steeped dangerously between the waves.

All they could do was wait out the storm, holding on for dear life—trying not to be swept overboard as the waves crashed over them. There were many women and children aboard between the benches and chained together. All of them unsure whether they wanted to survive the storm or not... all prisoners of war and sold slaves to the *Nordmainn* in the Dublin markets, who were sending them off to unknown fates.

One of the young women, Saraid Ní Conrí, sat in the far back. Just before they set off from the piers, the Nordmainn savagely took each adult male of their tribe and slit their throats, pushing them off the pier. They only kept the women for breeding, and the children to work their fields. The horror of their circumstances was now only dissipating with the danger they now found themselves in. As the slavers made sure their chains were steady, she pulled out her tin whistle that hung from her belt by a leather strap and started playing a melody, hoping to help soothe her fellow Irish-man. The women and children were crying—some even unable to see her in the mists—but many of them simmered as they heard her sweet music.

But even she stalled as she thought she saw something in the mists. It was dark, but something out there glowed with a green phosphorescence along its slick, massive body. It rose between the mountainous waves—a serpent with barbed teeth and prodigious jaws. Its spiked dorsal fins were larger than sails. Tendrils roiled around behind its head and around its many aquatic arms and legs.

It dove back down, and its three massive tails swished back and forth through the air, making cracking sounds as they swung about before disappearing altogether under the waters.

It happened all so fast, but the serpent's horrible visage remained burned into her mind.

Saraid gasped and looked around to see if anyone else had seen it. She caught the eye of one old woman, who nodded knowingly back at her.

"Tagann Nathaira dúinn," she said. *Nathaira comes for us.* "Let this life go with a loving heart."

There was a powerful roar in the darkness. It wasn't the storm. It was the throat of the serpent itself. Everyone heard it this time, and all waited in silence to catch the sound again, or to glance at its presence.

Nothing. They waited a long time for another sound.

Lightning flashed overhead—dancing on the black swells around them.

Nathaira roared again in the darkness.

"Tagann Nathaira!" the old woman shouted.

Natharia comes!

A single girl-child began wailing loudly.

When the lightning clawed the intemperate waters again, lighting up the gloom, Saraid screamed. The serpent was just a few feet beyond the vessel—her giant silver eye there, gazing at them, just before her large jaws came up from the sea, pouring water down on them like a waterfall.

Yes, she had hoped for death, but could one ever be ready for their finality?

Saraid continued to scream as the serpent's jaws wrapped around the boat, and after that, there was crushing darkness. Her lungs needed air, but there was only water.

Saraid opened her eyes. She was once again on the *MacTíre Mara*, but now the waters were silent and the fog around them seemed eternal. Even the slavers wept.

Oarsmen put their oars back into the water and began to paddle together as the chief of the *Nordmainn* counted out.

"En, to...En, to...En, to..."

Saraid was already at peace with her life on the Éire. Her family. Her friends. Her lover. Nathaira slipped beside the boat so that Saraid could see her closer. The serpent's colorful blue and purple fins opened wide before descending beneath the waters.

Saraid knew this was death and was comforted by it all.

II. Elf Shot

May—1941
Galway

1

In bed, Nora was sketching in her charcoal as the morning light glowed golden in her room through the half-open window. She was only wearing her loose, white cotton shift that she had worn to bed. The warm breeze played over her, so she held down the paper against the drawing board in her lap with her free hand as she worked. Her thin legs were crossed, and she was hunched over her work, trying to shade in the dark recesses of the effeminate and serpentine body she'd drawn there.

She was humming out loud, saying the words in her mind:

Out of the waters of the western sea,
Covered in algae and covered in slime,
With a hook made of silver and steel from oft Other,
She hacks and she hacks until she snatches away...
Heads for the taking, heads for the claiming—
Those are the treasures she hunts from the shores.
She comes from the brine, and feels cold and clammy,
What a horrible tale: the terror of Seagrass Maggie.

Out of the waters of the western sea,
Hellish of fervor and hellish of mind,
Hunted by Fomorians and plotting her time,
She hacks and she hacks until she snatches away...
Heads of your best mates, heads of your children—
Those are the trophies she hunts in the dark.
Beware of the shorelines and where it's oft craggy,
What a horrible tale: the terror of Seagrass Maggie.

The old sea chanty mingled with the breeze, and she could feel gooseflesh crawl over her skin. She looked at her drawing again, tilting her head a little to make sure the proportions all looked right. It was partially a self-portrait but layered with all the things her mother, Bridget, had always described to her: the petite frame, the spiked fins running from the top of her head, down her back and to the tip of her tail. The pointed ears and sharp teeth. And all over her body, there were ancient Irish symbols scarred purposefully by the Fomorians themselves—symbols older than the Iberian Gaels and the ogham they later developed. Spirals. Organic stars. Crescents. Eels. And others.

If she had colors, she would have painted Seagrass Maggie a sea green with the dark Irish red hair. Her scars would glow in a teal or soft blue-green. Her fins would gradate from blue to purple.

Red blood would pour from her mouth between her long, wicked teeth.

When Nora was fourteen, about four years ago, her ma started telling her what she'd learned of the sea creature. Stories from other fishermen up and down the western shores.

"Usually, she hid amongst the crags and cliffs, searching for victims. Picking one out to keep her company, she'd stalk them and drag them into the sea. With her powerful teeth, she'd gnaw through their necks and then tear from them their heads. Most of the bodies were never found. The sea drew them far out into the ocean to never be seen again. But Seagrass Maggie kept the heads, so she could talk to them. For you see, Seagrass Maggie knew the ancient ritual of the token head. Like the warriors that first set their feet on these shores—known in those times as the Milesians— once a head was won, it was kept so that the successful warrior could take its secrets and its powers," her ma had said, holding her in her arms.

"But Ma, if she's from the sea, did she not hunt the fishermen?" Nora remembered asking.

"Aye. Them, too. And still does to this day."

"How many years has it been since she's haunted the shores?"

Her ma was as blond as they come, and it glowed in the firelight the night she'd told Nora the story. She would have been beautiful, if she hadn't been frowning.

"Some will tell you that Seagrass Maggie has been stalking the shores for centuries, but that's not true. It's only been since nineteen twenty-four—twelve years ago. That's when the stories started. But I'm not trying to tell you all of this to scare you." Her ma gave her a loving squeeze. "I...used to know Seagrass Maggie."

Nora's mouth dropped. "No. Really?"

"Aye. Before she was changed by the Fomorians forever," Bridget said. "Do you care to hear the story?"

Nora's heart skipped. "Yes, please."

Continue reading about Seagrass Maggie in

A Graveyard of Ships

Book III in the Seagrass Maggie Trilogy

About the Author

Charles Allen has worked as a game designer, filmmaker and photographer but telling stories comes most natural to him. He is the author of the tabletop roleplaying game VICTORIAN GOTHIC and SEAGRASS MAGGIE. He resides in northern Idaho with his wife, Jen, and youngest son, Bentley, a mixed Terrier (Murphy), a Havanese (Chewy), and two tabby cats (Oscar and Winnie).

The Seagrass Maggie Trilogy

Seagrass Maggie (2023)

The Order of the Red God (2024)

A Graveyard of Ships (2025)

"Allen is a great world builder and provides complex characters with intricate plots."

— Chanticleer